Ode to Damnation

A Legacy of Devils novel

Viktor Bloodstone

FORTRESS PUBLISHING, INC.

WWW.FORTRESSPUBLISHINGINC.COM

Ode to Damnation
© 2025 Fortress Publishing, Inc.
ISBN: 978-1-959797-06-7

Edited by: Catherine Jordan

This book is available for wholesale through the publisher,
Fortress Publishing, Inc.

PUBLISHED BY:
Fortress Publishing, Inc.
1200 Market Street
Unit 17 / Box 137
Lemoyne, PA 17043

WWW.FORTRESSPUBLISHINGINC.COM

CHAPTER 01

Sometime in the 1860s – I ain't too sure of the exact year – there was a nasty fella named Silas Worthington. Sounds like a name full of gold, don't it? Trust me, that man ain't got nothin' but dirty oil in his veins pumpin' from a pitch-black heart. Ain't a good bone in his body. If he ever had any good ones, he woulda sold 'em to the church and then spent the tithings in the nearest casino or brothel. Instead, Silas stole to get what he needed. Didn't matter none if it were money, goods, or women; he just took what he wanted when he wanted. 'Course, that's why we're here right now.

At the Devil Tree.

Yep, that big ol' chunk of wood sproutin' from the ground with a wide, gnarled trunk that splits into two horns. Damn tree is big enough to hide a whole family inside. A couple of branches reach out here and there, but nothin' like them horns. Two swirlin' knots twisted themselves right below where the branches split, lookin' like eyes. One big hole at the base, a mouth ready to swallow anyone fool enough to go pokin' around inside. The real kicker is when the sheriff tosses a lit torch in that there hole to shoo away any rattlesnake nests. The trunk is so thick and wet that the fire don't last, but when it burns, it's like the devil himself is laughin' out flames from his belly. That there is the Devil Tree. You know what else they call it?

The hangin' tree.

When it comes time for a hangin', the sheriff, his deputies, the townsfolk, and a pastor or two – I ain't never considered a man of the cloth a member of the regular townsfolk, since they always put themselves above everybody else – all bring the accused to the Devil Tree. No need to sully the streets of the town, when they can string 'em up at this cursed place far from their homes and farms.

Yep, I said that there Devil Tree is cursed. No one got the guts to say so out loud, but we all know it. This land ain't nothin' but scrub brush and itch weed for acres in any direction, and then you got this tree. A monster, biggest in the county, if not the territory, growin' leafless yet hearty. Ain't natural, and everybody knows. But what we don't know is why it's cursed. Some say witches doin' all their sacrifices on this spot. Others say the natives left it as a partin' gift for when the white man moved in. Ask any man of the cloth and he'll tell you with the certainty of sayin' water is wet that it came from the devil's own garden, an invite for wicked souls to join him. My guess? It's the witches. They's some nasty cunts, I tell you so! Livin' in the hills, talkin' to the plants and animals. Talkin' to ol' Scratch himself, I say. But the townsfolk made this the hangin' tree, addin' to the cursed land one villain at a time.

The bodies of eight prior, in different stages of rot, are still swingin' in the hot breeze. No one believes these men are proper enough to bury, and the coyote, wolves, and bears all leave the carcasses alone, not wantin' anythin' to do with this place. Other than nasty rattlesnakes, animals are all smarter than people, I say. But dumb ol' people keep comin' back. This time, they brung Silas Worthington with them.

I already told ya he is a no good son of a whore. Yep, he's a killer. Yep, he's a thief and a rapist and a cheat and a cuss. Rumor has it that the church is comin' up with new commandments 'cause Silas broke the first ten so many times! He usually did good avoidin' the law by runnin' when he felt fate was gonna take a piss in his beer. But then he got bit by… what's that fancy word for actin' like you're too big for your britches? Oh yeah… hubris. Hubris took a big ol' chunk outta Silas' ass.

Last night, Silas took a room at the inn and brung inside a young, wholesome girl. In Silas' twisted up mind, if she's old enough to bleed from God's graceful cut, then she's old enough to be considered a woman. Didn't matter none to him that she was only twelve. He had his fun, and gave her a right ol' scare before he tossed her cryin' face outta his room.

Guess the rest of the townsfolk didn't read from the same sheet music he was singin' from, 'cause now there are about fifty of them all screamin' and cussin' at Silas, accusin' him of rape as the sheriff brought him to the tree on horseback, noose all wrapped around his neck. The townsfolk don't stop there, neither. Now they're spittin' and throwin' rocks at Silas, ignorin' all the "Thou Shalts" they speak on Sundays. 'Course it amazes me how fast the good people turn from God in the name of God. The sheriff tries to calm 'em down with words 'bout justice and law, but Silas smiles a sick, slick smile and they get all riled back up again. The pastors are throwin' holy water by the bucketful, and this makes Silas laugh real loud even as the sheriff and his deputies are tossin' the long end of the rope over one of the branches shootin' off the left devil horn. The horse holdin' Silas ain't standin' too still, brayin' with eyes all wide and in a tizzy.

The pastor tries to say a few words, readin' from his little black book as if them words were magic enough to whitewash that bastard's black soul, but the people yell and shout louder than their shepherd. The deputies try to hold the crowd back, and they're doin' a fair job. But the girl's daddy slips through and rushes to Silas with a knife. Ol' Daddy yanks Silas down from the horse 'cause the rope ain't ready yet, and stuck him in the gut like a pig. Well, Daddy was a man blinded by rage 'cause if he had been seein' straight, he woulda saw he was way too close to the condemned's maw. Yep, Silas opens his villainous mouth and clamps down on dear ol' Daddy's ear.

And Silas ain't lettin' go.

The sheriff and his three deputies all run to the other end of the rope and pull. They yank Silas away from Daddy, but with animal effort, Silas takes the ear with him, blood sprayin' from Daddy's head. Ear still in his mouth, he's laughin' like a jackal as the lawmen pull him into the air. Dear ol' Daddy misses the action 'cause he's rollin' on the ground, gettin' his blood everywhere and smearin' Silas' belly-blood all over the place. Oh, what a gory sight this is!

Well, as things like this go, it ends with the hanged body givin' one last twitch. Everyone scrunches their noses with the finality – him fartin' and shittin' his britches. The townsfolk collect their wits and head back to their homes. Except Daddy and his family as they head to the doctor to get his head patched.

Me? How do I know all this? Well…

That dead fella swinging from the tree? Silas Worthington? Well, that's me.

And we ain't done with my story yet.

CHAPTER 02

Sean McCullough rocked in the chair on his porch, listening to the creak of wood that threatened to snap on the backwards pitch followed by the squeal of relief on the forward lurch. These noises had developed years ago, and he never once tried to determine if the creaking wood came from the chair or the floorboards of this old porch. The mystery didn't matter to him at all, more than happy to fall asleep every now and again on a soft summer evening to the rhythm created by the push and release of his feet. This was his last time on the rocking chair, and he wasn't going to ruin the magic or the memories by figuring out what caused the creaky lullaby he so loved. He'd miss these moments.

Sure, he could take the rocking chair with him, it was his personal property and all. His son wanted him to take it just to spite that bastard Wilber Boyle. But Sean couldn't bring himself to remove it from the only place it had ever rocked. Just because Boyle was kicking him out of his own home didn't mean Sean had the right to take the rocking chair. Instead, he was going to enjoy his last bits of time while he whittled away at a chunk of wood and thought about the upcoming election.

Ol' Hoover was going to face a tough opponent in Roosevelt come this November. Sean was voting blue this year. He didn't know much about the financial this-and-that mumbo-jumbo that the newspapers kept printing on and on regarding the stock market crash, nor did he claim to. He only knew Hoover was in charge when it happened. Hoover was in charge when the banks came knocking on Sean's door about what he owed them. Hoover was in charge when that bastard Wilber Boyle came onto Sean's property with a police escort and stated that he bought this farm from them banks for pennies on the dollar. Hoover was in charge when Sean felt nothing but helpless and hopeless.

Sure, his son got blessed by God's will and found himself a decent job on the west coast. Decent enough to move everyone with him and bid good riddance to this heap of New Mexico land. But still, it was the principle of the thing, and this was Sean's home. And the only home his grandson, Chester, had even known.

And Chester hadn't taken the news well.

Only six, the boy didn't understand the how or why of the matter, just that he had to leave. He was prone to crying fits and foot-stomping tantrums for the first week. His daddy let it slip that the banks and that bastard Wilber Boyle were the causes of their unwanted situation. "Bastard" was now a curse word allowed to pass over Chester's lips, the only one. The following three weeks lacked Chester's explosive outbursts, but the boy moped around the house and barn like a ghost, the occasional wail to boot.

Today was the day. The truck was almost full and it'd be rolling out within the hour. Sean knifed the finishing touches into the wood. What started off as a branch finished up as a soldier captured in mid-march. Right leg up, left arm back; left leg and right arm straight. A frown on his face. Sean didn't think it'd be a good idea to make a soldier with a smile. Plus, Chester could now have a friend to frown along with him.

Sean stood up, his knees, left ankle, and right hip all told him he had been sitting too long. This old rocking chair did his old bones no favors, yet he smirked at how something so comfortable could be bad for him. A tear rolled over his cheek as he stroked the chair's arm one last time. Foolish, him getting watery-eyed over pieces of wood. Tears were reserved for kin and dogs, that's it. Not wooden chairs and porches.

The three steps down the porch didn't help his hip, full throb by the time his feet hit the earth. He hobbled along the dirt path to the barn, stopping himself from swinging his left arm to propel his giddy-up. His gait was better by halfway there and he was thankful for that. He hated to look so feeble in front of his grandson.

*

Chester picked up a rock. It was only the size of a nickel, but it'd have to do. It was in the horse stall where Hercules used to live, before Daddy had to sell him. Hercules was his favorite horse.

Having already found all the bigger rocks, Chester would have to throw this one really hard. Probably no splash, but it might make a funny noise like some of the other smaller stones. He left the stall and hurried to the far corner of the barn, where the ground sloped to collect rainwater and make a big honkin' mud puddle. When it rained, Daddy would swear and promise to fix the ground or the spouts or both, but he never did anything about it other than toss straw on the mud. Now Daddy would never have to worry about the rain or the crooked land or the mud puddle ever again, thanks to Bastard Wilber Boyle taking everything.

Chester wound up his throwing arm, mumbled, "Bastard Wilber Boyle," and put all the anger from the last month into his throw. No splash. A tiny slorp and the rock disappeared. It was enough for Chester. It had to be. He kicked a pile of dirt toward the mud. On his quest for more rocks, he ran through the barn, and pulled up as soon as he saw his grandpa.

"Hey, Barn Boy."

This would be the last time he'd be Barn Boy. Grandpa would have to find a new name for him. He didn't know what it'd be, but it couldn't be Barn Boy anymore. "Hey, Grandpa."

"Whatchya doin'?"

Chester shrugged so big that his shoulders touched his ears. Normally, when he didn't want to admit to doing something he shouldn't be, he'd say something like, "Nothin'," or, "Just playin'." But if he were to get into trouble, what could Grandpa do? Forbid him from coming to a place he'd never see again? He said, "I was throwing rocks in the big mud puddle over there in the corner."

"Hunh," Grandpa grunted as he looked over to the corner. "Did they make funny noises?"

Chester wanted to laugh but wasn't sure if he were in trouble or not. He kept it simple. "Yeah."

"Well, alrighty then." Grandpa turned back to Chester and crouched down. "I made you somethin', Barn Boy. Here."

From behind his back, Grandpa handed Chester a wooden soldier, something he'd carved himself. Chester liked when Grandpa carved him toys. He was still stung about having to leave this home he loved, but the hand-sized soldier helped. Would Grandpa be able to whittle more toys where they were going? "This is the bee's knees! Thanks!"

"Bee's knees? Heh. I made it from that tree at the far, far, far end of the property."

Daddy didn't like that tree because nothing grew around it for hundreds and hundreds of paces, no matter what he tried to plant. Daddy swore a lot because of it. But Chester liked it, liked how it looked, liked that it was a big chunk of wood that split into two points. Daddy and Mommy and Grandpa all called it the fork tree. He called it the horned tree, because it looked like a big, nasty monster rising from the ground. It whispered to him when he was close enough, from the big hole that looked like a mouth. Not words, just scary feelings. And he touched it once. A few months ago, Daddy and a few hired hands were working the land near it – trying yet *another* crop – and they weren't paying attention to Chester. Daddy always said to stay away from it, but Chester couldn't help himself. As he played, he crept closer and closer. Finally, when no one was looking, he touched it. The bark didn't feel like wood, but like the cracked leather of the oldest saddle Daddy owned.

Grandpa mussed Chester's hair and stayed crouched for a long time. Right when his eyes started to get watery, he stood up, knees creaking like the old wooden porch, and mussed Chester's hair one more time before he turned to leave. "I know all the scary stories people tell about that tree, but it's nonsense to get all worked up about a chunk of wood, right? Anyways, you got about another fifteen minutes or so, Barn Boy."

One last adventure. And that meant the loft!

Chester ran to the ladder, thoughts of him and his new soldier finding a good perch to scout for enemy troops. Maybe even shoot a few before they could do any harm. But he got too fast, too careless, like Daddy always barked at him about. Chester forgot about the stray nail sticking out too far from where the third rung was attached. It sliced his hand from the top of his pinkie all the way past his wrist.

"Aaah!" Chester pulled his hand close to his chest. He had gotten worse cuts before, but this one burned and throbbed real wicked. And there was a lot of blood, enough to drip fast. And he was getting it on his new toy!

Now the pain behind his chest – the anger he felt after ruining his new toy – took priority. Stupid! So mad at himself. There were only a few drops on the soldier's chest and face, but it was enough to turn the cream-colored wood red, then brownish. Then… the stain disappeared as if the soldier was made from a sponge and not a tree branch.

Relief washed through Chester, happy that his new toy wasn't ruined, but… could it do that blood-absorbing magic trick again? He knew he shouldn't try it, because maybe it'd actually stain the toy this time, but… He held his injured hand over his soldier. Drip. Drip. Drip. The magic happened! The wood drank his blood faster than the last time. Too fascinated to feel the pain anymore, he squeezed his hand to make the blood drip faster. As soon as a drop hit the wood, it vanished. This was so neat! And getting neater, because the soldier moved!

It twitched only a little, at first. Then its right leg straightened while its left leg bent at the knee. The arms moved, too! Slowly, they reached from its body toward Chester. Excited that his new friend was reaching for him, Chester brought his bleeding hand closer. The soldier bent at the waist. Chester didn't know it could do that! He started laughing as the soldier sat up in his palm.

But he didn't laugh for long.

As quick as a blink, the wooden soldier lunged forward and shoved both arms into Chester's sliced skin.

Chester shrieked and let go of it. It clung to him, crawling deeper into his cut hand. Crying, he grabbed the toy and yanked it free, tiny globs of meat looking like mittens on its hands. He threw it on the ground, but as soon as it hit the dirt it scurried on all fours toward him – fast, faster than Chester could think. He stomped it like a bug when it got close enough. It squirmed under his sole, the little body rubbing against the bottom of his shoe.

"Grandpa!" Chester called out, but his voice didn't carry, too hoarse from crying. He ground his foot into the wooden soldier, no longer a toy, putting his whole weight into the effort. Sobbing, he clutched his pained hand – it hurt *really* bad – against his chest, not caring that he was ruining his shirt with his blood. A lot of blood! "Stop! Stop, you bastard, stop! Stop moving! Stop it!"

Body shaking from how bad it had hurt when this… this *thing* dug into his hand and how much worse it would hurt if it got out from under his foot, Chester started to pray. "Please, please God make it stop. Make it stop!"

The squirming lessened. This gave Chester a bloom of hope. Were his prayers answered? With a new burst of energy, angry grunts replaced his sloppy sobs as he ground his foot harder, more and more until the squirming stopped. Slowly, he lifted his foot, peeking under his shoe, foot poised and ready to stomp if it twitched. It looked like it did, so he stomped! And stomped on it over and over again. His fear-filled tears returned, and after one last stomp, he kicked it toward the mud puddle in the corner of the barn, hoping it would drown.

He ran out of the barn as fast as he could move his legs, happy to get in the truck and leave this place far behind.

CHAPTER 03

Amanda Winters had a sure-fire way to tell when the resin and the hardener were sufficiently mixed together – the nerve spasm in her right shoulder. Nothing too painful, just a slight flutter letting her know she had worked the thick liquid in the bucket enough. Ever since she stirred her first batch ten years ago, a little twitch would tap her shoulder right around the five-minute mark. Setting her wooden spoon aside on the workbench, she eyed her molds – thin plastic cubes with an empty space in the middle, the size and shape of a softball. Judging by the quantity in the bucket, she'd need four molds, and lined them up in a row on her workbench. She added a mouse skull to one mold, a rattlesnake skull in another, and scorpion carcasses in the last two.

All ready, she poured the colorless liquid into the molds, filling them to the top. She gently inserted a long, thin metal hook into the epoxy resin and carefully adjusted the mouse skull, moving it to the center of the sphere. After doing the same to the other three molds, she took a step back to scrutinize her work. These weren't items she found decorative; she'd prefer an interestingly shaped cactus or the occasional desert flower. But these were what the tourists bought whenever they stopped into Twila's Trading Post just outside of town.

The items were perfectly centered in the globes, so she moved them to the fan box that her husband, Hank, had built for her a few years back. A nice four-foot by four-foot box in the corner of her workshop with a fan to keep the interior cool and the humidity low enough for her resin projects to cure. After all, her workshop hadn't been designed to control the New Mexico climate.

Amanda's workshop started off as a storage shed many decades ago, then became a sad excuse for a one-car garage for a while, then back to a storage shed, and finally a workshop when her resin hobby became a side business that cleared enough to pay for the utilities and more than a few good meals every month. The ranch paid for the taxes, the mortgages, the insurances, the clothes on everyone's backs, and the more pragmatic meals. It also afforded them the ability to slip money into a savings account for the boys to start a college career. Although, the Aggies were interested in Riley's skills as a quarterback and the way Rand had been winning bull riding competitions lately, he had a legitimate shot to go pro, so there might not be a need to touch that money.

Amanda closed the door on the fan box and would let the epoxy resin cure for two days. She removed her filter mask and set it on one of the counters. The canisters gave it a gas mask look and Hank would always tease her about being able to survive an Agent Orange strike.

As she cleaned up her mess, Amanda stole a glance out the window, at the horse training corral. Javi Ramirez led the newest addition, Buster, a three-year-old chestnut, around the pen. WinterBorn Ranch received the horse a week ago, so they were in the early stages of their relationship. To give the stallion some exercise and a chance to meet the ranch-hands, Javi led the horse by the thin rope attached to the halter around its face. The young man stayed to the left of the horse and walked him around the paddock – four rails tall and forty feet in diameter with two doors; one leading in and out, the other leading to the bigger corral.

Riley popped out of the house and crossed the patch of dirt hardened from tire treads, hooves, and boot soles. His tee shirt and jeans couldn't hide the rounded muscles of an athletic teen who ate three solid meals and quite a few snacks throughout the day. Hair long in the front and short in the back, he swept it from his eyes with a hand. It wouldn't stay that way for long and Amanda chuckled at her son's style choice. He entered the corral and strolled along the perimeter next to Javi, the two of them with smiles on their faces.

A weight crushed everything behind Amanda's chest from the sadness of seeing her son struggle with societally imposed limitations and feeling the need to hide who he really was. He had never talked to her about it, but as his mother, Amanda knew. Sure, he was an entirely different person around his teammates than he was at home, but there was never a sparkle in his eye whenever his brother talked about the girls in their school. Even now, just talking to Javi, there was a brightness to his face, the joy of being free from the confines of a mask. To Amanda's surprise, Javi was the same way. They focused on each other as they spoke, constant eye contact as they talked and walked. Amanda loved to see Riley happy. He hadn't seemed that way too often lately.

Amanda went back to cleaning up her workbench. She put away the unused molds and took the mixing bucket and stirring spoon outside to rinse them with the hose. Curiosity getting the better of her, Amanda crept along the wall of her workshop to steal another peek at Javi and Riley. She wanted to see her son's smile again.

Standing in the center of the paddock, Javi and Riley faced each other. Both had the slouched posture of nervous uncertainty; Javi's hands clasped behind his back, fingers fidgeting while Riley's were submerged in his pockets, his head angled down enough for his hair to fall in front of his eyes. But no one was holding onto Buster's lead rope.

The horse now explored the space. Amanda hurried toward the pen, not wanting to make any sudden movements or unexpected noises. Unfortunately, Riley must have said something funny, because Javi released a honking laugh accompanied by a snort. Startled, Buster did a quick turn and darted away, his hindquarters slamming into Javi and knocking him off his feet. Slack face in surprise, Riley backed away as Buster bucked and jumped.

In a full sprint, Amanda raced to the pen. Up the rails and over, her left knee letting her know it would demand attention later. Buster whinnied and reared up on hind legs, front hooves kicking – too close to Riley. At six feet tall and two hundred pounds, he was five inches taller than Amanda and outweighed her by fifty pounds, but a mother's protective instinct was bigger and stronger, and she slammed into Riley's chest, driving him away from the flailing hooves. As Riley stumbled to keep his footing, Amanda said, "Open the gate to the Play Pen."

Riley struggled to catch his breath while running to the larger corral's gate.

Buster galloped around the paddock, braying and shaking his head. Javi was back on his feet, half covered in dirt, but otherwise he looked unharmed.

And terrified. His eyes were as big as the horse's, his hands out in front as if all he had to do was push should Buster get too close.

"Eyes down," Amanda said, loud enough for Javi to follow her command, but hopefully not so loud as to add to the confusion.

Following her own advice and not looking Buster in the eye, Amanda tried to predict the horse's path, arm out to grab the lead rope. Snorting, Buster turned, avoiding Javi, and his gait slowed to a feisty trot. Staying on his left side, she snatched the rope with a firm grip and hoped he didn't change direction too quickly or else she'd have a dislocated shoulder to add to the list of bumps and bruises.

"It's okay, Buster. It's okay. Nothing to fuss over," she repeated as she pulled the rope to guide him toward the gate Riley had opened, stroking his long muscular neck and silky mane along the way. But the closer they got, the more Buster shook his head. The halter – a few simple nylon straps with a quick release clasp – was clearly upsetting him. Buster picked up the pace and yanked his head away as Amanda reached for the clasp. At a full run to keep up, Amanda stretched her arm. If he made it to the big corral with the halter still on his face, he'd run around angry, and might hurt himself. The lead rope could catch on the fencing, or he could become distracted and twist a leg. The open gate enticed Buster to trot faster, forcing Amanda to sprint with her fingers wrapped around the lead rope. Shoulders burning, gate getting closer, Amanda stretched.

SNAP.

Off went the halter.

Amanda breathed a sigh of relief as Buster blasted through the gate, free from the straps.

Riley shut the gate, and Buster took advantage of the space, galloping along the perimeter. As Amanda had hoped, the stallion just wanted to let off some steam, seemingly content to run around the open space for a while. Now… about the young men.

Lips pressed together and nostrils flaring, Riley stared at Amanda. Even with his hair over his eyes, she could tell he was unsure about what level of trouble he was in. Tone as calm as dealing with Buster, she asked, "Are you okay?"

Riley nodded, and then glanced over her shoulder. Satisfied that her son was unharmed, she turned to Javi as he was jogging toward her. With a quiver in his voice, he mashed his words together while he explained. "Sorry, Mrs. Winters. It was my fault that Buster got spooked. I let go of the lead thinking he was more comfortable than he was and—"

Amanda held her hand up for him to stop talking, and he did so with an audible gulp. "Are you okay?"

The fear of being fired presented itself as tiny trembles along his face and body, but he nodded.

She could tell by the look in his eye that he wanted to continue apologizing and explaining himself. The poor kid didn't need to work himself up in a lather. "Good," she said. "No one got hurt and Buster just wanted to stretch his legs. We all lose focus now and again, even me at times, but as long as we learn from our mistakes, right?"

Both young men wore the same slack-faced look of confusion as they nodded in unison. Javi added a, "Yes, Ma'am."

Offering a soft smile, Amanda was going to suggest they tend to the horses and their stalls to give them a chance to be alone, but a familiar cloud of dust caught her attention. Hank and Rand pulled up in the F-150, back from bull-riding practice.

At six-foot six with shoulders broader than the barn, Hank took an extra few seconds to work his way out of the driver's seat, holding his Stetson to his head. Rand had Riley by an inch or so but with less meat on his frame, though Rand's taut and wiry muscles held their own against Riley's bulky form whenever the boys ended up wrestling, whether for fun or to settle a score. And all three of Amanda's men had the same deep dimple in their left cheeks. Hank's was a little harder to see thanks to his thick mustache, black as his hair and just as lightly sprinkled with gray.

Hank greeted Amanda the same way he always did – a soft kiss on the lips lingering long enough to flutter her heart, and a, "Hello, Gorgeous." After looking over her shoulder to the corral, he said, "I'm guessing there was some excitement by the look on those two boys' faces, and from the way Buster's running around the Play Pen."

The brothers greeted each other the same way they always did – a medium punch to the shoulder, even with Rand carrying the giant duffle bag full of gloves, pads, and a practice helmet. Far enough away that she couldn't make out the whole conversation, Amanda was close enough to hear a few words from Riley extoling how much of a badass Mom had been during the ruckus.

Amanda adjusted Hank's Stetson. "Nothing to write home about. Young Buster just needed to kick up his hooves."

Hank grunted, a noise that carried many statements. Twenty years of marriage told Amanda that grunt meant, "Dang it, I was hoping he'd be further along. We'll have to keep him in his stall while the movie people are here." He instead looked down, tucked a lock of hair behind her ear, and said, "Glad you're okay from whatever happened."

She reached up and put her hands on his cheeks. "Don't worry about the movie people coming in next week. We've had guests before."

Hank's big grin created the dimple. "It's like you can read my mind."

"That's because I can." She punctuated her sentence with a wink.

"Then you know I'm not keen on guests. They'll be here for at least three weeks, maybe four."

"I know, I know, but they're paying us good money."

Her sons made their way into the house, leaving Javi alone in the walking paddock.

"Our bills are paid on time," Hank said, "and we eat well. We're far from being in dire straits."

"Hank, with the amount they're paying us, we could take the entire year off and be in the exact spot we're in now. A full scholarship for Riley isn't guaranteed, and the rodeo circuit for Rand could be tough if he wants to go to school as well. Amateur winnings are nice, but bird seed compared to college costs."

Hank rolled his eyes. "I know. But New York types on our land? Ugh."

"They're from California."

"Are we sure that's any better?"

"Being snooty to those who are snooty makes you snootier than them."

Hank reeled back and contorted his face as if she had topped his cherry pie with liver. "Have the epoxy fumes got to your head?"

"It means don't be judgmental." A quick swat to his rump yielded a cloud of dust. "Now get inside and get cleaned up. I'll take Buster back to his stall."

He tipped his hat. "Yes, Ma'am."

Hank joined the boys and headed to the house while Amanda made her way to the walking pen. As nervous as a long-tailed cat in a rocking chair convention, Javi fidgeted with the halter and lead rope. He handed her the rope and mumbled, "Sorry again, Mrs. Winters. Are... Are you going to tell my dad?"

At forty-five, Amanda had played enough cards around town to read people. He wasn't asking if she was going to share with his father that he had been distracted. Rather, why and how he had been distracted by her son. She put her hand on his shoulder and squeezed, a sign of support. "Javi, it's not my story to tell. Now, head on home. It'll be dark in an hour. I'll get Buster, okay?"

The worry-wrinkles melted from his forehead. "Thank you, Mrs. Winters."

As Javi rode away on his bike, Amanda collected Buster and led him to his stall. After locking up, she noticed across the way that one of the Boyles, Amos she assumed, was feeding the pigs.

She stretched her arm out and pinched her fingers together, fitting Amos within a one-inch gap between her index finger and thumb. But he and the pigpens were still too close for her taste. And she could see the gaudy Boyle house, too. In her opinion, the other neighboring house belonging to the Tomlins, was nicer.

The sty's proximity was an intimidation tactic by the Boyles. The stench and grunts were too close for her liking, and for common courtesy. Every farmer knew to keep a pigsty out of sight and smell from their neighbor. The Boyles knew this, too. Yet...

She had always taught her boys to keep hate out of their souls, but when it came to the Boyles... Well, that family challenged her principles. Every human being had dark places in their hearts where they stored feelings they ought not think about. Her dark places were solely occupied by how she felt about the Boyles.

On the horizon, as small as a toy from Amanda's viewpoint, sat the Tomlin house, north of the Boyle property and the only other neighbors they had. The cursed property had been purchased two months ago from those snakes, the Boyles. Whenever the unsuspecting Tomlins learned that the land was no good, and they eventually would, then the Boyles would undoubtedly swoop in and buy it back for pennies on the dollar.

From this distance, Amanda couldn't see what Amos was feeding the pigs, but the air faintly carried the smell of rot. They snorted and squealed, as if happy for the rare treat. It wasn't old vegetables, that much she knew. What was he feeding them? Amanda turned and hurried to the house, trying to outrace the spine-tingles chasing her.

CHAPTER 04

Little Jack Tomlin peeked around the hallway corner. Down the stairs and in the living room, his parents were arguing.

"I can't believe you bought this property sight unseen," Mommy said, her voice scary.

"I did my research!" Daddy matched Mommy's loudness.

"Not enough, obviously."

At only seven years old, Jack didn't know what they were arguing about. He didn't know much outside of the numbers and words he learned at school. He knew 1996 was supposed to be the year it all gets turned around, according to Daddy, but from the way his parents had been arguing ever since they moved into this house two months ago, Daddy might be wrong. Jack also knew that the stairs from the second floor to the first floor in this old farmhouse squeaked something fierce, so he needed to time his escape perfectly.

"Ain't my fault! I asked all the right questions."

"Then how did you not know what Archibald Boyle did to the last owners? He sold them this land for two hundred thousand, and then bought it back from them for fifty within a year."

"I was told the last owner didn't have the proper fortitude to work a farm."

"No one has the fortitude to work a farm that can't grow no crops!"

"I didn't know this land can't grow nothin'!"

"And they weren't the only ones. Archibald did that *twice* before them!"

"That's the fuckin' lawyer's fault for not tellin' me that!"

Jack didn't know who Archibald Boyle was or what a lawyer was, and he certainly hated when his parents argued, but he wasn't going to pass up an opportunity to sneak to the barn. They yelled over the creaks as Little Jack dashed down the stairs and out the back door.

The barn stood before him like a castle. An old, faded, wooden castle, but a magical place anyway. Magic came from the unknown, and there was plenty he didn't know about this barn. His dad had told him to stay away because the people before them used it as a dumping area for trash. Mom was worried about tet-tennis, something bad he could get from stepping on a rusty nail.

There were no lights, but the late afternoon sun was plenty bright to expose what the shadows held. Inside, the barn looked simple enough. Stalls to the left, a big open area to the right, and a loft on each side. Jack paused long enough to think about where he wanted to start – on the ground or climb up to one of the lofts. There was too much stuff on the ground *not* to explore. He'd get to the lofts later.

Old appliances were scattered about. A rusted oven here, a rusted wash machine there, a big ol' rusted sink a few more feet over that way. No nails stuck out on any of them, so there was no fear of tet-tennis. Little Jack ran his hands over each appliance, wondering how old they were. Maybe older than his parents! That thought amazed him as he headed for the back corner of the barn.

He passed by an old mower and wanted nothing to do with that. As much as his dad complained about mowing the lawn? No thanks! But the stack of four tires looked fun. Jack ran to them, his head full of thoughts about bouncing them high enough to hit the ceiling. He did the mature thing first and looked for rusty nails, proud of himself as he did so. Only layers of dirt were on the tires – nothing harmful. But they were heavy. Super heavy. Grunting and sweating, he finally pushed the top one off the pile – and it bounced! Not as bouncy as he was expecting, but it did leave the ground a couple times, and then rolled to the very back, darkest corner of the barn.

Jack chased after it, kicking up dirt from the uneven ground. It was weird – the closer he got to the corner, the ground changed from hard dirt to soft, to thick mud. He almost fell when he stepped on something. He lifted his foot – a tiny piece of wood laid right in the center of his footprint. A stick? No. Jack crouched down and poked at it. Bigger than he thought and smushed deep in the mud. Between his fingers, he grasped at whatever had

been sticking up and wiggled it out. Something not too big. Something that…
looked like a wooden statue?

Using dirty fingers to remove chunks of mud, Jack stood and uncovered
what looked like a toy soldier, a wooden one, its tiny hands outstretched. This
was a mystery, and mysteries outweighed heavy tires. Jack rushed into the
house, past his still arguing parents, and up the stairs. In the bathroom next to
his bedroom, Jack took his new discovery to the sink and turned on the water.
Little by little, he cleaned away the dirt.

The toy was a little weird, like no soldier he had ever seen before. Not
that he was an expert on wooden toy soldiers, but the ones he'd seen in toy
stores were never posed like this. This one had a straight leg and a bent one,
like it was running, arms out like it was reaching for something. Its face was
weird, too! Like it was yelling. Or afraid? Or angry? Jack knew what would
cheer it up – some friends.

Jack's bedroom had a big ol' closet, about half as big as the whole
bedroom itself. Not only plenty of room for his toys, but plenty of space to
play. Since this was a soldier, Jack rummaged through his toy boxes and
pulled out all his plastic army men and any action figure that resembled a
soldier. But the one he really wanted to show to his new friend was Army
Guy 2000. The super-duper action figure was almost as tall as Jack and was
made forever ago, like maybe in the 1960s. That had to be old because Army
Guy 2000 used to be Daddy's toy, and he'd go on and on about how it was
better than the other big army toys, because this one was painted wood, not
dumb old plastic. Army Guy 2000 – or Guy, as Jack called him – had a hollow
wooden body and head with a smiling face, a little silly for a soldier, which
made Jack giggle if he looked at it at the right angle. Another silly part about
Guy was his super big feet and hands. He had toes and fingers, but his fingers
were curled into fists. His elbows and knees and wrists and ankles didn't
bend, because they were painted wood, too, but his green army clothes were
pretty cool. No boy parts under the clothes – Jack had checked.

"Okay, Guy, this is our new friend…" Jack stroked his chin and looked
skyward, like he had seen adults do on television while thinking. A name

popped into his head. "...Silas. Now, Guy, no laughing. It's no sillier than your name."

Jack held up Silas so Guy could see him better. Neither soldier did anything, their expressions frozen in place, Guy smiling at Silias' silent scream. "Okay, soldiers, I'm going on a mission back to the barn, so I need you to—" A thought struck Jack so hard he almost fell over. "But first, you need to see something."

Jack ran to his bed and crawled underneath, grabbing his shoe box of treasures. It only contained four things: A perfectly round and smooth rock, a black feather with a white tip, one of his baby teeth, and the item he was most excited to show to his soldiers – a pocketknife.

"Now, Mom and Dad don't know I have this, so I order you to never tell them," Jack commanded as he returned to the closet. Sitting cross legged, he fussed with the knife. It was so hard to open! "Every good soldier... nnnngh... should be...guuuuh... prepared and have... nnnngh..." Jack's thumb pried into the little groove, snapping open the knife, but the tip sliced his index finger. The knife was plenty sharp.

Wide-eyed and holding his breath, Jack wondered why the bloodied cut running the length of his finger didn't hurt as bad as it should. He winced at the sharp pain that should be coming any second now. But then something weird happened. A drop of blood fell onto Silas, at least he thought it did. Jack didn't see red anywhere. And while he looked in wonder, a few more drips from his bleeding finger fell onto Silas. The wood immediately absorbed the blood. This went from curious to cool!

Jack's finger started to sting and burn, but the pain didn't matter. He rubbed his oozing finger over the wooden soldier. The red streak slowly disappeared into the wood. Suddenly, the toy soldier moved, twitched in Jack's hand. Not only had he found a cool wooden toy soldier in the barn, but it was magical! What other magical items were in the barn? Then the soldier sat up.

Startled, Jack released the soldier, but the soldier didn't release him. The wooden toy jammed his tiny hand into Jack's cut. Jack's finger exploded with pain, panic flowing through his chest. He screamed but only hoarse squeaks came out of his mouth. He shook his hand, the cut now bigger and bloodier, but Silas wouldn't let go, until Jack used his other hand to pull with all his might and fling the wooden toy to the floor, close to where he had dropped the pocketknife. Noise came out of Jack's mouth this time, but his screams were short lived.

*

Ahhh…Existence. Silas was aware of his own existence. Awake again. He had been woken from his slumber before, by some stupid little kid. Who was he kidding? All little kids were stupid. Never listening to their parents. Playing where they ought not to, with things they shouldn't touch. If little kids were *too* stupid, then they'd end up like him, and no one wanted that, right? If Silas knew only two things, it was how to spread a woman's legs and stupid little kids would find ways to be stupider. Then again, the last time he awoke, it was Silas who had been stupid.

But he didn't know better last time. He had been floating in darkness and then suddenly he was aware, awake, and being held by some stupid little kid. It was the kid's blood that brought him back into existence and he needed more. Not thinking, just doing, he sucked up as much blood as possible, as quickly as possible. But that hadn't worked out so well.

Tossed into the corner of a barn, Silas faded away – aware of his existence, but unable to do anything about it in that moment of consciousness right before sleep took over. That moment stretched out forever. Until now. Thank God for stupid little kids.

This time Silas told himself to be patient, and to figure things out *first* before acting. He could see and hear, but in a muted fashion. The world around him was blurry and the noises muffled, like he was underwater. He could feel, too, but a level of sensitivity was lacking. He had felt the pressure of the stupid little kid's grip, but nothing else – no painful squeeze from the grip, no contact against his skin. Why was that? And why was he so damn small?

His thoughts were clouded as well, slow and thick like wagon wheels through mud. But now his mind raced with a jolt as if he'd drank a whole pot of coal miner's coffee.

Wood. Blood. He was made of wood and needed blood to move. He remembered learning that the last time he was woken. It made no sense, but he knew he needed more blood. Patience this time. Allow the stupid little kid to be a stupid little kid.

As sure as God made little green apples, the kid came through, willingly smearing blood all over Silas. More! Yes! The blood had seeped into his wooden body, and he became more and more alive. But...he shouldn't be made of wood! He should have a real body.

And looky here, this kid had a real body, didn't he.

The idea of being trapped inside a kid didn't appeal to him, having already been one so many years ago. How long ago was that? Didn't matter at the moment, taking over the kid's body did. But how? No better way than the direct way, so Silas shoved his hand into the kid's cut.

The sudden gush of blood invigorated him, but it didn't help his goal none. The kid was only a kid, but Silas was a wooden toy, too small to overpower anything other than a good idea. Bless his lucky stars, because the stupid little kid threw him right next to the pocketknife. It wasn't much, but it did the job. Silas was barely larger than the knife, but he was able to use it to shut the kid up. Now, to take over his body.

The knife was sharp. Few things worse than cutting hide with a dull blade. It took only one pass to slice a hole at the base of the kid's neck big enough to fit through. Silas crawled in and...

The blood energized him, made him feel like he could run around the world in stiff boots, but nothing else happened. He thought he'd get inside the kid and magically take over, like some kind of possessing ghost from the stories he'd heard while sitting around campfires. If he wasn't some kind of ghost, then what was he? He certainly wasn't human no more, though after measuring his heart and deeds, it could be argued he wasn't ever human to begin with. But right now, he was wood in the shape of a human. The only other thing around here like that was the kid's other wooden toy soldier. Silas got a bright idea. Well, an idea brighter than all the other stupid ones going through his head.

That other toy soldier was almost as tall as the kid. Its feet and hands were comically large, and it wore the goofy smile of someone who got hit in the head with a horseshoe. But when Silas touched it, there was a connection. He couldn't feel how hard the wood was or if it were cold or warm, but he felt that it could be an extension of himself. A way to be better, stronger, like riding a horse by becoming a part of it.

Silas pushed the big toy soldier over, needing a great amount of effort because the damn feet were so big, but it toppled nonetheless. The torso was hollow, empty echoes bouncing around inside when Silas tapped on it. He climbed on the toy and with the aid of the pocketknife, he split the shirt. It fell away, exposing its back. Right in the center was a hole, big enough to fit Silas' hand.

It took effort, but he tore away a small chunk of wood. After removing a few more pieces, the ragged edged hole was now big enough for him to squirm through. He dropped into the darkness and...

Yes! It worked. Silas, as the bigger wooden soldier, moved his arms and legs to push himself off the ground and stand.

The world now seemed smaller. He could see and hear, though only well enough to make out his surroundings. His first steps were wobbly, and his next few were a struggle. His arms and fingers weren't responding to his wishes. More blood. When he inhabited the smaller body, he needed blood to function. Made sense to him that a bigger body needed more blood. Luckily the kid was still right there. Silas was never much of a forward thinker, because if he was, he might not have done half the stupid things he'd done, especially with the last little girl that got the town all riled up enough to hunt him down and hang him.

After considering a few stray facts, he concluded that he'd need more blood. It had absorbed into the wood and helped him move, but the effects eventually wore off. He'd need to leave this closet and find more people. Gripping the pocketknife and looking at the dead kid, Silas got a bright idea. Well, brighter than all the other stupid ones bouncing around in his head.

*

Jeremy Tomlin hated fighting with his wife. Not only did he usually lose, but he always felt stupid about it. She was smarter than him, by a lot; her family told her that all the time. They were right. And wrong.

Yes, it was his fault for buying the farm without telling her, but she'd given him the okay when he'd first brought up the idea of them becoming farmers. He'd busted his ass to get his HVAC license, but hated the work. Awful conditions, a bad boss, and even worse customers. Coming from a small town, he'd known plenty of farmers and always wanted to be one. His wife had said okay, so he'd jumped at the opportunity.

Nothing made him angrier than paying the price for not knowing something he couldn't have known. He'd done the right thing – he'd found an affordable farm and talked to a lawyer. How was he supposed to know that dirtbag was going to screw him over?

But he hadn't gone to his wife before signing on the dotted line, which was the whole point of their argument. During the exchange of words, he didn't feel like that was *her* point, though. Every time they argued, she attacked his intelligence. Of course, that meant he'd say things he didn't really mean. Things he hoped Little Jack didn't hear.

While his wife was cooling off outside, Jeremy trudged up the stairs to talk to his son, to explain the situation as best he could.

Another thing about this house his wife didn't like… how quickly it became gloomy whenever the sun crept close to the horizon. Upstairs, the closed bedroom doors shut off any light from the bedroom windows, painting the hallway in darkness. Jeremy took a moment to let his eyes adjust, then jerked back as a dark shape formed at the end of the hall.

His son.

Something was wrong. There was all kinds of talk about women's intuition. Everyone knew that a mother's sense was almost supernatural, but men knew things too. A father could sense when something was wrong with his child.

Jeremy flipped the light switch, but nothing happened. His wife told him to change the bulb a week ago, and now he regretted his laziness. Jack was just a shadow at the end of the hallway, but he wasn't standing right. His posture was off. And he seemed... shorter? "Jack?"

"Daddy?"

The hairs on the back of Jeremy's neck stood up and his skin prickled along his arms. That was his son's voice, but it wasn't him speaking. Instinct told him to run, but what kind of father runs from his own son? A weak one, and Jeremy wasn't weak, despite what his wife's family said.

Jeremy approached, taking short, cautious steps. The closer Jeremy got to his son, the clearer Little Jack became, but what he was seeing didn't make sense. A strange expression was pasted on his son's face, and his body.... Was he naked? It was like clothing, but it was also like he wasn't wearing any. Jeremy couldn't make out what should have been familiar, the shadows playing tricks on his eyes. "Jack? Everything okay?"

"I don't feel so good."

Neither did Jeremy. Fear scooped away his guts, leaving a cavernous hole in his belly. His hands shook and he didn't know why. Confused about his feelings toward his boy – this was his son, right? – he crouched down and said, "It's okay, Jack. Come here."

Jack took awkward steps, like he'd forgotten how to walk. As he got closer, Jeremy saw him better, could see his son's face. And skin.

Like a robe that hadn't been cinched, Jack's skin hung loose and flappy from his body. Not a human body. More like a doll. A painted wooden doll – the toy soldier, the Army Guy 2000, that Jeremy had given him.

"The fuck?" Jeremy said, taking in the scene, looking this, this *thing* up and down as it waddled closer toward him. His knees burned from squatting, but he couldn't bring himself to stand. His throat closed and burned, his eyes wide. He tried to talk to his son, ask about what the hell was happening, but nothing came out of his mouth, not even breath.

Jack came closer with outstretched arms, the two ragged flaps of his chest moving like an unbuttoned shirt, his legs moving in wrinkled skin pants too big for him.

"Daddy, I need a hug."

His son's face was a mask over the doll's head, painted black eyes where his son's blue ones should have been. Yet, they held life, and emotion. Anger. Evil.

By the time Jeremy noticed that Jack was holding a pocketknife, it was too late.

CHAPTER 05

"You are what you eat."

Johnny Ghastson cringed. He hated that statement, yet people hurled it at him constantly. For the fourth time today, he considered his life choices, looking around at the pristine walls and neatly organized shelves of his little shop – a place for holistic, unique, and natural medicines and remedies – called Soliterraneous. It took years of Johnny explaining that it meant "not of this Earth" for people to understand. Usually, they'd simply give up asking what the word meant.

Stacks of loose, precisely lined up gemstones caught the light as the sun streamed through the windows, casting ghostly images across the face of the loose-leaf tea display on the opposite wall. Meditation bowls of various sizes lined the shelves signed with, "Ask for assistance," so kids wouldn't run around gonging the expensive brass with the little wooden mallets. The idea was to have the bowls sing, not annoy. Posters referencing chakras and the importance of maintaining optimal balance peered out from between floor-to-ceiling wooden bookcases. Dozens of various tarot cards and velvet bags of rune stones sat in glass cases by the register – both easy targets for shoplifting.

In the back corner sat several matching brown leather chairs, most of them wrinkled and cracked with age – he'd picked them up from Goodwill and yard sales. The chairs huddled close together as if entreating an enclave to take up residence around an oak coffee table topped with boxes of colored candles and strong scented incense cones.

The store was an affront to the senses: awash in a kaleidoscope of colors and thick with an amalgam of swirled aromas. It was a bleak existence for Johnny to be contained by these four walls, trapped with the same handful of constant customers all bleating for his attention, each with their own trigger points. Ms. Johnson, for instance, could be launched into a virtual tirade just by mentioning the state of the country under the sitting president.

"Arkansas," she winced, "never produced anything worthwhile." In the same breath she brashly proclaimed to those within earshot, "Unlike our beautiful state of New Mexico." But people like this were a lucrative necessity for Johnny, who had a bevy of his own expensive hobbies.

Johnny tried not to engage his clientele in any conversation beyond the items displayed in his store or things that he could order. Rich to a fault and maligned by ailments both real and imagined, Johnny applied his background in psychology to expose his clients' fears. Drawing from his medical background, he plied them with unrefined salves and natural balms as a mithridate against the pollution of physical toxins and the frenetic electrical bursts of frayed nerves.

"Isn't that right, Johnny? Isn't it?" his current sheep-like customer bleated. "You are what you eat."

Johnny was transported back to his college days. He'd gotten embroiled into an argument with his Nutrition 101 professor, a tall, thin Asian woman of indeterminate age. The nutritionist had stated for the umpteenth time, "You are what you eat." It was a ludicrously simple statement to sum up the human existence, and he'd told her exactly that. The ensuing contretemps lasted half the allotted class time, ultimately resulting in Johnny's cessation of that class. How he hated that stupid, *You are what you eat*, mantra.

Surely human beings were far too complex and exist on more than just a physical plane for such a ludicrously simple statement to sum up existence.

"Mr. Ghastson? Uh, Mr. Ghastson, isn't that right?"

Johnny looked up from his reverie to find himself standing at the register, with Gladys Steckler's sycophantic smile fixed upon him, the need for his approval evident. He offered a weak smile in response. "Why, Mrs. Steckler, that lip balm I set you up with last month is really making a difference."

"Really?" Gladys crowed in on him with fake humility, the kind that twisted every nerve under Johnny's skin. "I didn't want to say anything, hoping you'd notice. You're such a flatterer. Can you auto-reorder? Say, once a month?"

Johnny pulled his Palm Pilot from his pocket and smiled. "I will make a note in your account… once a month… you're all set. Thank you for your business, Mrs. Steckler."

"Gladys. Please call me Gladys, Johnny. Say, do you have one of those herb poultices?"

"I'm sure I can put one together for you. Let me go in back for the lip balm and I'll get the herbs, too. Anything else you need while I'm back there?"

"Do you still have those protein bars from that little company a few towns over?"

"Peanut butter, right?"

"Yes, please. They're so good. A half dozen if you have them, please."

"Give me five minutes," Johnny said. His frozen smile did not melt until he had crossed the store and put his hand on the backroom door. He cast a glance over his shoulder to make sure no one was watching as he swung it open just wide enough to slither through.

Behind the door was the stockroom. He grabbed the lip balm, then proceeded down the narrow hallway past his office, and entered the adjoining area. Herbs were pinned to a clothesline drying. He grabbed a few, then glanced at the moveable room partition that stood beyond. Taking a few quick steps, he peeked beyond the partition. The smile returned to his lips, a genuine one this time.

"Comfy?" he asked. "I'll be back soon."

There was no answer from the corpse lying on the dissection table behind the ersatz wall. Ragged grey hair framed a well-worn and weathered face, the forehead splayed open, flaps of skin pinned neatly back to expose a sawed open cranium, which served as a bowl for sliced and diced brain matter. Cold, blue eyes fixed the ceiling with a vague, frozen stare. Johnny reached toward the corpse, pulling on the bottom jaw so the mouth hung open as if in astonishment. He smirked before spinning around and walking back to the store's main room.

Johnny used a marble pestle and mortar to crush various herbs, added a tablespoon of liquid from a bottle behind the counter, and continued mixing

34

until the blend became a thick paste. He scraped the cataplasm into a plastic jar, sealing it tight before dropping it into a bag with several wrapped strips of cloth and the other items Gladys had requested. When finished, he called her to the counter and accepted her payment with a flourish she undoubtedly expected after making it known that the left-over change was for Johnny. "Keep it as your tip," she said.

As if he needed the old lady's two dollars and thirty-five cents.

"Don't forget to heat up the poultice before application, Gladys."

"Thank you. You're such a good boy. The world needs more people like you, Johnny Ghastson."

Johnny smiled. "And enjoy the protein bars. I tossed in a sample of the new berry flavor for you to try."

"You are what you eat!" she responded, clearly proud of herself.

Johnny stifled a cringe as he waved goodbye to her, disgust welling within him. When she was no longer in sight, Johnny sat down and waited out the last hour of his day before flipping the "open" sign to "closed." He pulled down the half shade and locked the door.

After he reconciled the cash drawer, Johnny set himself to prepare the cadaver in the backroom for disposal. A thick, plastic bag over the head, cinched tightly about the neck with a piece of nylon cord ensured that no blood or brain matter went astray while the body was transported. There were no other incisions on the body. Johnny was a focused surgeon and his interest in *this* body was solely on the forehead.

"You aren't a very good sneak," Johnny said without turning around.

"I barely made a sound," his newly arrived accomplice said with protest. "No way you heard me."

"I don't need to hear what I can smell from the other end of a city block," Johnny replied, wrinkling his nose. He couldn't get used to the smell of hog that pervaded every piece of clothing Amos Boyle owned.

"Sorry. Extra showers would tell everyone I'd be going out, and you said I shouldn't draw attention to myself."

"Yes, thank you for following my instructions so closely, Amos. It simply wouldn't do for anyone to find out the nature of what we were doing here. Illicit experiments need to remain a secret, after all."

"Sure, sure. Did you find what you were looking for here?" Amos asked.

"No, this one was a dud."

"I might just be a hog farmer and all, but I'm pretty sure we all have the same basic body parts."

"Unfortunately, Amos, that is not always the case. At least not in this one. This poor sod is among about three percent of the population that lacks what I need. Good thing I don't play the odds, eh?" Johnny grinned at his own joke.

Amos was on the tall side, which made him appear thinner than he was, but his leanness was not to be denied. A lifetime of farm work and heavy lifting ensured the muscles attached to his lanky frame. And if Johnny hadn't known how much of a rube he was, then Amos' eyepatch would have given him a sinister flair.

Johnny looked over the cadaver, which was on the relatively small side for an older and presumably undernourished male, before working the table levers that dropped one end of the table to the ground, positioning the cadaver like it was practically standing on its own two feet. Hinting for Amos to get on with the deed, Johnny asked, "Do you need help with this?"

"No, I got it." With barely a sound, Amos lifted the dead man up onto his shoulder. "Out of curiosity, what is it you're lookin' for? What didn't this guy have?"

"Oh, well, I don't want to go into details about my work, so let's just say the poor bastard suffered from aphantasia."

Amos paused from his spot near the store's backdoor, and looked at Johnny as if he suddenly sprouted a third eye in the middle of his forehead. "The heck you say?"

"If one suffers from *aphantasia*, then one cannot visualize within their own mind. Simply put, the man slung over your shoulder has no mind's eye," Johnny replied.

Amos chuckled and pointed to his eye patch. "What a coincidence. I got no left eye."

Johnny sighed, and then gestured toward the exit. "The night isn't getting any younger, Amos. And the hungry piggies need time to make this morsel disappear."

"Right."

"Don't be seen, Amos."

"Got it." Amos disappeared out the door, which Johnny latched and locked behind his tall acquaintance. The sound of a truck engine followed moments later, then faded in the distance.

Johnny went to his office and slumped into his chair. The experiment had been a failure. No, the dead man was the failure. Johnny wasn't to blame. It wasn't his fault that there was no mind's eye present in this specimen. He couldn't have known that without opening him up.

He would simply need to be patient until a new cadaver could be procured. One with a mind's eye. Scientific hypotheses have led researchers to consider the pineal gland as the so-called "mind's eye." But that was too simple for Johnny to accept. There was more to the mind's eye than a pea-sized gland at the back of the brain. He needed proof of something more responsible for visualization. *Something that directly ties into the way we translate sight and sound and suggestion, something responsible for more than the simple physical mechanics of the human body, since we are more than physical beings. Something that brings unity to the physically and emotionally and mentally impressionistic beings that we truly are. Something that would help me shoot down the ridiculously simplistic notion that we are what we eat.*

"We are what we *consume*," he muttered to himself.

CHAPTER 06

The Ford-150 squeaked somewhere in the passenger side wheel well, where Riley sat, every time it hit a large bump. Dad had bought it new ten years ago, and "sold" it to Rand last year for a hundred bucks. Riley often wondered how much he would have been charged. Probably Kelly Blue Book value. Even though Riley had to deal with the noise, it made him feel better that Dad and Rand couldn't find the squeak no matter how often or in depth they searched. Riley sighed. Wasn't Rand's fault that he was Dad's favorite.

"What's up?" Rand asked from the driver seat.

Riley rolled his shoulders. "Good day at the gym. How was practice today?"

"Great!" The truck hit a rut deep enough to elicit two squeaks. "Rode Cyclone three times. Hit eight seconds each time."

"Nice!" Riley's enthusiasm was authentic. No matter what friends he had made over the years, none compared to his brother Rand. There had been plenty of disagreements and misunderstandings that led to a scuffle or two and the occasional fight. Nothing a couple days of quiet introspection followed by a mumbled apology couldn't fix.

Another bump, another squeak. The roads through the plains from The WinterBorn Ranch to Sandia Mountain were easy enough, even when the terrain morphed from sparse brush to thick forest. The rutted and gutted road to the clearing in the woods for the party was a different story. The closer they got to the clearing, the tighter the knots in Riley's belly twisted. He hadn't talked to Javi since the incident with Buster yesterday. The knots didn't loosen in the slightest when he thought about telling Rand a truth he learned about himself not so long ago. A realization, an admission *to* himself *about* himself. He now needed to hide that truth. But for how long? He needed to tell Rand but couldn't bring himself to say the words. His parents? Even harder to think of when and how, or how they'd react. Mom would accept him. Dad? Dad loved him, but they weren't... close. Not in the way that Dad was close to Rand.

One last truck-squeak broke Riley from his thoughts, and the truck lurched to a stop. "Here we are."

Riley blinked and looked around as if awakening from a dream. He'd been to the clearing plenty of times, saw the same banged up cars and used pickups from the vehicles afforded by teenagers. "Cool."

Rand turned off the engine and pocketed the keys as he turned in the seat to face Riley. "Hey, you okay?"

Riley frowned. "Yeah. Why?"

"You seem upset these last few days. Hell, you've been kinda out of it for a month or so."

Two and a half months to be exact from the day when the rising sun's rays lit up the inside of the barn and made Javi's skin glow. "Just a lot on my mind."

Rand's hand on his shoulder, grip tight, felt comforting. "Look, I get it. There's a lot going on. I'm graduating this year, you'll be a senior next year, we got them movie people coming day after tomorrow. But if there's something else eating at you, you can always come to me. You can tell me anything."

Does he know? No. Impossible. I didn't even know until a little while ago. Riley forced a smile. "Thanks. I do have something to tell you."

Rand leaned closer, priming to hear a whispered secret. "Yeah?"

"Yeah." Riley leaned in as well. After a tense few seconds, he belched and blew it in his brother's face.

Grimacing, Rand pushed Riley's face away. "Horse's ass!"

Both laughing, the brothers hopped out of the truck. They strode past other parked pickups, toward the center of the clearing, where a few other juniors and seniors from school were tossing logs and branches onto a pile rimmed by a circle of stones. They had about an hour before twilight descended, and the fire wasn't needed yet. But the keg was ready, and that was the place to start.

Rand filled a red plastic cup halfway and handed it to Riley. A furrowed brow was the only response Riley gave. Rand filled his own cup only halfway as well. "C'mon, you know the rules – be smart because being stupid could ruin this for everyone."

Taking a sip, Riley rolled his eyes. Their mother hated the monthly party, but she let them go because back when she and their father were teenagers, these parties gave them an opportunity to have fun and it's where they discovered their feelings for each other. Their father had a more "boys will be boys" attitude. "Yeah, yeah, yeah, be smart."

Rand tapped his cup against Riley's. "Exactly. Cops don't bust these parties because they were here when they were in high school, same with their parents. How many decades of the monthly party without incident? God knows I don't want to be the one to mess that up by getting drunk and stupid. Do you?"

Begrudgingly, Riley tapped his cup against his brother's. "Nope."

After a quick sip, Rand looked past Riley and smacked his shoulder. "Alright. Be smart. Now, I see Maribeth by the tree-line. Meet at the truck in three hours, no excuses."

Once Rand was far enough away, Riley added a couple more ounces of beer to his cup. Not a big fan of beer, it would probably be warm by the end of the night, doubting he'd even finish it. He mostly carried it around to keep people from asking why he wasn't drinking. After all, he'd been faking it for his entire life.

Across the clearing, a few of his football teammates congregated, whooping and baying at a moon that had yet to show itself. To keep up appearances, he started in their direction, conjuring a howl in the back of his throat. It caught, causing him to cough, when he saw Javi.

Feet frozen to the ground, Riley stared, watching Javi laugh and converse with a group of five other students. Javi had graduated last year, but he still knew enough of these high schoolers to keep him coming to the party. When Javi noticed him and smiled, warmth bloomed within Riley's chest, strong enough to liquify the rest of his insides.

Too far away to hear what they were saying, Riley watched in silence as Javi said something to his friends, and then strolled toward the forest. None of his friends seemed to notice his foray into the dark woods, so Javi must have been subtle. Riley snapped out of his stupor and blushed, as if every eye of the party were watching him. But he slowly turned in a full circle, and not a single laughing, talking person seemed to have noticed his presence. Perfect!

When he was on the football field, Riley had speed and power, no need for stealth. Now, he scurried across the clearing as catlike as his large form allowed. Once he crossed the forest's tree barrier, he paused and looked behind to make sure no one was watching or following. Heart pounding harder than after throwing a touchdown, he continued farther into the woods. Plenty of light filtered through the thin canopy of leaves, so he had no fear of losing his footing on the uneven terrain. Deeper into the woods, the mountain asserted itself, sloping and rolling in random ways. The slope grew steep. Riley's calves tightened as he ascended, and he grabbed hold of sturdy saplings for support as he climbed to a flatter area near a patch of trees by the mouth of a small cave.

Javi was leaning against the trees, hands in his pockets. "Hey."

"Hey," Riley replied as he set his cup on the ground and put his hands on Javi's waist.

"Sorry about screwing up with Buster."

"S'alright. My mom got him under control, so it's all good."

"I meant the reason why I messed up. You don't think she suspects, do you?"

"She doesn't."

"I don't know. She might—"

Riley pulled Javi closer, chest to chest. "I don't want to talk about my mom right now."

Javi smiled and threw his arms over Riley's shoulders.

They kissed. And it felt right.

Their first kiss had happened behind the barn, a week ago. It was so surprising that Riley barely recognized what was happening. But it felt right.

Anytime he had kissed a girl, he felt like he was warming the bench, just waiting for his chance to put on his helmet and take the field. With Javi he was off the bench and playing.

Time melted away as if they were the only two people in the world, alone with the soft forest noises. A click and the soft whir of a tiny motor. Unusual, but not enough to stop. Until Riley heard the sound again.

Breaking away from Javi, Riley's heart turned to ash when he saw Mercer Boyle and Caleb McTavish. Polaroid camera in hand, Caleb clicked it a third time and handed the picture to Mercer. Lightning blasted through Riley, his reflex's taking over. Fast enough to grab the camera and throw it against the nearest tree, shattering it, but not fast enough to snatch the pictures from Mercer as he jumped back. Before he attempted anything else, another click; Mercer's switchblade popping open.

And yet another click; a switchblade in Caleb's hand. "Not so fast, pretty boy."

The Winters weren't overly religious people – the phrase "Christian enough" used by all four family members – but they had values. Hate wasn't a word that touched any of their lips, even in jest or hyperbole. But Riley hated Mercer and Caleb.

He hated all the Boyles. A lot of people did, but Mercer was in his class even though he should have graduated with Javi's class. He shared the same forward slouch as the rest of his kin, though his father, Archibald, hid his under fancy clothing, and his Uncle Amos diverted attention with his unsavory appearance. Mercer's frame was that of a condemned outhouse ready to topple over – thin and ramshackle – and his facial hair had been present since the fifth grade and was still just as wispy. Caleb's thick face had thick features. It was no secret that his parents were cousins, nor was it a secret that he did horrific things to animals using firecrackers and gasoline.

Facing two switchblades, Riley could only clench his fists and seethe.

"Well, well, well, who knew pretty boy Winters was a faggot?" Mercer's nasally voice came across as cartoonish, most likely from him trying to sound more sophisticated than his lineage allowed. He looked at the half-developed pictures and continued, "I sure didn't until two minutes ago."

"I did," Caleb said with a grunt, his voice deeper than the county majority. A flick of his tongue across dry, scaley lips. "He's so pretty."

Riley took a step closer, eyeing the Polaroids. Both Caleb and Mercer asserted their control with the switchblades. "I could take you both on."

"Oh, I bet you could, faggot. In fact… You want these pictures? That's what you'll have to do."

Javi gasped and Riley frowned so hard that his nose hurt. "What are you saying?"

Caleb dropped his pants first and held the knife tip uncomfortably close to Riley's neck. Mercer dropped his next. "Oh, I think you know what we're saying."

Riley sneered. "I didn't think you were gay."

"Getting a blow job don't make us gay," Mercer said.

"Getting one from another guy absolutely does."

"Pfft. I've stuck my dick in watermelon, honeydew, and cantaloupe. That don't make me a melon-lover."

"An' I put my dick in worse," Caleb said, chuckling.

Riley shuddered. He wondered if he could swat Caleb's knife away fast enough. Or could he lunge at Mercer before getting slashed? He didn't need to tackle him, just push him. Or—?

Mercer laughed. "You ain't that fast, pretty boy. I can see your thinkin' all over your face. We cut better people than you, Winters. Even if we ain't cut ya, we'll get in a few good hits. Rough terrain might twist your knee. At the least, you beat the shit out of us, and we go to the cops. Whatever chance you got at a scholarship disappears."

Scholarships. If Mercer and Caleb leave with those Polaroids, Riley would be done with football, and his scholarship chances would go up in smoke. He had no choice.

A gurgle bubbled up from his gut and popped at the back of his throat, acid burning hot and starting the water in his eyes. He clenched his jaw to keep his chin from quivering, tight enough to send a throb between his temples. Javi grabbed his arm and said, "Don't."

Riley grimaced at what he had to do and made one last plea. "Why? Why are you doing this? Do you want money? I can get money."

Something darker than the shadows cast by the setting sun came across Mercer's face, the monster within roiling up from oily goo. "'Cause you're a Winters and I'm a Boyle, and it's about time we got the better of you. I'll be the first Boyle to get a Winters on his knees, and I don't care if I can't tell no one about it. And all the better if I get a tear or two out of you."

Riley wanted to run and hide and make this all go away. Everything he'd done and shouldn't have done that led to this moment flipped through his mind like the pictures in Mercer's hands, a portfolio of regret. There was only one way to get out of this with his scholarship still intact, and he damn sure wouldn't give Mercer or Caleb the satisfaction of seeing him cry.

Riley got on his knees, the sounds of Javi sobbing behind him.

CHAPTER 07

Night fell with a thunk, crushing out twilight's existence. *Perfect*, Silas thought. *Time to see what I can see.*

"See" was a subjective term at the moment. Silas didn't have eyes. Well, not in the normal sense.

He didn't know exactly what was going on, but in the last day he learned himself a few things. As far as he could figure, his soul was trapped inside this toy soldier. Actually, he figured his soul was trapped in a small hand-carved wooden toy, but then – as the small wooden toy – he moved on up in the world by merging with the larger toy soldier. As far as Silas figured, he might be a ghost of some sort – he was hanged after all – but instead of possessing people, he moved his afterlife into toys.

No, not toys. The wood.

The first few hours after killing little Jack were chaotic at best. Being a ghost and possessing things had rules, none of which he knew until he surmised that the wood he inhabited needed blood. Thirsted for it, the way he used to thirst for a beer and a shot after a long day of riding across the plains under a cloudless sky. Little Jack sure supplied enough to get the joints moving, allowing him to walk around. And to kill Jeremy.

Silas learned Jack's pa's name because that's what Ma screamed when she first saw Silas wearing her son's skin, and "Jeremy" was the last word she spoke. Shame that Silas had to kill her before he could use her as God intended, as cute as they come and a great set of milkers. Real shame. But Silas got over it, on account that he had nothing on his body that would bring him pleasure. That was when he learned a few more rules about being trapped in wood.

He saw the world as he once did from where eyes would be on the toy. His soul must have had something to do with that, like it remembered how to see out of instinct. And hear, too. Everything was muted, but he could make his way around in this new world he found himself in. Touch was a different story, though.

When he removed little Jack's skin from his bones, he judged the right pressure to hold the knife and make the best cuts possible, but he couldn't feel the texture of the boy's soft skin or the meatiness of the little bits of muscle beneath it. He didn't necessarily wish to do what he did, but when he witnessed the image of himself in a mirror – and he most definitely felt a *coldness* within himself – the image told him, that ain't right. It ain't right wearing the skin of a boy like the hide of a deer, but it was a more natural step up from watching a big marionette move around with no strings.

On a lark, he cut the talk-box out of Jack's throat, and held it up to his own neck, and it worked. Using the boy's voice fooled Jeremy, and then again fooled Ma. It was a clever trick, but he had a more pressing matter than fooling around with other body parts. He needed to contain the blood.

The washroom. It was stranger than any he'd ever seen before – for starters the pisspot was a permanent feature, like they moved the outhouse inside – but he recognized the bathing tub. Different, like everything else in this world, but he figured out the stopper on the chain clogged the drain hole quickly enough. Then he learned one more thing about his new self – his strength.

Stronger than his size should allow, he had no issues dragging Jeremy and Ma into the washroom, but not strong enough to heft them into the tub with one motion. Arms and head over the edge first, he then lifted and pushed as best he could until he got them in. The lack of height was burdensome, but sure as God made little green apples, he was stronger now than when people knew him as Silas Worthington.

After getting Jack's dead parents into the tub, Silas afforded himself a breather, which gave him the sick kind of chuckles after hearing a nasty joke, since he hadn't taken a single breath after waking up from the long slumber. How long, though? Thought he saw some newspapers lying about.

Sure enough, in the corner of the kitchen – even though they looked unusual, he recognized the oven and ice box – laid a stack of Albuquerque Journals. A dozen or so, all with dates of mid to late April in the year of the lord, 1996. Had he any lungs to hold breath, it'd have been taken from him. The machinations of numbers never appealed to him, but he conjured enough mathematics to know it was well over a hundred years between this sunset and the last one he'd seen.

If Silas knew two things, whatever happened to him wasn't natural and had he the propensity for fear, he would have felt it now. Wanton desires had been in the forefront of his motivations, yet desires sometimes had to be put aside for survival purposes. This was one of those times. He had no inclination for any of the sciences, but he needed to pay attention to when he started to stiffen and how much blood was necessary to loosen back up. From the time the sun went down yesterday to sundown today, he needed to call upon absorbing blood twice. The amount he needed for the full day was what he had drained from little Jack's ma. In between, he spent the hours learning about this new world.

Same world, different time.

Since he was able to use little Jack's voice by holding the kid's voice box to his own wooden neck, he then tried the same technique with other body parts. He needed more than a pocketknife for that and the kitchen held remarkable marvels – the ice box had very little ice but still managed to keep oddly packaged foods cold; cupboards kept food and spices as well as plates and bowls; alien devices were laying on the countertops. The drawers contained more cutlery than was available in the entire county back in his day. His immediate need, though, was for a more suitable knife than the pocketknife he had used on little Jack and his folks, and the drawers held aplenty.

He grabbed a spoon to pop Jeremy's eyeballs from their sockets like grapes squirting from their skins, and sure enough, when Silas held them against the toy soldier's face, his vision improved. Taking a moment to use the knife on his wooden skull, Silas cut grooves deep enough to hold the eyeballs. An ear pressed to the side of his head helped him hear better, but the need for pristine hearing was low on his list. He was happy enough about the improved vision, but it only lasted the day.

When the eyeballs stopped serving their purpose, there was nothing Silas could do to rejuvenate them, no matter if he poured blood over his head or plucked them out and dunk them into a crimson pool. When the eyes were done, they were done; the grapes turned to raisins.

Good to know.

What wasn't good was running out of what he needed to move, to live, to haunt.

Now that the sun fell away, it was time to see what changed in the world outside the house and to find more blood. With one of Ma's freshly plucked eyeballs stuffed into the socket of his wooden head, Silas ventured into the night.

The land felt familiar, the star-specked sky recognizable. He couldn't feel much, but something unnatural twisted inside him, like whenever he'd eaten meat past its prime. He wasn't standing too far from where he had been hanged. This house hadn't been here back then, nor had the barn now filled with junk instead of animals, nor these two covered wagons made of metal. Somewhere in the distance, the Devil Tree waited, called to him. Silas walked the other direction.

The sickle-shaped moon and twinkling stars offered enough light to show Silas the darkened brush around him and the slight shifts in the flat terrain. Not a problem even if the celestials hadn't been helpful. He'd walked this land back in the day; maybe not this exact path from this farm to the next, but he'd worn out the soles of his boots aplenty. Even on a night like tonight he could almost see the ground's crumbled rust color. Though it unnerved him not to feel the air drop from warm to cool, nor the breeze. He still wore the cloak of little Jack's skin, a flesh and meat robe, but unlike Ma's eye, it added nothing to the senses. Should he be seen, it camouflaged him enough to get the jump on his next unsuspecting victim, much as it did with Jeremy and little Jack's ma. That opportunity might come soon enough; Silas saw a large house with a light on.

Big ol' kitchen knives in his hands, Silas walked faster, then trotted, then ran, hopeful there'd be another family there with enough blood and spare parts to keep him moving for a few more days. Then a feeling hit him hard enough to make him stop in his tracks, like an invisible hand reached down from the heavens and slapped him. A… smell? Not quite – he couldn't smell. He thought about what would've happened if he had cut off Jeremy's nose and held it over the wooden one he had. That fleeting thought didn't matter one hill of beans, so he tossed it from his head and concentrated on the… awareness? Something with no words or sound called to him. Blood. He sensed blood.

The alluring pull came from close to the house, but not quite the house. Silas continued fast of foot, but not a run. Had he been this cautious when he was alive, he might have avoided the hangman. A structure away from the house – a barn? It was smaller than a usual barn, but the closer he got, the one shape became two. No roofs, no solid walls. He wondered why the structures were so far away from the house, but as he got closer, he thought he heard snorts. Pigpens?

Not bringing an ear with him was a regrettable decision, since he needed to get closer to be sure he heard swine. There were a half dozen pens from what he could reckon, grunts coming from most of them, but he was more interested in what he was sensing than what he was hearing. There was blood, and it came from only one pen.

Silas crept closer, reminding himself to look around, trying to be wary of any farmer or family member still out at this hour, but his curiosity was too great. Thick wooden slats formed the walls of the pen and climbing them was easy. Draping one leg over the top, Silas got himself secure before looking into the pen. And he almost fell over from what he saw.

A trio of round bellied, thick thighed boars snorted and slobbered while tearing at a body. A human body.

Silas hoisted himself over the top of the pen and landed with a splash in ankle-deep slop. The pig-dinner used to be a man, an empty cavity where is guts should be. The hogs worked the hands and feet, crunching bone loud enough for Silas to hear without extra ears for assistance. What mattered to Silas, though, was what he saw – glistening blood.

Sure, there was mud on the man, but who hadn't eaten something off the ground before? Silas wasn't a particular fellow, and he craved blood too much to care. A man this dead didn't have much to give, but a few drops was better than none, right? Two hogs munched on the legs, one on the left arm. When Silas tried slipping himself in a gap between the hogs for a go at the body, one of the boars took exception and shifted its bulk to block him.

Stronger than usual or not, Silas doubted he was even thirty pounds. No match for about three hundred pounds of hungry animal. Well, then. *A two for one dinner*, he thought as he tightened his grip on the knives. Staying close to the pen's wall, he crept around the pig, eyeing up its fat neck. The knives were plenty long to reach its jugular – all Silas had to do was survive the initial strike. Each step closer, he set his footing. Then he heard a familiar sound, one that hadn't changed much in over a hundred years – the clack of a shotgun. "I recommend you stop what you're doin' you weird fuckin' kid."

Silas froze. He turned toward the voice. The amber flare of a puffed cigarette glowed. The dim moonlight shone enough for Silas to get the gist – a thin man had dropped into the pen, the gun butt tucked under his armpit, finger on the trigger. He had enough tight muscles to do farm work, shoulder length black hair oily enough to run a lantern for a few hours, a stubbled chin a person could use to light a match, and an eye patch. He held a strange stick in his free hand and was pointing it at Silas. Light! Bright, painful light came from the stick!

Silas raised his hands to cover his face, unable to blink.

"Whoa," the man said. "You ain't no kid now are ya? What the fuck are you? You're... somethin'... else."

The man kept the beam of light on Silas while walking closer. The pigs continued to grunt and munch and Silas assumed that the man coming toward him was responsible for the dead body since he paid it no mind. The swine scooted around the body to make way, lining up next to each other. Silas was thankful – the beasts just gave him a path to the dead man's head. Blessed be! The pigs hadn't defiled the neck.

Moving quickly as possible before the man's trigger finger got itchy, he cut out the dead man's throat. Surprised he hadn't been blown away yet, Silas pressed the pulpy mess – the blood absorbing into his wooden hands felt invigorating – to his neck and turned to the man with the light and the gun. "Wait. Don't shoot."

The man looked at him with his head cocked and jaw slacked, his eye holding the wonder of a curious child ready to poke a dead bird with a stick. This man wasn't scared. He was marveled.

"Name's Silas," he continued, moving his wooden jaw. "I need blood to survive."

The man's smile moved across his face like a spreading infection. "Nice to meet ya, Silas. Name's Amos. And I can get you blood."

CHAPTER 08

Every new dawn brought with it something different than the previous, especially life on a ranch. This was one reason why Amanda loved it so much. Rand would say that every day on a ranch was like a Magic 8-Ball while Riley only focused on the monotony of the chores, and whenever his frustrations boiled too hot, he'd express how excited he was to leave for college. There was enough routine to give Amanda comfort, but moving beyond the tasks of feed, clean, exercise the horses, she never knew what to expect from one day to the next, sometimes from one hour to the next. These experiences were wide and varied, ranging from near tragedy to unequivocal happiness, each adding to her preparedness for the next dawn. What she hadn't been prepared for was the possibility of her husband using obscenities, let alone shouting them while looking out their bedroom window.

"What in the God damn fucking hell am I looking at, Mandy?"

Eyes going wide, surprised to hear such language leave Hank's mouth, Amanda finished buttoning her blue flannel shirt as she joined him by the window. A caravan of vehicles was driving through the entrance, between the massive cedar posts holding the hand-carved "The WinterBorn Ranch" sign. A shiny Dodge Ram led the way, followed by four pickups each towing a moving trailer, then a Lincoln Town Car, six RVs, and a bus. "If I'm not mistaken, we're looking at the movie people, Dear."

"They're early! They said around lunch time, not breakfast!"

Amanda believed he was madder at himself for being prejudiced toward those who lived on the west coast, joking last night that they'd show up after today's dinner. However, his next gripe was legitimate. "Why the hell are there so many vehicles?"

"That, darling, is a great question."

"No. No no no. This was not what we agreed to, and this will not stand."

Hank marched toward the bedroom door, but Amanda had to stop him before he embarrassed himself. "Hank. Clothes."

Sill in the start of his morning routine, with nothing more than a towel wrapped around his waist to stop him from showing off the secrets God had given him, it tickled Amanda to think about the high-n-mighty movie people getting the what-for from Hank while dripping wet from his morning shower. But it would only make the situation more inflammatory. She needed water to put out a fire, not gasoline.

Hank grunted and stormed to the closet. Amanda left the room saying, "I'll see what I can find out." Hank grunted again.

The lead Ram parked and two men barely a decade older than her sons hopped out, the rest of the vehicles lining up next to each other. At least they were smart enough to park away from the barn and paddocks. Javi's father, Ramos, led Sunny Day around the closest paddock while keeping a curious eye on the happenings.

Amanda greeted the two men with a smile. "Good morning. Welcome to The WinterBorn Ranch. I'm Amanda Winters. How may I help you?"

The driver hurried toward her, hand outstretched to either stab her or greet her. The look in his wide eyes didn't help, neither did his twitchy smile. "Hi, Amanda! How the hell are ya? I'm Miles Pennypacker, the producer. Great name for the guy with the checkbook, right? I'm the movie producer. Sorry, did I say that already?"

"You did, Mr. Pennypacker, but no sin in that." Amanda paused before her next question, stunned by the chemical warfare assaulting her nose. "Oh. Oh, my, that's quite a significant amount of cologne."

Sunny Day snorted then sneezed, as if affirming, and gave no resistance as Ramos led him back to the barn.

"Safari by Ralph Lauren. Guess I must've overdone it, huh? I didn't know what to expect coming to a ranch. I've never been to a ranch before. I barely leave L.A. other than to go to Vegas or Miami, so I didn't know what to expect."

"Miles, calm down, will you?" the other man said. A few inches taller, he seemed to have a more relaxed way about him yet looked no less out of place. Miles wore smooth gray slacks and black shoes that had an expensive shine to them. His glimmering shirt, a shade of blue God had no hand in creating, was unbuttoned to his sternum, revealing enough of his smooth, tanned chest to show a life lived without a single day of manual labor. The tightness at his round belly, thick arms and thighs, showed that when he sat at the dinner table, he enjoyed foods finer than the average man's paycheck could afford. This other man wore a sleeveless "Metallica" tee shirt, black jeans, and a black Stetson adorned with an ace-of-spades playing card, a bullet casing, and a skeletal snake tail. His cowboy boots were nice, though, black snakeskin with pointed silver tips.

An inviting smile cut through the field of stubble coating his lower face and neck, Adam's apple bobbing as he spoke. "Howdy. I'm Nixon Lang, the director. I apologize for Miles' behavior. He's just very excited about this movie. Which is why we're here so early."

"A little too early by my watch," Hank said, striding tall toward the conversation. As simply as brushing away a stray hair, Amanda fixed the collar of his denim shirt.

"Hi, Sir, Nixon Lang." The director offered his hand to shake. If nothing else, the director was polite, though it wouldn't surprise Amanda if it was an act. "I'm the director and this is Miles Pennypacker, the producer. We do apologize for the disruption of arriving a few hours early."

Frown softening, Hank looked at Nixon's hand like it was a snake ready to strike. Asserting himself, Hank grabbed it and squeezed tightly. "Apology accepted, but it doesn't explain why there are so many vehicles. Looks like ya'll are planning to live here."

Nixon scowled at Miles, the classic look of indignant surprise. Sweat beading along his hairline and ready to cascade, the producer stepped forward. "Hey, hi. Yeah, about that... Our scouts scoped out different areas. We didn't find any place more suitable than your ranch. You advertise 'a great western experience,' so we thought we'd book all your camping sites during our time here while filming."

Hank's muscles tightened as if he wrestled a five-hundred-pound steer. "First off, we don't have camping sites. None of our customers stay the night. They come, ride some trails, and then go. Second, you said you wanted to film scenic views, not the whole county."

"But you have plenty of space here for us to set up a ghost town —"

"Set up a ghost town? There are a few close to Santa Fe, just a little north of here."

"Yeah, but they suck."

Nixon put his hand on Miles' shoulder, tagging into the conversation. "What he means to say, is that while they are certainly authentic, they lack the *je ne sais quoi* that we can manufacture on a temporary set. We know this is a major inconvenience for your family, so on the way here, Miles and I discussed upping our fiscal offerings."

"Double!" Multiple rivulets of sweat flowed along the length of the producer's face. "Double our original offer."

"And the construction crews can be your choice," Nixon added. "We didn't bring any carpenters with us because we wanted to give back to the community by using local labor. If you have friends who want to make a quick buck by putting up the façade of a fake town, call them and we'll pay them more than their going rate."

As discreetly as possible, Amanda looked into her husband's eyes and whispered, "Hank, this is *a lot* of money we're talking about."

Hank's jaw muscles worked as he chewed on the new offer. "I don't know."

Miles looked like a child caught sneaking a cookie before dinner – he knew it was wrong but didn't know why. "No worries, no worries. The good news is, you're not the only ranch in the area. Our scouts told us there's a nearby farm – the Boyles' farm, right? If there's no deal here, we can head on over to the Boyles. I mean, they're your neighbors, right? So, we can just jump back in our pickup and go have a chat with them. The Boyles."

A shadow cast over Hank's face, a darkness summoned by the threat. Miles' tone was spun from cotton candy, but his words were coated with poison. Whoever these scouts were deserved a bonus for digging deep enough to uproot the local family rivalry. The darkness washed away all emotion from Hank, his face a blank slate. He spat in his hand and held it out to Miles.

As giddy as a kid seeing a real, live horse for the first time, the producer smiled, spat in his own hand – a string of saliva trailing from his bottom lip to his chin – and eagerly shook Hank's. "Great news! Oh, this is gonna be awesome! I love this! This place is awesome, the movie is going to be awesome, you're awesome. And huge! I'm liking how your 'stache is almost starting to curl into a handlebar. If you want, I'm sure we could work you into the script."

Chuckling, Nixon gently pulled Miles away by the shoulders. "I don't believe Mr. Winters has those kinds of aspirations."

"Yeah, no. That's cool. How 'bout them kids? They're handsome and strapping. They'd look great on the screen. They yours?"

Backpacks slung over their shoulders, Rand and Riley headed closer to the conversation. Rand's glee hung from him like gaudy jewelry and Riley's sour demeanor was on full display. Yesterday, other than eat and do his chores, Riley had stayed in his room, his eyes pink from crying. Something had happened at the party the night before, but he wouldn't talk about it and Rand claimed he had no idea why his brother was so angry. Hank assumed he was simply hungover, and gave him no flack about it since he had similar mornings back in the day. No Sunday hangover lasted until Monday. Something was wrong, but Amanda wasn't in a good position to play mother. For now, all she could do was answer Miles. "Yes, these are our sons, Rand and Riley. And, no, they don't have those aspirations either."

"Okay, yeah, no, that's cool. That's cool. Being in movies ain't for everyone, right?" Miles turned his attention back to Hank. "Okay, so we're gonna do this. Very excited. Where should we tell the crew to keep the vehicles?"

"I think it'd be best if you move all the vehicles to the southern part of the property."

"Not the north part?" Rand asked.

"No. The land is a little rougher there, so I think it'd be better for them to use that part of the property for filming."

"Filming? They're going to film on our property? Awesome! Are they going to get any local shots elsewhere in the area? Like Graffiti Rock? Getaway Gulch? the Devil Tree?"

The sun itself couldn't match the sudden brightness in the producer's eyes. "The Devil Tree? Sounds amazing! What's the Devil Tree."

"Not on our property." Hank's sternness ended that line of questioning.

Riley smacked Rand's arm with his elbow and grumbled. "We leaving or what?"

"Later," Rand said to everyone. Hands in his pockets, head down, Riley followed his brother to the truck without another word.

Once the boys drove away, Miles clapped his hands and rubbed them together with a hunger in his eyes, ready for a feast. "Okay, Hank. How about we head over to the crew and you can show them where to go?"

Amanda knew her husband well enough to know his answer would be, "To Hell," but his grace and fortitude kept those words in his mouth as he walked Miles toward the rest of the vehicles.

More sheepishly than the ewes two farms over, Nixon approached Amanda. "I am really sorry for all the surprises today, Mrs. Winters. Miles and I go way back and have talked about bringing life to this movie for a while. He can be a bit much and is easily excitable. I, personally, appreciate and respect what you're doing for us. Thank you."

Mustering her best fake smile, Amanda replied, "You're very welcome, Nixon. I appreciate the niceties, but I'll need you to pass along a message to the crew, and especially to Miles since he's the producer."

With a soft smile that would make many a woman coo, he said, "Absolutely. Anything. What's the message?"

Wiping under her nose with her thumb and index finger a few times, she said, "We do not tolerate drug usage or possession on our property. If we even suspect drugs, the authorities will be notified. And every stereotype you've heard about the locals in hick towns controlling the law enforcement? They're true."

A shade of pink touched his cheeks. He nodded. "You got it."

As he walked away, a car door shut behind Amanda. From the Lincoln, a man with a swoop of graying hair poorly swept over his bald spot exited. This guy's suit was more modest than Miles', but the way he sneered while eyeing the property made Amanda's skin prickle. From behind him, a blonde woman about Amanda's age with a made-up face that desperately tried to eliminate a decade, took unsteady strides in her heels. Aiming right for Amanda.

Wiggling her fingers, the woman called out, "Hello! Hi! Are you Mrs. Amanda Winters?"

Resisting the urge to reach out a steadying hand – Amanda had long since stopped feeling responsible for women who wore inappropriate footwear to a ranch – and waited until the woman stood in front of her before answering. "Yes, I am. How may I help you, Miss….?"

"Brett. Mrs. Brenda Haddon is my name. My husband and manager, Joel Haddon, is the man grousing around by the car. But I go by Brett. At least, that's how my fans know me. Afterall, I'm the lead in this movie," she said as she looked away, pretending to be humble, the same false humility Rose Sumter displayed every time she won the annual church baking competition, thanking God and her long-since-passed grandmother for giving her grace in the kitchen, when everyone knew her secret was a nuclear quantity of butter.

"It's nice to meet you, Brett," Amanda lied. "What can I do for you?"

"Well, as I'm sure you know, my character is a tough-as-nails farmer and after watching how you and your husband handled Miles and Nixon so effortlessly, I now know that you are my muse. I need to study you. I have to follow you around to absorb your essence and mimic your motivations. Oh, Amanda, this is going to be a hoot!"

Amanda glanced to Hank who was with Miles and the crew. She needed to summon the images of her boy's bright future to the forefront of her mind, because she now desperately wanted to call the whole thing off.

CHAPTER 09

"Okay, I have to go. I'll talk to you later, Mother. Bye."

Johnny thumbed the "off" button on the handset and placed the phone back on the charging cradle. He let out a small sigh, resigning himself to the fact that a child's first job was to carry out his mother's wishes. Even if she was a bit of a perturbance. Of course, as perturbances went...

"Amos, I'm off the phone now," Johnny said. "What do you need or are you just here to touch every product in my store?"

The lanky man scratched at his stubbled chin. He took a moment to return the crystals he had been admiring to their respective baskets. Judging by the many times he had inquired about them, he was probably unsure about the ruby's power to stimulate his sexual ability or the sapphire's ability to stimulate his artistic creativity, but desirous of testing the veracity of both claims. Taking a few steps from the alcove toward Johnny, Amos quickly turned back and snatched a ruby.

"Amos?"

"Yeah," he said, his long strides carrying him through Soliterraneous, within a scant few steps. "I need to talk to you about something."

Amos held out the ruby, and Johnny wanted to laugh, but there was a quality deep within his associate that he found interesting. A curious quality he wanted to investigate non-intrusively. He took the stone and transcribed the purchase details in a ledger, before slipping the ruby into a small, cinch bag. Pushing a bill of sale toward Amos, he asked, "What's on your mind?"

Amos fished in his pocket for money. "I think you should do another one."

"Another what?"

"Another thing. That thing you do. The thing."

Amos was naturally awkward, but this was beyond his normal scope. Johnny wasn't sure he wanted to be a part of where this might be going, especially if the motivation was as plebian as revenge or just some banal criminal intent.

"It's too soon, Amos. Patience is key."

"I... you, that is, don't have time to be patient. You're on the brink of something. Discovery can't afford to be delayed, I think I heard you say once."

Johnny knew he was being used, or, at the very least, set up. He began to consider the nature of their relationship and the value he had placed upon Amos. He wanted to know the motive behind this sudden need and considered himself more than capable of seeing through whatever veil Amos was trying to hold up. "Well, I'm touched. I had no idea you were so concerned about my needs, but there would be a much longer delay if 'we' were to get caught, so I still think the research needs to wait a while. I have a good memory and take copious notes. I don't forget details."

Amos hesitated, clearly considering his next words. "It seemed like what you did a few nights ago took you a big step forward. I know you didn't find what you were looking for, but you found what not to look for, right?"

Why was Amos so impatient? What could be so pressing? Was he in league with someone else? Was he trying to expose Johnny, maybe working with law enforcement and having some sort of plea deal in mind? Or, considering the purchase of the ruby, could this be some sort of sick fantasy, some dark urge that propelled him toward the malefic, even if by proxy?

"Why don't *you* do it, Amos?"

A blind man traversing a minefield would have been less nervous. "What? Me? I never..." Amos voice was increasing by octaves. "Why would *I* do it?"

"I don't know, but clearly, you're not willing to listen to reason, so if this is important to you, then be a man, be your own man, and take matters into your own hands. Your brother, Archibald... he is a doer, not a procrastinator. He wouldn't hesitate, wouldn't wait on another to satisfy his needs."

Mentioning Archibald, the owner of the pig farm where Amos worked and lived, was akin to using him as a weapon, a symbol of jealousy to be held aloft, a waypoint that could never be reached.

"Wait. What?" Amos hunched his shoulders forward, his hangdog expression drooping his entire body. Johnny suppressed a smirk. This was going all wrong for Amos. The simpleton was losing the situation, failing to seize upon an opportunity. "Johnny, look, I'm trying—"

"To manipulate me? To fulfill a sick need that you can't fulfill on your own?"

"What? No! Not at all. That's not it at all. I'm thinkin' about the needs of lots of people and the good you could do for society—"

"My research might never be accepted by society. And your denial is a little too vehement. I think that's it, Amos. I think this is one of your dirty, little cravings. You wouldn't want the world to know about them, now, would you? I assure you, I can make life very uncomfortable for you if you push me to that point."

"Wha... What do you mean?"

"Well, just that if people came nosing around about things, I might get nervous and slip up by mentioning unmentionables. If word got out about your predilections, then who knows what could happen."

"Predilection? I don't know that word. Are...? Are you threatening me? I could tell people things about you, too, but I don't and never would."

"That's right. You never will. Because, after all, Amos, who do you think people would believe? You or me? Your silence buys my silence."

Their argument was interrupted by a knock upon the front door.

"Johnny? Johnny, are you there, dear? It's time for you to open and I do need my tea."

Mrs. Jeffers. A store regular. Took tea – a far eastern blend – to aid with her blood pressure. Johnny wasn't sure if the promised effects were real or if it was a placebo effect, but the money she paid was both real and believable.

"Sorry, Mrs. Jeffers," Johnny called out. "Lost track of time putting away a new shipment. Be right there." Turning his attention back to Amos, he spoke in lower tones. "So, what will it be? Are you walking out the front door or slipping out the back?"

Johnny was determined to base his next course of action on Amos' decision. If he walked out the front door, then it was an act of defiance, which meant he was planning to betray Johnny, and Johhny would make Amos the next cadaver for the surgeon's scalpel. If, however, Amos slunk out the back door, then the man's motives, grisly though they might be, were solely his own.

"I'm opening the store, now, Amos. Time's up, I'm afraid." As he slowly reached for the door latch, he turned back, but Amos was no longer there, his long, quiet gait having led him out of sight. His slipping out the back door was a relief – he preferred foolishness over defiance. Johnny sighed, as if the exhale powered his shift in demeanor.

"So sorry, Mrs. Jeffers. Hope I didn't keep you standing out there for long. Please come in. Have a seat by the window and I'll grab your tea. One box or two?"

"Two, dear," she answered. Her tiny teeth barely showed through a wide smile, vomerine in nature, mostly hidden within thick gums. The expression stretched her gaunt face to its virtual limits, sending her age spots into a well-choreographed dance.

Johnny nodded politely, though her physiognomy appalled him, and he set off to grab her order. He exchanged insipid pleasantries while trying to rid himself of the thought of using a scalpel to play connect the dots on her face.

"Here you are," he said, bagging her purchase. "Put them on your account?"

"Oh, you're such a dear. Yes, please," she answered, standing slowly. "These little concoctions are such a help, dear. I feel twenty years younger. You're such a good boy for recommending them."

As Johnny walked the old lady toward the door, his phone rang again. He opened the door and waved goodbye.

"Thirty days?" she asked.

"Yes, Mrs. Jeffers. I will set a reminder on the calendar to re-order them at the right time."

"Goodbye, dear."

"Goodbye," Johnny said, closing the door after her. The phone continued its persistent ring, so, despite wanting to make note of Mrs. Jeffers next order, he diverted himself.

His mother. Again. "Hello, Mother."

"Son, I need to ask you something."

He sighed, wondering why she hadn't asked him on their last phone call.

"I just came back from my power walk around the block, and you'll never guess what I saw," she continued. "A homeless man."

"You called again to tell me you saw a homeless man?"

"Yes, Johnny. He was big and dirty."

"Because he was dirty, you assume he was—"

"I'm not making assumptions. He is what I said."

"Okay, what was he doing?"

"He was being homeless."

"Look, Mother, I'm kind of b—"

"And leering! He was leering at me, making faces and strange noises and acting all out of sorts."

"Are you sure this wasn't your imagination taking over?

"Johnny, do not patronize me. I know what I know. He was menacing me, Johnny. Me. Your mother. I can't walk down my own street now."

"Mother, you know he has a right—"

"To be gone! He has the right to leave. *You* need to make him leave."

"Mother, now is not a good time. Maybe you were just a little startled and would benefit from quiet time and a few sips of wine."

"Am I not capable of good judgment? Do you think I am unsound?"

"I didn't say that, Mother."

"I think you should come by for a visit. See for yourself, since I'm so incapable. When do you think you can come for a visit?"

Johnny sighed. For whatever cosmic reason, the Fates decided to taunt him and grant Amos his wish.

"Tomorrow. How's tomorrow?"

CHAPTER 10

Power. Riley had learned over the past seventeen years of his life that power came in diverse forms and actions. He preferred physical power. It made sense. Be stronger than the opponent to win the game. Simple concept. Workout, practice, train to get stronger. He knew of other power, too, like influence and sway and clout. The influence his dad held over him, manipulating his emotions by giving attention to Rand. But Riley could sway his mother through smiles and hugs, by listening and asking questions. Yet, his mother had clout over his father through subtle expressions or shifts in conversational tone. Those forms of power confused him. How could he break free from the power his father had over him, and could he ever wield the same power as his mother?

Then there was the power of decisive action. His strength came from action, from the most direct path between cause and effect. Two nights ago, he had been powerless. He was at the wrong end of two knife blades. More importantly, he was at the wrong end of a camera lens.

When he was eleven, he tried riding a mechanical bull because his older brother had tried it, liked it, and excelled. Always large for his age, Riley had bulled through elementary school, but when he tried to employ what he knew about strength to the padded machine, he had failed. No matter how he pulled, squeezed, or tugged, he still found himself at the losing end. That was the last time he felt powerless. Until Saturday night.

Mercer and Caleb had left Riley on his knees. Laughing, they zipped up their pants and tossed the Polaroids at him. A cold electricity had burst through his chest, the adrenaline-fueled relief that it was over, that the knives weren't used, that he retrieved the evidence. Then came the shakes, the cold sweat percolating on the back of his neck, the hot ball of acid spinning in his gut. A few seconds lost in his own mind, his own body. Javi dropped to the ground and threw his arms around him, sobbing. Riley pulled away, stood up, and ran.

Sprinting through the forest, up the mountainside and away from the party, Riley cried, each teardrop sizzling like hot iron, burning from the forge behind his chest. Fists clenched, he wanted to punch. Punch the trees he ran by. Punch Caleb and Mercer. Punch himself. He couldn't handle his own tears, his own pain, so how could he handle Javi's?

After a half hour of sitting behind a moss-covered boulder, crying and swearing, thinking dark and disgusting thoughts, Riley composed himself enough to return to the party. No one was staring at him. No one was pointing, laughing, whispering about him. A few teammates held up red plastic cups and whooped a greeting. Riley wanted to find Caleb and Mercer, bash every bone in their bodies, and toss them into the bonfire. Then sparks of rationality and glimmers of his potential scholarship flickered in his mind like fireworks.

"Hey," Rand said, tossing his cup into an empty cardboard box, a makeshift trashcan. "I was thinking about heading home."

Scanning the sea of classmates one last time – no Caleb, no Mercer, but no Javi either – Riley shoved his fists in his pockets and stormed toward the truck. "Let's go."

Rand followed on his heels. "You okay?"

Riley grunted, and Rand didn't ask again.

Rand didn't ask again on Sunday as Riley snarled his way through the day.

Nor did he ask this morning when they drove to school, though Rand was so taken with the movie crew, the movie was all he babbled about.

Which was good, Rand not giving much thought to Riley's disposition. Because Riley didn't want Rand to know he had revenge on his mind. He was going to get Caleb and Mercer back, with the power he knew. But there was another power – inaction – which confounded him the most.

On the way to lunch, Riley aimed for Caleb in the hallway. At his locker with two other scuzzy yokels. Fists clenched so tightly these past two days, Riley wasn't sure if they'd ever revert to open hands again, he stood next to Caleb and stared at him. There was no doubt in his mind that Caleb would reference Saturday. Heated words would turn into an inferno and after a righteous explosion, Caleb would be on the ground bleeding. Riley had his speech to the principal and his parents all ready, highlighting that he was defending his honor from the lying, no good snake. The one scenario he hadn't thought of was the one that played out.

"S'up?" Caleb said and nodded. Collecting his books and shutting his locker, he and his hick friends turned away, one of them mumbling, "Pretty boy sure is being weird."

"I know, huh?" Caleb replied as they strolled down the hall.

Didn't seem like Caleb had told his scumbag friends. Then again, if he or Mercer told anyone, it would look just as bad for them. No way either of them would tell a story that might turn into a rumor about them being gay. And no one who mattered would believe them anyway. Either of those two could stand in a park on a sunny day and tell people that the sky is blue and the grass is green, and not a soul would believe them.

But Riley wouldn't accept that they'd told no one.

Hours later, Riley was off to the last class of the day, and he knew he'd pass Mercer in the hallway. Every other day, Mercer called him pretty boy or uttered some nonsensical insult loud enough for others to hear. Today would be one of those days, Riley felt it. They started at opposite ends of the hall, aiming right for each other. Mercer was walking alone, looking away, but had that *I'll shit in someone's lawn and be proud of it* grin on his stupid face. Riley walked right down the middle of the hallway, his bulky form an unstoppable locomotive ready to roll over the dumb cow standing on the tracks. They'd meet at the halfway point and no way Mercer was going to pass up an opportunity to slam his shoulder into Riley's. That'd start his motormouth running. One thing would lead to another ending with Mercer on the ground, blood covering his face. A few more steps to light the fuse. Mercer looked at Riley, their eyes locked, and... Mercer looked away and side-stepped to avoid contact as they passed.

What the fuck?

The volcano in Riley's gut erupted and he had to swallow down lava. He now understood how unreleased stress caused severe heartburn. Which led him, a couple hours later, outside of school with Coach, waiting for Rand.

End of school-day Monday routine was Rand jumping in the pickup and driving off to riding practice, leaving Riley to make full use of the weight room for the next ninety minutes or so.

When Rand pulled up to the curb and rolled down the window, his eyes went from Riley to the football coach. Rand kept his tone light. "Hey, Coach. How's it going?"

"Good. Good."

"Everything okay?" he asked, eying Riley.

"Yeah, yeah," Coach said, chuckling. He shook his head. "Nothin' bad. Just wanted to suggest that you invest in a heavy bag for Riley here."

Rand frowned and smiled. "Yeah? Why's that?"

"Well, Riley is ready for next season. After an hour in the weight room, he told me he needed something in the equipment room. So, I gave him the key and after fifteen minutes or so, I went to check on him. I… ummm… I found him beatin' the ever lovin' snot out of one of the blocking sleds."

It was the only thing in the school with enough padding to absorb a hit or two or a hundred. A few teammates had joined him in the weight room and he'd gone along with the camaraderie as best he could, but every smile he faked, every fist bump shared, drove a wedge between him and them. The words, "Mercer's lying," were primed on the tip of his tongue, a bullet in a gun with a cocked hammer. Did they know? If they did, then they were setting him up for something. He had to get away, needed to be alone.

Rand glanced down at Riley's hands. Gym bag in one fist, the other by his side, knuckles a scraped mess of pinks and reds.

With a chuckle, implying that he'd seen this a million times, and a smile as warm and friendly as a freshly paved road, Rand said, "No worries, Coach. I think we're all excited for him to take us to states next year."

When Coach patted Riley on the back, worms wriggled in his guts, an unusual reaction. Head down, he hurried to the passenger door and jumped in.

They drove toward home, Rand giving Riley a few minutes of silence before asking, "So… Who was the blocking sled?"

Riley hadn't planned on saying anything, but the question was so direct with no preamble that the words flew out of his mouth before he could tether them. "Mercer Boyle."

Rand nodded. "Something happen at the party?"

Crushing his jaw tight to keep unwanted statements from escaping, Riley turned to look out the passenger side window. Rand took that non-answer as a, "Yes."

"You know I'm here for you whenever you're ready to talk, so I won't go on and on about that. Just let me know what you want me to tell Mom and Dad should they ask about your knuckles, okay?"

Riley grunted in response. The only other noises between school and the ranch were the engine and the mystery squeak when they hit a big enough bump. Crossing under the "The WinterBorn Ranch" sign was like crossing into the circus. Ramos, Javi – Riley hadn't seen or talked to Javi since Saturday night, but he was happy to see him – and the six other ranch hands had most of the horses out. Some blonde woman was talking to Mom by her shed-turned-workshop. Dad was gesturing to the producer and director in between shouting instructions to the ranch hands. A dozen random strangers milled about, a few smoking cigarettes, sure to be raising the hackles along Dad's neck. Pickup trucks hauled lumber to the northern part of the property while others returned with empty beds, all flowing like ants.

This was an absolute nightmare for anyone who wanted to be alone. Surely, Rand was excited by the activity, ready to be a part of this alien invasion. Riley worked up a few snarky comments for the sole purpose of antagonizing, but swallowed them when Rand asked, "You wanna go to the Devil Tree?"

Surprised by his brother's question, Riley whipped his head around with open-mouthed shock. Sure enough, Rand was focused on him, not the excitement and wonder happening outside the truck. Only him. "What? Are you serious?"

"As serious as a snake bite. Yeah, it's just a silly legend, but it might make you feel better. And if something ill were to befall Mercer, then all the better. Plus, legends are legends for a reason, right? So, who knows?"

"But... But Mom and Dad would never let us—"

"I don't know if you've noticed, baby brother, but Mom and Dad don't even know we're here yet. Now, you gonna get something for the tree, or what?"

Riley felt alone, like no one would understand what he was going through. But Rand was trying. A quick nod, and Riley ran from the pickup to his room. He dropped his backpack and gym bag at the foot of his bed and rushed to his desk, shaky fingers fumbling with the drawer. Pressed against the back of the drawer were the three Polaroids. *Don't look. Don't look. Don't look.* But he did. And his heart broke.

He wanted to kill Mercer and Caleb – literally wrap his hands around their throats until their faces went blue – and he hated how nice the pictures turned out. Javi's smile. His smile. Happiness found only in daydreams and magazine pages. How could these beautiful pictures come from something as ugly as blackmail? Summoning the strength to do what he must from his hatred of Mercer and Caleb, Riley shoved the Polaroids in the front pocket of his jeans and ran back to the pickup before Rand changed his mind or their parents noticed that they were home. Kicking up dirt, the truck peeled away.

Getting to the Devil Tree meant taking a barely-there strip of pavement off the main road to a packed dirt road to a trail that faded away after a mile. After another half mile of jostling to the point of whiplash and heads smacking against the ceiling, Rand stopped the pickup. Panting hard, harder than after his last workout, Riley took a moment to catch his breath. Hand on the door, he turned to Rand to see if he planned on coming with him to the Tree. Seat belt strapped and engine running, Rand showed no sign of leaving the vehicle. His brother held a serious expression, one Riley had rarely seen, as if what Riley was about to do carried earnestness, as if he knew that Riley's wish would come true. Did Rand wish Mercer dead as well?

Riley grabbed the hunting knife from the glove box and hopped out of the truck. The Devil Tree stood a football field away, alone, the single strand of black hair on Satan's blistered head. His feet were heavy as he walked, the cracked, red ground so dead that it leeched life from him. The barren earth didn't have a single scrap of life; no brush, no weeds, no insects, no animal remains. There were no twigs or leaves or skeletons – everything avoided this place, the welcome mat to Hell.

There were more rumors about this tree than stars in the sky and Riley had heard them all. He discounted the more extravagant ones, not quick to believe in witches or demons or aliens or the supernatural. The stories about it once being a hanging tree, he believed. Even though he never fell for superstition, the idea of vile criminals dying here gave him gooseflesh. Yet, here he was doing what he'd laughed at others for doing – coming to the Tree with a sacrifice and a dark wish, asking for a favor that would lead to harm. Divorcées seeking revenge on who divorced them. Victims of abuse wishing harm to those who hurt them. Business partners getting back at those who screwed them over. "Did you hear about So-N-So? They went to the Devil Tree and now Such-N-Such is in the hospital." Or broke. Or dead.

Mouth as dry as the White Sands desert, Riley approached the tree. The gnarled bark, so brown it looked black, twisted and flowed in ways never seen on a tree before. Scarred skin instead of wood. It was warm to the touch.

Knife tip digging and cutting into the tree, making a notch for the Polaroids, Riley whispered, "Mercer Boyle and Caleb McTavish. They wronged me in ways I can't speak about. Take them. Take them, kill them, damn them to Hell so the devil can make them suck his dick."

After tucking the photos in the newly cut notches, Riley ran the blade across his meaty palm, under his thumb. Blood pooled along the slice. He then ran his palm over the Polaroids and smeared blood on the tree bark.

A surge of nausea roiled through his stomach. The air in front of him rippled with heat vapors. Riley leaned into his forearm, against the tree, to keep from fainting. Fire and ice chased each other from his head to his feet. Eyes closed. Deep breaths. Relax. When the odd feeling subsided, he opened his eyes. Using his forearm to swipe sweat off his forehead, he noted the time on his watch. 6:46. He took a deep inhale and hurried toward the truck, but paused when he heard unusual scraping noises, wet and dry like chewing, as if tree-bark was munching on something. Breath shaking, he turned to look.

The Polaroids were gone.

Riley sprinted back to the pickup.

CHAPTER 11

Amos Boyle was a born lackey. Silas could smell the need to serve all over the rube, even though he had no sniffer for sniffing. Not that he was complaining! Silas loved himself a good lackey. If not for Amos, Silas would lack the knowhow to understand the modern devices found all over the Tomlin house. Electricity had come a long way, now found in every room of every house. A switch on the wall for lights and holes close to the floor to accept plugs attached to all sorts of mechanical trinkets. This was akin to witchcraft in Silas' mind, but he accepted what Amos told him, especially after learning about the flashlight and those heavy little things to power it called batteries. Batteries made all kinds of things work, like clocks – including clocks worn around wrists – music boxes, things called remote controls, children's toys, and in gasoline powered vehicles.

All too willing to help, his curiosity that of a backwoods boy poking at a bloated dog's corpse with a stick, Amos had collected the blood from the dead body in the pigpen, barely enough to coat the bottom of a metal pail. "Coulda got more had I known I'd be hosting company for dinner," he'd said, checking his wrist clock. "I gotta take you back to the Tomlin house. Can't have you stayin' at my place. It ain't mine. My brother, Archibald, owns it. Owns the farm and the livestock on it, too. In a month or two, he'll own the Tomlin property. His son, Mercer, lives with us as well. Neither of them know about my side business." He cackled like a man who either worked in coal mines or smoked too many cigarettes. "And they sure as hell wouldn't be willin' to help you the way I am."

And help he did. It took about an hour to learn the magic of the Tomlin house. A kitchen for cooking and an outhouse inside, neither of which appealed to Silas in his current state. They found books, but Silas was never much of a reader, only enough to know how much was being offered for his capture on "Wanted" posters.

That Saturday night, before Amos returned to his place, he taught Silas about the black square with the glass face located on the opposite side of the room from the couch. The square – and plenty of other things in the house – was called plastic. The glass was still glass, though. Combined, the materials formed something called a television. Had Silas believed in Heaven, this would be it.

Using a plastic stick full of buttons – a remote control, Amos called it – Silas could summon images of the outside world. Everything from beautiful people in beautiful places to the ugliest of the ugly wallowing in nastiness. Amos called the ugly nastiness "the news," and Silas continued to "flip through the channels." He stopped on channels with the prettiest faces and the biggest milkers.

Monday came around and so did Amos with a small, sickly-looking pig. "My brother ain't gonna miss this one much," he said. "Let's see if pig blood does what people blood does."

In the Tomlin barn – Silas didn't like the barn, a storage space of the abyss and bad memories – the pig left the world with a slit throat and a squeal. Amos made sure to collect the blood in a plastic bin. Plastic sure was handy for quite a few things, Silas learned. Then he dunked his wooden hand into the pig blood and learned something else – soaking his wooden hand in blood worked, but it wasn't... satisfying? Nourishing?

"Well?" Amos asked. "Is it working?"

Silas held the pulp of Jeremy Tomlin's throat against his wooden neck and said, "Sorta. It ain't right, but it'd do in a pinch."

Jaw jutting as if from real thinking, Amos nodded. "Alright. I stopped by and talked to my friend, the one who supplies the special food to the pigs, and tried to get him to get more."

"What does your friend do?"

"It's hard to explain, but—"

A sudden blast of pain and ecstasy struck Silas like lightning, crumbling something deep within his chest, his soul. Had he any lungs, this desperate and tragic feeling would have knocked the air out of them. The delicious taste of blood coated his tongue. *Do I even have a tongue in this body?* Didn't matter. The pain disappeared almost as fast as it struck, and he dropped to his knees.

Amos rushed over and grabbed Silas by the shoulders, giving him a little shake. His wrist clock rattled before his eyes, the time glowing 6:46. "You okay Silas? What was that all about?"

Names. Three names appeared in red through the blackness of Silas' mind, dripping like they were written in fresh blood. Mercer Boyle. Caleb McTavish. And... "Winters?"

"Winters?" Amos asked, standing and helping Silas balance on his short, wooden legs. "Us Boyles don't like them Winters very much."

Silas didn't care about family drama horse shit. But he did wonder why the hell those names flashed in his mind. And why it felt like God drove a hatchet into his head right beforehand. "Who are the Winters?"

"Our neighbors to the east. They're all so high-n-mighty, lookin' down their noses at us regular folk, actin' like their shit don't stink, all too happy to throw their weight around and try to keep us Boyles down."

Silas freed himself from Amos' grasp. Looking to the east, a vast field of sad looking greens ran in straight lines, many turning yellow and brown. Silas didn't know what the crop was supposed to be, but he sure as hell knew that it had failed. A couple hundred yards away was a border fence – a simple line of two lengths of wood between each post. On the other side was movement. Lots of people milling about like scurrying insects from this distance. Too many for a normal ranch, even in this day and age. "What's going on over there?"

Amos gawked, mouth open. "Oh yeah. They're rentin' their land to some movie people. See? I told you they was sons-of-bitches. When money come knockin' on their door, they keep it all for themselves, never sharin' with no one."

"Movie?"

"Yeah. Shows and movies. Like what you been watching on the television. It takes a lot of people to make just one movie. Lots of money to be made in them, as the Winters now know."

None of what Amos babbled about mattered. It was the blood. *Is this what wolves feel around a clutch of rabbits? How buzzards know where the carrion is? And what about them names?* It was mighty coincidental that Amos' nephew was one of them names, and he'd never heard Caleb McTavish pass over the rube's lips, but the biggest question mark was the name Winters. A tingle ran around the inside of his wooden body anytime that surname skittered through his mind. "I wanna go over there."

Amos chuckled. "I hate to break it to ya, but there ain't no way someone sees a moving wooden toy wearing the skin of a little boy without freakin' the fuck out."

"I have an idea." Silas walked back into the barn, to the vat of pig blood, and knelt beside it. "Now, listen good. My soul, or whatever the hell keeps hold of my badness, is in a smaller wooden soldier which is inside this bigger wooden soldier. I don't know how any of this works, but when a smaller wooden soldier pops out, it's me, and you're gonna put me in your pocket."

The sensation of separating the body of the smaller toy soldier from the body of the larger was odd, like shooting out of his ma at birth fully capable of cunning and conniving. As the tiny soldier, he crawled along the bigger toy to the vat and jumped in. Though it was inferior to human blood in every way, the pig blood fed him, energized him, allowed him to move. Unable to absorb any more, he crawled from the vat and stood upon the larger toy's shoulder.

"Whoa," Amos said, looking into the vat. "Look how far that level of blood dropped. You sure drank a lot."

Maybe it took two or three times as much animal blood to equal human blood? Silas would chew on that later, he had more important things to focus on, like the eyeball in the larger toy's head. It popped out easily enough and he needed both hands to hold it against his wooden face, but seeing clearly through it still worked. The throat was too big, so he hoped there was enough spark of smarts within Amos' head to figure out what needed to be done along the way.

Amos slid Silas in his flannel shirt pocket and jogged over to the Tomlin house. He grabbed a ring of funny-looking keys from a hook on the wall by the door, and then hurried back into the barn to some kind of vehicle. Silas had seen enough motorcycles on television and this thing looked like two of them mushed together – four wheels, one seat, one set of handlebars. A turn of the key and it fired up.

The speed was exhilarating, faster than any horse Silas had ever stolen. He'd have to question Amos about this thing later, but as they headed east for the northern part of the Winters' fence, the yearning to get closer to the people began to overshadow any other thought he had.

Once they were close enough to the commotion, Amos parked the vehicle by the fence and hopped over. He blended in with the activity of about two dozen people who were piling planks of wood pulled from the beds of pickup trucks.

Silas held the eyeball to his head sparingly, only when confident his action would go unnoticed. Amos was a rube, but he was right in his thinking about how unkindly these people would react should they notice a wooden toy toting around a human eyeball. During one of his lookie-loos, Silas spied something useful.

Certain his actions would go unseen, Silas tugged on Amos' shirt to get his attention, then pointed toward a set of modern-day wagons covered in plastic with a couple of windows and more than a few tires. One of the wagons had its doors open with racks upon racks of clothing around it. Silas found it curious that the clothing on the racks matched what people wore when he was alive and kicking rather than what he'd seen people wear nowadays.

He forwent the use of the eyeball as Amos ambled closer, but Silas made enough sense of the blurry world to see two women fuss over dressing a man. One approached Amos and said, "Hi! Are you one of the actors?"

"Just an extra, ma'am," Amos replied.

"An extra? We're nowhere near ready to start filming. We don't need extras yet. Is Miles making decisions again? God, he should just mind his own business and let Nixon do his thing."

Amos shrugged. "Yeah, I know, huh? What can ya do?"

Silas didn't understand a lick of what they were going on about, he just wanted a better look at the setup. He shook his tiny head thinking that plastic was so prevalent in this world that it was now used to make people. But upon further investigation, they were just fancy dress-forms. And one of them dress-form caught his eye.

"This is a cool looking mannequin ya got here," Amos said.

Amos, though a rube, must've figured out why Silas had wanted him over here.

"The wooden one?" one of the women asked, walking to the faceless mannequin, the woodgrain bold and running vertical.

"Yeah. It looks like it got joints at the elbows and knees."

A sing-song excitement in her voice, she said, "It does! I do a lot of sketching to create my outfits, so I use this wooden mannequin for unique poses. Plastic ones can't do that. Are you sure you're just an extra? The eyepatch is a good look for this movie."

"Oh, yeah? What kinda movie we got goin' on here?"

"None of your concern, Amos," snapped a stern voice. A woman had stormed around the corner of the plastic wagon with another woman in tow. Silas debated bringing the eyeball out to get a better look of these two, because his insides tingled again, even though he had nothing on the inside to tingle.

"Well, Mrs. Amanda Winters, I saw the commotion on your property, and as a concerned neighbor, I thought it my duty to investigate."

"I doubt that very much, Amos. I think you need to leave before Hank sees you."

Amos tipped an invisible hat and started to walk away. "You got it."

The gaze of leery eyes stuck to them like warm horse shit on bootheels as Amos strutted back to the vehicle that brung them here. Before he called it to life, he said, "Don't worry, Silas. I'll come back later and get that wooden mannequin for you. And I'll contact my special friend. I think he's gonna wanna meet you."

Amos Boyle was a born lackey, and Silas was excited to use him to the fullest.

CHAPTER 12

Amanda stink-eyed Joel Haddon, Brett's husband and manager, as he flipped open the cellular phone, antenna pointed to the sky. She struggled to keep her very non-Christian thoughts about the man out of mind. He and the rest of the movie people had been here for well over ten hours and this was the seventh time he tried to use his cellular phone despite every stitch of evidence pointing to the lack of service. A slow exhale through pursed lips to mitigate the potential for a biting tone, she asked, "Still no service?"

Joel grunted and lowered his arm. He stared at the device as if it had suddenly and inexplicably failed him. He poked the buttons, the action made more comical by sweat flowing from his salt and pepper hair over his reddened face. Amanda wasn't sure if the tomato color was from sunburn or because he stubbornly refused to remove his tie and unbutton his shirt. Even Miles Pennypacker had removed his jacket long ago and unbuttoned his shirt embarrassingly low.

Amanda forced a smile. "Try for the eighth time in an hour or so. Or head into Albuquerque. You should be able to get a signal there."

Joel grunted again and poked the buttons harder. Nixon shared a quick glance with Amanda and rolled his eyes. Miles shook his head and put his hand on Joel's shoulder. "I don't know, Joel. Maybe we try our luck in Albuquerque."

"You're right. Good idea," Joel said as he snapped the phone shut and tucked it into his jacket pocket.

Amanda pursed her lips and sighed with irritation. Was he signaling her out as someone to ignore, or was this his normal behavior? It had been quite a while since a man had ignored her so aggressively. When she was a younger woman starting off in ranching, plenty of old-timers didn't care a lick for her opinion, but time and temperance made her voice heard. Families were different from country to country, state to state, and even house to house, but the idea of Brett encouraging this man's sexist behavior by staying with him chapped Amanda more than a long day in the sun with no lip balm.

Joel looked around at the barn, paddocks, and house as if they had suddenly sprouted from the dusty ground. "I just want to make sure I'm not missing any calls from studios looking to hire Brett. Where is she, by the way?"

"I'm here, sweety, no need to get your underwear in a bunch," Brett said as she exited the house. All eyes were on her as she strutted across the porch and down the stairs. Even the horses in the paddocks stopped to stare.

When Brett had told Amanda that she was to be her new role model, Amanda's first instinct was to jump on the closest horse and gallop away. Brett had insisted that if she were to play a cowgirl, she needed to learn all she could from a real, true, authentic cowgirl.

"Lesson number cne, Mrs. Haddon – I'm a rancher, not a cowgirl."

"Lesson number one for you, Amanda, I'm Brett, not Mrs. Haddon. And even though the name on all my important paperwork is Brenda, I insist on being called Brett. Lesson number two, you need to lighten up, because we're going to be the best of friends." Her glistening smile was practiced, her words more sugary than the cubes Amanda occasionally treated to the horses, and the woman had the audacity to punctuate her statement by booping Amanda's nose with her index finger. Amanda called forth some unpleasant words, about to teach a hard lesson number two, but the blustery Hurricane Brett had moved on.

Over the next few hours, a certain level of calm worked its way into Amanda. As she fielded questions ranging from awkward – "Why are they called horseshoes?" – to insightful – "How do you handle a horse with a temperamental personality?" – she realized that they were coming from a place within Brett searching for knowledge. Maybe even searching for something more?

A woman from wardrobe had come over to discuss setting up a time to meet with Brett for fittings. "Not necessary, sweety. Amanda and I are all but the same size. I'm sure she wouldn't mind lending me a few outfits. That okay with you, Amanda?"

The presumptuousness rankled Amanda's hackles from tip to tail, but she escorted Brett to her closet anyway and left her there to savor a moment or so of peace. That was an hour ago, most of that time spent witnessing Miles being a bootlick for Brett's husband, Joel. Nixon's layers of diplomacy wore thinner as time passed. Now, the three men looked at Brett through different sets of eyes: Nixon like an adult watching a toddler play dress up, Miles like a wolf stalking a tasty sheep, Joel like an owner fussing over a piece of property. All the other men in the vicinity were transformed into moths flitting around a glowing bug-zapper.

"All but the same size" was now the most laughable statement Amanda had heard all day. A pair of jeans she had always described as comfortable were painted onto Brett's rolling hips as she sashayed closer. Though Brett had chosen to wear a yellow version of the same flannel shirt as Amanda, it looked remarkably different. Amanda's blue flannel was untucked, and it flowed casually over her torso. Brett had tucked her shirt into her tight jeans, top two buttons open to expose a vast expanse of cleavage and the third button valiantly losing a battle to keep the rest of her chest contained. A blue handkerchief was tied around her neck and the pink Stetson that Amanda had received as a joke present four birthdays ago topped Brett's flouncy blonde hair. Still wearing high heels, she took her unsteady time making her way across the packed dirt to her husband. "Well, Joel. What do you think?"

"I think it'd be better without this..." He pulled away the handkerchief. "And this." He undid the third button, the top half of her chest bursting free like a popped canister of premade muffins.

"Joel!" Amanda scolded. "Don't you think that was rather inappropriate?"

"What's inappropriate is how much I paid for them."

"I guess that means he owns them, huh?" Hank whispered into Amanda's ear from behind.

She jumped and spun around. How a man the size of a bear could sneak around like a house cat baffled her. Always glad to see him, but more so after witnessing the kind of man Brett felt the need to endure, Amanda all but leapt from the ground to hug him. She whispered back, "I missed you."

Chuckling, Hank gave her a tight enough squeeze to spark the comfortable and tender parts of her heart. "I've been gone for only two hours."

"Felt like two years."

They gently separated, and Hank glanced at the four others and muttered, "I bet it did." For the sake of those very four, Hank gestured to his pickup truck. On a trailer attached to the hitch were three porta-johns. "I'm back from my errand."

Miles' jaw positively looked as if it'd fall right off his face. "I thought he was joking."

A shit-eating grin from ear to ear, Nixon put his arm around his friend and said, "I told you on the way here, no way they'd let us use the bathrooms in their house."

"I didn't think they would, but I thought they'd have some form of restroom for their clients. I mean, where do they go, your clients, when you take them horseback riding on the trails?"

With his own shit-eating grin, Hank swept his arm through the air with a grandiose flair. "See all the brush and occasional tree? Any and all of those are available."

Miles sneered. He placed both hands on his lower belly. "Joel? Is it okay if I use the trailer we got for you and Brett?"

"Absolutely not."

"I'm the producer and I'm paying for the damn thing!"

"You can't really expect the star of your movie to respect you if you go into her trailer and defile its toilet, can you?"

Miles slouched, defeated. With the eyes of a whipped puppy, he looked at Hank and asked, "Where are you going to set those up?"

"Southern part of the property, where the trailers and tents are. Hop in the back, I'll give you a lift."

Miles turned to Nixon, a silent request for help in his wide, pleading eyes. The director sighed, walked to the pickup's bed and waved Miles over. With Miles foot on the tire, both hands on the bed, it took three attempts and one final shove to his rump from Nixon to get Miles up and over the bed. The director was far more graceful with a hop, step, and leg-swing into the bed.

"Why didn't they just put the tailgate down?" Brett asked Amanda.

"Either ignorance or ego. Been my experience they're interchangeable."

"Amen, sister." Brett turned to Joel and said, "Why don't you join them, sweety. You might have better cellphone reception down there."

After an eyebrow-knitting look of confusion, as if wondering how she could possibly understand the complexities of cellular phone technology, Joel grunted his affirmation and joined the others in the pickup, though he opted to ease his efforts by lowering the tailgate. Once the tailgate was shut, Hank kissed Amanda, jumped in the truck, and drove away.

Something wistful took ahold of Brett's eyes as she watched the men go, like the look of a zoo animal dreaming of life beyond the bars.

Sympathy touched Amanda. "Now that the men are gone…"

Brett snapped out of her trance and turned on her brightness as if flipping a switch. "Yes, you're right. Girl time! Okay, first…" She put her hands behind her back and struck a pose accentuating every curve along her "S" figure. "How does this look on me? I know you'll tell me the truth, because you and Hank are the only two honest people on the ranch. Do I look the part?"

It took Amanda a beat to realize that the part to which Brett referred was that of a rancher. She almost pulled a muscle stifling a laugh. "Well… Isn't the movie set in the early 1800s?"

"It is."

"Oh, Brett. Jeans weren't invented yet. And it took a long, hard-fought time before it was socially acceptable for women to wear them."

Brett's posture relaxed, a slight pout tugging at her lip. Amanda decided to let someone else break Brett's heart about the pink Stetson. Then the actress chuckled and shook her head. Her mask fell away and she said, "Damn men. Always holding us back, right?" She then looked down at herself and made a sweep of her hands. "I'm sure I look quite ridiculous. I think the saying you'd use is 'shoving ten pounds of shit in a five-pound bag.' Right?"

At first, Amanda thought Brett to be weak for being so dependent on her husband, allowing him to treat her like property. She sensed strength within her, though. Brett had made it abundantly clear during the course of the day that her knowledge and skill-level on the ranch were lacking. That didn't mean she was useless and without other talents. The first thing she had said to Amanda was that she wanted to learn from her. Maybe it was for more than just a movie role?

"Actually, I'd never use that expression," Amanda said. "You are way too pretty and strong for that statement to come to mind. Maybe trying to put seven muffins in a tin made for six?"

They shared a laugh. Brett then took Amanda by the arm, and they headed toward the northern part of the property. "I like the way you put things, Amanda. Now, if you don't mind, let's get wardrobe to peel me out of this and put me in something more realistic."

At first Amanda thought Brett was just using her for balance, but she still held her arm while walking along the flat patches of land. If someone else's horse found its way onto her property, she'd feed and care for it until it was time for it to go on its way, so she made no attempt to free herself from Brett's desperate grip.

The flora was sparse in this part of the land, but the brush was full enough after the horses made their meals. Yet Hank was none too thrilled about the crew clearing it away to create the illusion of a dirty, dusty town. With sundown only a couple hours away, the construction crews busied themselves stacking up material to create the stereotypical "olde west" town – simple one-story buildings with four single room, square stores each.

Miles had become excited when he learned that Amanda and Hank owned three hundred acres, though he wasn't entirely sure what that meant. Amanda explained that their property was basically a rectangle that ran about a half mile east-west and almost a mile north-south. Miles then "coalesced an idea" for six stores on one side, six on the other. Hank balked at having such useless structures, especially after Nixon said they'd only need three different interiors, so the rest of the stores would be all but empty. They'd compromised.

Miles had whipped out yet another contract compensating for land use. Hank was satisfied with the paperwork, but the fact that Miles was able to pull one out the way most farmers pulled a handkerchief from their back pocket made Amanda wonder if Miles used his contracts the same way.

"You're such a strong woman," Brett said as they ambled closer to wardrobe. "I mean, not just toss-around-hay-bales-strong, because your arms are like pipes and you could make a ton of money if you ever wanted to teach a class on that, but you hold your own with the men."

"Well, my instruction for any kind of class would be short – like you said, it's tossing around hay bales, as well as many other chores. With men, they respect authenticity and accuracy. Know what you're talking about before you talk about it. If you need to know something, ask proper questions instead of making improper guesses."

Brett laughed. "Well, that's a hell of a secret."

"It's no secret. It's what I teach my boys."

"You sound like a great mother. I could stand to learn more about that, too."

At the moment, Amanda didn't feel like a good mother – almost 7:00 and she didn't know where her sons were. She'd swear on the front, back, and inside of the Bible that she had seen them come home, but with the overwhelming amount of activity buzzing around the ranch today, she had difficulty mustering any details about anything.

"You don't think you're a good mother?" Amanda asked.

"Oh, I *know* I'm not a good mother. My daughter, Dakota, turns eighteen in a few days, and she refused to come along with us."

"You left her home by herself?"

"I had no choice. Joel is my manager and agent, so both our careers are tied to me. This movie was the only part offered… I mean, of all the choices of movie parts available to me at the moment, this was the most lucrative."

"How does Dakota feel about you two not being there for her birthday?"

"I doubt she cares. If she did, she'd be here. I'm sure she's going to throw a party and look for trouble with her friend, Calista. I'm not a big fan of that girl. But then there's Melody. She's the sensible one, and I trust her."

Amanda leaned on the opinion that boys were easier to raise than girls, so she reserved her judgment for the umpteenth time today. As much as she benefited from reaching deep within herself to help Brett – at the very least, it gave her a safe space to express herself – Amanda was happy to get to the wardrobe trailer and pass her off.

As the wardrobe women fussed with nineteenth century dresses, pulling them from racks and getting them onto mannequins, an irritatingly familiar voice asked, "Oh, yeah? What kinda movie we got goin' on here?"

"None of your concern, Amos," Amanda snapped. If his brother, Archibald, weren't so quick to sue anyone who looked at a Boyle cross-eyed, she'd have punched Amos square in his mouth. That, and Brett had cast a favorable light upon her, so she shouldered the responsibility of living up to that perceived standard.

"Well, Mrs. Amanda Winters, I saw a commotion on your property, and as a concerned neighbor, I thought it my duty to investigate."

"I doubt that very much, Amos. You need to leave before Hank sees you."

Amos tipped an invisible hat and started to walk away. "You got it."

Once he was out of earshot, Brett asked, "Who was that?"

"A snake named Amos Boyle."

"What do you think he wanted?"

Amanda watched Amos ride away on his four-wheeler. But instead of heading for the Boyle property, he headed toward the Tomlin's. "I don't know, but it's never anything good."

CHAPTER 13

The sun was still about an hour away from peaking over the mountains when Johnny pulled into Chuck's Convenience store. Normally he eschewed caffeine, but had a thirst for a tall, black coffee – it was going to be a long day and Johnny needed chemical assistance to make the most of it.

Functioning on autopilot, Johnny slid back into the car's driver seat and realized he had no recollection of entering the store, much less pouring coffee or paying for the transaction. Briefly, he wondered if there'd been dialogue with the clerk, but when he couldn't even put a face to the person behind the counter, he wondered if he had paid at all. But no one was yelling, "Thief!" or running out the door to stop him, so he started the vehicle and headed back out to the road. Guess he really needed that coffee. Johnny giggled – Chuck's Convenience store – where one shops without memory of stepping foot in the trashy establishment, which was the ultimate in convenience.

Johnny managed to stay alert for the drive to his store, even though his mind wandered to the tasks he had accomplished so far early this morning.

Removing the subject from the realm of the living had been done in the darkest hours of the morning, not taking preparation time into consideration. A homeless person was the easiest test subject to procure, but the process was hardly effortless, much to his mother's consternations. He had forced himself to be mindful of the details, but not of the passage of time. Two hours of slumber were all Johnny could afford, and he was dealing with the after-effects.

Now, back in his store and midway through writing an order list, a knock at the front door interrupted him. Drawn from his reverie, Johnny suddenly realized the sun was blazing around the edges of the drawn curtains. A glance at his watch confirmed that he was four minutes late opening the store. He expected to find one of his regular customers on the other side of the closed door, but opened it to reveal a tall, gaunt figure, jacket hood pulled down over his face.

"Amos!" Johnny stole a quick glance at the parking lot and surrounding area, relieved that no one else was there. "What are you doing here?" Johnny asked, pulling him inside, relocking the door behind them.

"You will never believe this—"

"What I don't believe is that you're here when it's not time to collect the cadaver. I have yet to prep it let alone perform any form of surgery. And it hasn't been lost on me that you've been here quite often as of late. And coming through the front door? People recognize your truck, you know."

"I took the Tomlin's car. It's a Taurus... practically invisible."

"For the sake of brevity, we'll discuss whatever that means later. Why are you here?"

"You will never believe what I found."

"Amos, I have to open the store!"

"Okay, okay... say you will come with me tonight. Don't operate on your new patient yet. I'll come by after you close and pick you both up. It's amazing, I promise."

"What's amazing?"

"You have to see for yourself."

Johnny tensed with annoyance, mashing his lips as he considered the meaning he hoped to convey with this his next statement. He needed to end this little theater, but the man before him clearly relished his part in the unfolding drama and appeared happy to prolong the mystery.

"What am I going to see for myself? If you wish to have me as a voyeur while you feed the hogs, then I'm afraid—"

"He's... it's... alive..."

"What is? What are you talking about?"

"The little... man," said Amos, eyes wide with excitement. "The little wooden man."

"Like... Pinocchio? Please tell me that you haven't started to believe—"

"No," Amos moaned. "No, this is goin' all wrong."

"You get one more sentence to explain yourself. Then you leave," Johnny said.

"If what I show you tonight isn't the most amazin' thing you've ever seen, then you can use me for your next experiment."

Without hesitating to think it through, Johnny nodded in agreement and reached to unlock the door. He pushed Amos, bristling with excitement, out the door.

"Tonight," said Amos, pulling his hood back down over his face. It was as if shielding himself from the New Mexico sun, or prying eyes, were more important than overheating on an eighty plus degree day.

As he closed the door, the tintinnabulation of the small door chime a pleasant distraction, he considered the absurdity of Amos' appearance. Pulling back the curtains, Johnny watched the tall man disappear into the distance. He did not want to go with Amos tonight. Positively did not. Despite the zero inclination, it had been Johnny's experience that Amos rarely got excited about much of anything, so something was clearly afoot. After a few minutes of deliberation, Johnny resigned himself to accompany Amos as his first customer came to the door.

"Good morning, Mrs. Bauers." Johnny smiled. "How can I help you today?"

One after another, customers visited Soliterraneous, and Johnny greeted each of them with professional mien. Despite the burgeoning use of computers, he preferred writing out orders and bills of sale. He used expensive pens and wrote with a flourish, his hands shaped out of marble and his fingernails more beautifully manicured than a lawn tended by a crew of workers.

As Johnny helped the last customer take her special-order packages to her car, distant church bells rang – one, two, three, four, five, six times followed by a pause. Angelus, a six o'clock Catholic devotion accompanied by the ringing of annunciation bells. Johnny set about closing the shop for the day. To his ears, the door chime sounded as cheerful at the close of the day as it was at the beginning, as if it never tired of its own voice. Johnny pulled the curtains shut and settled into his chair to finish up the day's paperwork. And to wait for Amos to return, a torturous task considering the request not to operate on his new subject.

Darkness came and Johnny, still sitting at the desk, turned on a light. He liked the dark and frequently tried to work in it, until he found himself squinting at his own writing. Another hour passed before the sound of a truck engine caused Johnny to stir. He stood, arching his back to relieve the cramping, and opened the back door, allowing Amos to enter.

"You ready, Johnny?" Amos asked.

"I suppose I am. I admit that I do not look forward to whatever you have planned, Amos. I've come to expect secrecy from you, but this urgency is not like you at all. You do not wear it particularly well. Still, if it must be done for me to get a moment's peace from you, then let us be at it."

Amos loaded the cadaver into the pickup with ease, and they drove out into the middle of nowhere, passing several homes and structures that seemed to be placed haphazardly along the route. Moonlight was the only illumination afforded them, though it was plentiful in this desolate surrounding. Johnny was vaguely aware that the pig farm Amos called home was around here. Perhaps that was their destination?

It was bad enough driving out in the boonies, but the powerlessness of being at someone else's instruction was damn near intolerable. It wasn't his plan, not his idea of a good time. He was about to tell Amos that this was a bad idea and to turn around, but then Amos parked the truck in a remote area. Johnny got out, and followed Amos in silence. A simple farm. What crop grew upon this land, Johnny neither knew nor cared.

"In here," Amos said, opening the barn door and slipping inside.

Johnny looked around and, seeing no one, followed Amos inside the building, easing the door shut behind him. It was dark inside and Johnny heard fumbling. He assumed it was Amos searching for lights. Moments later, followed by a cuss, then there was light. Amos stood against the side wall, hand still lingering over the power switch.

"You might have left the door open until I got the lights on," Amos said with admonishment.

"I thought you wouldn't want half the state to see the light spilling out the door," Johnny said. "What are we doing here?"

"This." Amos directed Johnny's attention to a small wooden doll, about three feet tall with cartoonish hands and feet. Judging by the general shape, Johnny assumed it was a military toy from decades long gone for boys to dress and play war with. "Isn't it great," Amos asked as he stood beside it, gesturing to the rudimentary face carved into wood.

"You found an old army toy and thought, 'Hey, I have to show this to Johnny.' Why on Earth would you think that I have any interest in this, Amos? Have you lost your mind?"

Amos, who had been running his hand across the top of the statue's head, let out a sudden yelp and yanked his hand to his mouth, muttering something about splinters, before examining his hand for slivers.

"Howdy, Johnny. Nice of ya to make it. Amos said he'd bring ya. He said you'd help me."

Johnny stared in disbelief. The voice sounded like it came from... but it couldn't be... Amos wasn't a ventriloquist, not as far as Johnny knew. The figure's jaw opened and closed, and the words didn't seem to be created by electronics. Johnny blamed sleep deprivation for not having first noticed the pulpy mass of bloody flesh it held at its neck. He grimaced.

Amos' madness is catching, Johnny thought, wondering briefly if Amos drugged him with a hallucinogen. When? He hadn't anything to eat or drink, hadn't touched Amos. How could've he drugged him? And why? But then he saw a frown form on the wooden figure's face.

"So... Amos," the wooden toy spoke again, cocking its head at Johnny. "You said he's some kinda genius, but I ain't really seein' it."

Amos placed a folding chair next to Johnny and said, "Don't worry. He's just a bit surprised. Johnny, have a seat. I'm gonna get the subject from the truck and then you'll *really* be amazed."

Fumbling for the chair, Johnny kept his gaze fastened on the talking toy, the grotesque mass pressed against its neck. If there was anything more amazing than this, then Johnny knew he'd be changing the scope of his experiments.

CHAPTER 14

Riley paced his bedroom, twisting his pillow. Saturday night. Nothing to do but pace his room and stew. All week at school he watched Caleb and Mercer, hoping beyond hope that the Devil Tree would be his avenger. He daydreamed about a painful event, like their crotches spontaneously exploding, or a freak Bunsen burner accident in Chemistry class that fried their dicks off. Very unrealistic, Riley was aware of that, so his fantasies shifted to them falling down the stairs.

Or being pushed down the stairs.

Riley stopped pacing, his fingers dug deep into the pillow. Heart throbbing from his chest to his chin, heat radiating to his ears, he wondered, *Could I do it? Do I have what it takes?*

No, he decided. Cool tingles replaced the fire that had flashed in his gut, a weird sense of relief. He just wanted to beat the shit out of Caleb and Mercer, but instead of trying to instigate them like he'd done at the beginning of the week, he decided to observe them, giving the Devil Tree plenty of room to do its thing. But… time had passed and nothing happened. Not even something like a coincidence, like someone else beating on them. But maybe he could pay someone to beat them up?

Squeezing and pulling the pillow like an accordion, Riley continued his pacing while contemplating that idea. Names of potential candidates flipped through his head as if he thumbed through a rolodex, making notes of the pros and cons. He didn't realize how into the idea he was until Rand showed up.

Knocking on the door frame, Rand said, "Hey. Good to see you smiling."

Had he been smiling? Riley scrunched his face back into a frown. "Oh, hey. What's up?"

Rand strolled into Riley's bedroom and picked up a football from the floor. After spinning it a few times, he lobbed it. Riley tossed the pillow back to his bed, freeing his hands to catch the football. "Mom and Dad are out,"

Rand said, "so I wanted to go to the lower part of the property where the movie people are hanging out. They're having a party and I need you to come along."

After giving the football a squeeze, Riley tossed it back. "What? No. Why?"

"Come on. It'll be fun."

The thought of going to a party twisted something deep within Riley's gut. "I doubt it. Where are Mom and Dad anyway?"

Rand lobbed the ball back to Riley. "Date night. Dad said the devil himself couldn't stop date night let alone a bunch of entitled shits from California. Did you notice he's swearing more?"

Riley chuckled, for reasons too deep to think about. "You just want me along so you don't get in trouble by yourself."

Rand's smile was a devilish one, exciting and inviting. Many people had fallen victim to that smile. "No one's getting in trouble. Mom and Dad will be out for *at least* three hours. We'll be back in one. Even if we do get caught, I'll just tell them we were checking to make sure the movie people were adhering to the strict no drugs policy."

Riley tossed the football. Even though it was underhand, it had enough zing to slap Rand's hands when he caught it. "I smell bullshit."

The intensity of Rand's smile increased. "Fine. Fine, fine, fine. I'm curious about them, the whole movie making process. Aren't you?"

"You just want to meet the pretty girls."

A shoulder shrug. "I mean, what's wrong with that? Have you seen the wardrobe girl, Valencia? Super cute, and I think she's only a couple years older than me."

It was Riley's turn to shrug.

Rand's expression changed and Riley didn't like it. The smile disappeared and his eyes squinted, lips drawn tight. He looked like a mountain lion stalking prey. "But, if you have your eye on Valencia, there are plenty of other cuties. What do you think about that production assistant with the green hair?"

Riley looked away and mumbled the same thing he always said whenever someone suggested a girl at school, "She's not my type."

"There's the other wardrobe girl, the brunette with a dozen earrings in each ear. How about her?"

Riley clenched his fists. "She's not my type."

"Okay. How about the *other* wardrobe girl, the redhe—"

"Not my type!"

"Yeah? Then who is?"

Forearms burning from crunching his fingers into fists, Riley's heartbeat thumped at the base of his throat. "None of the girls on the movie crew."

"How about the girls at school?"

Riley wanted to punch Rand to make him shut up so the stinging between his nose and his eyes would go away. "None of them!"

"Come on. There has to be at least one girl there."

"No!"

"Then how about Javi?"

Riley felt a giant fist closing in on himself, crushing his chest and head and guts. He wanted to say, "Yes," but the truth evaded him; he wanted to say, "No," but he didn't want to lie to his brother anymore. The tears came, his sobs quivering as his entire body shook. He tried to make them stop, tried to gulp them back or grind his jaw harder, but that made them flow faster.

Rand hurried across the room causing Riley to flinch and turn, readying for the inevitable. The beating. The anger. The cussing. He wasn't ready for his brother to embrace him.

Head buried into Rand's shoulder, Riley continued to cry, half of him waiting for a sudden betrayal, the other half feeling like he had disappointed his brother. The only words he could get through his clenched teeth were, "I'm sorry."

"Nothing to be sorry about. If anything, I'm the one who should be sorry for pushing you into something you're not ready to talk about."

"I'm sorry for being so different. For being so... wrong."

"Different ain't wrong. Different is good."

Riley finally allowed his body to relax enough to return the hug. "I'm so alone."

"Not anymore. I'm right here, baby brother, and that will never change."

A few seconds was all Riley allowed himself before he started to reconstruct the walls. He pulled away and used his shirt sleeve to wipe his nose. "So, you're not... I dunno... disappointed? Mad?"

"Yeah, but not at *you*. I'm disappointed with myself for not paying enough attention and I'm pissed at the world for making you feel the need to hide."

"I hide because—"

Rand put his hands on Riley's shoulders and squeezed. "I get it. I mean, I know why you can't tell anyone. But, once you get to college, things might be different. If you go to a big enough school, one in a bigger city, then maybe you'll have a better opportunity to open up about yourself."

Riley sighed. The slightest bit of relief tickled the back of his head. He hadn't thought of that, or about being around people where he could be himself. It was... nice. Then his breath hitched as another thought hit him hard. "Why did you mention Javi's name?"

Rand smiled like a prideful guardian angel. "I see things, baby brother. The last couple weeks, you and Javi have been getting along real good, then you two met up and disappeared at the party last week, but afterward you were really pissed. You said you wanted to visit the Devil Tree because of Mercer, but you and Javi have been at opposite ends of the ranch all week."

Love for his brother claimed his whole heart, happily surprised that he took so much interest in his life, but a cold ice pick slid between his eyes, fearful about how obvious he might have been. Shaking his head, he said, "I'm not mad at Javi. It's—" He stopped himself, the rage still too great to articulate any other feeling yet.

Rand shook Riley's shoulders just enough to make Riley look up. "Hey, no need to hold back now. I told you, I'm here."

The thought of letting his brother down resurfaced and Riley took a deep inhale followed by a shaky exhale. "Caleb and Mercer. At the party last week, they made me... made me... do... something to them."

Rand's smile disappeared, anger forging hard lines across his iron face. His grip on Riley's shoulders tightened before he released him. Hands wringing together, Rand started to back away. "Well, obviously I'm gonna go kill them now."

"No," Riley grabbed his brother's arm and almost knocked him off balance. "All that will do is expose who I am and ruin your future. I thought about it, too, Rand. Thought about beating the ever-living shit out of them. But that'd get me suspended, kicked off the football team, and no chance for a college scholarship."

Rand's jaw muscles worked, chewing on Riley's reasoning.

Riley continued. "The pictures I took to the Devil Tree? That was the only evidence Caleb and Mercer had to expose me. That's it, nothing else. If either of them tried to spread that kind of rumor about me with no proof, no one would believe them. They're shit-heels, Rand, to the point that literally no one trusts them."

Being a hothead ran in the family, a trait Riley blamed on their father, and there was nothing more terrifying than an erupting volcano. Running both hands through his hair, Rand paced in tight circles before releasing something between a growl and a scream. "Okay. You're right. Me or you putting them in the hospital will only jeopardize our futures. But… God Damn… we can't just let them get away without paying."

"Yeah. I've been thinking about that, about what to do."

Nodding, Rand stroked his chin and sat on Riley's bed. "Alright. Let's lay out what we can come up with and see which plans we like the best."

"What about the party? I don't want you to be late or—"

A flick of his hand, Rand shooed away Riley's words. "Pfft. There'll be others."

Probably, but not many more with people from Hollywood. It might just be a group of people drinking beer around a campfire, but they'd have unique stories to share, ones Rand wouldn't hear otherwise. And Rand had an uncontrollable smile when he mentioned Valencia and the other cute girls. He'd be touring in a rodeo circuit soon enough, but unless he shot past the best bull riders and a movie was made about him, it was doubtful that Rand would ever have access to a behind the scenes experience like this ever again.

"We're going to the party," Riley said. "It's a ten-minute walk. We'll plan how to get back at the shit-heels on the way."

"You sure? We absolutely do not have to go."

Riley looked into Rand's eyes and reiterated. "I'm sure."

Flashlights in back pockets for when it came time to walk back to the house, they exchanged dastardly ideas from putting itch powder in their jockstraps – unfortunately, neither of them had gym class with either Caleb or Mercer – to pushing them down a flight of stairs. Just as Riley had suspected, it'd be murder should they die from the fall. Riley brought up paying someone to beat them up. "I like it," Rand said, "but we need to remember, we're not just paying for the service, we're paying for silence from whoever does it. We need to think of a list of names we trust."

Before they could explore the idea further, they came upon the party.

Rand smiled, his excitement infectious, as they approached a couple dozen people around three small campfires, loosely bordered by the bus, a few of the RVs, and a handful of tents.

As they approached, they were greeted by cheers, smiles, and plastic cups of beer. During the week, Rand did his best to meet as many of them as possible. Valencia bound over to Rand barefoot, wearing a flouncy skirt made of layers of thin material that fell to her ankles, and a loose blouse that exposed her midriff. Spirals of blonde got thicker as they extended from her head to her waist, and she wore a smile that could rival Rand's. "Hi! Glad you came!"

"Hi," Rand replied. "Glad you invited me."

"Hi, Riley!" She waved enthusiastically and Riley was impressed that she knew his name. She started to tug Rand toward the farthest campfire where only a few people sat. "Come on over here."

A wink and smirk were all Riley needed to give Rand as permission, and off those two went with Rand's smile leading the way, changing all fortunes to his favor. Even though Riley could bench press a horse, Rand was stronger, so he'd be fine on his own.

Riley thought about heading back to the house, but as he took a sip of beer, he glanced over to the campfire where three people held their sticks in the direct flame, burning the crap out of the helpless marshmallows. A young woman, the right side of her head shaved, the left side green, with metal hops through her left nostril; a young man with a mop of blue hair and earrings in both ears; another young man with a shaved head, black boots, and a rainbow patch sewn onto the sleeve of his olive-green jacket. They were failing miserably at smores, but they were laughing and enjoying each other's company. Enjoying who they were. Maybe Rand was right? Maybe there was a place for him in this world?

"Hey, Doe Eyes," the young man with blue hair called to Riley. He held up his burning snack, half of the stick on fire. "You wouldn't be willing to help us out, would you?"

"Sure," Riley chuckled as he took an empty lawn chair next to them. As he sat down, Riley noticed something move behind a nearby patch of brush. There were always critters scurrying about and he was looking forward to letting his problems go for the next hour, so he decided not to investigate.

CHAPTER 15

Amanda checked her watch. Five minutes. She and Hank had been standing at the edge of the fake town, Hank wordlessly shaking his head in disbelief, for five solid minutes. She'd been holding his hand the entire time and, blessedly, he never once squeezed too hard in frustration.

"Mandy, what the hell have we allowed into our lives?"

Amanda pulled Hank's hand closer to her chest and patted it. "Financial security, Hank, distasteful but necessary. Kind of like a dose or two of cough syrup – nasty on the tongue for a few minutes, but the results are welcomed."

"This kind of nasty is going to last a lot longer than a few minutes, I'm afraid."

"That may be true, but the results will be more welcome than just a good night's sleep. C'mon, let's take a nickel tour."

It took a tug to get him moving, but Hank finally crossed the border of Fake Town with Amanda. They strolled side by side, among more than three dozen individuals buzzing about, moving from place to place at varying speeds.

Fake Town consisted of a hundred-foot stretch of dirt-worn road with two structures on either side, each structure divided into four stores. A plank-wood porch ran the length of each structure, lined by banisters and posts. Both buildings had a saloon, each saloon marked with three-quarter height swinging doors. The "stores" on the left were complete, two of the four rooms finished. Artists worked on painting the completed storefronts, weathering the walls, floorboards, and posts while others crafted signs in "old west" script to signify the wares available through the doors they'd be hanging over. The structure on the right was more complete: carpenters sawed and hammered away at the flat roof, the final coat of paint drying on two of the storefronts, the third getting a new coat.

Even though it was not an entirely accurate facsimile of how things appeared in a century long gone, Amanda couldn't help but admire the aesthetic. No plumbing or electricity inside these structures, no interior decoration either. Just a shell, an estimation of early 19th century urban sprawl. Should she wish to suspend her disbelief and squint just a little, she'd envision the world as it once was. In a playful tone while conveying sincerity to her cranky husband, she said, "I don't know, Hank. I think Fake Town is looking kind of cool."

"It's going to be a nightmare tearing this down after they leave. Or I might tell Miles to do it, get his soft hands working."

"Maybe we keep it and incorporate it into our 'southwestern experience' for the tourists?"

Pace still at a leisurely stroll, Hank cast a side-eye gaze to his wife. "You serious?"

"Miles said they're going to need to complete the interiors of two or three storefronts for filming. Maybe we charge an extra fifty bucks a head to bring tourists through Fake Town and give them a looksee."

"For a genuine old west experience? This set of buildings has a blacksmith shop in between a bank and a saloon. The other set of buildings has a haberdashery. Really? A haberdashery?"

Stroking Hanks arm to pacify his growing frustration, Amanda said, "I think Mr. Miles Pennypacker had learned a new word and was desperate to flaunt it."

A twisted chuckle became a snort and ended with a disapproving head shake. "Maybe they should spend more time asking us questions about what an old west town actually looked like and not so much time forcing Brenda Hadden to follow you around like a puppy."

"Now, Hank, Brett is a very sweet, if not often misguided, woman. She has a genuine willingness to learn... when she's open to the concept of listening. I think you're upset that *you* don't have a protégé."

Another snort. "I think that director wants to be. What's that boy's name again? Wait... Don't tell me. Named after a president. Nixon. Nixon Lang. Sometimes that kid follows me around like a shadow but doesn't say a word."

"That's because he's too scared to approach you, you big dummy. You can give off a mighty unfriendly vibe."

Hank looked down at Amanda with a twist to his face, even his mustache seemed confused. "Scared of me? I'm plenty approachable and friendly. Watch."

Hank turned to the structure on the right. Fingers tucked into the corners of his mouth, he gave a shrieking whistle and garnered the attention of all six workers on the roof. Goofy smile on his face, he waved his meaty hand slowly, inviting, like the animatronic cowboy outside Simpson Tucker's used car lot, conveniently located just outside of Albuquerque and ready to accept any trade-in. All six workers paused in their pounding and sawing to return the gesture.

Hank took Amanda's hand in his and continued their stroll. "See? I don't know a single one of those fellows."

"Henry Bartholomew Winters, you know dang well that you just compared apples to oranges. You might not know who those gentlemen are, but they certainly know who you are. They all work for your good friend, Sal Diego, and each one of them knows that your friendship with Sal got them this job, a job so lucrative that Sal has given all his workers a bonus. They were all smiley and waving to you because you're the man who made that possible."

"I'm also the man who made this movie possible for Pennypacker and Lang, yet neither of them react to me the way the roofers did."

"Have you once smiled at either Mr. Pennypacker or Mr. Lang?"

Hank's silence answered her question. Under his breath he said, "I don't like that Pennypacker."

"I know, but we all need to like him just enough. So far, every single check he has written has cleared."

"I'm a little surprised by that."

"I am, too. But if the rumors are to be believed, he is sinking every nickel, dime, and quarter he owns, and quite a few he's begged and borrowed, into this project. He has quite literally everything riding on this, and we all know that kind of pressure can make a man a little squirrelly."

Looking skyward, Hank huffed the same way a toddler would when confronted with eating broccoli before leaving the table. "Fine. I will try my holy darndest to be more approachable and friendly to Pennypacker and Lang."

"And their crew."

"And their crew."

Hank's newfound efforts were going well until they rounded a line of buildings while heading back toward the house, and caught a distinct whiff of skunk. Two long-haired young men were leaning against the back of the structure. One had a bottle of water, the other puffed away at a joint.

"Hey!" Hank shouted. "If that's what I think it is, get rid of it now! I told Pennypacker to make sure y'all knew I don't want that shit on my property."

Deep and commanding, Hank had the kind of voice that penetrated skin, bone, and soul. Whoever he directed an order at felt compelled to follow. When he said, "Jump," no one asked how high, they'd just start jumping until it met Hank's parameters. The boys called it his "Bible Voice," because the Good Book was the only point of reference for a voice like Hank's.

So startled by Hank and his Bible Voice, both men stood ramrod straight while the one with the joint crushed the lit end between his finger and thumb, then tossed it into his mouth. He grabbed his associate's water bottle and chugged until empty. Skin tone a little greener than a few seconds ago, he and his coworker dropped their gazes to the ground and hurried away.

Once they cleared the scene, Hank closed his eyes and took a deep breath, inhaling everything the land had to offer. After a whooshing exhale, he opened his eyes. "Starting *now*, I will try my holy darndest to be more approachable and friendly to Pennypacker and Lang and their crew."

Amanda laughed. Sure, she felt a little bad that the love of her life had to navigate the rough waters of social discomfort, but one couldn't sail across the ocean on still waters. "I have faith in you."

"Good to know."

The fifteen-minute walk from Fake Town, on the northern part of their property, was peaceful enough to be enjoyable. A smile lingered on their faces while they held hands, strolling arm against arm, the silence reaffirming. When they got to the house, Hank kissed Amanda, and then said, "Despite my promise, I have a list of errands to run. Interested in accompanying me?"

Amanda returned the kiss and said, "Absolutely. However, I just noticed that Brett is riding Miss Misty. She isn't scheduled for a lesson until later today. Give me a minute to figure out what's what and then we'll head out, okay?"

"You got it."

Hank headed toward the house while Amanda ambled to the corral.

Brett sat on the horse straight as can be, shoulder, hip, and heel all in line, confident and controlled. However, Ramos held the lead rope, guiding the horse to an easy trot around the perimeter of the paddock.

Near the paddock and the barn, Javi had Buster in the big corral, brushing his coat. Outside the corral, Riley cut chunks from an apple and fed them to Buster. The two young men said nothing, not even looking at each other, their awkwardness made more so by Javi's father standing so close by. Amanda assumed it had something to do with the party the weekend prior. The boys needed to work through whatever was causing their silence and Amanda decided to help by shooing away Ramos. Her presence wasn't optimal, but it sure as sunburn in a desert was better than Ramos'.

"Yeeeeehaw!" Brett squealed, waving to Amanda with a smile brighter than the sun overhead. The yelp and sudden shift in her saddle triggered the panic muscles accompanying a novice, her free hand grabbing the horn of the saddle. With shaky-brow embarrassment, she released the horn and grabbed the reins with both hands, adjusting her posture, soldier straight. As flat as a shaken soda, Brett repeated, "Yeeeeehaw."

Amanda slipped into the corral and matched Ramos' pace as they walked with the horse. Squinting against the sun, she looked up to the actress and said, "Please don't ever do that again."

A head-bob accompanied her sing-song voice as she said, "I know. Keep both hands on the reins. It won't happen again, promise."

"No, I meant that silly yeehaw you did."

Perplexed, as if hearing up was down, Brett asked, "Ranchers and cowboys don't say yeehaw?"

"In movies of lower quality than the one you wish to make. Only time it's said in real life is by drunk college girls riding mechanical bulls in western -themed bars."

Amanda saw right into the wheels of Brett's brain as it spun in mud for a good few seconds before acceptance got her unbogged. Another side-to-side head-bob and her smile returned. "Never say it again. Unless I find myself on a mechanical bull knee-deep in my third margarita."

Ramos buried his mustache in his armpit to stifle a chuckle. When he regained his composure, Amanda gestured to take the lead rope. "We'll have you at that skill level in no time, Brett. But... I didn't think we had a riding lesson until later today?"

"We don't. I was supposed to have an intense fitting with one of the wardrobe girls, but she's nowhere to be found. I overheard the crew say that when they were partying last night, Bo Ellsworth, the leading man, showed up. Rumor has it she makes bad decisions around him. Anyway, one of the other girls is going to take over, but she needed a few hours to look over notes and 'coalesce her vision.' She said that while holding a full pot of coffee, so I'm thinking that was a euphemism for 'nurse a hangover.'"

"Excuse me?" Riley said, his worry-eyes leading the way. "Did you say one of the wardrobe girls is missing?"

"I did, hun," Brett replied.

"Which one?"

"Her name was something sort of exotic. Valentina? No, Valencia. Her name's Valencia."

"She's the blonde, right?"

The horse continued around the corral's perimeter with a lethargic gait, keeping the metal barrier between Brett and Riley. Almost as if wanting to have fun at Brett's expense, the horse turned and began to sidestep, making Brett look over her shoulder, though no matter which direction she chose, it was the wrong one. Like a blonde windsock in a storm, she repeatedly whipped her head from one side to the other. "That, she is, hun."

Riley shared his concern through his eyes, as if it were a tangible sack of anxiety he passed to Amanda. "I... umm... I need to see Rand about something." With a giddy-up in his step, he hurried to the house.

Javi watched in slack-jaw silence. Amanda was just as confused by Riley's reaction to what Brett had to say. And Rand was involved. What the heck were her boys up to?

CHAPTER 16

Silas lay on Johnny's "operating table", a big ol' slab of thick grained wood on a sturdy set of wide legs. He inhaled with such gusto that his breath sounded like a cyclone racing through a canyon.

"Fascinating," Johnny said, his eyes roaming over Silas.

Fascinatin' is a word for it. One that Silas would never have thought to use but it buzzed out of Johnny's mouth as common as a horsefly in summer. *Fuckin' miracle is another word.*

Amos had said that Johnny was into experiments and learning. One thing Silas had learned was that the body parts he borrowed had a time limit of about one to five days before they stopped working, no matter how much blood he soaked them in.

The operating table had come from the Tomlin's dining room and got itself relocated in the center of the barn. Silas objected when Johnny floated the idea – the barn held bad mojo – but ultimately understood that the inside of a house was no place to be slopping around blood and guts. And lungs.

"How do the new windpipes feel?" Amos asked, standing beside the table, opposite Johnny.

"Weird," Silas replied, inhaling and exhaling. Also weird – Silas had a different voice than Jeremy Tomlin.

Ol' Amos had stolen the wooden mannequin, Silas' new body, the night after Silas met Johnny. Only about five and a half feet tall, but blessed be, things like eyeballs and ears fit better. Now, he had the homeless man's voice box. It fit better, too, thanks to Johnny keeping plenty of skin attached to the throat and tacking it to Silas' neck. He hoped it'd last a good five days or more, though it might only be a few.

Silas couldn't make rhyme or reason about how long it might last. Neither could Johnny who was "fascinated" by the skin not going blue then black as it should. For now, the stretch of skin keeping the homeless man's windpipe strapped to Silas' neck was the same shade of a healthy white man's. The voice sounded like rode upon gravel, but Silas sure as hell was not going to use the voice of the girl they brought in last night. He was perfectly fine using her lungs, but he wasn't about to go around sounding like some whore.

"Can you actually feel them?" Johnny asked.

"Sorta. I mean, who really feels their lungs? I can breathe. I can... sense them, I guess you'd say."

"Interesting."

Silas sat up a bit, propping himself on his wooden elbows, and looked down. Johnny had become excited, as excited as this sack of wet rags got, when he first discovered that the mannequin's torso was hollow. With the deft hands of a surgeon – though back in Silas' day, a surgeon downed more numbing spirits than the patient before attacking the afflicted area with a hacksaw – Johnny cut a nice hole in Silas' chest, plenty of room for a set of lungs.

Not sure why Johnny wanted to start there, Silas kept his yap shut and let the man do what he thought was right. Silas had gotten lost along the path to where Johnny's words were taking him, mostly due to getting bored by the man's long, nonsensical language as he rambled on and on about lobes and trachea and cartilage. Silas offered no complaints, too busy thinking about the next steps. After cutting the lungs out of the movie girl – what was her name? Oh yeah, Valencia, as Amos called her – Johnny had held them up like a proud papa, a sheet of slime flowing over his hands and arms. Butterfly shaped, meaty pink wings and a bony tube of a body. Johnny went to work on tacking the bonelike tube inside Silas' chest cavity. Abracadabra, now Silas could breathe! Yes sir, Johnny was a hell of a surgeon. Not that he referred to himself as one. He called himself something else, that kind of rhymed. Oh yeah...

The Chirurgeon.

Johnny was an odd bird, all right. The way he talked. The way he carried himself. The way he looked at the world. The way he looked at people. If Silas had a spine, then it would have turned to jelly the way Johnny looked at other people. Silas was more than willing to admit that he didn't always love and respect his fellow man, especially when "fellow man" was a woman. Yeah, he might have looked at more than a few women as meat, and almost as many men as obstacles to the guilty pleasures of what made life worth living, but he still recognized each and every one of them as a human being.

Not so with Johnny. He looked at people like he had no idea what they were, other than a form of animal to break open and learn more about. Silas even began to question if Johnny was human, or some greater creature wearing a suit of skin to blend in with lower lifeforms.

Johnny used a scalpel to work on Valencia's hand, making a precise cut around her wrist as he released the skin from the meat, peeling it back as he went along. No doubt in Silas' mind that Johnny thought of this as removing a slimy glove and nothing more. Even though he didn't go any shade of green that most men would have turned – probably getting too used to seeing this type of stuff – Amos still turned away. Johnny took his time so as not to damage the skin while pulling it from the fingers.

After a belch, Amos asked, "So, Johnny, why do you think Silas is the way he is."

"I'm sure there is a reason, though I haven't given one any thought."

"Not curious enough?" Silas asked, watching Johnny.

"The reasonings of many, many things interest me, but it does no good to focus on too many at once, especially when I know so little about the variables."

"Variables?"

"I know nothing about you or your past. How old are you? Where are you from? Were you a human before this?"

"That last one, I can answer with authority. Yes. I mighta been a miserable cuss, but I was a human, like you and Amos."

Johnny paused from his cutting to eye Silas with a disapproving look, as if saying that man and ant were much the same. Back to freeing the girl's thumb from her skin, Johnny asked, "How old are you?"

"Don't know that none," Silas answered. "Never knew my Pappy, and my Mama died before memory. The nuns at the orphanage said I was ten the year right before I ran away with the traveling carnival that swept through town. Half a decade with them, I recon, before a handful of us split away with a few horses, deciding it was easier to ask people for their belongings while holding a gun to their face than to develop the art of flimflam. Maybe two decades and a few dozen different members of my gang before I was caught and hanged."

"You was hanged?" Amos asked. His face stretched into wide shock.

Silas chuckled. "Sure was. Made quite a ruckus about it, too. A little plaything couldn't keep her big mouth shut none, and told her daddy. Well, the whole town took his side and strung me up. Her daddy made things entertainin' by stickin' me with a knife before the sheriff could get me danglin' from the Devil Tree. 'Course, I couldn't go quietly, so I chomped his ear real good and tore it off. We made such a bloody mess!"

"What year did that take place?" Johnny asked as casual as discussing the weather with a stranger.

"I believe it was eighteen-sixty-somethin', the year of someone's Lord."

"How did you survive?" Amos asked.

"I didn't."

Amos stepped back as if bowled over by that statement. It even gave Johnny pause right before he cut the last little red bits that held the skin of Valencia's hand to her fingers.

Amos wobbled over to one of the stalls and leaned against it for support. With a whisper of wonder, he asked, "You been to the other side?"

Johnny went back to his particular task.

"You ever been asleep?" Silas asked Amos. "Well, 'the other side' began much like that. Then, outta nowhere, I woke up in the little wooden body you found me inhabiting, the little wooden body inside this one. I learned that blood made me move, but I didn't go back to sleep when I ran out of it. I just lay awake in a pile of mud, unable to move."

As single minded as an eagle hunting a rabbit, Johnny held the skin-glove in his hand. Running his fingers over it, he brought it to his face. After a minute of studying each side, he dipped it into a small pail of blood by the table. "Hold your fingers straight and apart."

Silas obliged. Johnny slid the skin over Silas' hand, the wood tingling as it absorbed the blood. Valencia had small hands, but the skin fit nicely, not too snug, because Silas' mannequin-body was a size somewhere close to hers.

"Wiggle your fingers," Johnny ordered.

They wiggled just fine, the dangling flaps by his wrist dancing around.

"Now touch something."

Silas reached out and shook Johnny's hand. Soft. Clammy.

The look on Johnny's face, like that of one wrangling a live snake, was priceless. Tone flat, Johnny said, "Now touch something else."

Silas brought his new hand to his face and felt wood. Hard. Cold. "Well shit in my pants and call me sloppy! I can feel everything."

"Fascinating," Johnny said.

Oh, there's that word again!

Amos meandered to the operating table, staring at Silas' wriggling fingers. "Fascinating," he said, a hitch to the word like he had never tried to say it before.

"Hammer and tacks," Johnny said to Amos.

The yokel followed the order, scurrying to a table of tools and returning with the request. As Johnny began tacking the loose skin to Silas' wooden wrist, Amos shook his head and said, "Magic. It's gotta be magic, right?"

"Could be a variety of reasons," Johnny replied.

"Fella like you probably don't believe in magic none."

Johnny turned and regarded Amos with the first look of emotion on his face Silas had seen. The slightest hint of a frown, a light twitch of his right eye. Johnny was insulted. "Of course, I believe in magic. What fool doesn't?"

"Didn't think you to be the religious type," Silas said. Reason and logic never guided him, sometimes even when his life depended upon it, and he knew better than to upset the one man who worked diligently on bringing him closer to the lifestyle he once knew, but seeing a reaction like his to the mention of magic? Oh, Silas needed to explore that. "But I mean, half the shit in that special bible book is all magic, right?"

Dang it! Lost it, Silas thought as Johnny's face shifted back to an unnerving neutral expression.

Returning to tacking the flaps of skin down, Johnny explained, "There's no magic in religion. Just overly simplified and made-up answers to complicated questions."

"Obviously, you're a man of science, lookin' for answers."

"I'm looking for reasons, not necessarily answers. Through experiments, science looks for answers by finding replicable equations. But when science finds satisfying enough equations, it stops looking for the reason behind them. A human can't be created in a laboratory even though science has every equation for a human's chemical makeup. Why is the proportion of men to women almost half? Why are some short and some tall? Why are some born with deformities? Why do some have a mind's eye and some do not? We all know the *answer* is genetics, but that's not a satisfying *reason* for all these variable occurrences. If the reason were truly that simple, then it should be replicable; science should be able to recreate short or tall, blue eyes or green." Johnny paused, frozen in thought and mumbled, "or a mind's eye so I wouldn't have to go on a quest for it." Back to tapping away at the little nails, he continued, "You asked me if I believe in magic? That is the magic. A coven of dirt-covered witches dancing naked around a cauldron and adding necessary ingredients to summon a spell is no different than a group of scientists in lab coats huddled around a microscope."

Silas chuckled. "You lost me a few thought-trails back."

Johnny sighed. "If the *answer* to the question of why you are the way you are is magic, then so be it. It's magic. But there is a *reason* it happened."

"A reason why it happened," Amos muttered.

Johnny finished tacking down the skin-flap. Silas sat up, using his new hand for support. He felt the wood of the table and the pressure of wrapping his fingers around the edge. "I don't much care about the reason or the answer. I just wanna get back to having a normal body. Or at least a human enough body to get back into the world of other people."

"I still need to do more experiments," Johnny said. "So, we'll need another body."

Silas and Amos both looked at the remains of Valencia, folded like a gory ragdoll in a metal trough, her leg dangling over the side. After draining her blood, Johnny had instructed Amos to drop her in the trough, and then he took what he needed from her. Her skin had a gray tint and her chest was open like a shirt, all her organs – minus her lungs – in a sloppy heap around her hips. Two gaping holes in her face where her pretty blue eyes had been, now in Silas' head.

With a bit of reverence, Amos said, "I'll find another one tomorrow night."

Amos had a taste of the pie Johnny ate from, and Silas wondered how far he would go for more.

CHAPTER 17

Riley took the stairs two at a time and almost faceplanted when he hit the second-floor carpet. His momentum didn't stop until he slammed into Rand's door frame. "Valencia's missing!"

Reclined on his bed, thumbing through the latest issue of *Sports Illustrated*, Rand looked as confused as a cat being told to fetch. "First, baby brother, take a breath. Second, what are you talking about?"

"I overheard Mrs. Haddon talking to Mom and she said Valencia's missing."

"Valencia?"

"Yeah, the blonde wardrobe girl."

Rand sat up and tossed the magazine at Riley. "I know who she is, dumbass. I made out with her last night."

"Sorry, just worried. We've never had a guest go missing before."

Rand hopped off his bed and stretched. He smacked Riley on the shoulder when he squeezed past him out the door, and said, "Technically they're not guests. And, even though she's not much older than me, she's an adult, so she's free to come and go as she pleases. But I understand what you're saying. Come on, let's head down to their camp to see if anyone is concerned."

"Yeah. Yeah, good idea."

Riley followed Rand down the stairs and out the front door. Mom and Javi's father were too focused on giving horse riding lessons to notice them. Javi led Buster deeper into the Play Pen, presumably to let the horse run off steam, unaware of Riley heading to the southern part of the property. Which was all for the best, since Riley didn't have time to answer any questions or fill in backstory as to where he was going and why.

"Have you talked to him yet?" Rand asked.

Riley's first response was, "Who?" but since he was walking forward while looking backwards, feigning ignorance was stupid. Shoving his hands in his pockets and casting his gaze to his feet, he mumbled, "No. Don't know what to say."

"Speak from your heart. It's usually smarter than your brain."

"I feel like I need to apologize to him, but not sure for what."

"You don't. He knows what happened and he knows you're hurting because of it."

"I just… I don't know… feel bad, I guess, that he had to be there. That he couldn't do anything."

"Well, I'm sure he feels bad for you for the same reasons."

"I feel bad that I've shut him out all this time."

"He'll understand. I don't know him as well as you do, but I know he'll understand."

Riley stood straighter as they walked, thankful for his brother's words. After a few minutes of silence, something Rand said earlier struck him. "Wait, you said you made out with Valencia last night?"

"Yeah. For about a half hour before you and I went back to the house."

"Nice. Did you get to second base?"

Rand chuckled and shoved Riley hard enough to stumble. "God, you're such a football player."

"Oh, like you bull riders are more sophisticated?"

"In comparison, yes."

"Big brother, comparing football to bull riding is like comparing chess to checkers."

"Ha! No one on your team can spell chess, let alone play it."

"Then how is it that I kick your ass at chess every time we play?"

Rand scoffed. "You always catch me on my off days or right after I get back from practice. You need to challenge me when I'm at my strongest, not my weakest."

"Whatever." Riley ended the conversation with a shove and a chuckle.

Something was different about the crew's living area, but Riley couldn't put his finger on it. At first glance, it looked just like how he saw it last night, except now it was daylight. Three circles of charred ground from last night's campfires – thank God the guests at least had the common sense to encircle each area with a ring of larger stones – each about twenty paces apart, four Porta-Potties a hundred feet away, trailers parked haphazardly…

The trailers. Unless Riley's eyes were playing a trick on him, there was one more compared to last night. And in front of it was a shirtless man talking to Miles and Nixon. Standing within their orbit were three people, PAs – Production Assistants. Riley had met them last night – the young woman with the half-shaved head of green hair and pierced left nostril named Tilde; Barnes, the young man with earrings in both ears, his disheveled blue hair looking extra messy; and Sasha, the guy with the shaved head who explained what the rainbow patch on his jacket meant. When Riley had asked what a PA did, Sasha said, "We're dedicated to helping whenever we can in whatever way possible." As Barnes described it, "You know the expression, 'shit rolls downhill?' Yeah well, we're the morons at the bottom of the hill with buckets ready to catch it all."

Riley and Rand approached PAs. Arms crossed and hip cocked, Barnes smiled. "Welcome back, Puppy Dog Eyes. Had a blast last night, but now we're waiting for the real fun to begin."

"Hey," Riley replied. "Who's that guy?"

"The ripped hottie with the eight pack abs, chiseled face, and pissy attitude? That's Bo Ellsworth, the leading man. Got in late last night, partied hard, and now he's taking his hangover out on everyone."

"Hunh," Riley grunted as he and Rand stepped a little closer to the conversation with the lead actor, director, and producer. Since they were holding it in front of everyone with no attempt to hide it, then it must be available for all ears, including Riley's.

"… It isn't about me. It's about her," Bo said, hands on his hips.

"Her? Are you talking about Valencia?" Riley asked, eliciting gasps from Tilde, Barnes, and Sasha.

"What?" Bo snapped at Riley. "No! Who the fuck is Valencia? And who the fuck are *you*?"

Stepping into the center of haphazard group of people, Nixon gestured to Riley and Rand. Using the tone of a frustrated teacher scolding his least favorite student, he said, "This is Riley Winters, and he's Rand Winters. If you didn't catch their last names, they're members of the family graciously allowing us to use their property for filming."

Running his hand through a head of hair fuller than a bush of summertime thickets, Bo glared at Riley, ending with a dismissive snort. "Okay. Who's Valencia?"

"One of the costume designers," Rand said. "Long blonde hair. Dresses kinda like a hippie."

"Oh, her. Yeah, we hooked up right after I got here."

"Dude, come on," Nixon said, shaking his head.

"What? Look, I rolled in around ten." An hour after Riley and Rand had left. "Partied for a few hours or so. Blondie was hot and ready, so we went back to my trailer for a bit, then she left. What's the big fucking deal?"

Rand was great at poker, a small smile playing on his face to hide his thoughts and feelings. Zero surprise or shock. Carrying the burden of betrayal for his brother, Riley stepped forward and hurriedly said, "Well, she's missing as of today. Thought you might want to call the police."

"Whoa, whoa, whoa!" Miles waved his hands, trying to erase the implication. "No need for police."

Nixon rolled his eyes as if all too familiar with having to drag his friend out of embarrassing situations, something he probably had done a million times before. "He's trying to say that police won't be necessary. We've worked with Valencia before. This is not the first time she's disappeared. Honestly, we were hesitant to use her for this movie because this is so habitual for her. We appreciate your concern, and thanks for letting us know, but we don't want to bug the police for something like this."

"Oh. Then who was the 'her' you were talking about?"

"Not that it's any of your fucking business," Bo said, rubbing the heel of his hand against his right eye, the universal sign for trying to keep it from popping out while fighting a headache. "But we were talking about Brett."

"No need to be rude," Nixon said to Bo. He then turned to Tilde and asked, "Would you be able to fetch him some water?" He swung back around to Riley and Rand. "Bo hadn't read the details of the paperwork he'd been sent, so he wasn't aware that Miss Brenda Haddon was going to be his costar until about half an hour ago when he woke up."

"She's supposed to be my love interest," Bo said.

Rand shrugged. "She's a pretty woman. Maybe even prettier than Valencia."

"Brett's too old!"

"Age doesn't matter," Nixon said.

"She's almost fifty and I'm not even thirty yet!"

"She's forty-two and you're thirty-three. Your last girlfriend of six months ago was barely twenty-one."

"My last girlfriend was an international model," he mumbled.

Tilde offered him a water bottle, and he snatched it from her hand. The closest thing to a "thank you" came when he unscrewed the lid and handed the cap to her. After a few audible gulps, he wiped his mouth with the back of his hand and said with a whine, "Is she at least going to get her tits out?"

"What does that have to do with anything?" Nixon asked.

Bo paused mid-chug to sneer. "Seriously? It's the best part of her."

Nixon crossed his arms over his chest, jaw muscles tightening. "No, she doesn't get naked at all."

Miles reeled back as if the director had taken a swing at him. "Really? Why not? She gets topless in literally every movie she's ever done. Rumor has it she got fired from a TV pilot because she couldn't get the concept that she needed to keep her tits covered."

Nixon punched his shoulder. "Dude! Go. Right now."

"But—?"

"Nudity is not in her contract for this movie, and we are not going to ask her to do that. Now, get outta here. In fact, go find her and let her know that Bo is excited to work with her."

"I never said that!" Bo snapped as he tossed the empty water bottle to Tilde. "And you have no right to give him orders. He's the producer!"

"It's in the producer's best interest to make a successful movie, which means that sometimes Miles needs to step away from certain aspects. As his friend, I need to remind him that sometimes his biggest obstacle is himself."

Drooping his head to stare at his expensive shoes, Miles muttered, "Yeah, Nixon is right."

Riley wanted to laugh when the actor – a grown man – stomped his foot and said, "This is bullshit. I'm the lead actor and I should have a major say about my role and the other actors in the movie. Don't make me pull out the contract!"

Like a hawk targeting a field mouse, Nixon swooped to Bo, almost nose to nose. At first Riley thought the director was going to take a swing at the actor, or crack foreheads, and found himself more than a little disappointed when Nixon used only words. "Go right ahead and grab a copy of the contract, Bo, but before you do, let me remind you what's in it. It states, with your signature at the bottom, that you are an actor in this movie. It makes no mention that you're the lead, just an actor. So, that means I can give the lead role to anyone I want, maybe even him." Nixon pointed at Rand. He then added, "You know what? The more I think about it, the more I like that idea. He looks and acts the part of a cowboy waaaaay better than you. If I'm not mistaken, there's a stableboy in the script. Maybe that's the part I give you, Bo? Contract also states that if you say 'no' to any part I offer, you're axed with no pay. I'm no lawyer, Bo, but maybe next time you sign a contract, how about you try to be sober?"

Bo turned to his trailer, his gaze locked on Rand, and said, "I'll be in my trailer." He then turned to Barnes. "Blue hair kid – I need some coffee. I'll be reading the script and getting ready to go for the lead."

Barnes smirked at Riley and winked before he went off, presumably to find coffee. Riley wondered if he'd spit in it.

"You need anything, Nixon?" Sasha asked.

Nixon removed his black Stetson and ran his forearm across his forehead. "Despite it shaping up to be a hot day, I could use a coffee, too. Thanks, Sasha. Not awake enough to deal with Bo's bullshit."

"Got it," Sasha said. He waved to Riley before wandering in the same direction as Barnes. Tilde shrugged and joined the other PAs.

Returning his hat to its rightful spot, Nixon pressed his hands together and bowed toward Riley and Rand. "Thanks again for letting us know about

Valencia. I deeply apologize for Bo and Miles' behavior. Now, if you'll excuse me, I have an ego to stroke. *Namaste.*"

"What a bunch of weirdos," Riley mumbled to Rand. His heart sank when he turned to see his big brother looking at the trailers with stars in his eyes. "Rand?"

"Yeah?"

"Whatchya thinking?"

"He said I could be the lead in a movie."

What the Hell? "Rand—?"

Waving his hands, Rand's smile assured Riley that he was of sound mind. Well, he at least thought he was of sound mind. "I know he said it to threaten Bo, but he wasn't lying. I could hear it in his voice, that I could be in the movie. It doesn't hurt to ask, right?"

Yes. Yes, it did. "Rand, come on. You saw what just happened, right?"

"Yeah, yeah, yeah. Drama. But there's drama in school. Drama in the rodeo circuit. Drama on the ranch. I'm gonna run up to the house, take a shower, dress a bit nicer and see if I can find Nixon later, after everyone cools down, to get a copy of the script. Hell, he said there's a scene with a stable boy. That's good enough."

"Seriously?"

Grabbing Riley by both shoulders, Rand hit him with a smile that made the idea of jumping off a bridge sound fun. "I'm not gonna give up anything or change my life or run away to Hollywood. This is a chance to be in a movie, something I never thought about. Ever. It's stupid. It's silly. But how often will this opportunity come knockin'? I'm gonna answer the door when it does."

With a step faster than usual, Rand started back toward the house. Riley looked skyward for guidance and when Heaven kept its advice behind the clouds, he looked to the trailers, then to the brush and small trees specking the lands. Two rows of scuff marks that could be mistaken for tire tracks caught his eye. They led from the other side of the fence separating the camp site from the Boyle property and faded away into the open lands. He thought about giving them a closer looksee but decided to hoof it to catch up with his brother.

CHAPTER 18

On his knees, Amos vomited into the toilet.

"What got in his guts?" Silas asked, pointing to Amos.

Johnny remembered his first kill fondly. It was a cat, when he was ten, followed by a homeless man a month later. No vomiting, though. "The body in the back of his pickup truck – it's his first kill."

Johnny had waited in the passenger seat of Amos' truck, there strictly for moral support and as a necessary instructor while Amos perpetrated the deed. It had been six days since Amos had observed Johnny kill Valencia, the young blonde woman, so now it was his turn. Much to Johnny's surprise and delight, Amos was effective as well as stealthy when it came time to kill the young man with a shaved head and an olive-green army coat from the movie production.

But as soon as they stepped foot into the Tomlin house, Amos scuttled directly to the bathroom.

"Ha! Popped your cherry, did ya?" Silas said, laughing. Johnny observed how the simulacrum's mouth moved – the lips, the jaw – and paid particular attention to the teeth and gums. A few hours here, a few hours there during the evenings after closing the shop for the day, he had painstakingly used a Dremel tool to shape the mannequin's head. The chest cavity was hollow, but the head was solid. A bit smaller than the average human head, and the lower portion needed significant modification to accommodate teeth, but Johnny admitted to himself that he had done a fine job. The homeless man's face over Silas' head frowned after Amos spat into the toilet, and said, "Fuck off."

"Silas?" Johnny said. "Would you get the body from the back of the truck and move it to the barn?"

The outlaw from a time gone by sneered. Despite the expression of unpleasant thoughts, Silas did as asked. As the mannequin body with human face, hand, and foot ambled down the hallway, Johnny watched how the skin adhered to the wood along the edges of the body parts, how it stretched and pulled, how it clung as if desperate for life, no longer needing tacks to stay in place. Johnny smiled, happy with his work.

After a flush and a mouth rinse from the sink faucet, Amos swiped the back of his hand over his mouth and mumbled, "Fuckin' asshole."

"I believe Silas is curious about why you had such a reaction. I must admit, I'm rather curious about that myself."

Amos journeyed to the kitchen. "It's 'cause I ain't never killed no one before."

Johnny followed. "But you've killed many a pig, Amos."

Crossing the threshold, Amos glanced over his shoulder. "If you don't know the difference between a pig and a person, then there's something wrong with you."

"Is there?" Johnny asked. "A real difference between man and animal?"

Amos shook his head as he opened the refrigerator. After shifting items around, he grabbed a can of ginger ale. "Man's a man, and animal's an animal."

"Man is an animal. Didn't you learn that in school?"

"Course I did! I didn't make it all the way through high school, but even you gotta admit there's something special about man. How we think. How we feel."

"What about when I kill people? Does that bother you?"

"Of course it does!"

"Judging by how you seem to relish disposing of the bodies, I question your statement."

Amos gulped from the can, then looked out the kitchen window as if the contention he sought was out in the night. "I'm fascinated," Amos said, "about why some of us can withstand so much, while others can withstand so little."

"Elaborate."

Emptying the can after a few more gulps, he peered into the pop-top opening as if he could see certain events in the dregs. "My brother, Archibald, is a nasty piece of shit. Always had been, since the day he came into this world. Takes after our pa in that way. Well, Pa knew my fate as well as he knew Archibald's. Even as kids, I tended the pigs and Archibald tended the money stuff. As punishment anytime Archibald acted out, Pa would make him work with me for a few hours. Archibald always did what Archibald wanted – Mercer takes after him that way – so one day when Archibald was twelve and I was ten, he did somethin' to piss off Pa. I don't know what, probably giving him lip over somethin' or other, but after school, Pa sent him to help me feed the pigs. As always, Archibald took his punishments out on me. This time, it was flingin' pig shit in my eye." Amos pointed to the eye patch as if Johnny couldn't deduce which eye was the topic. "My cryin' only pissed off Pa, and the next day when I told him I didn't feel no good, he told me to quit bein' a sissy. After throwin' up for three days straight and going blind, he let a doctor look at me. A month in the hospital and Pa tellin' everyone it was my fault for being careless was what I got for Archibald's punishment. I missed so much school, I got held back. The first of three times."

"Now you understand," Johnny said as he wandered to the phone on the counter. Next to it laid a pencil and a small notepad.

"Understand what?" Amos snapped.

"What I'm looking for. I'm fascinated by the same things, sort of. I need to explore, examine, experiment to determine these magical qualities that humans have. Many, many people have died from the same infection you had. What about *you* made you stronger? Amos, although you are not typically seen as a peak specimen, you have managed to survive circumstances that healthier individuals might not withstand. You beat parasitic microbes. Yes, you had the benefit of modern medicine, but according to your own words, your access to it was hindered. You overcame obstructions when others faltered."

Amos took a step back. "Does that mean you wanna cut me open?"

"On the contrary. It's obvious you have moxie. Something inside you gives you more determination than others. Moxie is another item on my growing list of what to search for when I operate."

Amos crumpled the empty can, then tossed it into the nearby trash bin. He ran his hands over his face, one after the other, as if pulling notions from his mind before speaking. "I ain't never thought about how you can just kill all willy-nilly. But now that I've... ya know, done just that... I still can't help wondering how you do it? How can you do that?"

Johnny grabbed the pencil and wrote a word on the notepad. He tore the sheet from the pad and held up the blank side toward Amos. "How I turn people into experiments is a quick and easy process. I make no elaborate plans to end them, I don't set up Rube Goldberg machinations to bring about their demise. What I do is quite simple. If it takes such little effort to remove them from this plane of existence, then what right did they have being here in the first place? And if they're so weak and expendable, then that means they are..."

Johnny flipped the paper to the other side, presenting the word, "Worthless."

Scratching the stubble on his cheeks, Amos squinted. His jaw muscles flexed as if he was chewing words to find which ones tasted better. He nodded. "I get it. I get it, Johnny."

"Excellent." Johnny crumbled the paper into a ball and tossed it into the trash can. He clapped his hands together, signaling for an end to the discussion, and then started toward the hallway. "Obviously, experimenting on Silas takes priority. He's... fascinating."

"Yeah, that's for sure," Amos whispered while drifting toward the pencil and pad.

Curious, Johnny paused to observe.

A monomaniacal expression etched upon his face, Amos picked up the pencil and wrote the word, "Archibald," on the pad. He tore off the sheet, crumbled it, and tossed it in the trash.

CHAPTER 19

Riley inhaled deeply. He didn't know what shampoo Javi used, but the smell was "fresh." The start of a morning. Beginning. New, yet as comfortable as slipping on his favorite old shoes. *Okay, not going to compare Javi to my old sneakers. Maybe freshly washed blankets on a cold night.* Riley rolled his eyes at his own thoughts; he'd never be a poet. Anyway… no words described how nice it felt to lie in the barn's loft with Javi's head on his chest. He had almost screwed this up, having spent the last two weeks unable to put his anger into words. "I'm sorry."

"You said that already," Javi said into Riley's tee shirt. "And I said this already – you have nothing to be sorry about. I'm sorry you had to go through what you went through and I'm doubly sorry I was too weak to help."

"Weakness had nothing to do with it. We were caught in a tornado with no ditch to dive into. And I'm sorry it took me so long to say I'm sorry."

Javi shifted, overlapping his hands on Riley's chest for a place to rest his chin. "You needed time to process, to heal. I wish I hadn't pressured you into thinking you had to apologize."

Wrapping his arms around Javi, Riley studied every curve of his face. "Well, too bad we have to be who we are in secret."

As if the universe needed to prove Riley's point, Javi's father walked into the barn. "Javi? You in here, Son?"

Holding his breath, Riley released Javi. With worry etched on his face, Javi said, "Yes! Be right down."

Javi got to his knees and grabbed the small bale of hay positioned at the loft's edge for this very reason. He tossed it over the short railing and then hurried to the ladder. Right before he disappeared from Riley's view, he winked.

Riley hated that Javi had to leave but understood the ramifications if he didn't. The exchange between father and son was in Spanish, so Riley caught less than half of what was said. The tone was more important than the words – casual, jovial... Good

With Javi gone, Riley smelled nothing but fresh hay, old straw, dust, and faint mustiness coming from the far corner where water ran during big rains. And an onion-smell warning that his deodorant was on the verge of conking out. Saturday morning chores had a habit of doing that. Especially when he had to cover for Rand, as a favor, while doing a few of his own.

Begrudgingly, Riley rolled over to get back to the world outside the barn, but froze when he heard footsteps, the dry scrapes of boots scuffing against boards.

"Riley?" Rand whispered from below, though the volume was no softer than his regular voice. "Riley? You in here?"

Riley immediately felt stupid for playing possum; with Javi gone, he didn't need to hold his breath or hide. He crawled to the edge and looked over. "Yeah. Why you whispering?"

Rand shrugged. "I dunno. Just in case you weren't alone?"

"So you think if you whisper, they wouldn't hear you, but I would?"

Rand rolled his eyes. "Shut up and get down here."

Laughing, Riley swept a clump of loose hay over the edge, enough for Rand to shout, "Horse's ass!"

When Riley reached the bottom of the ladder, Rand was still brushing hay from his billowy white shirt and dark brown pants held up by suspenders. "What in God's name are you wearing, big brother? Did someone steal all your clothes?"

"Ha ha. It's my costume for my movie role."

"This? This is why I helped with your chores?"

"Hell yes, baby brother! I'm the stable boy."

"What century is this movie set in? Because it sure as hell isn't early nineteenth century America."

Rand smirked and kicked up hay and dirt at Riley. "I'm in the movie and that's all that matters."

Riley laughed. "We need to talk about priorities."

"I don't need a quarterback to lecture me about priorities. Anyway, that's not why I'm here. Your friends, Tilde and Barnes, are looking for you."

"Yeah? Did they say why?"

Rand gave a head nod for Riley to follow him out the barn door. "They did not. Now, come on."

As they walked, Riley eyed Rand again and shook his head, chuckling. "God, they did you so wrong."

"The costume girls did they best they could."

"We could hit the thrift shops in Duke City and do a better job."

"It's not about the costume, it's about the character."

"So, Mr. Method Actor, what's your character's name?"

"He... ummm... he doesn't have one, just 'stableboy' in the script. Although, Mrs. Haddon has been calling me Percival..."

Riley sneered as if his brother had just farted in church. "Jesus Christ, Rand, you can't be serious."

"Hey! I'm not shitting all over your dreams!"

Rand's words nailed Riley's feet to the ground. "Wait... Are you saying you're really dreaming about becoming an actor?"

Hands in his pockets, Rand shrugged and cuffed a stone with his boot. "No, but maybe? I don't know. I mean, I'm not gonna run away with the movie crew when they pack up, but... You got me thinking. In about a year and a half, you're gonna be in college. College encourages you to ask questions about yourself and your future. I mean, don't get me wrong, I love this home and ranch, and I love being a bull rider and I really do want to go pro. But it's, I don't know, years and years of being in the same place. I know I'll travel, but it'd be to places just like here with people just like the ones in places like this one. Am I making sense?"

As the younger brother, rarely had he been turned to for anything. Maybe to help with math homework and chores now and again, but nothing like real feelings. Real concerns and fears. Grabbing Rand by the shoulders, Riley gave him a firm shake to get his eyes up and focused. "You're making all the sense in the world, big brother. Plus, there are no old bull riders, but plenty of old actors."

Rand's eyes glistened as he nodded. "I promise I'm not gonna throw away my bull riding career. I just want to have something else in my life."

Those words didn't sound like they were meant for Riley, but as practice for what Rand would eventually tell their parents, so he squeezed and shook his older brother again, harder this time to elicit a chuckle. "I'm going to be here, and support you, no matter what. Got it?"

Rand knocked Riley's hands away. "Yeah. Yeah, I do."

"Good. Now let's—"

"There you are!" Tilde interrupted as she and Barnes jogged across the field to join the brothers.

"Hey, Doe Eyes," Barnes said. After a couple deep inhales to catch his breath, he continued, "Hey, Smiles. Either of you seen Sasha?"

"Is she the new costume girl?" Rand asked.

"*He* is the third P.A. The one with the shaved head and an army jacket. The new wardrobe girl who did you dirty by dressing you in that tragedy is named Matilda."

Rand grinned as if he'd just shared a joke with close friends. "Sorry. Sasha, P.A.; Matilda, wardrobe. Good to know."

"I haven't seen him," Riley said.

Tilde ran her hand through her green hair and paced in a small circle, avoiding eye contact with the men. "He's missing. We haven't seen him since last night. We've looked everywhere."

"We know he's a big boy and can take care of himself," Barnes said, "but we're still a little on edge from Valencia running away. And we're nervous, because he's, you know, different. Like us."

Riley swallowed as a lump formed in his throat after hearing the word "us." Did Barnes include Riley in that grouping, or did he mean just himself and Tilde? And how would he know about Riley anyway? Did he give off a vibe? Should he be able to recognize others like himself, did he have… what'd he hear it called? Oh yeah… gaydar? "Yeah, small town New Mexico is not what people would call progressive, so I understand the concern."

"Did you ask anyone around camp?"

"We did some light asking."

"Light asking?"

"Yeah," Barnes said. "Dropped subtle hints here and there. Asked Bo if Sasha got his coffee, asked Brett if she needed anything from Sasha. Little things like that."

"Okay. Let's go talk to Miles and Nixon again."

Barnes puckered his face, spraying a bit of spittle when he said, "Oh, fuck that!"

Rand gave a reassuring nod. "Alright. I hear ya. Follow me."

Riley didn't believe he could string enough words together to help Tilde and Barnes feel any less worried about Sasha, so he kept his mouth shut. Of course, that meant he didn't ask Rand where he was going until his older brother marched right up to their mother, inside the paddock with one of the horses. Not thinking it possible until this very moment, Riley's admiration for Rand skyrocketed. Dressed the way he was, Rand was exposing a truth about himself for the benefit of a few people he had met only two weeks ago.

"Well, if it isn't Percival," Mother said with a smile of mockery. The horse let out a stuttered whiney as if in on the joke.

Rand didn't usually blush, but on this occasion, his cheeks hit the hue of pickled beets. He moved closer to Mother and mumbled, "Sorry."

The production assistants had the courtesy to look away and take a few lingering steps to the side. Riley expected to witness a tongue lashing, but instead Mother laughed. "I think it's healthy to expand your horizons. I just wish I didn't have to find out from Brett."

"Sorry," Rand said again. "Does Dad know?"

"Not yet, but you're going to tell him today, right?"

"Yes, Ma'am."

Placing her hand on the back of his neck to bring his eyes to hers, she said, "You can tell us anything. It may take a moment to process, but we're your parents and we love you no matter what."

She then glanced at Riley, and the cold insects of getting found out skittered through his chest. *Does she know? Of course she does! She's Mom!* Before his mind spun out of control with potential scenarios of what would happen should he decide to tell his parents the truth, Mother released Rand

and stepped closer to Tilde and Barnes. "Judging by the worried looks I see on your faces, it seems like you might have something to tell me?"

Barnes fidgeted with his fingers while Tilde did the talking, "It's Sasha, the other production assistant, the one with the shaved head. He's missing."

"I'm assuming you haven't told Miles or Nixon."

"No, not after the way they reacted when Valencia disappeared the other day."

"You don't think she left like they suggested?"

Barnes shrugged his shoulders. "Valencia? Maybe, maybe not. But now that we can't find Sasha... I don't know."

Mother looked toward the northern part of the property and squinted as if she could see the happenings of Fake Town. "Okay. Percival, tell your father I'm going to call the police. The rest of you, follow me in the house."

Color poured out of Rand's cheeks like spilled wine. He looked like he'd rather run naked through a cactus patch. He took off toward Dad, none to happy with the comments he'd receive from their father about what he was wearing and why. Tilde and Barnes both sighed with relief, clearly encouraged by Mother offering to help. *Yes*, Riley thought. *Telling her was a good idea.*

CHAPTER 20

Amanda hovered close to Hank as Sheriff Pete Cunningham – Petey, when he wasn't in uniform – strolled through the ankle-high brush of the southern part of their property. He was Petey when Amanda and Hank saw him in the grocery store shopping for his infirmed mother, in the bar with a beer in one hand and pool cue in the other, and at the Albuquerque food bank helping when he can. He'd been a guest at the Winters' dinner table on more than one occasion, but never on their property in any official capacity. Nor, to the best of Amanda's knowledge, had he performed any detective work beyond helping hungover people, who woke up in his drunk-tank, find their vehicles. Now, she felt Hank's frustration wash over her like waves on a beach anytime Sheriff Pete crouched down or grunted as if acknowledging a clue.

"This is the same man who confessed to us that he once locked himself out of his own cruiser," Hank whispered to Amanda.

"No one else needs to know that," Amanda whispered back. "Right now, he's the calming factor everyone is looking for."

Sheriff Pete stood to investigate brush a few yards away.

Hank looked around at the small gathering that had made a police appearance a spectator event. Rand and Riley stood beside Tilde and Barnes, exchanging tense whispers among themselves. A half dozen others involved with the movie wandered around and shared furtive suspicions and theories. Nixon stood apart from everyone, arms crossed over his chest. Amanda couldn't tell if it was a pensive stance of frustration, or if he was hugging himself from apprehension.

"The longer Sheriff's here, the worse it looks for our ranch."

"Hank. Think about what you just said." The terseness in Amanda's tone conveyed her feelings.

Hank huffed and shook his head. "Half the people here are barely older than Rand and Riley. I get that they're concerned, but motives are fleeting for young people. Heck, there's probably no reason why they've gone missing, other than that they are. I bet they just ran off somewhere."

"You think Valencia and Sasha just left? Without telling anyone?"

"The logic of young people is as straight as a moth's flight path. Just like it was for us once upon a time, if you remember correctly."

"Oh, I do. But doesn't this feel... different?"

Hank huffed again and then gestured with a nod toward Pete. "C'mon. Let's go see what he's found."

Hands in his pockets, Sheriff Pete stared at the ground as if expecting something to pop out any second. "These look like footprints to you?" he asked as Hank and Amanda approached.

Only the sturdiest brush dared to grow from the hard ground. The reddish dirt was too dense to hold the impressions of anything that walked or traversed over it. The indentations Pete referred to were suggestions at best.

Amanda replied, "Sort of, only because you put that idea in my head."

"Yeah, this ground likes to keep its secrets, doesn't it?" Sheriff Pete said as he half-turned, gazing at another patch of ground. "If they are footprints, then they kind of lead here, don't they?"

Twists in the dirt, a gouge here and there, as if someone turned this small patch into a dance floor.

"What are you suggesting?" Amanda asked.

"Nothing, actually," Sheriff Pete said, pointing to the other side of the tongue-in-groove fence. "Could be anything, right? How about over here, on the Boyles' property? More possible markings, two straight lines. A branch or two of brush seems to be broken. Tire tracks?"

"Seems it," Hank said. "Course you could hold a monster truck rally here and this land would show no evidence of it taking place. And there's no way we're gonna hop the fence to look any closer. If Archibald saw that, he'd have lawyers up my ass."

"Mine, too." Sherrif Pete added a sad chuckle to his words. "The point I'm trying to make is... you know the land as well as I do. Familiarity can make us see what we want to see. We can't be sure what's going on, especially with all these people camping here on the southern part of your property, and all the commotion and whatnot."

"Well, you should know by now, Sherrif, we gave them all kinds of rules to follow."

Sherrif Pete strolled behind the port-a-johns and nudged a cigarette butt from the tiny field of finished smokes. "I know you well enough Hank to know that you probably told your guests not to smoke on your property, right?"

"Damn movie people," Hank mumbled.

Sheriff Pete offered a tight-lipped look of sympathy. "Sorry, but I don't have much to go on, and what I did find, can be explained away without much thought."

"Sorry for bringing you out here without offering you a meal," Hank said as the trio headed back to the trailers and tents.

"Well, this being a professional visit and all, I think it'd be best, under the circumstances, if I come over out of uniform for one of your wife's pot roasts."

Under the scrutiny of curious eyes, Sheriff Pete approached Nixon and pulled his pen and small notebook from his shirt. "I'm sorry, Mr. Lang, but I didn't find any evidence that the missing fellow didn't leave on his own accord."

Indistinct mumbles flowed along the onlookers.

Pen to paper, Sheriff Pete said, "I have plenty of statements regarding Sasha, saying that he would not leave without telling anyone. But the more I think about it, it's quite a hike down the driveway to the main road by foot. Are any vehicles missing?"

Nixon removed his black Stetson and ran his hand through his hair as he looked over to where the RVs and trailers were parked. "I don't know. At the moment, I can't remember what all we brought and—"

"Shit!" Tilde blurted out. "The black pickup."

"Huh?" Nixon asked.

A hangdog look on her face, Tilde answered softly, "The black Ford pickup, the one the PAs arrived in? Miles let us drive it, because it fit all three of us. We used it to transport a bunch of props."

As Sheriff Pete wrote in the notebook, Nixon pulled his walkie-talkie from his back pocket. A crackle of static until he pressed the talk button. "Hey, Stew? It's Nixon. Is the black pickup by you guys?"

A crackle. "I don't see it but let me ask around."

"Hey, guys, what's going on?" Miles asked, appearing so suddenly that everyone jumped, even Amanda. And that was before she got a good eyeful of him. Always in slacks and nice black shoes, though they had dulled quite a bit over these past couple weeks. Half the buttons of his fancy blue shirt were unbuttoned, a few too many for Amanda's taste. Rolled up sleeves did nothing to alleviate the dark sweat circles that had spread well behind the confines of his underarms. Perspiration brought curls to a few locks of his hair, quite a bit of it plastered to his forehead.

"What the hell, dude?" Nixon said to Miles. "You look like you just sprinted a marathon."

With a chuckle that seemed a bit too rehearsed to Amanda's ear, Miles patted his belly. "No, no, no. Nothing like that. Those delicious green chilies from Hatch that I can't stop eating? Well, they sometimes get the better of me. Anyway, I see we have an officer of the law here. Is everything okay?"

Pen primed over the notepad, Sheriff Pete said, "Just responding to a missing person call. And you are?"

"Miles Pennypacker, sir. The producer of the motion picture we're filming on the Winters' property." He turned to Nixon and asked, "Who's missing?"

"Sasha," Nixon said. "Tilde and Barnes said he was with them last night but gone this morning. They were concerned because they said he wouldn't leave without telling anyone. However, we just noticed that one of the pickups might be missing, so I'm checking with the crew to see if it's by the set."

"One of the pickups—?" Miles started but the crackle of the walkie-talkie interrupted him.

"Hey, Nixon? Stew here. Yeah, no sign of the pickup. No one's seen it."

All heads swiveled to Sheriff Pete. "Year, make, model, and plate number…"

Miles reached out for the pad and pen. After a quick scribble, he handed it back. "Here you go. I included my cellular phone number. Call if we can do anything to provide further assistance, though, as I'm sure you're aware, cellular service isn't the best out here."

"Noted," Sheriff Pete said as he jotted a few more items into his notebook before tucking it into his shirt pocket. "I'll have Albuquerque, Santa Fe, and everyone in between keep an eye out for it. Unfortunately, that's the best I can do for now. Feel free to reach out should anything pertinent arise."

Sheriff Pete shook Hank's and Amanda's hands, and tipped his white Stetson to everyone else as he made his way back to his cruiser.

Hank glared at Rand. With head hanging low, "Percival" joined his father for a long, and undoubtedly uncomfortable, walk back to the house.

Miles gained everyone's attention with a startling clap. "Alright everyone. I'm sure Sasha just ran to town for supplies or something and I'll have to apologize to the sheriff for wasting his time, so let's all get back to work."

"Tone it down a notch," Nixon said to Miles as they turned away from Amanda. "And towel off, dude."

Miles gave a salute, soaked in more sarcasm than his hair was with sweat, and then headed to his trailer.

The PAs glared at the producer's trailer the way Red Riding Hood looked at her grandmother's eyes and teeth. Amanda didn't blame them. During his entire stay here, Miles rejected Hatch's green chilies every time they had been offered.

CHAPTER 21

Silas wiggled the fingers of his right hand. Perfect, no more difficult than... well, wiggling fingers. He chuckled, the sound in his ears different than the last time he chuckled. It was a different voice box attached to his neck, after all. But he frowned when he looked at his left hand.

Technically, he didn't frown, not having the proper facial features to do so since he no longer wore anyone's face. But looking at the skin covering his left hand, progressing from green to gray these past couple days, triggered anger and disappointment. The skin was dying and when he touched index finger to thumb, he felt nothing. *Fuck it*, he thought as he ripped it off like a used glove, the flimsy skin pulling from the wooden wrist like rotted cloth. He tossed it toward the corner of the barn.

"Shall I assume you no longer find any use in it?" Johnny asked, his words as sterile as an alcohol-cleaned scalpel, and just as cutting.

"A day-old corpse would look more alive than that skin," Silas said.

Johnny held a pail of blood in front of him. He wore a green surgeon's mask and latex gloves.

"Technically, it was from a corpse over a week old, so all things considered, it looked better than it should've. Now, dunk your hand in this."

Too many questions crashed into each other around the inside of Silas' mind. Was this to be his new normal? How could he rejoin the world outside the Tomlin property if he had to change parts every week? How long would this hand last? But he kept his words to himself and dunked his new hand into the pail. Wet. Warm. Soothing?

Johnny's approach to this hand differed from the last. Cutting from fingertips to palm, then from palm to elbow, he had removed the bones from the unwilling donor. With the meat still attached to the skin, Johnny worked Silas' wooden hand in through the cuts. A simple sew job to close the openings. The skin itched and burned, a minor irritant Silas would cope with if it meant gaining the sensation of touch. Now, after dipping his hand in the bucket of blood, the discomfort subsided.

The cuts were gone, as were the threads once holding the skin together, but the impression remained. Not scars. Silas received plenty of those during his years as a living breathing man, so he'd become quite an expert on how bad decisions made their permanent mark. The lines on his hand now were faint enough that they could be missed at first glance. "Fascinatin'."

"Indeed." Not wasting any time, Johnny moved back to the donor and grabbed a hacksaw. He then wandered to the metal tub holding the bald guy with a woman's name, the person who Amos had kidnapped and killed from the movie set. Once the chirurgeon started to give the business to the dead man's upper thigh, Silas was suddenly thankful that he had no stomach, or else it'd have turned and turned again. To his surprise – Amos watched with intent.

No longer going green gilled like he had been when this bloody work had all began, Amos took a few shuffling steps closer, his eyes glued to the leg as Johnny removed it from the tub and dropped it on the operating table next to Silas. The rube's staring didn't go unnoticed.

Had Silas been asked to conjure a time when Johnny showed even the slightest bit of mirth, this would have been it. While wiping a long, thin knife usually found in a slaughterhouse with a clean cloth after dousing it with non -drinking alcohol, Johnny approached Amos and said, "Care to operate?"

As if awakening from a nightmare, Amos backed away with his hands out and shaking his head. Blubbering to the point of spraying his words, he protested. "No. No, no, no. That ain't for me none. I was just... Umm... Just..."

"Curious?" Johnny said, finishing Amos' sentence. "Wondering what secrets lay beneath and within the layers of skin and fat and muscle? What mechanics make the machine of man? What tiny nuances separate us from animals? You have operated on animals before, correct?"

"Operated? No. Nothing like that."

"No? You work and live on a pig farm. I'm assuming you know how to skin and gut and chop up a piggy. You should be able do those actions with your eyes closed."

"Yeah, but I wouldn't call it 'operatin'. That's butcherin'."

"Nonsense." As simple as running a pencil over a piece of paper, Johnny slid the tip of the knife along the top of the leg. Down the thigh. Across the shin. Over the foot. The skin spread to expose a crimson valley. Even though the body had been drained of blood, the meat still glistened. "You dig deep into the essence of the specimen. You know what's used for what. You break down, remove, rearrange." Placing the blade in his gloved hand, Johnny offered the handle to Amos. "You know exactly what to do."

Nervous as a schoolboy going in for his first kiss behind a church, Amos accepted the knife with trembling hand, and approached the operating table. After an audible gulp, he followed the same cuts Johnny had made. Offering no words of encouragement nor words of derision, Johnny instructed Amos where to cut and why. Slice after slice, Amos followed Johnny's commands, his actions more deliberate with each cut. With Johnny's assistance, he removed enough meat to pull the leg bones out with a slurp.

"There. Now you, too, are a chirurgeon," Johnny said, the pride in his voice reserved for a proud papa. Chunks of residual meat jiggled as he tossed the bones in the tub holding the donor; part of a big ol' meal for the Boyles' pigs later.

Johnny instructed Silas to lay back on the table and extend his leg. Amos shaved away muscle from inside the donor's leg, helping fit it around Silas' wooden leg. After a few minutes with the two men working in perfect silence, they got it looking like a fleshy stocking.

"Now you're a chirurgeon, too," Silas said to Amos, meaning it as a snide tease.

Judging by the punch-drunk smile on Amos' face, he was too stupid to take it as one. With a point of pride sharpened into his words, he said, "Thank you. Much obliged."

"Hold the seam together," Johnny said as he grabbed the pail of blood. "I want to test a theory."

Starting at the foot, Amos squeezed the two halves of skin together while Johnny poured a controlled stream of blood into the meat canyon. Like lovers who had been apart for too long, the two halves fused together. The two men continued the process up Silas' new leg, Amos pressing the skin together while Johnny followed along with the blood, the crimson liquid flowing over the skin and splashing to the table.

The process became more interesting at the top of the thigh. Skin grew over the exposed meat and wrapped around the wooden hip, bonding the new leg to Silas. Even a small-minded cuss like Silas Worthington was mesmerized by the miracle. "Well, I'll be."

"Fascinating," Johnny whispered, removing his mask, his eyes locked onto the last few twitches of skin bonding to wood. "Absolutely fascinating."

Silas hopped off the table, and dirt and grit from the rough wooden floor dug into his foot. He couldn't wiggle his toes none – the mannequin feet had no such appendages to begin with – but the leg was strong and sturdy. He felt the barn floor with every step he took as he walked to the door. Sun warmed both his hand and leg. Starting at his knee, he ran the finger of his skin-covered hand along the crease in his leg. The closer he got to his hip, the more he ached for what was missing. "I need a body. A whole damn body. I need to walk outside this property. I need to walk into a bar and drink everythin' that makes my tongue burn and fight the first asshole who pisses me off and then fuck every whore in the goddamn place."

Johnny slowly poured what remained in the bucket over Silas' head. The blood flowed over his neck and shoulders, the wood soaking it up like a dry sponge, fully absorbed by the time it reached his chest. Johnny placed the empty bucket next to the metal tub holding the corpse's remains. "I'd like to run a few more experiments. Maybe with another two or three donors. We'll need to space them out about a week or two."

"No!" Silas pounded the door frame. He had used his skin covered hand and it hurt. "I need a body now! I need both hands and feet and a face and a dick! I need a dick! Find me another body – a whole body – and put me in it."

Johnny sighed, a hint of a frown playing across his face. Despite being as sour as vinegar, Silas found a tiny bit of joy in making Johnny express emotion. "Very well. We'll put your body into the next donor we get."

Wiping away his anger as easily as Johnny wiped the blood from his knife, Silas turned to Amos. "Ya hear that? Go back to the Winters' place and get me a new donor."

Amos shook his head and waved his hands, his whole body disagreeing with the request. "No. No no no. It ain't a good idea."

"Why the fuck not?"

"I jumped the guy whose parts you're wearing two nights ago, so yesterday, the Winters called the cops. And it's gettin' weird over there."

"How do you mean?"

"My nephew said one of the movie guys gave him a hundred bucks for a ride from Duke City to the Winters' ranch yesterday."

"That sounds like nothin' having to do with nothin,'" Silas said.

"Isn't that the kind of thinking that led to you being on the wrong end of a noose?" Johnny asked.

Damn him and his emotionless reasoning. Silas wanted to punch him, plant his brand-new fist right in Johnny's smug puss. "Ain't you funnier than a court jester." Done with Johnny's smart mouth, Silas turned his attention back to Amos and asked, "You're implyin' that what you just said ain't normal?"

Amos laughed, exposing a couple gaps once inhabited by teeth. "No, it is not. No one willingly associates with us Boyles, especially Mercer Boyle."

Pain blasted through Silas' head. The name "Mercer Boyle" was an ax splitting it in half. Running his new hand over his throbbing head, he checked for cracks. "What in the Hell?"

Johnny and Amos glanced at each other before turning to Silas. Not needing either of them to ask, Silas explained. "I felt a big punch to my brain... Well, a big ol' pain where my brain ought to be, and in the center of it, the name 'Mercer Boyle' flashed like a lightning bolt."

"Why is my nephew's name dancin' around in your head?" Amos asked.

"If I knew, I'd kick it out."

Johnny removed his rubber gloves and tossed them into the small trashcan by the operating table. "Was the experience similar to when the Winters' name suddenly popped into your head a while ago?"

"Yeah. But this was like a rattlesnake coiled up behind a rock, waitin' for the right time to strike, when Amos said Mercer's name. It don't hurt no more, but it's taking up a lot of space between my ears."

"Fascinating. Are there other names?"

"No. Well, maybe. I don't know. I feel like there's somethin' there, somethin' that goes along with Mercer and Winters."

Amos laughed. "Trust me, the only thing that goes with Mercer Boyle and any of the Winters, is their mutual hatred for each other."

"How about other relatives?" Johnny asked. "Maybe friends?"

"Anyone who is not a Boyle is friends with the Winters, so there's too many to list. Anyone who Mercer can bum a smoke or a drink from, he'd consider a friend. But he only got one that he hangs out with – Caleb McTavish."

Silas screamed, well beyond what the throat attached to his neck could handle, and clamped his hands to his head to keep it from exploding with pain. Like a desert thunderstorm, the pain left just as soon as it came. And the inside of Silas' head felt just as wet.

"What in the Hell?" Amos asked.

"Are you alright?" Johnny asked. There was no concern in his voice or gaze, just the coldness of collecting data.

"Yeah. Yeah. Fit as a fiddle," Silas answered.

"I'm afraid to mention any more names around you," Amos said, stepping back as if proximity equaled intensity.

Silas waved his hand, shooing away everyone's concerns. Well, Amos' concerns since Johnny had proclaimed that his concerns were found in science, not people. Strange, but Silas felt the same way he'd felt after a few unpleasant grunts in an outhouse after downing too many Mexican peppers. Relieved, hungry, and ready to go. "I'm pretty sure that all the names needing to be said have been said."

"And you have no idea what they mean to you or why they had those effects?" Johnny asked, wiping his knife with an alcohol-soaked rag.

"No. Them names appeared in my head a while ago. They never really left. It's like wantin' a steak after not havin' one for a spell. Real, mouth waterin', belly hurtin' hunger hits and all you want is a steak."

"Very well, then. My work here is done for the day." As if attaching body parts to a moving chunk of wood in human form was as normal as running errands, Johnny left the barn.

"He's weird as a goose that flies south for the summer," Amos mumbled after Johnny left.

"Can't disagree none about that," Silas replied. Testing out his leg, he walked over to Amos. It felt good, as natural as the leg he had when he was alive. With his new hand, he grabbed the sleeve of Amos' flannel shirt, the cotton coarse from time's wear and tear. "I still need a body, though, Amos. I *need* a body."

The dummy missed the threat; the look in his eye mimicked that of a friend consoling another friend over the loss of their dog.

Amos gently pried Silas' hand from his sleeve and patted it. "Don't you worry none. I'll think of somethin'. You go on back inside the house and relax. I'm gonna head home and think upon your problem."

With another pat on the hand, Amos exited the barn. Once he was far enough down the property to be the size of an insect, Silas said, "You better. Or my problem becomes your problem."

CHAPTER 22

Amos trudged up the steps to the wraparound porch of his house. Well, it ain't his house; it's his brother's. Archibald let him live there for free as long as Amos did enough around the pig farm to earn his keep. Their pa made Archibald take that oath when he handed the business and farm and property over to his eldest son. And smartest son, according to Pa. Well, according to anyone who had enough sense to know up from down and that rain was wet.

Key in the front door's lock, Amos paused and chewed on that sentiment a bit. *He's smarter than me now, but who says I ain't got what it takes to eventually be smarter than him?* Amos knew of only one way to outsmart him – solve problems. Archibald always said that smarts ain't nothing more than solving problems. All Amos had to do was solve the biggest problem before him now – where to get the next body for Silas and Johnny.

Sucking his teeth, Amos shook his head to scratch the itch inside his mind from all this thinking. But he had to keep thinking to get smarter than Archibald, to prove he was worthy of the Boyle name and property. And this house.

Amos didn't know what the word "antebellum" meant, but he heard Archibald use it to describe the house. If Archibald used that word while bragging to others, then it was a snooty word, all smell and no taste. He once heard an older woman in the grocery store say with a lip curling snarl to another woman that the house was "ostentatious". Didn't know exactly what that word meant neither, but it sounded like a much better descriptor. Who the hell needed four thick, white columns for a two-story house on a pig farm?

The insides didn't make much sense to Amos either. The front door opened to a big – *what was that French word for it? Oh, yeah* – "foyer" of thin slatted hardwood. A stupid big staircase took up a lot of the foyer and shot straight to the second floor, most of it exposed. Upstairs is where the house's four bedrooms were. Well, only two were used as bedrooms – one for Mercer and a super big one for Archibald. The other two were offices; one for the pig business and the other for personal use, such as whenever Mercer decided to do homework. Amos knew homework never got done there, just Mercer using the computer for porn and other mindlessness.

Amos' room was through a door in the back corner of the kitchen, often unseen by anyone laying eyes upon the kitchen for the first time. Another door to his room was in the dining room, but he'd always hit the kitchen first for a snack. It once was a large pantry, back when six or seven people living here needed that quantity of food and supplies. Now with only three people living here and Archibald eating lunches and dinners in restaurants more often than not, the large pantry got converted into a small bedroom for Amos. It was a place to lay his head, nothing more. Not a bad place, should Amos ever really reflect upon comparing it to other places where he'd woken up, but there was one main drawback – sometimes Mercer was in the kitchen.

Caleb stood in the kitchen with Amos' nephew, both laughing while waiting for the microwave to finish its humming.

"Oh, hey pig fucker," Mercer said when Amos entered the kitchen, the greeting as friendly as it got.

"Hey pig fucker," Caleb repeated like a parrot. Well, a parrot that got hit in the head with a hammer.

Amos didn't respond, not wanting to encourage the nickname. Not that it discouraged them none, but it was better than getting into a spat which Amos would undoubtedly be on the losing end of with these two.

The microwave dinged and recaptured their attention.

"Hey!" Amos snapped when Mercer opened the microwave door. "Are those my burritos?"

Mercer chuckled as he gave one of the two burritos to Caleb, biting into the other himself. "Didn't see anyone's name on the box."

Amos hurried to the freezer and damn near tore off the door. "The box is gone."

"Maybe that's why I didn't see a name on it." Mercer and Caleb shared a laugh.

"I bought it just yesterday. There were six in the box and I didn't have a single one."

"Well, pig fucker, they were mighty tasty." Mercer held up his, toasting Amos with the injustice, then walked out of the kitchen.

Caleb followed, mimicking Mercer's toast, and said, "Mighty tasty, pig fucker, mighty tasty."

Amos slammed the freezer door hard enough to rattle the fridge's contents. Didn't give a good God damn if he broke anything. He marched out of the kitchen, stopping in the hallway beside the stairs. Mercer and Caleb lurked in the hall leading to the foyer, stomping in tight, angry circles, like spoiled little children who didn't get their way. They hadn't seen Amos, so he hugged the wall along the staircase and became part of the shadows, curious about what might have caused such sour pusses.

"The party's a little more than a week away, and you're still in charge of getting the beer even though you fucked up our situation" Mercer said, and then took an aggressive bite from Amos' burrito.

"I didn't fuck nothin' up," Caleb snapped back.

"You had a guy all lined up to get us beer, but now you don't. Sounds like a fuck up to me."

"Pffft. Ain't my fault he got busted."

"Don't matter. You got one week to get beer."

"I'll think of somethin'," Caleb said, heading for the front door.

"You better." Mercer's farewell.

Like lightning striking him in the ear, a plan formed all at once, and Amos hurried through the kitchen to the back door. Once outside, he ran around the house as fast as his legs could carry him. Trying not to suck wind, he made it to the half rusted pickup truck by the time Caleb stepped off the porch. "Hey."

"What the fuck you want, pig fucker?" Caleb asked as he strolled to the truck.

"I heard you and Mercer talkin' about getting' beer for a party," Amos said.

Caleb paused at the driver-side door, frowning. "You spying on us? That's fuckin' creepy, dude."

"Ain't like you two were whisperin'. What happened to your regular guy?"

Caleb rolled his eyes, like now all of a sudden Amos was a coworker to whom he confided while bitching behind the boss' back. "Pffft. The prick got busted by Cunningham for speedin', and he had a shit-ton of pot on the passenger seat. Like the fuckin' idiot he is."

"Fuckin' idiot. But I can get you a case or two of beer."

Squinting did no favors for Caleb's dull eyes. A tone as dubious as his expression, he asked, "Yeah? Why?"

Like he'd seen cool characters on television do many times, Amos shrugged one shoulder and looked away, mysterious. "I need a little help with somethin'."

"Go on."

Caleb had taken the bait, and now all Amos had to do was reel in the line. Easy enough. A lazy gaze punctuated by a head nod toward the Tomlin property. "Word is," Amos said, "the Tomlins are gettin' desperate to sell."

"Yeah? Well, it's their own damn fault for buying that shit property from your brother. Your brother's smart, though. He'll buy it from them cheap in no time and sell it again to the next idiot, like he always does. You should be smarter, Amos. Like your brother."

I'm aimin' to be, you fuck-head. Smarter even than him. "Exactly. They gathered their valuables to sell. Word is they've been askin' prices from Santa Fe to Duke City every night. That means they ain't home right now. I wanna hit the place, but I don't wanna use my truck." To make sure even someone as stupid as Caleb knew what he was hinting at, Amos strolled closer to the passenger door and ran his hand over the roof.

Caleb smirked, his right eye widening three times the size of his left, looking like some kind of palsy victim. "Maybe I just take my truck up there now and leave you behind in my dust."

It was Amos' turn to smirk as he reached inside his pocket and pulled out a set of keys. He jingled them after every other word. "You could, but who'd help you with the TVs and gun safe and ice box? Plus, you'd have to either bust the door down or pick the lock. But if you bring me, it'd be so much easier."

Caleb frowned again, cracked lips pursed. "What's the split you're proposin'?"

"Fifty-fifty."

"Fuck you! I want half!"

Amos chuckled. After returning the keys to his pocket, he opened the passenger door and said, "You drive a hard bargain, but you got yourself a deal. You get half."

"Fuck right I do. I make sure to get what I deserve."

Amos couldn't stop his laughter as Caleb got in the truck and started the engine.

CHAPTER 23

Silas' heart raced. Or rather, Caleb's heart raced inside Silas' wooden chest. The wind flowed over his arm covered with Caleb's skin, tickling the hairs haphazardly growing along it, and he broke out into a big ol' smile of contentment.

When Amos had brought Caleb to the Tomlin house, the look on the poor sap's face after taking a good look at Silas and his wooden body covered with random body parts was kind of funny. Amos then gave the boy a few whacks over the head with a cast iron pan – a couple more than necessary – but it killed him good and kept the blood inside his body, allowing them plenty of time to move him to the bleeding trough. Johnny came right over and started the surgery.

Johnny and Amos took their time removing the bones to make room for Silas' mannequin body. When certain parts of the mannequin, like arms or legs, were bigger than the bones, then more muscle had to be trimmed away. Johnny cleared out the inner hollow of Silas' chest and added the new lungs and heart. Silas liked the sensation of breathing and of a beating heart.

Had there been a rooster nearby, its crow to the rising sun would have been just a few clock ticks after Johnny finished this morning.

Caleb was a couple inches taller than the mannequin, but once Silas got tucked inside and Johnny had poured the blood along the seams, Silas swore that his body shifted and accommodated the new height.

Sitting in the passenger side of Caleb's pickup truck – technically his pickup now, since he was wearing Caleb's body – he held his arm out the window while Amos drove on something called Old Route 66. Amos said it ran parallel to U.S. 40, whatever the hell that was, and they were heading to Chuck's Convenience store. Silas wanted to go to a bar, but his two flunkies shot that idea down faster than a gimpy horse, saying some bullshit about "legal drinking age" since he was now inside the body of a teenager. *Weird fuckin' laws 'round here.*

Silas pulled his hand back into the truck and side-eyed Amos. "You and Johnny said I can't buy no hooch since I'm wearing Caleb, so now that means I am Caleb, right?"

"Yep," Amos answered, keeping a tight grip on the steering wheel and his eye forward.

"Then that means this horseless carriage is mine, so why ain't I drivin'?"

A half frown over his good eye, Amos glanced at Silas and huffed, "'Cause you don't know how to drive."

"Gotta learn somehow, sometime."

"Let's get you learned on how to be around people first, especially Mercer."

Silas grunted and went back to watching the world outside the windows whiz by. Not sure why Mercer was so damn important. He and Caleb were attached at the hip, according to Amos. Though, every time Silas thought too hard about Mercer, the taste of blood traipsed across his tongue. It tasted good and he wanted more. *If nothin' else, maybe I'll figure out why when I meet Mercer.*

After a few more minutes of Silas enjoying the miracles of this new world, Amos turned the truck into the parking lot of the general store.

Two other cars were parked by the single-story establishment called Chuck's Convenience Store drowning in lights, and another car was parked next to what had been explained to Silas as gas-pumps. He found this place disappointing compared to the general stores he'd seen on television. "This don't look like a place where there are a lot of people."

"That's the whole point."

Silas frowned, his face contorting with exaggeration. It'd been over a century since he could control the features of his face. The hard squint brought pain between his eyes and over his forehead, and it felt glorious. As much as he hated the discomfort back in the day, he sure missed it when he had no face to do it. "The whole point is for me to get back into the world. You and Doctor No Fun told me that this Caleb fellow is school age. I should have gone to the schoolhouse today."

"And what was the first thing you did after the surgery?" Amos asked.

Amos was as sharp as a marble, but that question along with the sour expression made Silas feel stupid. Yes, he now had a body. A living, breathing, functioning body. And the first thing he did was run to the washroom and take care of the animal urge. Twice. "Nothin' you wouldn't have done in my position."

"Yeah, yeah, yeah. Can't have you runnin' around the high school tryin' to slick your stick with every girl that got near you. I know that's high on your list of wants, but you need to start slow. Plus, this convenience store is where kids like to get gas and snacks after school, which is why I'm certain Mercer will show up."

"Fine." *Bullshit*. "Now what?"

Amos pulled all the way up to the store, at the far corner away from the other cars, and parked. "Simple. Go inside and try not to stand out. 'Course lots of people know your face, and none of them are a fan of it. Don't talk to any women and do *not* steal anything. Sheriffs and cops today are way different than what you're used to from back in your day. Mercer should be along any minute. If he ain't along in half an hour, come back out."

"Yeah, yeah, yeah. No attention, wait for Mercer. Got it." Silas slammed the door, giving zero shits that the half-rusted thing simply bounced back open. A ringing chime sounded when he opened the door to Chuck's Convenience Store and by the time it faded, so did his sour mood.

The door was a gateway from the old and used yesterday to the new and virgin tomorrow. Bright lights from the ceiling shined on everything in the store like a smile from God. All kinds of foods individually wrapped in colorful packaging lined the shelves. A few looked familiar from the commercials on the television. Bottles of drinks were kept behind glass doors along the back wall. To the left was a counter surrounded by cigarettes and lottery tickets. The grumpy-looking shopkeeper behind the counter growled. "Keepin' an eye on you, McTavish."

Maybe Amos wasn't exaggerating the feelings others held about Caleb McTavish? Silas shrugged and decided to try a popular greeting he had heard. "Wha'sup?"

The shopkeeper rolled his eyes, grunted, but watched Silas like a circling hawk. Not caring about that none, Silas started down the first aisle. On the right were small containers and big containers. Automotive fluids, according to the labels. Must be for cars and trucks. Lots of little bags of mouth-watering morsels dangled from hooks along the shelving to the left.

Silas didn't know what any of these snacks tasted like, but judging from the pictures on the bag and the descriptions, he assumed something akin to fried chicken or pig skins, or the overcooked potato shavings that got stuck to the bottom of a skillet. Silas gulped down a pool of liquid hunger, something he hadn't done for quite some time. Another stupid little thing he never thought about until now. Yep, he'd love to try a few bags, but Amos gave him no money and added dire warnings about stealing. Much as it went against Silas' nature not to just grab and go, he had the shopkeep's eyes on him. And he wanted to learn about the bottles of assorted liquids behind glass doors.

Every color of the rainbow, and more than a few Silas couldn't recognize, cans and bottles all lined up in neat, nifty arrays. About a third of them had the word "beer." Oh, what he wouldn't give to pop the tops and guzzle! But Amos' nagging voice cut right between his ears, fussing about being too young. He stopped himself as he reached for the door handle and then looked to his left to see a man with a mouth-hiding mustache and a few hints of gray in his black hair giving Silas stink eye. Silas lowered his hand and nodded. "Wha'sup?"

"'Sup," the man grunted and opened the glass door. He retrieved a red and white cardboard carrier with the word "Budweiser" on it holding six brown bottles, and left. If Silas couldn't drink that, or the other beer, then what could he drink? The kid two doors down answered that question.

About Caleb's age, from what Silas guessed, the kid opened the door and grabbed a bottle labeled "Jolt." He shut the door and jerked when he noticed Silas staring at him. Silas went with what he knew and said, "Wha'sup?"

The kid looked around as if confused about who Silas was talking to. He mumbled, "'Sup," then walked to the front of the store.

Two girls, again about the same age as the skin he was wearing, loitered nearby in an aisle. They glanced up from their shopping and Silas flashed the best smile this face could muster. "Wha'sup?"

Both girls scowled as if he had just dropped his trousers and treated the floor like an outhouse. One of them said, "Ew, gross." They hurried away.

Concerned that his skin costume developed flaws or fluids leaking from the seams, Silas moved toward the glass doors, close enough to garner his reflection. No blood or other fluids, no sloughing. Then he got a better look at what he was working with as far as this kid's looks were concerned. When Johnny had finished the operation, Silas had been too excited about being human to take real notice of what he looked like. Long, thick head with a bottom jaw and forehead that stuck out too far. Eyes too close together and teeth too far apart as well as ears floppier than a prairie hare's. An ugly fucker for sure! He might need to find another body if he ever wanted to get his stick wet again.

Too busy critiquing his ugliness, he almost jumped out of his skin when a face appeared behind him in the reflection and yelled, "Where the fuck you been?"

Silas almost swung a fist as he turned around, but at the last second he recognized the kid.

Mercer Boyle.

A sudden pain stabbed between Silas' eyes. The pain flowed down his neck and chest all the way to his guts, inside the hollow cavity of his mannequin frame. He felt them guts twist and twitch, almost like hunger. A thought suddenly chilled him – he had no guts for those feelings to twist.

"Sick," Silas said.

"Bullshit. I went by your trailer yesterday and you weren't there. Your old man had no idea where you were. Though, as shit-faced as he was, I'm surprised he knew where he was."

Silas chuckled. No surprise this Caleb kid had a drunk father.

"I ain't fuckin' around, Caleb." Mercer snarled as he stepped closer, aggressively. "Where've you been?"

150

Always quick to run whenever bullets or blades might be involved, Silas never backed down from a dispute that could be settled with fists. A quick check and it seemed like Mercer had neither gun nor knife, so Silas stood tall and leaned into the conversation. "I said I was sick."

Mercer stepped back, looking at Silas as if he were waving a red-hot branding iron. He cleared his throat and though his face still held the expression of someone who'd just eaten rotted fruit, Mercer softened his tone. "Yeah? Well, you better not be sick for the party next weekend. You know what this party means to me. You get the booze yet?"

"Workin' on it."

Mercer glanced at the glass doors and then at Silas. "Yeah? You thinkin' about getting' it here? Whether you try to buy it or steal it, we both know Chuck ain't gonna let you leave the store with it."

A man with long hair and half-closed eyes strolled up to the glass door beside Silas and grabbed a six-pack of Miller Beer. Silas nodded and said, "Wha'sup?"

"My buzz, real soon," the man replied, and left.

Under the heavy gaze of Mercer's confusion, Silas said, "I'm workin' on it. Need me to say it a third time?"

Clearly Mercer was the wolf used to eating first, because whatever Silas had done to twist Mercer's sense of being upside-down had worn off. Clenching his fists, Mercer stepped forward and growled. "I don't know what the fuck you been up to, but your bullshit's gonna—"

Mercer suddenly stepped back. Silas looked to see what had spooked him. Two kids, around their age. Both blond; one a hint shorter and thicker in the chest, the other a hint taller and wiry. They both eye-balled Silas. He figured, *why not?* and said, "Wha'sup?"

"Are you serious?" the shorter one said.

That voice. Silas knew that voice, though he had never heard it before now. That voice once said, pleading, "*Mercer Boyle and Caleb McTavish. They wronged me in ways I can't speak about. Take them. Take them, kill them, damn them to Hell.*"

"What the fuck is wrong with you?" the taller one asked, fists clenched as tight as his pinched face.

Silas knew those faces. He was connected to them. He wanted them. Hot desire ignited a furnace in his wooden gut and spread quickly, turning his tree-bone skeleton to ash all the way up his body, stopping when hit with an explosion of sun right between his eyes, seeing the branded word in his brain: "Winters."

Pressing both hands against his head, Silas slumped against the glass case. The pain was brief, and in no time his vision cleared enough to see three sets of eyes stricken with bewilderment, as if witnessing the unnatural horror of sheep giving birth to a cow.

"The fuck *is wrong* with you, McTavish?" Mercer asked.

Silas pushed himself from the glass door, his wooden hand slipping around inside the fleshy glove of Caleb McTavish's hand, no longer connected to the meaty bits. Curling his fingers, he hid his hand behind his back and waved dismissively with his other hand. "Nothin'. Just a headache. So…" Not sure what else to do or say, he went with one thing he knew about the Winters. "How's the movie comin' along?"

Silas wasn't sure how it was possible for either of the Winters boys to scowl harder, yet they did. The taller one looked as if he could rip through Silas' skin as well as his wooden insides. "What the fuck is that supposed to mean, McTavish?"

"C'mon, Rand, these pieces of garbage ain't worth our time." The shorter one wrapped his arm around his brother's shoulders and guided him to the front. They paid for whatever they had in their hands and exited the store.

Mimicking the same frown on the Winters boys' faces, Mercer stepped close enough for Silas to smell the stale tobacco on his hot breath. He fought the urge to smile from the tickle of joy that came with having a working sniffer again as Mercer growled, "What the literal fuck is wrong with you, talkin' to them after what we… *you*… did to Riley?"

Silas didn't know a damn thing about whatever Mercer was talking about, so he galloped along with the limited information he had. A shoulder shrug. "What we did to Riley is what we've done to everyone. Ain't no big deal."

Mercer jumped back, eyes wide as if he'd narrowly dodged a lightning strike. A few heartbeats and a gulp that made his Adam's apple wiggle was all it took for Mercer to slip back into a hungry coyote. "I don't know what fuckin' game you're playing, but it's a stupid one, especially if you think I'm—"

"Hey, Boyle!" the shopkeeper shouted, something black in his hands. Wait, Silas knew this from the television – a telephone! "Your uncle is callin'."

A finger point to punctuate his words, Mercer said to Silas, "Quit actin' all fuckin' weird. And you better have the booze for the party."

Silas stood in silence while Mercer went to talk on the phone. He thought about the Winters boys the way he'd once thought about wantin' a perfect pair of boots while the ratty ones on his feet pinched his toes. Those boys were his destiny.

Mercer handed the phone back to the shopkeeper, waved to Silas with a middle finger, and stormed out of the store.

Silas took one last longing look at the beer in the glass cases and decided that if he couldn't have any, then there was no reason to stay in the store any longer. The shopkeeper said nothing, the heat in his stare scalding as Silas left. No sign of Mercer outside, Silas got in the passenger side of the pickup and Amos popped up from slouching under the steering wheel. He asked, "How'd it go with Mercer?"

Silas shrugged. "Blew a bunch of hot air, then left."

Amos nodded and started the truck. "Yeah, I figured as much, so I called from the payphone over there to get him outta the store."

"I also met the Winters kids."

Wide-eyed, Amos snapped his head around. "And?"

"And I have a new plan."

CHAPTER 24

The kiss was nice; Riley hated to end it, but he needed to get to school. Rand would wait for him as long as possible, but he had no qualms about taking off and letting Riley deal with the wrath of Mom and Dad for taking time away from their always busy morning to get him to school.

"Sorry for holding you up," Javi said, smiling and gripping the bottom of Riley's shirt with both hands. "But I hate letting go. I hate not looking into your eyes."

Riley's cheeks warmed. "Don't worry, I'll be right back here after school. And then it's the weekend."

Javi released Riley's shirt and wandered to the closest horse stall. "You better. Though, with the movie people, who knows what the weekend will bring."

Riley rolled his eyes. "I know. So much drama."

Javi chuckled. "Well, drama is literally their business."

Another eye roll. "You know what I mean. It's a weird circle – Miles is too intense and makes a crew member run away, then that makes him more intense and another crew member runs away, making him even more intense. I bet someone else will run away soon."

"You think those two really ran off without telling anyone?"

Riley shrugged. "I didn't know them well enough. Tilde and Barnes are convinced that something bad happened to Sasha. Either way, I can't wait for the movie to be over with and for them to leave."

"For things to go back to normal?"

The fear behind Javi's words broke Riley's heart. "No. For us to figure out what to do next."

Javi smiled, warm, inviting. "Okay. I like that plan. Now, get going to school."

Grabbing his backpack, Riley left. He cut through a patch of land so seldomly used that a few weeds were brave enough to grow along the weakly tramped footpaths. It was the quickest way from the back of the barn to the driveway, where Rand sat in the driver seat of the pickup, tapping his hand against the outside door and bobbing his head to whatever song played on the radio. Riley picked up speed and trotted along past the toolshed, then slowed when he overheard a voice. Tense. Stilted. Familiar.

Quiet as a jackrabbit sneaking around sleeping rattlesnakes, Riley crept to the corner of the shed. Someone was behind it, holding a one-sided conversation. Watching where he placed his feet, he crept along the outside wall, then leaned forward to peek around the back. One glimpse, no more than a second, was all he needed to see Miles on a mobile phone.

The drama that had been the conversation topic between Riley and Javi was evident in Miles' voice. "No, Maddox, you don't need to come to the set." A pause. "Yes, Maddox. I have everything under control." Another pause. "I know you put a lot of money into this and— Yes, I know it wasn't *your* money, rather your boss' money, and yeah, I know who Roger Templeton is, which is why— No, please, Maddox, you don't need to come down here. I know what's at stake. I'll get the movie done and make everyone a lot of money. I'll— Hello? Hello? Maddox? Gone. Fuck! Fuck! Fuck! Fuck!" Miles pulled at his hair as he stomped away.

Riley tightened his grip on the backpack straps and held his breath, ready to sprint while waiting for Miles' foot stomps to fade as he gained distance. Satisfied he wouldn't get caught, he scurried along the side of the shed, and about ran into his father when he turned the corner. "Oh! Dad!"

"Son."

Random heartbeats in the snowy frost of his cold heart spread to his fingers and toes. He didn't know physiology well enough to know which organ, gland, or other mysterious internal mechanism lurked undetected in the base of his neck, but it flared anytime he got in trouble. Right now, it bulged to the point of discomfort when he gulped. "Yeah, so, I just wanted to make sure Javi had everything he needed to start the day."

"I..." Dad said, his voice commanding, even when his words were weak with uncertainty. "I... Son, I know what you and Javi were doing in the barn."

"Just getting things ready for the horses." Riley was never much for thinking on his feet, so he talked as fast as he could, throwing as much information against the proverbial wall to see if anything stuck. "The movie people being here have messed up everyone's schedules, so I just wanted to pitch in where I can, when I can. I'm just—"

"Son…" Dad put his hands on Riley's shoulders. "I *know*."

"I just… I… But…" *Run.* The only word that Riley could functionally understand. Run.

"It's okay."

"I… huh?"

"I know what—" Dad cut himself short, an angry grunt accompanying a quick headshake. "Who. I know *who* you are. I know. And I know how hard it must be for you. I know what kind of world we live in and that a lot of the people in your life aren't hospitable or make you feel comfortable for being who you are. I love you, Riley, and as God as my witness, this is always your home where you can be who you are."

Dad had said everything Riley wanted to hear, needed to hear, but he was paralyzed with fear, wondering if the nightmare would begin or if Earth would split open and unleash the fires of damnation, his punishment for turning to the Devil Tree and not the church, his punishment for being who he was. "Dad?"

"Come here, Son." A hug. A big, crushing hug. A validation of his father's words. The Earth didn't split open; God wasn't punishing him.

Riley hugged back, partly to keep himself from floating away with the released secret. As if he had been holding his breath for months, he used the newest air in his lungs to say, "I thought you'd be mad."

Separating, Dad grabbed Riley by his arms and squeezed. Riley couldn't look anywhere other than his father's intense eyes, dark and eternal. The vibrations of Dad's voice ran through his body down to his boots. "I love you. I get why you'd be scared about telling anyone about who you are. I'm not gonna lie – I don't understand it. What I do understand is that love is a God damn dictatorship, Son. You have no choice about who you like, who you're attracted to, who you love. I can't turn on and off my love for you mother. Or your brother. Or *you.*"

Averting his eyes, Riley wiped away his tears and ran his forearm under his nose. "Thank you. I love you, too."

With the slightest twist of Dad's lips, which was considered a huge smile from him, he squeezed until Riley looked back into his eyes. "Don't forget… It's better than wanting to be an actor, like your brother. Now *that* is a choice."

Dad shared a joke with him – a joke meant only for him – and Riley chuckled, and momentum turned it into a laugh.

Dad gave a quick exhale, which was considered laughter from him, and said, "I didn't mean to hold you up from school, but I needed to tell you what I needed to tell you. Alright, get going before Rand starts laying on the horn."

Riley nodded and ran to the pickup.

Rand put it in gear and hit the gas before Riley shut the door. "What the hell took you so long? And what's with the goofy smile?"

"Dad needed to talk to me, dumbass."

"About what?"

"About how he hates that you want to be an actor."

Rand scowled and smacked the top of the steering wheel. "Damn it, Dad! I don't want to be an actor. I just want to be a part of the movie because it's something special that's happening on the ranch. He doesn't listen."

"Actually, he does."

*

Riley shared the whole conversation between Dad and himself with his brother. Even though Rand expressed nothing but joy, Riley could tell he was a bit bruised on the inside about Dad's views on anyone associated with Hollywood.

The school day was a blur, Riley's mind floating around like a boat at sea, stopping at some ports to revisit the memories of this morning, and then heading for the deeper, unknown waters of future potential. Too much stored energy begging for release, he opted to stay after school and hit the weight room while Rand went off to bull riding practice. The workout was what he needed, feeling clearheaded and ready to head home when Rand returned.

Riley stepped off the curb as Rand's pickup rolled to a stop. As he reached for the door a voice barked from behind him. "Hey!"

At the far corner of the school, Mercer leaned against the faded brick wall and waved him over.

"The fuck?" Rand asked. "Is that Mercer?"

"Uh… Yeah, I think so," Riley replied.

Mercer waved again, this time accompanied by a frown. "Come here."

"Fuck off!" Rand yelled, leaning across the passenger seat to make sure his words were clear as crystal.

"What he said," Riley yelled back.

Mercer pushed himself away from the wall and gestured for them to join hm behind the building. "We need to talk."

"Do I need to repeat myself?" Rand yelled.

"Riley gets a free shot." Mercer tapped his cheek and meandered around the corner of the building.

"This is a setup, right?" Riley asked.

Rand turned off the engine and leaned across the passenger seat to open the glovebox. After retrieving the hunting knife, he hopped out. "If it is, then it will be his last."

Riley's emotions alternated with every step: step one, he worried that his brother might do something irreversibly rash; step two, he hoped that he would; step three, back to worry. When they rounded the corner, Mercer was standing next to the filled dumpsters, his hands by his sides, fingers splayed. "Knew you couldn't resist that offer."

"What's this about, Mercer?" Rand asked, his hands behind his back, undoubtedly ready to brandish the knife at Mercer's first screwy movement.

"We need to talk about Caleb."

Riley laughed and shook his head as he turned to leave. "No, we don't."

"Free shot," Mercer practically yelled, taking a step closer and spreading his arms out even further. "I know what we did was wrong. I'm… Fuck, I'm not a good person, we all know that. Half the fucking state knows that. I ain't got no other excuses or explanations for doing what I did. I guess I need to apologize, but I ain't got the functioning morals to do it right, so... I know Riley wants to pop me good. I can see it in his eyes. So, here I am."

Riley exchanged a look with his brother, silently asking for permission. Rand shrugged, giving consent. As Riley approached Mercer, he looked around – no sign of any other life in this seldom used area behind the building. Fists clenched, his Christian-enough morals whispered all forms of paranoia. Everything from this being an ambush, to hidden cameras, to a random teacher appearing out of nowhere for no reason, to tarnishing his soul from being unable to grant forgiveness. But the closer he got, the easier it was to tell his Christian-enough morals to fuck off, and when he got within striking distance, he whipped his fist in an arc with devastating purpose.

One punch dropped Mercer. But Riley couldn't stop with that. A foot to Mercer's gut while he was on his hands and knees. God, that felt good, the release. But there was too much rage to snuff with only one kick. One more kick. Another. *Another!*

"Riley!" Rand yelled, wrapping his arms around Riley's waist and pulling him away. "Enough. For now."

Way too much anger still in the tank, Riley twisted and shoved Rand away. "Get off, Rand! That's nowhere near enough!"

Rand approached with his hands out, as if dealing with a spooked horse. "I said, 'for now,' baby brother. I know he deserves more, but right now, we should hear what he has to say."

"I call bullshit on that!"

Rand pointed to Mercer, writhing on the ground with both arms wrapped around his gut while blood streamed from his nose. "He wouldn't just lay there and take it if he really didn't have something important to say."

Mercer coughed, then gave a pained yelp as he climbed to his hands and knees. "Didn't know you had it in you."

"Got more than that," Riley growled, tossing his hands in the air to throw away his frustrations. "Say what you gotta say."

On one knee, Mercer took a wheezed breath before saying, "Somethin' weird's goin' on with Caleb. He ain't right."

"So, something weird is happening to Caleb. Sounds like Caleb's problem."

"Caleb's problem could be our problem if we don't figure out what it is."

Riley snorted and spat on the ground. "Doubtful."

"When one of our pigs gets a sickness, we take it away from the other pigs. If it's a sickness that our doctor can't figure out, we take it off our property and shoot it. How about your horses? When one gets sick, do you keep it in the same barn with the others?"

"People are different from livestock, Mercer."

"Yeah? How is keepin' us in school any different than shovin' pigs into a pen or linin' up horses in a barn?"

A comeback for that escaped him, so Riley simply clenched his fists and turned to Rand for his reaction. Rand dragged a forearm across his brow and looked away, like the answer was somewhere out in the prairie running with the rabbits. Mercer must have deemed the silence as a weakness in their defenses, and asked, "Have you seen anything weird? People actin' as if they ain't them?"

Riley looked to his older brother for guidance.

Rand sighed and shrugged, implying, *You may as well tell him.*

"A couple people from the movie have disappeared," Riley said. "Some of their coworkers feel that it wasn't like them to run off. Even Sheriff Cunnigham came to ask questions after the second one disappeared."

Mercer spat a glob of blood to the packed dirt and Riley felt that was in reference to the police rather than clearing out his mouth. "Alright. Anything else? Anyone else?"

Rand swept his long hair from his face and asked, "When you say Caleb is being weird, what do you mean?"

Finally getting to his feet, after negotiating a slight wobble, Mercer ran the back of his hand under his nose and studied the amount of blood – not enough to worry anyone. "Like he forgot how to be Caleb."

"Yeah? How so?"

"His old man says he hasn't been home for days. At Chuck's, he snapped back at me. Hell, you saw how he tried to talk to you, like he didn't know you. And he was lookin'... I don't know... weird. Not normal Caleb-weird. Different-weird."

Rand chuckled. "So, Caleb is finally standing up for himself and you say he ain't Caleb anymore? I think Riley and I heard all we needed to hear from you." The brothers turned to leave.

"It's more than that," Mercer said, stopping them with a tone in his voice that Riley had never heard before. Concern? Fear? Whatever the reason, his tone intensified the more he spoke. "The whole... I don't know... Vibe? Feeling? The air around him is different, wrong. And the way he moves now... Like his skin is just a set of too-tight clothes."

"Mercer, come on, we're—"

"He's not remembering things."

The desire to go back to beating Mercer within an inch of his life coursed through Riley from fist to fist. Still might happen depending on his answer to the question, "Like what?"

"Like..." A pause to chew his thoughts, jaws muscles working hard. "Like the party we've been planning next weekend."

"He forgot about... a party?"

"It's more like he forgot how important it is. Steve Scallard—"

"Scumbag Steve?"

"Yeah, Scumbag Steve – his cousin is in a band and comin' into town for the party. The band is lookin' for a roadie. Desperate to the point where Steve said if his cousin likes what he sees, I might be able to leave with them."

Rand must have heard what Riley heard, that if Mercer got his wish, then he'd go away. "So... What are you thinking?" Rand asked. "What do you want us to do?"

"Just... I don't know. Keep your eyes open? I'm gonna follow him around this weekend to see where he's stayin' if he ain't stayin' with his old man. You two know more people at school than I do, so keep a lookout for anythin' not right. If Caleb's sick or whatever, he might not be the only one."

Rand furrowed his brow, then looked to the heavens for guidance. He snorted at whatever answer he received, and started back toward the pickup. "Meet us at the southern fence corner where our properties touch after school on Monday."

Giving Mercer one final glare, Riley jogged up to Rand. "You think that's a good idea?"

In the pickup, Rand fired the ignition. "I don't know. I'm just going by the whole, 'keep your enemies closer' thing. If he's up to something, then I want to see it in front of me, not behind me."

"Can't wait for these movie people to leave," Riley mumbled.

"Yeah, but I got the feeling things will never be the same again."

That morning, Riley would have considered that a good thing. Now? He had no idea.

CHAPTER 25

Amanda entered the kitchen and poured herself a cup of coffee. The mug was a squat white thing reserved for taking up forgotten space in the back of the cabinet. Dishes mounded in the sink. She opened the dishwasher. Full. She got mad at herself for forgetting to run it last night – after all, how hard was it to push the "start" button?

Give yourself a break, she told herself. *There's been too much going on lately.*

As she brought the mug to her mouth, her hands started to shake. Fearful of spilling hot coffee down the front of her, she set the mug on the counter. Eyes closed and leaning onto the counter for support, she drew a deep breath in through her nose and called upon words her mother had spoken quite often. "Strength isn't always muscle and backbone. It's willpower. Fortitude. Smarts. That's why women live longer."

The shaking stopped. *Way* too much was happening on the ranch, but Amanda was strong enough to weather the storm. She had the willpower. The fortitude. The smarts. Time to show her strength to the world. She grabbed her mug and hurried outside to fix whatever needed to be fixed today. Sure enough, her family was at the top of the list.

Rand was still in the driveway, testing the time limits of garnering a tardy from school. Both hands on her mug, she marched toward the driveway. Questions first, then a possible warning second. But she didn't get halfway before seeing Riley scurry from behind a seldom used tool shed, across an overgrown stretch of land, to Rand's pickup. Her mind kicked up more curiosity than Rand's truck kicked up dirt when Hank emerged from behind the shed, heading in the opposite direction.

Hands clenched, Hank strode toward the northern part of the property and Amanda hurried to catch up. Still behind him, but well within earshot, she said, "Hey, handsome."

No response.

"Hank?"

Still nothing, his stride singular of purpose.

"Hey!" she shouted.

Hank jolted to a stop and turned around with a startled look on his face. "Amanda?"

"Been calling your name for half a mile now. Just thought a 'good morning' from your strong, capable, and surprisingly beautiful wife might cheer you up."

Taking a second to register her words, Hank smiled. The big smile-line rippled along his cheeks, emphasizing well-deserved crow's feet while slightly shifting the brown Stetson on his head. Amanda loved that smile. He closed the gap between the two of them and placed both hands on her face, surprisingly gentle and soft despite the farm-grown callouses. His lips against her forehead sent warmth through her entire body. The depth of his voice traveled along her arms and she felt it in her bones. "Nothing cheers me up more than my strong, capable, exceptionally beautiful wife."

"Good! Glad to hear it." Amanda brought her coffee to her mouth, then lowered it when she saw how unsettled he was behind his eyes, as tumultuous as ocean waves under a hurricane. "What's going on?"

With a shift in his mustache, she inferred that there was something big he was trying to pass off as small. "Sorry, just feeling like I'm getting swept away by what's happening around here with the movie."

"Such as?"

Sinking his hands inside his pockets, he lowered his gaze to give the best "Aw, shucks" smile that a broad-shouldered, six-and-a-half-foot tall man could muster. Amanda was legitimately surprised that he didn't kick one of the nearby pebbles when he said, "I don't know. All of it, I guess. Starting with Rand wanting to become an actor."

Whenever Hank faced more than one issue, the one he started with was rarely the one he struggled with the most.

"Has he said he wanted to become an actor?" Amanda asked.

Hank cocked his head, giving her the look reserved for what he considered a silly question. "He's in the movie, ain't he?"

"As an unnamed stable boy who everyone has been calling Percival. Has he expressed wanting to quit rodeo to become an actor?"

"No. Quite the opposite, actually."

"Then you're overreacting. You're getting all riled up from imagined conversations, and making Rand feel bad even though he hasn't taken part in them. He's our son, Hank. If he wanted to quit rodeo to move to Hollywood, he'd tell us. We'd give advice, and he'd listen, because that's how we work as a family. He'd do foolhardy things only if he felt like he had no direction and no other choice."

Brow furrowed, Hank looked to the rising sun as if watching a hundred different futures unfold. He was smart enough to know how life worked. Whatever he saw, Hank gave a satisfied sigh and looked back to Amanda. "You're right. I need to stop making him feel bad about having a little fun."

"And to listen to him when he speaks?"

"And to listen to him when he speaks."

"Okay, that's one son. What about the other?"

Topping the many reasons Amanda loved her husband was his forthcoming nature. Never a secret between the two ever since they were high school sweethearts, so it was somewhere in between whimsical and hysterical to see Hank try to keep a secret from her. The way he fidgeted with his hat took her all the way back to those very high school days when he tried to muster the guts to ask her to prom, their first date. The way he stammered as well. "Umm... Riley? I... What about the other son? Our other son? Riley?"

"I saw you both around the old tool shed just a bit ago."

"Well... I needed to talk to him. Just... a conversation before school, is all."

Amanda smiled if only to stifle a laugh from his squirming. She reached out and squeezed his arm. "Hank. I know."

"You know...? About...?"

"I know about our son, Riley. I know about who he is."

"Oh? How?"

It was Amanda's turn to twist her expression in response to his silly questions. "Seriously? I'm his mother."

Hank chuckled and shook his head. "Yes, you are. And a great one at that. A better mother than I'm a father."

"Why on Earth would you say that? Do you still love him?"

"Of course I do. It's just..." Hank looked to the horizon again. He took off his hat and ran his fingers through his salt and pepper hair. "I'm scared for him."

"Because this environment may not be the best place for him to flourish."

"Yeah." A sadness swept through him, through his entire body as he slouched. "I can't help but think about when I was younger. The things I'd say about people like our son. The comments. The jokes."

"Do you feel bad?"

"Absolutely, I do."

"Are you gonna make those comments and jokes anymore?"

"Course not."

Amanda smacked her husband's arm and smiled. "That's called growth, Sweety."

Hank stood straighter. "Yeah?"

"Yeah. Riley will have to keep secrets and as his parents we will be there to help lighten the burden every time it gets too heavy, in any way we can. We have great sons, Hank. And all we have to do is let them both know that we are, and forever will be, there for them."

A twist in his lips, and then Hank nodded. He returned the Stetson back to his head and ran his hand down Amanda's arm, ultimately squeezing her free hand. "Damn, I do have one helluva a strong, capable, exceptionally beautiful, *and wise* wife."

Amanda pinched his cheek. "I know."

Hank kissed Amanda's forehead and made her insides wilt. "I don't tell you that often enough."

"You show me plenty, Sweety."

"I'm heading to Fake Town to make sure they haven't turned it into Fake City. Wanna join?"

"Maybe this afternoon. I'm going to hide in my workshop, enjoy my coffee, and pour resin."

"Sounds like a plan. Love you."

"Love you, too!"

Amanda brought the mug to her lips, distracted by watching Hank walk away, his jeans fitting particularly well today. It had been too long since she and Hank had any alone time for her to enjoy what the denim covered. Before she could take a sip, she heard voices coming from behind the barn. Ramos, Javi, and the other ranch hands had most of the horses in the paddocks, getting them exercise. According to the movie's schedule, everyone should be at Fake Town, filming. She lowered her mug and made her way to the back of the barn. She spotted Miles and Nixon, and both men were frowning.

"You don't fucking understand who we're dealing with," Miles said, voice low but heated. Amanda marveled at how sweaty he was hours before the noon sun had its way with him.

"I do," Nixon whispered back, the frustration in his voice evident. "Trust me, you made it very clear who Maddox is."

In his signature black jeans, concert tee shirt, and Stetson, Nixon was like a statue with his arms crossed over his chest while Miles frantically paced a semicircle around him, hands dancing around his head like moths flittering around a flame. "I'm not talking about Maddox. Well, of course I'm talking about Maddox, but I'm not *just* talking about Maddox. I'm talking about his boss."

"You never mentioned that Maddox had a boss."

"Well, I'm fucking mentioning it now, aren't I?"

"Jesus, Miles. What have you gotten us into?"

Miles abruptly halted his pace, sending a few droplets of sweat forward. Index finger poking Nixon's chest, the producer snarled. "Remember bringing me a script saying you'd do anything to bring it to life, to make us millions? Well, I got us what we needed for you to bring it to life. Now, go make us those millions."

Uncomfortable with eavesdropping, Amanda was ready to clear her throat, but Miles stormed off in the other direction, leaving Nixon to look skyward while hugging himself.

After a minute of silence, Amanda sauntered toward Nixon. "Oh, hey. Didn't see you there. Morning, Nixon."

The movie people must have been on the ranch too long, because Amanda's innocent act easily fooled Nixon. Without indicating that he suspected his conversation with Miles might have been overheard, he smiled politely and said, "Good morning, Mrs. Winters."

Amanda often wondered how he got mixed up with Miles in the first place. Sure, he was artsy – plenty of artists in Santa Fe – but he had manners and was even-tempered. Miles possessed none of those qualities. If not for the siren call to spend time in her workshop, she would have asked him questions about his past. Instead, she kept it simple with, "How are you this morning?"

Nixon uncrossed his arms, leaving behind red indentations from where his fingers had been squeezing, and slid his hands into his pockets. A wistful gaze in Miles' direction, he said, "Not too well, actually." He then tensed as if a snake had slithered over his boot. He slowly turned to Amanda with a touch of pink in his cheeks as if he hadn't meant to give voice to his thoughts.

"Trouble with the movie?" Amanda asked, again testing her skills as an actor, feigning ignorance.

Jaw muscles rippled under his tight skin. His soulful, brown eyes seemed to darken from the thoughts and emotions piling up behind them. Finally, he sighed and nodded. "You could certainly say that. From making my partner mad, to a lead actress wanting to do too much, to a lead actor wanting to do too little, to crew members upset by the recent disappearances, to having no clue what's going on around me… Yeah, I'm *definitely* having trouble with the movie."

Gripping her mug with both hands, the coffee rippled as she fought to styme a tremor. *Oh, I am doing the Lord's work today, aren't I?* "May I share an observation?"

Eyes wide, Nixon took a step closer and Amanda worried that she'd have to fend off a hug. "Yes, please. I'd love to hear your thoughts."

"The fact that you listed the problems you have means that you know they exist, which means you *do* know what's going on around you."

A spark flickered behind his eyes. "Yeah. Yeah, that makes sense."

"Does Miles do anything directly with the movie? I mean, if he takes the day off, would anything regarding the movie be impacted?"

Nixon cocked his head and leaned closer. "No…?"

"Alright then, don't waste one ounce of worry about him being upset. I know you two are friends and all, but from what I know of him, it seems that a smooth-running production would make him less upset. If you pull your focus from the movie and place it onto him, you'll make matters worse."

Nodding, he now looked hungry. "You're right about that, too."

"For the rest of them – the best thing is to remember that *you* are the boss. Steer Brett's energies where they belong. Don't take crap from Bo and keep reminding him that he's replaceable. If you get the actors moving in the right direction, then the crew won't focus on their coworkers leaving."

A smile crept across his face while the fire behind his eyes burned brightly. With a deep bow, he removed his hat. "I can't thank you enough, Mrs. Winters. How can I repay you?"

By finishing this damn movie and getting this circus out of our lives. "No repayment necessary, Nixon."

He replaced his hat to his head and pressed his palms together for a second bow. "Thank you again."

"Go get 'em," Amanda said as he hurried away, toward the northern part of the property.

Mug still in hand, Amanda held off trying to take a sip, deciding to wait until she could savor its warm flavor inside her workshop. She doubted she'd get to drink it at all when she found Brett standing in front of the workshop door. With a six-pack of beer in her hand.

"Brett? What are you doing here? Day one, I've told everyone that this space if off limits."

Amanda didn't like how harsh and admonishing she sounded. And she certainly didn't like the look of hurt in Brett's eyes as she lowered her head.

"I know. I'm sorry," Brett said. "I just… Between my husband and Bo and Miles, I just wanted to get away from men for a minute, and the other girls on the crew are so…" *Young. Too young to connect with.* "… inaccessible sometimes. I just… Well, honestly, I'm just feeling a little alone right now and wanted to hangout. I see men do this all the time." She weakly held up the six-pack, just another prop in the theater of life.

"Honey, it's barely past eight in the morning," Amanda said, her voice now holding more pity than annoyance.

Sulking like a scolded child, Brett shrugged. "When guys go fishing, they start drinking before the sun comes up."

"Don't you have to be on set?"

"Not today. Some kind of backstory for Bo's character."

Amanda looked at the coffee in her plain white mug, now cooler than she preferred. Resigned that this would be the only way she could enjoy it, she chugged it in a few audible gulps. She then chucked the mug over her shoulder and grabbed the keys from her pocket. "Fuck it. Let's go inside."

Strength isn't always muscle and backbone. It's willpower. Fortitude. Smarts. That's why women live longer.

CHAPTER 26

Silas stared at the ugly face staring back at him in the bathroom mirror. Caleb's slack face. He'd seen Caleb's living face only once, right before Amos smashed a skillet over his head. The boy's face had distended into a scream as a wooden mannequin with a few stumpy body parts attached to it rush toward him. So, Silas had no idea how slack Caleb's face should be. Back when he was a full human being, Silas had consorted with a few gape-mouthed pig-fuckers. If Silas knew two things, gape-mouthed pig-fuckers never got free pussy, and right now he was wearing the face of one.

Bracing himself on the sink, he leaned closer to better examine himself. His skin looked like loose fitting clothing, like a teen boy wearing his pa's britches. Fingertips under his left eye, he pulled down on the skin, bottom lid sliding down further than he thought right. Deep pink mucus shimmered, but Silas could still see the wood grain of the mannequin behind it. The skin did not snap back into place when he let go. "Damnation."

Five days. He'd been in this body for five days and it was already past its prime. With his index finger, he pushed the skin back in place. A crimson droplet rolled from the corner of his eye to his finger.

Pushing away from the sink, he put his finger in his mouth. Nothing. No taste of blood, no hint of salt from his skin. His tongue barely recognized it had something on it. He looked down his naked torso at his dick and admonishingly thought, *Well, that's another thing not workin'.*

Yesterday, all feeling in his crotch had disappeared. Frustrated that he didn't have a chance to use it on a woman, he slapped it. Still nothing. It wasn't his dick's fault that he hadn't been with a woman yet. It wasn't even Johnny's fault with confounding rules and forbidding Silas from leaving so he could be observed, studied. It was this damnable face. Taking one last rueful glance in the mirror, he left the bathroom.

"Oh, tarnation!" Amos exclaimed, bringing his hand over his eye when Silas entered the hallway. "Put some damn clothes on!"

"Ain't never seen what long-johns been hiding?"

"Sure have, but I don't want to see yours. And the skin you're wearing belongs to someone I known since he was a child."

"Aaaaaw, you goin' soft about him bein' dead?"

Amos dropped his hand and stepped closer, the earnestness in his eye inescapable. "I'm glad that piece of pig shit is dead. I'm glad I killed that ugly fucker."

Silas hadn't been much to look at in his previous life, but he could catch the eye of a woman or two whenever he walked into a crowded room. The look of disgust from the girls in the general store still lingered in his mind. He didn't like it. "You ain't nothin' to look at, yourself, Amos, so watch who you callin' ugly."

"Least I can get some."

"Yeah? Well, I'm sure it's..." A thought struck Silas silent. Maybe his dick wasn't working due to a lack of proper motivation. "... It's whores, ain't it? You're as ugly as me, and nowhere near as charming, so that means you use whores."

Amos' eye widened and he blushed all through his cheeks and forehead. "Wha...? I... What?"

"Stop tryin' to play dumb, even though dumb is your strongest quality. You use whores. How do you find them?"

Slumped shoulders made him resemble a withering corn stalk ready to blow away with the first strong breeze. "I call them."

"On the telephone? Like how you contact Johnny?"

"Yeah."

"Well, call some!"

"I gotta get back to the farm. I told our hands not to come in so I could tell Mercer we're short staffed to keep him workin' more than usual. He's been a little squirrely lately, and I think he knows something's up with Caleb. He's workin' today and I told him I'd be home an hour from now."

"I don't give a shit none about that. Give me the number and I'll call 'em."

"No."

"Don't make me threaten you, Amos. I've been growin' to like you. It'd be a shame to change that."

The taller man stood straighter, a strong posture ready to support strong words. It took a few seconds of digging around in the muck of his brain to search for those words, judging by the dancing brow and lip curls, but ultimately Amos huffed and said, "Fine. I'll run to the house and get the number."

"Fine!" Silas yelled to Amos' back as he stormed away.

Alone in the Tomlin house again. Despite the mind-relaxing comfort of the television, Silas was getting pretty darn sick of the place. He needed to get out, needed to carve into a piece of the world around him, needed to get his dick wet by a woman. Ugly or not, he couldn't hole himself up in this house any longer. When he was living, he'd sometimes take a woman when she didn't want to be taken and so what if he'd have to do it again. To hell with rules and Johanny and his observations!

A tee shirt, overalls, and boots were all he needed to wear to be accepted into public places. There was the challenge of getting to such places, but if a dummy like Amos could drive an automobile, how hard could it be?

Keys. Amos usually kept the keys in the kitchen.

Silas stormed from the second-floor master bedroom to head on downstairs but stopped right before he reached the staircase – the front door opened. From this angle, the wall hid him, but he crouched to look between the banister posts. The door was open just enough for a person to poke their head in. And that person was Mercer.

Had Mercer been around when Silas was his age, they'd have been good friends. Mercer had a temper like dynamite and lacked whatever was inside good men to make them say "no" to bad situations.

After a few seconds of lookie-loo, Mercer crept into the house and carefully shut the door behind him.

It being a few hours before the sun fell from the sky, there was no need for lights and the closed blinds didn't stop the outside light, just dulled it some. The living room was to the left of the foyer and the first room Mercer explored. Silas waited patiently, wanting to see if Mercer would wind up with valuables in his hands. After a few minutes, the young man exited empty-handed, a quizzical look on his face. Guess he wasn't here for thievery.

Across the foyer was the dining room. Mercer spent even less time in that room, returning to the foyer, then headed for the back of the house.

Once he disappeared, Silas started down the stairs, but the creak of bowing wood echoed through the quiet house.

In an instant, Mercer reappeared in the foyer. "Caleb? What the fuck, dude?"

What was the term Silas had heard Amos use? Oh, yeah… "I've been squattin' here."

Mercer's head snapped back as if Caleb's words had been live snakes. "Squatting? Doesn't someone live here?"

"Heh. Yeah. Me."

Lean muscles rippling under his tight tee shirt, Mercer prowled toward the stairs like a mountain lion, his foot poised on the bottom step. "No. I mean someone moved in here recently. A family. Tomlin. Yeah, the Tomlins. Where are they, Caleb?"

Silas looked down on him and shrugged. "Heard they was dead."

"Dead?" Being wide-eyed and slack-jawed from the news didn't stop Mercer from taking another step up toward him. The third. The fourth. "Where'd you hear that?"

"Around."

Mercer frowned, but it didn't seem like he was angry. "Look, man, I know your dad's a piece of shit, but hurtin' a family to hide in their house and get away from him ain't right."

"*You* hurt people all the time."

Two more steps and Mercer was now perched on the step below Silas. "Not like this. Nothin' permanent. Look, I've been talkin' to Rand and Riley."

Pain blasted between Silas' ears, the inside of his head on fire from images of Riley and Rand Winters. Why did that happen? He had to be connected to them in some way, shape, or form. But how? He had to know. He… He wanted… needed… *their* bodies.

"I know, I know, a Boyle talkin' to the Winters ain't right," Mercer continued. "But you and me don't know any people who can help you. I'm gonna meet with them tomorrow after school. Come along with me now and we'll see if they can help."

There was no way Caleb's body could get the Winters brothers here for Johnny to operate on them, not while in this ugly, misshapen thing. But Mercer had been talking to them. Mercer could get the brothers to this house. Silas reached out and grabbed the kid's wrist.

"The fuck?" Mercer yanked his hand back, but Silas wouldn't let go. With his other hand, Mercer grabbed Silas' forearm, trying to wrestle his arm free. A tug, a tear, and the skin around Silas' wrist separated. Like rolling up a fleshy shirt sleeve, Mercer squished the skin along Silas' arm to expose the wooden skeleton underneath. Red goo dripped as chunks of gelatinous meat splattered to the stairs.

A guttural scream came from deep within Mercer. His hand now pressed against Silas, against his face. Fearful that Caleb's eyes might pop out should Mercer's fingertips find their way too close, Silas let go of his arm.

Stumbling, Mercer half-fell down the stairs, landing on his feet. Leaping over the handrail, Silas dropped in front of Mercer. Shoulder to shoulder, Silas knocked Mercer into the foyer wall. The young man bounced off the wall with arms outstretched, reaching for the front door. Again, Silas led with his shoulder, smashing the front door closed the moment Mercer had managed to open it.

Fistful of shirt, Silas thought he held enough to stop Mercer. After an impotent punch to Silas' face, Mercer pressed his hands against his chest and shoved. Flesh and muscle slid over his wooden frame. No rips in the skin, but the effort yielded enough for Mercer to escape his grasp. Though, it gave Silas an idea.

Mercer ran down the hall toward the kitchen where the backdoor would lead to freedom. As Silas gave chase, he pulled at the loose skin of his arm, working it off his shoulder. With strength in his wooden fingers that surpassed the attached muscles around them, he yanked a section of flesh and meat off his arm. Right when Mercer crossed the threshold into the kitchen,

Silas threw the mess. The few pounds of gristle smacked Mercer in the back of the head, hard enough to disrupt his gait. A trip. A fall. A collision with the kitchen table. Mercer fell to the floor.

Silas strolled into the kitchen.

"Fuck you, man!" Mercer yelled as he twisted on the floor, reaching for the counter to help him up. His feet slipped again and again in the gristle-slop, but he gained purchase with a hard twist of his waist and stood. Arms shaking, panting, and with blood flowing from his nose, he spat a glob of ruby phlegm at Silas. "What the fuck is wrong with you?"

Silas laughed. "Nothin' is wrong with me, Mercer."

Steadier on his feet, Mercer released the counter and formed fists with both hands. Silas knew more bold threats waited on the young man's breath, but before he had a chance to hear any of them, the back door opened, and Amos strode into the kitchen.

"Yes!" Mercer shouted as he hurried around the counter to his uncle. "Yes! Amos, I don't know what the fuck is going on with Caleb, but he ain't human no more. We gotta fuck him up. Grab that knife and let's show him what—"

Mercer's last word turned into a gurgle after a pained wheeze. The butcher's knife wound up between his ribs. The last look on his face was confusion, true disbelief that Amos had stabbed him. There must have been a glimmer of realization somewhere in his brain, because he didn't ask why, didn't fight, didn't try to run. He simply fell into gravity's embrace and collapsed onto the floor.

Amos stepped over him and handed a slip of paper to Silas. "Here's the phone number to the whores."

"Much obliged." Silas accepted the paper and continued, "But now we need to call Johnny. I have another idea."

CHAPTER 27

Johnny was scrutinizing the mannequin's chest. There was no way to access the organs he had inserted days ago. Sitting on a table in the Tomlin's barn – the operating room, as they had been calling it – Silas had stripped away the remaining pieces of the used form once known as Caleb, save for the eyes in the mannequin's head and vocal cords attached to his neck. Stray bits of pink, jellylike meat clung to a few jagged imperfections in the wood.

"Interesting," Johnny said.

"Ya know, Doc, I'm not much at ease when you use that word," Silas said.

"I'm sorry to hear that, but as one who eschews hyperbole, what I'm looking at is truly interesting, dare I say fascinating."

"Everythin' okay?" Amos asked. Halfway across the barn, Mercer's body lay face down on the sturdy wooden work bench, now a second operating table. For the past hour, Amos had been using a high-quality paring knife to remove his nephew's skeletal system, tossing the bones in a metal tub on the floor by his feet.

"I'm not entirely sure."

"Oh? What's goin' on?"

"Yeah, Doc, what's going on?" Silas asked. Even though the featureless face of the mannequin made the words a filtered monotone, Johnny heard the sarcasm as clearly as if Silas had lips and a tongue to accompany his wooden jaw.

"It appears that your ability to instantly heal isn't limited to your flesh," Johnny answered as he ran his gloved finger along Silas' torso, where he estimated the lines from his previous cuts should have been.

"Meanin'?"

"Meaning that the piece of your wooden chest that I had cut away to insert your lungs and heart inside has... for lack of a better word... healed. I cannot see one single cut-line."

"Okay, I'll give you that it is interestin', Doc. You'll have to cut me open again?"

"I will." When Johnny had inserted Caleb's lungs and heart, the cut lines from the prior operation had been visible. Not this time, though. Was Silas subconsciously becoming more acclimated to his bizarre living situation? Was Silas evolving? Johnny thought about breaking off one of Silas' fingers to see if it would grow back, and how long it would take, but considering Silas' volatility and monomaniacal desire to get inserted into Mercer's body, he opted to wait for a better opportunity.

"My wood parts don't feel nothin' anyway. And even though I can move and talk and whatnot without the organs in there, havin' workin' lungs and a beating heart... I don't know. They make me feel human, I guess."

"Fair enough."

"Hey, Johnny?" Amos called out. "I'm done."

"Already?" Silas and Johnny asked at the same time. Impressive.

Leaving Silas on the table, Johnny crossed the barn to examine Amos' work. He expected sloppy cuts, ragged flaps of skin, and gouges torn from the muscle. Wrong on all accounts. Straight lines along the flayed skin, muscle smooth and glistening. On a silver tray rested the eyeballs, and the internal organs were piled into a neat mound in a porcelain basin on the table next to the body. "Masterfully done."

"Thank you." Amos beamed, a smile so bright it was easy to overlook the missing teeth. "I still can't believe that we can transfer a wooden person into a human body and have it work. I mean, I seen it already, but it's still wild. I ain't never thought about anythin' like this before. Have you ever dreamed of anythin' like this?" Amos asked.

The back of Johnny's throat twisted, a physical pang caused by hearing one simple word. He knew very well Amos used the word "dream" as an aspirational goal stemming from flights of fancy. But Johnny's thoughts and reaction stemmed from the biological act that occurred during a deep slumber. A twitch, a shift in countenance, an uncontrolled noise. Some involuntary movement on his part betrayed his emotions and must have captured Amos' attention, because the rube asked, "Everythin' okay?"

Despite Amos' simplistic upbringing, he clearly strived to grow beyond it. Johnny had always viewed Amos as a minion, the person who disposed of finished experiments. But now Johnny wondered if he should consider Amos as something akin to an apprentice. If so, then Amos must play the role of confidante to learn the motivations behind Johnny's quest.

Glancing at the sitting mannequin to make sure it was far enough away, Johnny – under the pretense of further scrutiny – leaned closer to Mercer Boyle's deboned body. Amos leaned in as well, and then Johnny said softly, "I can't dream."

As backwards as Amos appeared to be at times, he at least understood Johhny's surreptitious intent and repeated in a whisper, "You can't dream?"

"No, I'm afraid not. Well, we all dream, but since I can't remember mine, it feels like I don't. I feel like that magic is missing within me. We're nothing more than sugar filled sacks of water globbed around calcium sticks, yet we move, we think, we dream. Well, some of us, at least. But that's the magic of human beings, isn't it?"

"Was that what you've been lookin' for? Dreams?"

"A bit more involved than that, but yes. See, I can conceptualize, I can recall, I can bring forth an image in my mind. But I can't build a world inside my head filled with different hued skies and oceans with creatures that don't exist. I can imagine a rocket only after I see one take flight. And never once have I remembered a dream. After extensive study of the human brain and how the mind's eye affects dreams, I've found very little information about the mind's eye itself. Therefore, it is up to me to find it in others to learn about it, understand it. I must say, though, the mind's eye is quite elusive."

One positive side-effect of Amos' simplicity was his lack of nuance. His eye positively sparkled, yet another mystery of human physiognomy. How a sphere of protein-packed water could sparkle was another human trait Johnny would eventually want to investigate. Obviously, Amos was willing to assist, the expression on his face a declaration of fealty.

"You guys ready yet?" Silas asked.

Johnny gestured to the flayed carcass with a stage magician's flair. "Yes, indeed we are. Care to join us, Silas?"

"I'm guessin' you found a sense of humor somewhere in Mercer's body, huh, Doc?" Silas grumbled as his wooden form ambled to the table.

Amos placed a sturdy stool at the back of the table. Johnny held Silas by the arm to balance the wooden man's step up. "Did you think you had a monopoly on humor?"

To Johnny's surprise, the weight of Silas' glare had more heft than expected, considering it came from a single pair of eyeballs with no other facial countenance. There was no trust within Silas, Johnny knew this.

Amos and Johnny helped the wooden creature into a kneeling position on the operating table, between the boneless legs of Mercer's face down carcass.

"We'll follow the same process used when we transferred you into Caleb."

"Got it." Silas tossed the clump of throat behind him, and then plucked the eyeballs from the small cups carved into his head. Each grabbing a shoulder, Johnny and Amos lowered Silas face-first into Mercer.

Johnny nodded to Amos, signifying that he should take the lead. Breaking into another gap-toothed smile, Amos carefully pulled the Mercer skin-mask over Silas' wooden head, tugging the thick black hair to adjust it. Johnny held the back halves of Mercer's scalp together while Amos lifted the pitcher of blood and poured along the seam. As instantaneous as before, the two halves fused together, leaving only the faintest scar.

Amos asked, "How does that feel?"

"I can hear and speak, if that's what you're askin'," Silas replied, using Mercer's voice. "I feel someone's fingers tuggin' my hair."

"All good things," Johnny said as he guided Silas' left arm into the open sleeve of Mercer's left arm. Amos followed suit on the right side, each chirurgeon adjusting the skin around the torso to accommodate the new structure.

Having learned on Caleb's body, Amos masterfully sliced away enough muscle tissue to accommodate the differences in shape between the human bones and the mannequin limbs.

"Bet you have them hookers comin' over soon, don't ya?" Amos asked.

"Not yet," Silas replied. "I gotta meet with them Winters boys first. I don't know why, but I can't get them outta my head."

Passing the pitcher of blood back and forth, Johnny and Amos closed the seams along the back of Mercer's arms. "Well," Johnny said, "I might have a theory about that. I wasn't able to perform this surgery yesterday because I went to Albuquerque for research. After reading over records and newspapers well over a hundred years old, I believe I found a connection between you and the Winters."

Silas turned his eyeless head toward Johnny. "Ya don't say?"

"The little girl you molested? Do you remember her parents' names?"

"Her daddy. I remember people shouting his name as they separated us after he stabbed me and I tore his ear off with my teeth. Remember the taste of his blood, too. I think... Yeah, I think it was Ezekial Williamson."

A smirk tickled along Johnny's lips as he and Amos tucked Silas' legs into the open slits along Mercer's thighs and calves. "Correct. Records showed that Ezekial Williamson's other daughter married a fellow named Rutherford Winters. So, Rand and Riley Winters are direct descendants of the man you bit into and shared blood with the day you were hanged."

"Well, Doc, to steal your word... That is interestin' indeed. You think that's why I feel such a strong connection?"

"I do, especially when factoring in the Devil Tree." Once he and Amos finished using more blood to fuse Mercer's legs around Silas', Johnny gestured to his surgical bag. Amos hefted it onto the table and held it open for Johnny to peer inside. There. His Dremel tool. Johnny focused on cutting a square piece from Silas' exposed back, the whine of the tool changing pitch while buzzing through the wood. Once finished, he handed the tool back to Amos to clean while he removed the freshly cut section. "You had mentioned that you 'awakened' twice from darkness to find yourself in the form of a tiny wooden soldier, correct?"

"Yeah? What's that got to do with anythin'?"

"Local lore and legends are started for a reason. There have been many documented cases of unexplained happenings around the Devil Tree. Maybe the tree does possess supernatural elements? Perhaps it absorbed what can be described as Silas' soul as his body rotted away to feed its roots? Now, how does the toy soldier come into play? Upon further research regarding this property, one of the many families the Boyles swindled were the McCullough's. I read an article about a small toy shop owner named Chester McCullough who mentioned living in New Mexico as a small child, sharing fond memories of his grandfather whittling toys for him. My hypothesis is this – Chester's grandfather might have used a piece of the Devil Tree, the tree that supported the noose where you met your demise, the place where your blood mingled with Ezekial's, to whittle a toy soldier."

Amos reached into the cavity of Silas' torso to scoop out the used organs, shriveled and pruned. "Wait. You're sayin' you believe the stories of the Devil Tree?"

Johnny shrugged as he dumped the fresh, slime-covered heart and set of lungs into Silas' wooden well of a chest. He replaced the square piece of wood he had cut away and poured blood along the seams. The wood bonded with itself, leaving no trace of the Dremel tool's path. Fascinating.

One final drizzle of blood to suture the skin along Mercer's back, Silas sat up and stared at Johnny with empty eye sockets. "Not sure I like the way you describe my final moments, Doc."

Johnny spread the eyelids wide with one hand and gently placed the eyeballs inside with the other. "My apologies. I meant no disrespect. How do you feel?"

A deft hop from the table and Silas gave his new body a perusal. "Feels good, Doc. Now, you two go to the Boyle house and get ready for another surgery. This body is temporary. The Winters boys... They're my permanent body. I can feel it."

Without so much as another word, Silas dressed in Mercer's clothes and stormed out of the barn.

As Johnny removed his gloves and packed up his surgical equipment, Amos smiled at him and said, "I can't wait to get back to the house. There's something I want to show you. I've been practicin'."

"Practicing?"

"Yeah. Your teachings. You're a really good teacher. You should do it more."

"Thank you. I have been thinking about taking you on as an apprentice."

Amos shook his head. "Not what I meant. There are others like me, who want to be like *you*. You taught me so much already, but I want to learn more about the magic within the science. I gotta tell ya, just thinkin' about what we're doin', thinkin' about what you're lookin' for… I ain't never been this excited about anythin' in my life. And I know there are so many more people who would feel the same way."

Johnny was taken aback. Few people shared his intelligence, and he had mistakenly tied intelligence to motivation. Amos was far inferior in many categories, but he certainly exhibited enough enthusiasm to be motivated. Were there truly others who shared such desires? Who wanted to traverse along the border between science and magic? Who had the same lack of compunction as to how they went about their experiments? This was something Johnny needed to ponder.

CHAPTER 28

No rodeo practice for today, but Riley didn't get much of a chance to talk to Rand after school – as soon as they had finished their homework, Rand got into his movie costume. Apparently, they wanted more scenes with "Unnamed Stableboy" whom everyone called Percival.

"Hey, if everyone keeps calling you Percival, there's a chance that Nixon will put it in the script, giving you a real movie credit," Tilde had said when the four of them met at the southern part of the ranch, by the crew's RVs and trailers, a few minutes ago.

"Really?" Rand asked, his smile brighter than his pickup's high beams.

"Yeah," Barnes added. "After your character gets named, then he might get a line of dialog or two. That'd be a few extra shekels more than the pittance you're getting as an extra."

"Oh, wow."

Not happy with the thoughts they were putting in Rand's head, Riley wished they'd shut up. Admittedly, they helped him be brave enough to talk to his family about who he was by simply being who they were, but the longer they stuck around on the ranch, the more damage they created. He had joined Rand for moral support, but on the way from the house to the trailers, Rand rambled on and on about how he thought it was a good thing they wanted to film another scene with him. Riley couldn't get a word in edgewise about meeting Mercer to talk about Caleb.

Monday's school day had been as plain and usual as a white tee shirt. The only nettle in the back of Riley's mind was the complete lack of either Caleb or Mercer. It added credence to what Mercer had mentioned about Caleb being more squirrely than usual, but detracted from Mercer's trustworthiness, the little that he had anyway. Or did it add to what Mercer was talking about? If Caleb was sick, was it contagious and had Mercer caught it?

Now, he was standing outside the lead actress' trailer with butterflies in his stomach while she, Mr. Haddon, Bo, Nixon, and Miles argued inside.

A weird feeling burrowed through Riley's gut, leaving behind a quivering emptiness. Not one to get into trouble often, this nervousness, the chilly dew forming along his hairline, the numbness in his fingertips, were all unusual experiences. On the football field, confidence warded off fear of fallout and kept him in control, even when a play broke down. This troubled feeling sucked and it brought to mind the need to keep his true self a secret.

Mom and Dad rarely argued, and never yelled at each other, so the war of words waging behind the closed door of Mrs. Haddon's trailer was a new experience for Riley, riling up unnamed and unpleasant emotions that made his skin crawl. Rand looked just as uncomfortable, wringing his hands together while staring at the trailer's dirty white siding as if it were a movie screen, one playing a loud, scary movie. Mrs. Hadden had been tearing into Mr. Hadden, Bo, and Miles. Nixon hadn't said much.

"C'Mon, Rand, we shouldn't be here," Riley said, his nerves vibrating from every syllable of Mrs. Hadden's shrill words.

Rand shifted his weight from one foot to the other, like a child afraid they had missed Santa because the milk and cookies had gone untouched. "I don't know, baby brother. I don't want to be hard to find when this meeting's over."

"Meeting? I don't think this is a meeting."

Putting a hand on Riley's shoulder, Tilde said, "That's just how they communicate with each other."

"Yeah, Doe Eyes. I'm surprised this has been the first big blowout since production started. One shoot I was at, the lead actor tore into the writers at least twice a week," Barnes said.

Riley appreciated them trying to make him feel better, but they weren't helping. Hands on his hips, he looked skyward hoping he'd think of a way to get Rand away from this. No help from the clouds in the sky, but there was help by the porta-johns – Mercer.

Leaning against one of the light green, plastic outhouses, Mercer wore a shit-eating grin. He tipped an invisible hat and waved. Riley wanted to punch that smirk right off his face so badly his knuckles sang righteously beautiful songs, but Rand had set up this meeting to talk about Caleb. Riley didn't give a pile of horse shit about him; he held onto hope that what Mercer had said about the party he and Caleb were throwing later this week was true. God, the idea of Mercer Boyle being gone in less than a week? Heavenly. "Hey, Rand, I need to talk to you about something that happened at school today," Riley said.

Without so much as a glance away from the trailer, Rand grunted, "Yeah? What?"

"I kinda feel like we need to chat in private."

"We can leave if you two need a minute," Tilde said.

"Nah, that's okay." Riley wrapped an arm around Rand's shoulders and turned him to face the porta-johns. "We can just head over there for a minute."

"Huh? Wha...?" Rand mumbled as if groggy from waking up. After he got a glimpse of Mercer, his tone changed. "Yeah. Okay. Yeah, let's talk over there."

Riley cuffed Rand's arm as soon as they were far enough away from Tilde and Barnes, though he doubted that the PAs would have heard anything over the angry voices coming from the trailer. "What the hell, man?"

"What the hell what?"

"C'mon, Rand. The way you're acting like a hungry dog wanting to be fed no matter whose hand you bite."

With a lip twist and an eye roll to dismiss Riley's concerns, Rand said, "Whatever, baby brother. I ain't biting no one's hands. The last scene I did was fun, and I just don't want to miss the opportunity to do another one, is all."

"Waiting out someone's argument seems... I don't know... Like a vulture waiting for a jackrabbit to die of thirst on the side of the road."

Rand shook his head and chuckled. "Damn, Riley. As dramatic as you are, you should ask for a part in the movie. Now, hush up about it. I'm sure

Mercer's gonna say stupid shit about my costume, we don't need to give him more fuel."

Much to Riley's surprise, the only comment Mercer made about Rand's clothing was a sarcastic, "Nice outfit." Those words also served as a greeting.

"For the movie," Rand replied. "So, what's up?"

Mercer jutted his jaw and looked beyond Rand and Riley, gesturing that they were too close to other people, and he pushed off the porta-john to walk to the border fence. A quick hop over and he was back on his own property. "It's about Caleb."

Riley exchanged a glance with his brother, relieved that Rand seemed focused and in the moment, his mind not off in la-la-land. They followed Mercer to the fence but stayed on their side.

"Alright, Mercer, no one can hear us or see us," Rand said. "What's up with Caleb?"

Arms crossed over his chest, a slight shiver struck him. He looked away and said, "Honestly, I ain't sure."

Riley had enough drama to last him a lifetime. "What's that supposed to mean? A few days ago you said he was acting weird. Has it gotten worse? Is he sick? Is he puking? God, I hope he's puking."

Jerking back as if the fence had shocked him, Mercer reached out with his hands, a plea for help stamped across his face. "I don't know if he's sick! He might be? Or might be possessed by the devil himself? I don't fuckin' know. That's why I'm here. I need your help. I need you two to come over and look at him."

Both Riley and Rand stepped back as if Mercer was the one infected. "What the hell did you say?" Riley asked.

Mercer ran his hands over his face and paced in a tight circle. "I know, I know. It sounds strange what I said, but I don't know what's going on with Caleb. He don't... He just don't *look right*. Like... Oh, you ain't gonna believe me."

"Why the hell you need us to come over?" Rand asked. "Just call a doctor."

"*You* know any doctors who make house calls?"

"Call an ambulance, dumbass."

Mercer frowned, blinking rapidly like the idea was foreign to him. "And tell the ambulance what? That my friend just don't look right? And would an ambulance come to my house? All the way out here?"

"Yeah. It might take a half hour to get here, and I honestly don't know what hospital they'd go to. But, yeah."

"A half hour? Hospital? Caleb's… Caleb's been actin' fishy. I don't know if he'd stay at my house that long. I don't even know if he'll be there when I get back, which is why I need your help. To see what you think of him, and keep him from hurting himself, or other people."

"Look, Mercer, we're really busy." Rand emphasized his point by taking another step back to get a better view of the trailer.

Riley hated Mercer and Caleb with every fiber of his being. His teacher said that atoms don't have feelings, but he swore his did, every single one of them hating Mercer and Caleb. The thought of being set up for some sort of ambush at the Boyle house was in the forefront of his mind, but if there was even a fraction of truth to what Mercer had said about wanting to leave town to tour with a band, then Riley had to take it. And, God damn, the spell his brother was under from this cursed movie needed to be broken. "You said he was… possessed?"

With weird enthusiasm, Mercer livened up, his hands wild as he talked. "Yes! Yeah. It's… I don't how to describe it. He ain't him. It's like this… this *being* is living inside of him, like Caleb ain't nothin' more than just clothing."

Rand rolled his eyes. "Mercer—"

"C'mon, guys. If I only know two things, it's that the Boyles don't like the Winters and the Winters don't like the Boyles. I'm wantin' to forget all that. I know you owe me no favors, but I just don't know how to describe what's wrong with Caleb. You need to see it to believe it. There's somethin' wrong with him."

"Should we take a look?" Riley asked Rand, his senses tingling. Something was up, that's for sure.

Teeth bared in a sneer, Rand snapped his head around to look at Riley. "You can't be serious, baby brother."

"If it helps Mercer get to that party this weekend..." Riley let the last word dangle, hoping his brother would remember that this could be an opportunity to get rid of Mercer for good.

Rand huffed and gestured in the direction of the Boyle farm. "No. Look, Mercer, we told you to meet us here to compare notes. Riley and I didn't notice anyone else missing at school or acting funny today. You aren't giving us any more details than when we last talked. If Caleb isn't right, then call the doctor. That's all I'm gonna say about it. You should head back home now."

Mercer opened his mouth for one more argument, but then closed it and held up his hands in surrender. "Okay. I hear ya. If you change your mind, you know where I live."

As Mercer walked off toward his house, Rand stormed back toward the trailer, Riley hurrying to keep up. "Rand, I think what he's saying—"

"Is horse shit."

"Really? Why would he let me beat on him at school last week? Why would he walk all the way over here and ask for our help if there wasn't some truth to his words?"

"I don't know, Riley. Maybe to set us up for—"

The trailer door slammed against the outside wall, and both boys stopped in their tracks. Even Barnes and Tilde stared wide-eyed as Mrs. Hadden exited like dynamite blasted her out, and screamed, "I can't believe you said that to me!"

Her husband popped out of the trailer and grabbed her hand. "I didn't mean it that way."

Without breaking stride, she yanked away from his grasp and kept walking. "There's no other way you meant it! Where's Amanda? I need to see Amanda."

Miles shot from the trailer next. "Brett! Hold on, we can still work something out."

"Fuck you, Miles!" She raised her middle finger as she marched away, keeping ahead of Joel and Miles.

Bo and Nixon exited next, the actor laughing as he said, "And you said *I* was difficult to work with."

"Well, seeing how this is your fault – Yes, you're very fucking difficult to work with," Nixon said.

"Whatever, dude." Bo flicked his fingers as if shooing away a meddlesome fly. "Unlike you, I'm going to help Miles."

"God damn it," Nixon huffed as he started up the same path as the others, but paused when he noticed he had an audience. "Oh, hey guys. I'm sure you already guessed, but it might be a while, maybe even the rest of the day before we start filming again. Sorry, Percival, we need to move shooting your scene to tomorrow." Nixon attempted a reassuring posture and tone, but Riley saw right through it. The director was probably worried about losing his actress and didn't stick around to explain any further.

Riley grabbed Rand by the elbow and tugged. "Good," he whispered, "That means we can go to Mercer's and figure out what the hell is happening with Caleb."

Yanking his arm away, Rand turned to the PAs. "What do you guys think? Should I stick around? Maybe head up to Fake Town?"

Barnes looked in the direction where everyone had stormed. "I don't know, Smily. This feels a little different than a regular Hollywood spat. Even if it turns out to be some behind-the-scenes drama bullshit, today's schedule will still be cut."

Tilde nodded. "I agree. Go chill somewhere. We'll find you later and fill you in."

After a huge sigh, Rand turned to Riley. "We'll see what Mercer's talking about with Caleb, and then tell them both to fuck off if things turn to shit. Then we're coming right back and heading to Fake Town to see where everything stands with the movie."

"Fair enough," Riley replied. They aimed for the fence, hopping over to follow Mercer. It disgusted Riley that he was willing to this just to get Rand away from the movie madness.

CHAPTER 29

Amanda placed the ham hock in the center of the Dutch oven and swirled the wooden spoon through the water-soaked beans. A billion white stars of minced garlic orbited the center of the soup-galaxy. After adding chopped carrots and celery as well as a bit of onion, the water would soon turn to broth. Once boiling waves rippled around the edges, she'd set the heat to simmer. In an hour, she'd remove the hock and add the ham cubes. Even if for some reason she got distracted, the soup would be fine.

She rolled her eyes. If there was a "some reason" it'd have something to do with the movie. Four dinners and two lunches had been ruined over the past three weeks, because she or Hank – usually both – got roped into one crisis or another. Overcooked steaks. Dried out chicken. A casserole that set off the smoke detector a few nights ago. That one called forth Hank's Bible voice when he told Miles and Nixon in no uncertain terms that he and his family were off limits after 6:00 P.M. So far, the movie people abided, but Amanda didn't put faith in their respect for the rules, or that it would last very long.

"Amanda!" Brett's shriek burst through the kitchen windows as if the panes of glass weren't there. "Amanda! I need you!"

5:45. Just under the wire.

Amanda wiped her hands on a kitchen towel and tossed it on the counter as she stepped out the side door, readying herself to receive Brett's drama, no matter how infinitesimal it might be. By the time she got three steps on the lawn, she was hit by the serious look in Brett's eyes.

The actress didn't look like she wasn't about to ask for a line of dialog to be validated for authenticity or a request to help her pick out which cowboy hat made her look fiercer. Though disruptive and egocentric, she always beamed like a child ready to play at recess. With Joel and Miles in tow? Anger. Amanda noticed Nixon and Bo jogging right behind him. This can't be good. Ramos and Javi were by the horses, close enough to witness the exchange, and random crew members drifted closer.

"Hey, Brett," Amanda said, her tone light, yet supportive. *Make no assumptions, let her come to you.* "What's going on?"

"I'm quitting the fucking movie and I've come to say goodbye."

"Whoa, whoa whoa!" Miles yelled as he hurried his sweaty body along the lawn to catch up to Brett. Winded from running, his words were uneven as he continued. "Don't be rash, Brett. We can talk about this."

"We already talked in my trailer. It's clear that you and *my husband* have agreed with Bo."

"I didn't agree with Bo!" Miles said, voice still unsteady. "I just said that it was an idea to consider."

"Not helping, dude," Nixon said, stepping forward, authoritative tone leading the way. He then turned to the other two men and held up his hand. "Stay quiet. Bo, don't say a fucking word. Joel, you're not part of this. Brett, we need to talk about—"

"Talk?" Brett wheeled around to focus her red-eyed rage on the director. "Talk about it? Now you're taking their side? Now you're agreeing with Bo?"

"I *am* a part of this," Joel snapped at Nixon. "I'm her fucking manager."

Nixon said, "I'm not taking anyone's side, Brett." He paused to look over Brett's shoulder at Amanda. She knew that look. A desperate man floundering in the middle of a lake, ready to cling to anything to save his life. "I'm just following Amanda's advice."

Amanda knew Brett held her in high esteem. Hell, everyone knew Brett all but worshiped the ground Amanda trod upon, which was obviously why Nixon had pulled her into this argument, whatever it was about. Instead of calming Brett down, the angry actress spun on her heel to aim her words at Amanda. "You? You advised him to agree with Bo?"

A weird confusion washed through Amanda, being accused of something she wasn't sure about. Had Hank been here, everyone would have been kicked off the property and forbidden to return once the first line of shouting had been spewed. Part of Amanda thought to follow through with that idea – good riddance to bad grief. Just because she wasn't as quick to anger as her husband didn't mean she had to act upon it. And all she knew about the situation was that Brett had been wounded by at least three people around her and lashed out as such. Placing both hands on her shoulders, Amanda stood between her and the rest of the world. "Brett, all I suggested he do was take charge. I have no idea what he did or what Bo said or who's agreeing with whom."

The deep lines etching hard emotions across Brett's face softened, obvious that she finally found the friend she had been looking for. With a nostril-flaring inhale, Brett said, "So... Bo decided to stay sober long enough to read the script. Of course, in his twisted, narcissistic, misogynistic mind, that means he's now entitled to give suggestions, and he decided to rewrite the love scene between my character and his. The original way it's written is more implied and happens off screen, making this one of the few movies where I'm not topless."

In an attempt to offer much needed solidarity, Amanda extrapolated. "I'm assuming his rewrites have your character go topless."

"Even worse! He not only extended the sex scene, he made it more graphic, and had the nerve to state that it should be unsimulated. An unsimulated sex scene, Amanda! That means real fucking!"

"Wait... What?"

"You heard correctly. The leading man, the producer, and *my husband* want me to star in a fucking porno!"

Joel huffed. "I didn't say you should do it—"

"You sure as hell didn't say I shouldn't do it!"

"My objection was implied."

"You said we should listen to what Bo and Miles had to say! How the hell does that imply that I shouldn't do it."

"Allowing them to finish their thoughts establishes a basis of context. We can't negotiate expectations unless we know the starting point."

Brett crossed her arms over her chest, looked away from everyone to the endless prairie, and tapped her foot. There were no answers out there, so she turned to Amanda and asked, "What should I do?"

By now, a small crowd had gathered. Ramos, Javi, and other ranch hands held a few horses still by the reins, scrutinous eyes on their boss. Tilde, Barnes, and a dozen members of the cast and crew were wide-eyed, undoubtedly wondering about their fate. Miles' face was slicked with greasy anger. Joel looked like an accused criminal waiting for judgment. Bo's smile was a handsome mockery of everything good and decent. Nixon seemed helpless.

Suddenly she felt everyone's eyes upon her, the full weight of their thoughts and feelings pressing down on her shoulders. Their ears were open and ready to hear her words. The last person who wanted to be involved with attention now found herself at the center of it. What words could she use to appease everyone? *Just listen to your heart*, she told herself. *Hunh. Well, that's some damn good advice.*

"Just listen to your heart."

Finally unclenching her jaw, tears rolled over Brett's cheeks as if her furrowed brow had been holding them in. A jut-jawed nod. "Yeah. Yes. Yes, Amanda, you're right. I should follow my heart. Joel, we're leaving."

"Yeah. That's a good idea. Let's go back to your trailer and—"

"No, Joel. We're leaving this set, this state, and we're going home. I'm going to apologize to Dakota for heading to a job on her birthday, drink a case of wine, and contemplate life."

"Honey, we can't just leav—"

"If you want to stay married, we absolutely can leave."

The air grew quiet. Miles glared at Joel with a "don't do it" look reserved for cats poised to paw a glass of water from the counter to the floor. With the snap of a soldier called into action, Joel turned his back on the crowd and headed for the trailers. "I'll pack the bags."

"Joel!" Miles snapped. "Joel, she has a signed contract!"

Bo laughed.

Murmurs ran along the perimeter of cast and crew, standing shoulder to shoulder.

Unaffected by anything else, Brett threw her arms around Amanda. Breath hot with desperation, her words burned into Amanda's neck. "I can't thank you enough. You've helped me when I didn't know I needed help. I love you for that and I am eternally grateful. Is it okay if I stay in touch?"

The timidity in Brett's question was heartbreaking, and this level of familiarity was uncommon in Amanda's world. She returned Brett's hug, though not as bone-crushing. "Of course."

Giving Amanda one last lung-deflating squeeze, Brett released her. "Please, please, please, if you find yourself on the east coast, let me know. I'll meet you anywhere."

"Brett!" Miles called out as the actress headed for the trailer, her head held high. Fingers wriggling as if getting limber for strangulation, he started to follow her. "You can't do this! You bitch, you can't do this!"

Appearing out of nowhere, like a golem made from the land, Hank stood before Miles and placed a massive hand on the producer's shoulder. "I know you're upset right now, but we don't tolerate that kind of treatment on this property."

The tone in Hank's voice flowed through everyone standing around him, a benevolent god offering an opportunity for a lost soul to do the right thing. Sweat percolated along Miles' lips as they twitched, the fire behind his eyes burning. Prudence won out and he stepped back, then made a half turn while pulling at his own hair, mumbling a string of profanities through clenched teeth.

"Hank is so cool," Barnes whispered to Tilde, Amanda close enough to overhear. She shuddered to think about what would have happened if Hank hadn't appeared and stopped Miles before he could get started.

Nixon looked up at Hank for a brief second, a loyal puppy in awe of its master, and then took a more active role in the situation. "Miles, man, you need to take a breath. Everyone's emotions are running high. Step away and let everyone recalibrate."

Nixon reached out a supportive hand, but Miles swatted it away. "Fuck off, or I'll show you how high my emotions are running."

It was obvious Nixon needed to vent because he wheeled around to Bo, who wore a sinister smile on his face, and snapped, "And you! What the fuck is this bullshit rewrite all about?"

With a level of arrogance reserved for deities, Bo sneered and chuckled. "Hey, you were all pissed at me for saying she was too old and now you're pissed at me because I'm saying she's not. Make up your mind."

"Make up my mind? Yeah, okay. I'll just fucking replace you, how's that?"

That sneer again. "Pfft. Good luck with that."

Pointing at Hank and Amanda, he said, "I don't need luck. I already have someone younger than you, way better looking, and far more willing to work with me – their son. Kid's got talent, Bo. With a little patience and practice, he can be better than you. Maybe in two days. Three tops. Plenty of time for me to get Brett on a plane back here."

A blast of heat from Hank washed over Amanda. She pressed against his arm as she placed a hand on his chest, and whispered, "He's not serious. He's trying to get his people in line."

Fists clenched, Hank didn't move and remained quiet, even as Bo glared at them. Seconds stretched to minutes and Amanda could almost hear the score music build to a crescendo, until a pair of headlights broke the tension. One of the production SUVs turned down the driveway to exit.

"You're not gonna replace me with that kid," Bo said as he watched Joel and Brett drive away.

"I'm not the one with a legendary drug habit, Bo," Nixon said, never taking his eyes off the actor. "You want the paycheck, you get Brett back."

One final snarl followed by a glob of spit onto Nixon's boots. "I'll call her in an hour or so."

As Bo stormed off, those who witnessed the collision of explosive personalities broke off into smaller groups and exchanged furtive whispers. Nixon stood alone, a statue in an earthquake, desperate to stand tall and not crack into rubble. Hank tensed, wanting to keep control of the situation, but Amanda pressed against his chest again. Sometimes people needed a moment with their own voice before they could hear anyone else's. It seemed as if Nixon's told him to go after his friend, because he was gazing in Miles' direction. After a rueful, "I'm sorry about all of this," to Hank and Amanda, he took off after him.

Amanda exhaled; according to the burn in her lungs and the relief accompanying the inhale, she'd been holding her breath. She struggled to grasp what had just happened, torn about how she should feel. If Brett's departure meant that the movie production was over, then her life with her family could go back to normal, but that also meant that the dozen or so people depending on this job would suffer. If Bo could somehow get Brett back, then everyone involved might get the paycheck they were hoping for, and that would add a few more days to a production that was already taking longer than originally promised. "Well, that was... something."

Hank's muscles relaxed under Amanda's fingers, and he shook his head. "These movie people. I'm glad Rand wasn't around to see this. Last thing we need is him thinking he's going to be the lead actor in this shit show."

Amanda agreed, hoping no one would spill the beans, especially Ramos and Javi. "Speaking of the boys...Where are they?"

"I... don't know. I don't see them. If they were around, no way they wouldn't have heard the commotion."

"Ummm...? Excuse me?" Came from Tilde as she and Barnes approached. "Both Rand and Riley went with their friend Mercer to his house."

If Amanda hadn't known that these two befriended her sons, she'd have been sure they were thinking of the wrong kids. "Did you say... Mercer?"

Barnes nodded and pointed in the direction of the Boyle's house. "Yeah. They followed him that way."

Ramos and Javi both gasped. Amanda looked to Javi for information, but the young man gave her a nervous head shake.

"Well, that is odd," Hank said. "Why the hell would they go there? With Mercer? I'm gonna head over."

"I'll join you," Ramos said.

Amanda watched the two men walk to Hank's pickup and wondered how much weirder the evening was going to get.

CHAPTER 30

A mansion. Riley didn't know the exact terms and conditions that marked a big house from a mansion, but he always thought of the Boyle residence as a mansion. And nothing looked more out of place on a pig farm than a mansion.

Thankful to be wearing work boots, Riley strode alongside Rand as they followed Mercer down a mucky path between two pigpens. Fences made of moldy pressure-treated two-by-sixes hooked into crooked four-by-four posts. Should the massive boars in the right pen really wish to get to the sows in the left pen, the rotting fence wouldn't stop them. Each nasty looking beast was pushing three hundred pounds, but they seemed content while munching their slop. But... What the heck were they eating? Black and white snouts stained pink, snorted and nosed through the last bits of red meat on bones.

Riley's gut turned. Something about those bones unnerved him

Rand called to him, "Hey! Let's keep moving. We don't wanna be here any longer than we have to."

A one hundred percent true statement. Riley added a dash of hustle to his step from the driveway to the wraparound porch. A three-car garage flanked the far end of the circle. Caleb's hunk of junk truck and a Ford Taurus were parked in front of it. The setting sun cast unsettling shadows off the garage, but Riley didn't know who the Ford belonged to. At first, he thought Archibald had bought a new car, but that made no sense since this one was way too plain. And besides, Archibald would've parked a new vehicle inside the garage, not outside. Didn't matter none in the grand scheme of things as he and his brother made their way up the steps and into the house.

How a pig rancher could afford this place was beyond Riley. The clean and shiny hardwood floors in the foyer probably ran all throughout the first floor. Dark wooden, intricately carved banisters flanked the wide stairway centered in the open entry, the steps rising to the exposed second floor. The chilling beauty inside was made even colder by the lack of lighting. Twilight muted the colors and created shadows that would probably disappear with the flick of a switch. Yet, Mercer made no effort to turn on any lights.

A vivid memory smacked Riley between the eyes when he wiped his boots on the rug set to the side for such things – he had been here once before. How old was he? Five? No, four. Rand was five. Their parents brought them, specifically Rand, over to apologize to Mercer for beating him up. It didn't matter that Mercer had started it by bullying Riley on the playground, but Archibald was going to press charges if an apology hadn't been made. At the time, Riley didn't know what that meant, just that the bastard Archibald Boyle lorded over Mom and Dad while Rand was forced to humble himself. And that creepy Amos lurked in the shadows like a ghoul. Riley was never sure if the feud between the Winters and the Boyles existed before then or not, but it began for him on that day. Now, he was in the house of his family's enemy.

"Where's Caleb?"

"This way," Mercer said as he put his hands in his pockets and strolled through the foyer, starting down the hallway toward the kitchen.

Rand grunted, but followed.

Riley paused and pushed down the fear that had been hiding within him for the past thirteen years. Even though he was much bigger since that last visit, the deep brown walls interspersed with panels of *fleur-de-lis* wallpaper seemed no smaller. He remembered that the long hallway led to the kitchen. The room to the left was a sitting room connected to the dining room, connected to the other kitchen entrance. The room to the right was a game room filled with taxidermized animal heads. The foyer's high ceiling might as well have led to the sky, Riley's neck pinching as he looked upward. The bowling pin shaped posts in the banister leading up the stairs and along the walkway looked like mishappened teeth of a bulbous mouth ready to chew him up and spit him out. Maybe this was a mistake after all. He had a sudden urge to turn and run right back out that front door, but Rand was too far ahead of him.

"Mercer, c'mon. Where's Caleb?" Rand asked.

Mercer didn't respond.

"Hey!" Rand yelled as he jogged a few steps to catch Mercer and tug his arm.

Mercer tried to yank his arm free, but Rand didn't let go. As the two crossed the kitchen's threshold, Rand yanked with more force, his muscles going taut as he pulled. Mercer pulled back and laughed, jerking Rand into the kitchen. Riley had heard that laugh before – over a decade ago when Mercer got ahold of a magnifying glass and found a busy anthill. Sick glee had thickened his chuckle.

Rand was right – this had been a ruse and a fight was coming. God, it was going to feel good to kick Mercer's ass. Fists clenched, Riley rolled his neck and started down the hallway.

When Mercer reached the kitchen counter, still in Rand's grasp, he grabbed a butcher's knife from the block, turned and slashed. Riley froze. Mercer was capable of unspeakable things, but an assault with a knife? Why lead Rand into the kitchen? Into his house? But... From Riley's angle, it looked as if Mercer cut his own arm. That couldn't have happened? Right?

Rand went rigid, back straight and pulling up as if stunned. Then the world slowed. Rand looked down at his hands, holding something that Riley couldn't see.

A thump behind Riley's ribs. Another. A few patters of blood splashed the linoleum between Rand and Mercer. Another heartbeat.

Rand dropped what he had been holding with a splat.

Skin.

That can't be skin.

On the floor at Rand's feet laid a sleeve of skin and muscle all gathered like a wadded-up towel in a slimy pink pile.

"What the fuck?" Rand yelled, a panicked squeak to his voice. "What the f—?"

The knife to Rand's ribs cut his statement short.

"No!" Riley screamed. Like a bad dream, his legs felt like they were stuck in sludge, his body unreceptive to his brain's command. Mercer had always been pig-shit on an old boot, but Riley never in a million years would've thought him capable of something like this. He needed to help Rand. He needed to stop Mercer.

By the time Riley got his feet moving properly, Rand had grabbed Mercer's neck and knife-hand, then drove him deeper into the kitchen. They rounded the corner, disappearing from Riley's view. He heard a crash. Rand's screams – the pain, then anger – tore Riley apart from inside. The slap of skin hitting skin. Skin hitting wood. Wood hitting skin.

Riley skidded into the kitchen, fists up and ready to punch. Again, his body wasn't cooperating, because his brain couldn't comprehend what he was seeing. Rand lay on top of the collapsed table, pieces of a broken chair on him. Still holding the knife, Mercer stood over him, but... Was it Mercer? A chunk of wood protruded out of Mercer's shoulder from where his arm should be. At first, Riley's mind saw a table leg or a piece of chair. It took a few rib-cracking heartbeats to realize that it was Mercer's arm. A wooden arm.

Blood bloomed, covering most of Rand's flouncy white costume shirt as he lay motionless on the kitchen wreckage. Wooden arm be damned, Riley lunged forward and grabbed Mercer's knife-wielding hand by the wrist. Screaming, he punched Mercer in the face, his fist a piston of hatred. Three punches tore Mercer's nose from his face, the mound of cartilage softer and weaker than Riley expected. But Mercer's cheek and jaw were harder. Hard as punching a tree. Three more punches and Riley heard a crack as the bones inside his hand shifted, a strike of electricity blasting up his arm to the base of his neck.

Staggering in pain, Riley released Mercer's wrist. He cradled his hand and through the blur of tears, Riley could tell that Mercer wasn't right. Wasn't human. Nose dangling by a moist flap of skin, the gash in his face revealed wood underneath – it was the same shade of dark brown as his wooden arm – same shade as his jaw under the strips of skin torn away from his face.

Mercer lurched forward with a lazy knife swing. Riley easily dodged it. This Mercer *thing* was toying with him. But Riley couldn't do much to defend himself. He wasn't close enough to anything he could use as a weapon, and pain made his dominant hand worthless.

Mercer took a step forward, then fell.

Rand had tripped Mercer. With both arms wrapped around Mercer's ankles, Rand looked to Riley, blood pouring from his mouth, and gurgled, "Run. *Run!*"

Riley ran from the kitchen, back the way he came. Down the hall. Into the foyer. Then skidded to a stop when he got to the door. Through the thin, frosted sidelights, he saw someone approaching.

Too primed to run, too freaked out by what Mercer had become, too much pain to think straight, Riley planted his foot and sprinted to his right. When he heard the click of the turning knob, he dove. Hit with a burst of electricity from landing on his shoulder, he spun to his back and slid across the hardwood floor into the sitting room. Loveseat, coffee table, and wall of books. The loveseat was against the wall but there was enough room for Riley to tuck himself behind it.

The front door closed, and Riley thought he was going to piss himself. Knees to chest, he brought his good hand to his face. As slowly as possible, he exhaled, his shaky breath hot against his palm. He inhaled and then held his breath again.

From where he hid, he couldn't see who had entered the room. No footsteps, no breathing could be heard. But Riley *felt* that someone was there. He listened for even the tiniest of noise – a squeak of a shoe, a creak from the floorboard – but struggled to hear over the thudding of his heart, so loud he worried it'd give him away.

The air turned cold. He focused on holding his breath, trying to control his quivering. Then the chilled sensation was gone. The air warmed and Riley knew with certainty that the person had left the room. He exhaled.

Crouching low, he eased out from behind the loveseat. The front door was the most direct route out of the house, but the foyer held dangerous mysteries. Was the other person there waiting for Riley to come out? Even if he could make it out the front door, could he do so without attracting attention? With the sun descending and the lights off throughout the house, what other dangers might ambush him? He studied the dark for another means of escape.

A massive archway in the center of the wall led to the dining room. Riley took a chance and crept under the archway. The dining room wasn't as big as he remembered, though it was still impressive with a grand table and eight chairs all positioned around it in the center. A set of closed folding doors led to a kitchen, and God only knew what Mercer was doing in there. To his left was another closed door, this one more substantial. Possibly a way outside? Or, if it was another room, then maybe there was a phone in it? Should he try his luck, or revisit the idea of the front door?

A quick brush of sweat from his brow with the back of his good hand, he decided on the mystery door. He duck-walked through the dining room, careful not to bump into any of the chairs, and gripped the doorknob.

He turned it, giving the door a slight push while listening for creaks or groans that might give him away. He opened the door a little more, then froze when he saw the room's light was on. For the longest seconds Riley had ever waited in his life, he remained petrified, listening, eyes roaming over what looked like a bedroom. No signs of life, so he opened the door enough to slip inside.

It smelled God-awful in there. Rotten. Like meat left out. Odd that this room was accessible through the dining room. Maybe it used to be a big storage room? Obviously, it was now Amos' bedroom. Nude centerfolds taped to the wall and the collection of empty beer bottles piled on and around the small nightstand had clued Riley in. He stepped inside and scanned the room for a phone. One had to be in here. But before he took any further footsteps inside, he jerked back when he noticed the lump on the bed. There was something under the sheets. Judging by the bumps and shapes under it – some*one*, not something. But they lay still. No rising or falling with breath. The source of the smell.

After what happened to Rand – *oh, God, Rand! No. Stop. Not now, don't cry about that now* – the level of evil in this house surpassed the limits of Riley's imagination. Whoever was under the sheets was a victim, no doubt in Riley's mind. They deserved justice. They deserved to be seen, recognized. Hand trembling, Riley grabbed the corner of the sheets and pulled.

Acid shot up from his stomach and he slapped his good hand over his mouth to keep from puking everywhere.

Archibald Boyle.

Laid out like a science class experiment.

Eyelids held open by metal clamps, the left eyeball missing, and his jaw wrenched open, the Boyle family patriarch stared at the ceiling in a perpetual, silent scream. Arms missing, flaps of skin flayed open and nailed to a plank of wood between him and the mattress. There was no rib cage – *where the fuck were the bones*? – between his organs and the outside world. The skin of his legs was spread open along cut seams in his thighs and shins, the skin nailed to the wood, exposing dull brown leg bones.

Riley had no love for Archibald. Any true consternation his parents ever had stemmed from this man instigating false rumors among shared customers, or spewing slanderous words around the community, or prompting litigious disagreements about property boundaries, or arguing about an escaped horse that had caused property damage. Archibald had released a million other little devils upon the Winters. Riley wished more than his fair share of ills upon the man, but… this? He didn't even know what *this* was!

"I needed to practice," came from behind Riley.

Fists up, Riley spun.

"Amos!"

"Lucky day," Amos mumbled. Lips twitching like an electrocuted frog, he smiled. "Silas only needed one of you, now he gets both."

Riley reeled back to punch, but Amos was too quick. A shove and Riley's breath left him as he toppled backwards. Into Archibald's open chest cavity.

Archibald squelched and shifted around Riley's shoulders and head upon impact. His injured hand popped painfully. He squirmed to get up and out of Archibald, to escape the oozy tube webbing of intestines. In one coordinated effort, he spread his arms wide and kicked both feet in unison. He bucked his hips and then clenched his abs to sit up.

Amos approached with knife raised. "You'll make the perfect body for him."

Riley had no idea which muscles he used, but he flexed and lunged from the bed, slamming into Amos, sending him careening off the nearby wall. Falling to the ground, the madman screamed, "He's here! He's still in the house!"

Riley hurdled over Amos and ran out into the dining room, heading for the sitting room, the way to the front door. But someone shot out from behind the folding doors and into the dining room. A small man with glasses. He sprinted along the other side of the dining room table, then threw himself at Riley.

As a quarterback, Riley had been tackled a million times while running, so he braced himself for impact with the floor. The man was way smaller, and all Riley had to do was push him away and get to his feet.

Then the doorbell rang.

Followed by door-shaking knocking.

"Boyle!" boomed from outside.

Dad!

Hope ignited behind Riley's chest as he got to his hands and knees. "Dad! I'm—"

A weight fell on his back, forcing the wind from his lungs and blowing away his voice. God, his throat and neck hurt – the attack had injured his Adam's Apple or voice box or who knows what. All he knew was that he no longer yelled beyond burning whispers.

Riley's instincts took hold as he flopped like fish to find Amos on top of him. An elbow to Amos' face elicited a stream of blood from his mouth. A second elbow strike and Amos relented enough for Riley to flip over. The smaller man with glasses stood by the dining room table, watching.

"Boyle!" Dad yelled again. "I don't like entering without being invited, but I'm going to open the door!"

Yes! Open the door! Riley tried to call out again, but only a raspy noise escaped his mouth. God damn Amos! Riley punched Amos repeatedly in the face. Harder, faster until he was able to shove the pig farmer off him.

The front door opened and Dad was louder, clearer. "Boyle! I'm coming in! I'm just looking for the boys. Rand? Riley? Are you here?"

"Yes! Yes! Fucking yes!" he whispered. Panic set in knowing his dad couldn't hear him. Riley flipped over and got to his hands and knees again. He planted his right foot to stand, but his left went out from under him. Someone had grabbed it.

And pulled.

At first, he thought it was either Amos or the guy with the glasses, but as he slid backwards on his belly through the dining room, he passed by both men. In a flash, he was in the kitchen, the folding doors closing in front of him.

Fingers gripped his hair.

His throat hurt.

He'd never speak again.

CHAPTER 31

Silas was panting, which was an odd feeling since his chest didn't rise on the inhale nor fall on the exhale. His lungs inflated and deflated within its sealed crate, breath moving in and out of a hole in his wooden face. He was tired and sore, weak from the need for more blood. "God damn, that boy was tough as a bucking bronco. Took all three of us to bring him down."

"Agreed," Johnny whispered as he scurried into the kitchen. He hurried to the sink and grabbed a large mixing bowl to collect the blood pouring from Riley's neck.

Hands pressed against his bleeding nose and lips, Amos entered the room after Johnny. Whispering as well, he said, "You ain't seen nothin'. Their father is here and he's bigger. Much bigger."

A quarter of his mouth missing from his tussle with Rand, Silas used what remained to smile. "Well, go get him for me."

"Fuck you," Amos snapped, spraying bloodied slobber, his voice flirting to rise above a whisper. "You don't know him like I do. You don't know what he's like."

Glaring at Amos with his nephew's eyes, Silas pointed to the kitchen doorway that led into the hallway. "I don't care none about that. I care about that voice of his. I want that throat to make my words sound like God Himself."

"Boyle!" Hank's voice was getting closer. Silas guessed him to be in the sitting room, close to the dining room. "Where are you? Any of you. I'm looking for the boys and I heard they came here with Mercer. Like I said, I'm not a fan of entering someone's house uninvited, but there's been a lot of weird things happening lately."

"You don't get it," Amos said, fear quivering in his voice. "Hank Winters is Pecos Bill and Paul Bunyan all rolled up in one."

Crouching in between Amos and Silas, Johnny whispered, "Like it or not Amos, we must deal with him. He is in the house and could enter through the kitchen doors at any minute."

"We let him enter," Silas said. "Ambush him and kill him."

Johnny shook his head. "No. Amos, you meet him in the dining room. Lead him back to the foyer; I don't care what you have to tell him to get him moving. Hold him there and I'll come from behind. Silas, you stay in the kitchen until it's time to engage him. You'll provide both ample surprise and strength."

"This is a shit idea," Amos muttered.

"You ain't got no better ones, so get movin'," Silas said.

Johnny grabbed his scalpel and slithered his way from the kitchen to the hallway like the snake he was. Grumbling, Amos straightened and wiped blood from his face with a nearby hand towel. He threw it to the floor and pushed through the folding doors into the dining room.

"Hey, Hank. You know my brother would frown upon this."

Amos purposely left the folding doors ajar, allowing enough space for Silas to looky-loo from the kitchen. Hank was a big'un, all right! A bull on hind legs. Silas would love to live a life looking like that, but he glanced over his shoulder at Riley's body. No, that kid's body was the one for Silas. And his eyes; those big, beautiful, endless eyes. Not his face, though. Rand's face, and that manipulative smile, was his destiny.

"I get that, Amos," Hank said. "But I'm looking for the boys."

"The boys?" Amos repeated, his voice swinging upward. Silas doubted Amos' skill as a poker player. "Why would the boys be here, of all places?"

"I heard that Mercer came by our ranch and collected the boys to bring back here for reasons unclear to anyone."

"Well, Hank, that doesn't sound like Mercer or your kids."

"No, it doesn't, Amos." Hank squinted and glanced around. "I can't help but notice, though, that the lights are off with nighttime beckoning. Even as such, I can still see that you got a good amount of blood coming from your nose and mouth. Add that with this dining room being in shambles, it's easy to believe that a fight happened here."

"Well, Hank, I'm sure I don't have to spell it out to you that it's none of your business."

"If my boys are involved, then—"

"Hank!" a shout from the far end of the sitting room. A Mexican looking man stumbled in from the foyer, grimacing with his hands covering a wound in the side of his belly. "Hank! Look out!"

Hank turned, growling like a lion ready to pounce. Johnny stabbed the Mexican in the back again and again, until he dropped to his knees. Before Hank could help, Amos grabbed the closest chair and threw it at him.

The chair bounced off the mountain of a man and then skidded into the sitting room, only to redirect Hank's attention back to Amos. Holding another chair with the legs pointed outward like a lion tamer, Amos yelled, "Silas! Silas, get out here! I need help!"

Silas opened the kitchen door and sauntered into the dining room. He paused; there was something about Amos' panic that plucked a humorous cord.

"Silas!" Amos screamed again, backing away as Hank advanced. The scared rube followed the corner of the table, removing himself from between Silas and Hank. The bigger man's eyes widened when he noticed Silas.

"Well, fuck it," Silas said to himself as he launched himself at Hank.

Hank's surprise lasted a heartbeat, then he swung a massive fist at Silas' head. And connected with the force of lightning striking a tree.

Silas wondered how his head was still attached to his body after that hit. Had he still been human, he doubted he'd have lived through it. Hank didn't stop, the man a living locomotive. With one hand, he flung a chair at Amos. As it crashed into the moron, Hank charged Silas and slammed him against the wall. Hank lifted Silas off his feet. Face souring as if he'd chomped on a lemon peel, he asked, "Mercer, what is wrong with you?"

"Nothing, old man. I killed your kids and stashed them in the kitchen, so I'm right as rain."

With a roar that vibrated everything inside Silas, Hank twisted and slammed Silas onto the dining room table. There was a crack of wood and Silas had no idea if it was him or the table. Somehow, he felt pain and started to think it was him. Leaving him on the table, Hank stormed through the doors and into the kitchen.

Silas had heard many cries before, most of which he had caused. Pain. Frustration. Sorrow. Anger. Never had one contained each of those emotions, nor been loud enough to shake a house. Until now.

"What'd the fuck you do that for?" Amos asked Silas, peeling himself from the floor.

Mercer's skin was all kinds of askew, none of it fitting as it should. An ache went from his shoulders to his hips, but Silas pushed past that and hopped off the table. The windows of opportunity were known to slam shut fast, so Silas had to be faster.

He grabbed two fistfuls of Amos' shirt. Right before shoving Amos through the folding doors, he said, "Lead him down the hall to the foyer."

"Fuck!" Amos screamed, stumbling backwards into the kitchen.

The noise of commotion would have been comical if Silas' survival was a certainty. Clangs of pots and pans hitting the walls and floor rang out as did Hank's animal screams and Amos' frantic profanities. The sounds indicated that Amos was following Silas' instruction.

Silas ran from the dining room, through the sitting room, past the dead Mexican slumped against the wall. If only he'd had time to collect the blood pouring from him… but he had to focus on his timing.

He hadn't known Johnny for long, but hoped he was as conniving as he came across. Sure enough, as Silas exited the sitting room, he spied Johnny crouching in front of the stairs, doing his best to use the banister post as a shield.

Hank was pursuing Amos hard, but Silas had enough time to push Amos into Archibald's game room, and not the kinda game room for cards and checkers. He had to prepare himself for Hank. As the beast of rage ran by the stairs, Johnny lashed out and sliced the scalpel across Hank's thigh. It elicited a grunt of pain, but Silas knew well enough it would take much more than that to stop him. Aiming low, Silas slammed into Hank. Burying his head into the larger man's ribs, he drove with his legs and pushed him into the game room, hoping Amos was waiting with an ambush. His hopes were dashed as Amos struggled to get to his feet in the corner of the room.

Hank set his foot and grabbed Silas by the back of the shirt. Silas flipped through the air twice before slamming face first into a built-in bookshelf. Only four books in the whole damn thing, but plenty of taxidermized small game on the shelves poked and dug into him. Hank must have been near the light switch, because the room lit up as Silas collapsed to the floor.

Heads of animals, ten times the size of Silas, peeked out from various places along the other walls. Things with horns and snouts and fangs looked down upon Silas as he clambered to his feet. "Blazin' Hell, Amos, we just gave him weapons."

Animal heads weren't the only trophies mounted on the walls. Antique guns long since discharged adorned the walls as well as swords and spears. The pompous ass Archibald even had a suit of armor. A pair of axes fit for Viking hands hung crisscrossed near the doorway, but they looked like trinkets when Hank grabbed them.

"We got weapons of our own," Amos said. Nothing but books and stuffed critters behind Silas. Was Amos planning on reading Hank to death? Or did he think throwing long-dead animals at the hulk would stop him? But the snarl on Amos' face told Silas the plan, a half-second too late. Amos shoved Silas toward Hank, and ran to the side wall.

A string of profanity flowed through Silas' head like sluicing logs. None made it out of his mouth; Hank took a step and swung both axes downward, sinking a blade into each of Silas' shoulders. Shirt and skin split wide, exposing the slimy wood underneath. The only person more shocked than Silas was Hank. Blessed be all the saints and sinners for that, because Silas needed a breather.

Brows mashed into a "V," Hank stepped back. "What in the name of Hell are you?"

"Your death!" Amos screamed as he charged toward Hank with a spear in hand.

The weapon was longer than Amos was tall and proved unwieldy since the tip pierced Hank's leg instead of his chest or belly.

Hank bellowed again yet had the wherewithal to grab the spear behind the tip and dislodge it from his thigh. Of course, donkey-ass Amos was too stupid to let go of the pole. With a roar like the bear-head mounted on the wall above him, Hank threw Amos.

Releasing the pole at the wrong moment, Amos crashed head over giblets into the suit of armor. And Hank wasn't done with him yet.

Grabbing one of the axes with both hands, Hank pressed the sole of his boot against Silas' chest and pushed. The blade burst free, taking chunks of wood and pieces of meaty skin with it. *Fuck, that hurt!* Silas stumbled backwards and crashed into a shelf, books toppling onto him.

The clang of metal against metal rang out, echoing in the confinement of the room. Hank hacked at the full body shield protecting Amos as he squirmed behind it on the floor.

Amos screamed, "Silas! Help!"

The thought of letting the devil take his due from that yellow-belly Amos crossed Silas' mind, but Johnny was nowhere to be found. Silas didn't want to face Hank by himself. Running wasn't an option. But neither was an easy attack.

Hank – beating the ever-living Hell out of the shield as each ear-splitting clang rang out to the beat of Mercer's heart within Silas' chest – stood between Silas and the wall of weapons. Silas had access to one weapon, though, and it was sticking out of his shoulder.

The mannequin chest might have been hollow, but the area running from shoulder to shoulder was solid wood that somehow had the ability to repair itself when damaged. The gouge made when Hank had ripped the first axe out of Silas' shoulder was now half the size. The wood surrounding the second axe-gouge, axe still embedded in that shoulder, had a bit of grip.

Silas wrapped both hands around the axe handle, made slippery by the pink goop oozing from between the cuts on his hands. The first tug, nothing. The second yank moved the blade, but a hand slipped free.

CLANG! CLANG!

"Silas! Hurry!"

CLANG! CLANG!

Doing his best to work a tighter grip, Silas grabbed the handle again with both hands and eyed the nearest wall to use for leverage. The bookshelf.

CLANG! CLANG!

"Silas!"

As hard as he could muster, Silas slammed the handle against the bookshelf, knuckles in between. *Hellfire, that hurt!* He wasn't sure how or why, but his fingers burned and his shoulder throbbed. No time for thinking about the pain, he smashed against the shelf again. And again. The blade eked a little closer to release, and he bashed himself against the wall shelving one more time.

The axe popped free – *Finally!* – and Silas stumbled backwards, almost dropping it. Time to save his fool minion.

Amos squealed like the pigs, kicking at his attacker anytime an opportunity arose. It did little to slow Hank's strikes against the shield, the thing now folded like a taco shell. Right as Hank reeled back for another swing, Silas drove his axe into the mountainous man's back.

With a roar between anger and pain, Hank backhanded Silas halfway across the room. Loosened skin flopping all over the place, Silas got to his feet and ran back to the fray. Amos might not have been as dimwitted as his nature indicated, because he took full advantage of the distraction and dropped the shield to pick up the spear. This time, he rammed the tip into Hank's gut. But the damned man still had fight left in him.

Silas reached for the axe, but Hank delivered a world-shaking punch, knocking Silas to the ground. But Hank was slower now, weaker. The suit of armor Amos had crashed into held a sword, one that he needed both hands to hold. Blood sprayed from Amos' mouth now that it was his turn to scream with rage. He lunged forward, pointy end first. Even a rube like Amos couldn't miss from that distance.

The blade went clean through Hank's thigh, the one untouched by Amos' earlier spear attack. Hellfire, Hank still had enough fire in his belly to send Amos backwards with a punch!

Everyone was panting and wary. The heavy breathing for all three slowed, but when Hank clenched his fists and grit his teeth, Silas felt a chill skitter down his wooden back. How did this man still have any fight left? Was he, too, made from some possessed wood?

Johnny – *finally he shows up* – ran into the room, carrying plastic bowls with a blue tarp under an arm. He placed the bowls on the ground and hurried to unroll the tarp behind Hank while the fire behind the rancher's eyes reignited. Both Silas and Amos hurried to grab the spear's shaft. In unison, they gave one final shove, driving the tip the rest of the way through Hank, punching it out of his back, finally extinguishing the flame.

At last, Hank Winters fell straight back like a chopped tree.

As soon as he hit the tarp, Johnny rushed to capture the flowing blood into the bowls.

Silas dropped to his haunches, laughing. "Well, boys, that was exciting!"

Blood flowing from his face, Amos limped over to Johnny. "Exciting ain't the word I'd use. Crazy. Reckless. Sloppy. You gotta stop killin' everyone all willy-nilly!" Amos yelled. "We need to come up with a plan on what to do with all these dead bodies!"

"I got a plan," Silas said.

"You ain't got no plan! You don't know the meaning of the word!"

"No? I made a plan and everything about it is going as smooth as ice over glass. In fact, I called the number you gave me for the hookers a bit ago. They're going to be here in two hours. You up for a challenge, Doc?"

Johnny looked around the room as if he could see through all the walls of the house. "I would have preferred more time, but I can do what you want me to do in the allotment given."

"Good attitude, Doc. How about it, Amos? Up for the challenge?"

Amos didn't answer; he simply crouched down and helped Johnny collect Hank's blood.

CHAPTER 32

The Boyle house doorbell rang.

Johnny stood at the top of the stairs, impartial and unmoving. Observing. Down the hall, a door closed; Silas had exited the master bedroom in his new, beautiful Frankensteined body.

"Doc, this is it. I feel complete, intact. This fits me," Silas said, his voice capable of commanding armies to their demise with an eagerness in his step. A rigid voice as old as the Earth didn't belong to a face so young, so malleable.

"Excellent. I am intrigued to see the validity of your claim."

Silas twirled, presenting himself to the doctor. Rand's head with his shoulder length blond hair and smile that altered the mood of anyone who beheld it; Riley's muscular body, as well as his eyes, attuned to the souls of everyone who looked into them. And the coveted piece of Hank he now possessed – his voice.

Silas slapped Johnny's back. "I gotta thank you for gettin' me set up so quickly."

Johnny didn't appreciate having to rush the job, but pride tickled him; he'd done an exceptional job under the circumstances, which included quickly exsanguinating the bodies, and then throwing a plastic tarp onto Archibald's bed to perform the surgeries. He also didn't like that they had to store the bodies in the master bedroom's bathtub, but they were pressed for time. The doorbell chimed again and Johnny said, "I believe the women of ill-repute are here."

Silas rubbed his hands together like a starving cur eyeing abattoir scraps. "Oh, this is gonna be good."

Johnny moved aside as Silas started down the stairs. He leaned his forearms against the banister. "Remember to keep them out of the master bedroom, lest we need to take care of them as well."

"Don't worry none, Doc. No more killin' for today."

Wearing only gray sweatpants, Silas opened the door with a flourish. "Welcome ladies! Oh, four of you. Even better." He gestured for them to enter.

Silas had ordered three prostitutes – one each for himself, Johnny, and Amos. However, Johnny respectfully declined the offer. With earlier events going the direction they had, Silas determined that Amos' swollen face would sour the lustful mood of the evening and ordered him to stay at the Tomlin property after relocating Hank's truck there. Johnny suspected that the motivation was more of a sadistic powerplay on Silas' part.

"Even though you're quite a hottie, it's just the three of us, Stud," the shortest of the four said while leading the women into the house. She blew Silas a kiss, her lipstick as brown as her chocolate hair. "I'm Babydoll. This is Jinx and she's Starla."

The ebon-haired beauty, Jinx, slunk into the foyer with eyes roaming. She took in the scene even as she paused to run her long red-lacquered fingertips over Silas' new face. Starla, the honey blonde with a friendly smile, clasped a gray portable stereo – a boombox, if Johnny recalled the correct term – by the handle with both hands.

"Yeah? Only three? Then who's she?" Silas asked, leering at the young woman entering last.

Johnny shifted from one foot to the other the moment he saw her. Lucid and focused – the other three had obviously smoked or drank or snorted a mood enhancement – her big glasses didn't hinder a single element about her face.

"Beth," Babydoll answered. "She's the one you pay after the party."

"She's also our bodyguard," Jinx said. "She makes sure everyone behaves."

Beth was armed. Her red sequined handbag plenty big enough to hold an arsenal of makeup as well as a handgun. She implied as much by her aiming her purse, finger on the zipper as a trigger. She then looked up at Johnny and smirked. He shifted his weight again.

As Silas led the women up the stairs he said, "I'm sure hopin' you ladies don't intend to behave!"

"Of course not, Stud. You're paying us to misbehave," Babydoll said.

"And to party," Starla added, holding up the boombox. "There're two more dudes, right?"

"Change of plans." Silas reached the landing, and extended his hands toward Mercer's bedroom. "Just me tonight."

Jinx walked by Johnny, gliding her red fingernails across his cheek. "Oh yeah? Then who are you?"

Silas placed a hand on the small of her back, encouraging her past Johnny and into the bedroom. "Him? That's Johnny. He's my bodyguard."

"Alright," Babydoll said as she entered the bedroom. "Let's get the party started!"

"Woooo!" Starla squealed and hit "play" on the boombox. An electronic beat started, and she danced her way into the bedroom. Laughing, Silas followed, throwing the door shut behind him.

Beth chuckled. "Starla has been on a Nine Inch Nails kick lately."

"I don't know what that means," Johnny replied.

Beth shook her head. She looked up and down the hallway. "There someplace we can hang out? Like a bodyguard lounge or something?"

Johhny appreciated her humor – nothing as uproarious as Silas' these past couple of weeks – and rewarded her with a soft smile. "Not quite, sorry. But there is a home office over here."

He led her into a small, square room with two wooden chairs – the same type of chairs found in the dining room – their backs against the wall by the door. A corner desk took up its share of wall space with a cheap black rolling chair parked in front of it. Three metal filing cabinets stood along the other wall. Johnny flipped on the overhead light, positioned a wooden chair in the center of the room, then sat.

Beth turned off the light, bringing darkness back to the room. The foyer chandelier made a weak attempt to stretch its light beyond the doorway. She sauntered to the room's lone window, and cracked the blinds to allow in slats of moonlight. "There," she said. "Now it's a seedy back office where all the bodyguards hang out. The shadows, a safe place for a couple of world-weary souls to share their dark deeds within the only home they know." She sat in the office chair and rolled to Johnny, their knees touching. "Maybe I've been reading too many cheap, pulp noir novels. I like to read. Do you like to read?"

"I do," Johanny answered. "Alas, my tastes don't lie in fiction, rather medical journals and reference books regarding the human body."

With a simple push of her foot, Beth pivoted, her right leg aligned against Johnny's left. She rubbed his thigh. "Reference books on the human body? I'm guessing that makes you quite the expert?"

As gently as extracting a butterfly with no harm befalling it, Johnny moved her hand from his leg to hers. "I apologize for the misunderstanding, but I am not partaking in tonight's festivities. I don't wish to part with any funds at this moment in my life and – pardon the lack of aplomb in my next statement – I'll be damned if I put myself into debt with Silas."

Beth smiled, offering a connection that Johnny hadn't seen for quite a long time. Another push with her foot and she wheeled behind him. Her warm breath flowed over Johnny's neck as she leaned in to say something, but stopped when Silas streaked by, naked. She giggled, then asked, "Where do we think he's going?"

"Probably the master bedroom," Johnny answered. "That's where the bathroom is."

Another giggle as Beth spun the chair again, her left leg now pressed against his right. Her hand slid onto his leg. Shoulder to shoulder, she whispered into his ear, her words tingling along the way. "The other three girls are 'working' tonight, not me. Everything I've done and said so far does not imply a transactional obligation. Including this." Beth moved her hand up Johnny's leg until she reached his crotch. She cupped his erection, which was painfully obvious.

Silas, sporting one of his own, dashed past the open door again. Mercer's bedroom opened to squeals of excitement that faded away when the bedroom door closed.

A half rotation of the chair was all it took for Beth to wheel in front of Johnny, intertwining their legs. Her fingers glided up his cheeks and delicately gripped the arms of his glasses. As she started to slide them from his face, he brought his hands to hers. "I feel helpless without them."

With a smile of encouragement, she pushed his glasses back to position. Tips of their noses only a whisper apart, she said, "Then I'll keep mine on, too."

"Okay."

She ran her fingers through his hair. "Do you like that?"

The infinitesimal number of times his mother had ever shown the slightest physical affection toward him as a child was whenever an ailment befell him. His fondest memories of childhood were the sweaty chills or the stomach cramps after vomiting, because those moments called forth bedrest and Mother's fingers through his hair. Beth was eliciting childhood memories, but the strongest memory was still when his mother had purchased a gleaming new scalpel after he had butchered his father. "Yes. That feels nice."

As Beth's thumbs drifted along his temples, down his cheeks, and gently over his lips, he realized that this was the most inopportune time for Mother to enter his thoughts, so he evicted her. Not a moment too soon as Beth leaned in and kissed him. It was light, playful, the tip of her tongue flicking the tip of his.

"Did you like that?" Beth asked.

"Yes. That felt nice."

"I like nice guys," Beth said.

"I could be a murderer."

"You're no murderer."

"How can you be so certain?"

"I see it in your eyes," Beth said. "I see that you could kill, but *only* if you deemed it absolutely necessary."

Uncertain why, an educated guess was that her gliding fingers set off tingles and torches that zapped his prowess to life, he felt the need to tell her, "I tackled someone today. It was the first time I ever tackled anyone. A man. Larger than myself."

"Yeah? Tell me about it."

"I'd like to, but... I can't picture it in my mind."

"No? Then tell me how it made you feel."

"Feel?" Yes, that he remembered. The images of Riley's size or the layout of the dining room were frustratingly muted in his mind, but the feelings? "Invigorating. Yet, vaguely frightening."

"That can be scary sometimes." Like he was clay for sculpting, she lifted his arm by the elbow and ran her index finger down a surprisingly ticklish part of his palm. All five fingers splayed at the sensation. Her fingertips to his fingertips, she flattened her palm against his. Less ticklish this time, she ran her hand down his inner forearm and said, "This hand isn't made for hitting. Why did you tackle him?"

"He stole something."

"Then it seems you had a good enough reason to tackle him." As she undid his belt, Johnny unequivocally understood her intentions. He had only performed this act once before, in college. Coitus never took priority in his mind, but a drunk girl at a soiree had aggressively expressed physically romantic interest. For the sake of experience, he went along with her carnal requests. Squishy and chaotic, he ultimately wound up where biology dictated. The girl? Once finished, she threw up and passed out. Johnny studied her for the following month as she repeated those exact actions at least twice a week, a different man each time. He assumed it was due to an overactive libido, so two months later he operated on her, hoping to find it.

"Do you believe that I had a good reason?" he asked.

Beth moved off her chair, her hands to Johnny's pants, her lips to his ear. She unzipped his pants, and said, "You did the right thing, Johnny. I can tell that you always do what you think is right."

When Beth moved away, she took his pants with her, sliding them down his legs to his ankles. The wooden chair felt hard and cold against his bare bottom, but she slid her hands up his thighs and over his erection, redirecting all of his sensation to his groin. She shimmed her skirt upward, over her hips, and then straddled him. Just as squishy as before, but nowhere nearly as chaotic.

Obfuscated by shadows, Beth moved her face closer to Johnny's, her red lips glinting when caught by a stray moonbeam. Such a vision, and he hoped he'd be able to remember it.

"Do you dream when you sleep?" he asked. "Sorry for the stupid question." His mind was muddled by internal sparks skittering around – more experiments would be needed to explain that phenomena. But not now. "I know every human being dreams when they sleep. What I meant to ask was, do you remember them? Do you recall the ethereal moments not meant for the waking world?"

"I do."

From the corner of his eye, Johnny saw Silas run past the doorway, naked and flaccid, streaking toward the master bedroom again. "Tell me about them."

Beth pressed her chest against his, one hand snaking around and finding a home on his back, her other hand burrowing deep into his hair. She pressed her cheek against his as she whispered, "Sometimes I'm a far-away person in far-away places. Other times I'm right here, right now. I even saw your face in one of my dreams."

Impossible. She was lying to him, but her gyrations mushed his mind. All he could muster was, "I don't believe you."

"Saw your face just once. Occasionally, I dream about a witch. She wears a different face each time. Old. Young. Weathered. Fresh. Soft. Wicked. But no matter how she looks, I know it's her. She shows me things. The far-away people. The far-away places. The here. The now."

Johnny gripped the sides of the chair seat. His thoughts became very wet. "Describe them."

"Forests and jungles, lush and dripping with life, every color of every rainbow rushing over trees and plants and flowers." Beth's voice seemed to function on its own as words flowed from her mouth into his soul, faster with every syllable passing over her lips. "Beautiful angels living in fire, their bodies pierced and tattooed, their wings too. Oceans and rivers and rain running red. Whole other worlds where the colors of everything are reversed, turned inside out. Lands made of metal and trees grown from glass. The stars beyond it all, big and bright, burning for millions of years, bounding through the dark, black space. Crashing. Smashing into each other. Again and again, and again until... everything... *explodes*..."

Beth's entire body quivered and she tightened her grip on him as his own orgasm called forth flashes of bright colors behind closed eyes. Nuzzling her cheek against his neck, slicked with sweat, she whispered, "Hold me. For a minute."

Through the gauze covering his mind, Johnny did as she asked, unsure as to why she made the request, but this was not the time to evaluate. He had certainly enjoyed this experience more than he had in college, the pleasure unparalleled. However, both times, the orgasm had temporarily muted his mental capacity, which was unacceptable, no matter how temporary. Never again could he allow his mind to be addled as such.

"Thank you," Beth whimpered.

Silas hurried by their doorway yet again, his new erection leading the way.

CHAPTER 33

Amanda watched the second hand tick smoothly from one number to the next on her kitchen clock. It was a simple circle with gold Roman numerals enclosed a wooden frame. She had no particular affinity to the clock; it was an alternative to what Hank had wanted to hang – a classic Texaco clock. No way she was going to allow a big red star that advertised petroleum products in her home. So, he'd hung it in the barn where he could visit it, thanks to him listening to reason. Amanda couldn't take her eyes off the hands creeping past eight o'clock – Hank and Ramos had been gone for over two hours, the boys gone even longer.

"The soup is delicious, Mrs. Winters," Javi said.

Amanda sat with Javi, Tilde, and Barnes around the kitchen table which fit nicely in the corner. The small table only sat four, and it was perfect for lunches and snacks. She never served dinner at this table; the dining room was for that. But the ham and bean soup had simmered long enough and it'd be a shame not to enjoy it while it was hot. She didn't know Tilde and Barnes well, but she doubted they'd eaten anything other than food from a box or a wrapper since they'd arrived at the ranch, and they were the only two people on the film crew that hadn't pissed her off these past few weeks.

"Thank you, Javi." A forced grin, but it was the best she could do under the circumstances. Afterall, his father had been gone for just as long as Hank. A twitchy smile played at his lips, and he went back to eating his soup.

Tilde and Barnes had a unique... style. Amanda wasn't sure how she felt about their green or blue hair or partially shaved heads, but they seemed kind. She appreciated their furtive glances of concern and sympathy. All three of her guests had finished their soup, which she also appreciated, though she barely had two bites from her own bowl – a testament to how distracted she'd been. "Please, no need to wait for me. Help yourself to as much as you'd like."

Bowls in hands, all three made their way to the pot on the stove and thanked her in unison. Amanda decided to make a more concerted effort to finish her dinner, but as she dipped her spoon into the broth, the phone rang. The call was a little late for a social call, and Amanda answered with a wary tone. "Winters' residence."

"Amanda? This is Sheriff Pete Cunnigham." Amanda would have recognized his voice right away, so her skin prickled at the formal introduction. "Apologies for calling at such an unusual time and I hope I didn't cause any undue concern, but my deputy and I are on our way to your ranch and didn't feel right about stopping by unannounced. See, we got word that the movie people's pickup was found in Duke City, so we wanted to swing by to deliver the news and see what that producer-fella wants to do."

"Hi, Pete." A warm sense of relief chased away a few of the chills, but not all of them. "That's wonderful news, and I appreciate the call."

"Is everything alright? You sound a bit tense."

"Everything is… Well, I was going to say, 'fine,' but that's not entirely true. It's a bit chaotic over here, even more so with the boys and Hank missing."

"Missing?"

"Missing might not be the right word, because I know where they went, they've just been gone way too long."

"Where'd they go?"

"The Boyles' house."

"Did…? Did you say they went to the Boyles' house?"

Amanda offered a sad chuckle of disbelief. "Your ears didn't deceive you, Pete. We were told that Mercer invited the boys over. Hank didn't like the sound of that, so he and Ramos went to check on things. Like I said, that was a couple hours ago."

"I tell you what – we're only ten minutes away, so we'll make a quick stop to the Boyles' to see what's what. How's that sound?"

"That sounds perfect. Thank you so much, Pete."

"No problem at all. See you in a bit."

Amanda hung up the phone and turned to see three pairs of eyes looking at her from the table. Having no appetite with her insides all squirmy, Amanda needed to get out of the house. "That was the sheriff. Apparently, the truck that went missing from the movie set has been found. He's on his way over, but I'm going to let Nixon and Miles know."

"Don't worry about cleanup, Mrs. Winters. We'll take care of it," Tilde said with a wide-eyed look of wanting to say more, do more.

"Thank you, Tilde."

Outside was far more chaotic than normal at this time of night. The house's floodlights, the barn lights, and a few other temporary movie lights provided plenty of shine on the lawn, driveway, and paddock. Like the star he was, Bo paced in the middle of all the glare. A black cellular phone with extended antenna pressed to his ear, he nodded while speaking. "I agree, Joel. She's being irrational. I only made that suggestion to help position her for contract renegotiation. Yeah. Yeah. Yep, I agree."

Miles also paced while on his cellphone, but at the perimeter of the lighting. Every few circuits, he walked past Bo, looking like a parody of a before-and-after photo. His whispered words were hurried, becoming louder and more desperate as his conversation continued.

Centered in the confluence of lights, Nixon stood in front of a semicircle of supporting actors, wardrobe people, makeup artists, and set designers. All sought answers from the one man who looked more confused than a priest at a nudist colony. Amanda hated to add more to his plate, but it was time he lay in the bed he made.

"We just want to know if we should pack up and head home," one of the girls from wardrobe asked.

"Look, the movie's not dead," Nixon replied. "You can probably see and hear Bo on the phone with Joel right now. He's been on and off with him for hours, and he says each conversation ends better than the last. Miles is on the phone with our investors, keeping them in the loop."

"And it's pretty late," Amanda added. "We're about equal distance between Santa Fe and Albuquerque, but either way you head, there'll be long stretches of empty land with no lights. It's in everyone's best interest to get a good night sleep here and see how the world looks with tomorrow's sun shining on it."

Members of the small crowd looked at each other sharing knowing glances, a few whispers, and head-nodding. The crowd broke apart, but no one left the general area, content to mill about and keep an eye on Bo, Nixon, and Miles. As the producer and lead actor walked in circles, Amanda approached Nixon and asked, "I thought reception was too poor here for cell phones?"

Nixon looked skyward, the brightness of the moon and stars muted by the electric lights. "Super clear night tonight, no humidity. They each have one bar, and a call will drop every once in a while."

Miles' voice quivered as he got louder. "No, Maddox, you don't need to call anyone. No, please, you definitely do not need to stop by. No, man, I'm sure. Yeah, everything is under control. Whatever you're hearing from anyone other than me is blown out of proportion. We're all good, man, we're— Hello? Hello? Fuck!"

Miles snapped the phone shut and shoved it so hard into his pocket that Amanda was surprised his pants didn't rip off. Pulling at clumps of his sweaty hair, he mumbled, "We're fucked, man. We're so fucked." His words might have been meant for Nixon, or he could have been talking to himself.

Amanda cleared her throat to get his attention, but he didn't give it to her. No matter. Loud enough for him to hear whatever his mind was focused on, she said, "Sheriff Pete will be here in about ten minutes to talk to you two. They found your missing truck in Albuquerque."

Nixon reeled backwards, eyes wider than a spooked horse. Miles glanced at her, a slight curl to his upper lip, a sneer of annoyance. Amanda dug deep to forgive his rudeness, reminding herself that the young man had put all his money, as well as other people's money, into this movie. He sulked away mumbling to himself.

Removing his black Stetson to wipe a few stray locks out of his eyes, Nixon said, "Thank you, Mrs. Winters, for the information about the van. And for what you said to the crew. You have a great way with people."

"Thanks, Nixon. Half the secret to dealing with people is being open with them. Show them what they might not be seeing."

Nixon worked his bottom lip, his bloodshot droopy eyes making him look sadder than a kicked puppy. Amanda knew that look and a knot formed in her gut.

"Well," Nixon said, "The crew haven't made their way back to their trailers, so maybe just sharing information isn't enough..." The end of his sentence dangled like a worm from a hook.

Amanda didn't take the bait. "Nixon, I appreciate the vote of confidence, but *you* are the director. *You* are one of their leaders. I already have two of your crew in my house, and my mind isn't the clearest right now with Hank and the boys not back yet."

Nixon nodded. He put on his Stetson, securing his hair from his face. "You're right Mrs. Winters. I apologize for the way things are going."

"It's okay. You're doing your best."

Standing a little straighter, the director headed toward a small group of crew members.

One problem off her plate, but so many more to deal with. Amanda walked back to her house, then paused and looked in the direction of the Boyles' house. She needed to get her shotgun ready.

CHAPTER 34

Johnny paid Beth, the night air bringing the pigpen stink into the house through the open door. Jinx sat in the driver seat of an old model hatchback, engine running and headlights on. Babydoll and Stella whooped and cheered as they skipped arm in arm to the car, Stella's boom box thumping with electronic music.

"Thank you," Beth said.

Johnny wasn't sure about proper goodbye-protocol, so he kept things simple with a standard, "You're welcome."

She kissed his cheek then headed toward the running car.

Silas joined Johnny at the door and put his arm around his shoulders. "Don't fall in love with your whore, Doc."

"I'm not entirely sure she is one," Johnny said. Beth opened the passenger door, then paused to wave at Johnny one last time before getting in. "And there's no worry about me falling in love with her."

Releasing Johnny, Silas laughed. As he grabbed a cigarette from the pack kept in the pocket of his sweatpants, he said, "Well, she certainly liked you. What kind of snake are you packin' in your trousers?"

Johnny ignored the question and shut the front door. "How are you feeling in your new body?"

"I feel..." Silas paused to take a deep drag from his cigarette. He then extended his arms in cruciform and blew streams of smoke from his nose. "Infinite."

"No looseness? Any parts sliding away from your wooden skeleton?"

Silas laughed and strolled from the foyer to the hallway, toward the kitchen. "Nah, Doc. I'm right as rain. And wetter, too."

"No ill effects at all?"

Once in the kitchen, Silas leaned against the counter and glanced at the closed door to Amos' room. "None more than what was in my head at birth. Speakin' of ill effects... You can come out now, Amos."

After a minute of silence, Silas barked, "I know you're in your room, ya circus geek. I told you to move Hank's truck to the Tomlin house but it's still outside."

The door opened with a creak and Amos limped out, face swollen and bruised, a droplet or two of orange plasma seeping from a cut on his cheek. "Ain't fair that I didn't get none. If it weren't for me, you woulda never had them girls here."

Taking another pull of his cigarette, Silas squinted at Amos, the new god of youth and immortality weighing judgement against his most faithful disciple. He let the ash fall to the kitchen floor. "And do you think they woulda stayed with you lookin' the way you're lookin' right now? Like a bull trampled on your face and pissed on it for good measure?"

Amos hobbled to the freezer and grabbed a bag of frozen peas to press against his face. "Archibald never allowed smoking in his house."

"This is your house now, Amos, according to your brother's corpse in your bedroom."

Amos stared into his bedroom as if he had never seen it before. Silas' words unlocked something inside him, a realization. "So what?"

Johnny wasn't sure to whom the question was directed, nor its subject, but he pounced at the opportunity to address his new directive. "So... I believe the next course of action should be more experiments. On Silas."

"Experiments?" Silas said. "Why in the devil's ass would I want more experiments?"

"Your quest to become human again – or at least take human form since I have yet to conceive of a measurable parameter to determine exactly what you are – has made you monomaniacal, leaving you blind to the other half of yourself."

"There ain't no other half, Doc. And I *am* human. I have human thoughts and human urges and human movements. There ain't no other 'measurable parameter' I need figured out."

"I believe you misinterpreted my meaning. I never meant to imply that you were something less than human. You are something *more*, and we have yet to unlock your full potential."

"More than human? Potential?"

Johnny strolled to the sink's counter and gently removed a paper towel, one of the few spots in the kitchen bereft of blood, and used it to clean his glasses. "Silas, I own a holistic medicine shop. Yes, I sell more than a few items that could be classified as snake oil, but my underlying intent is hardly charlatan. I look at the body as a whole, something more than just a sack of chemicals or parts of a machine, unlike pharmaceutical companies and most doctors. There is more that makes us run, a type of magic."

Silas crinkled his face and waved his hands to shush Johnny from expounding further. "Stop. Stop, stop, stop. I'm still ridin' high from getting' my stick sticky, so I'm in no mood for your long-winded hoo-ha. Just get to the point."

Johnny sighed, disappointed he couldn't traverse the winding path he started down. He so enjoyed sharing his knowledge and viewpoints. Maybe there was something to Amos' suggestion about him becoming some form of teacher? "Your other half, Silas. The half that's under your skin. The half that drinks blood like a thirsty man wandering the desert. Your wooden half."

Silas crossed his arms over his chest and chuckled. "Yeah? My wood half? What about it?"

"When you wore the face of Caleb, then Mercer, now Rand, your visage has always conformed to the exact shape of those persons."

"Meanin'?"

"A face's shape is held into place by bones, ligaments, and tendons, none of which I included while placing the face upon your mannequin-head. Clearly your skin and muscle are capable of altering, evidenced by your ability to heal with the assistance of fresh blood. But I believe the wood beneath your skin shifts to the necessary structure, accommodating the specific face you're wearing. When we remove the face, your mannequin-head reverts to its blank features. And have you not noticed that Riley was taller than the mannequin, yet now, you're almost as tall as he was? The same could be said for when you wore Caleb's skin."

"I don't give a golden tub of donkey shit about what you just babbled, Doc."

"Why are you limiting yourself to your current shape?" Johnny asked.

Silas frowned, but before any insults could be hurled, Johnny continued. "You first awoke as a tiny wooden soldier, then moved into a bigger wooden toy soldier. Then you graduated to the wooden mannequin Amos procured for you from the movie set. To the best of my knowledge, neither a child's toy nor a seamstress' dressing form contain magic. They're both just plain, ordinary wood. The same material that we're surrounded by."

Silas and Amos looked around the kitchen. The cabinets. The trim. The doors. *The problem with limited minds is their inability to comprehend their own limitations.*

Shaking his head, Silas tossed his spent cigarette into the sink and reached into his pocket, pulling out a crumbled pack – empty. He walked toward the hallway. "Don't your big brains got anythin' better to do than think of nonsense? With this body, I got more than I ever wanted. Right now, I need more smokes."

Amos watched Silas meander down the hallway toward the stairs and mumbled, "Damned fool don't know what he's got."

"That is a true and accurate statement. But do you?"

Amos turned to Johnny. Despite the cuts, bruises, and swelling, the answer on his face was obvious.

"You have a talent," Johnny said. "I reviewed the work you've done on your brother. Your lines were straight. Your separation of bones and joints was logical and organized. Now imagine what you could do under my tutelage with further instruction from me."

The flame ignited behind his eye, transforming his expression from a kicked puppy to a dog awaiting his favorite treat in his master's hand. There was a line between desperation and elation, and Amos crossed that line just as he crossed the kitchen. "Do you mean what I think you mean?"

"I've been giving it thought," Johnny said. "Significant medical breakthroughs are the result of collaborative efforts rather than the work of an individual acting in isolation. I believe sharing my current knowledge with others will help my endeavors."

Amos smiled, winced, then smiled wider, his grin displaying one less tooth than yesterday. "You won't be disappointed," Amos said. "I wanna learn everything you have to teach. And I can think of four... no, five... five other fellas who would want to learn what you have to teach. Learn about what's inside of us, look for all of life's secrets. Figure out why we are the way we are."

Despite the grotesqueness of Amos' face, Johnny had to admit that his enthusiasm was contagious. Initially, he planned to mentor a single protégé; however, Amos' eagerness prompted him to consider additional individuals. "Yes, Amos. That's the spirit."

Amos clapped and spun in a circle. "Hot damn. I ain't never been excited about school before!"

School? Yes, I guess it could be akin to going to school. I'd be providing a higher education, after all. "Before we start looking for classrooms, we need to figure out what to do with Silas, and contemplate the ramifications of tonight's—"

The doorbell chimed.

Both men hurried from the kitchen to the foyer; Johnny positioned himself to obstruct the kitchen's view while Amos looked up the stairs, most likely looking for Silas to tell him what to do.

The bell chimed again, followed by knocking. "Archibald? This is Sheriff Pete Cunningham. I was wondering if we could have a quick word."

Fingers twisting together, Amos looked from the stairs to the door to Johnny. He jumped when the sheriff knocked again. "Archibald? Amos? Mercer?"

Amos opened the door and smiled. "Hey, Petey. What can I do for you?"

The sheriff entered the house uninvited, accompanied by another officer. Both men wore distrust and concern, their eyes glued to Amos' mangled face. "Jesus, Amos," the sheriff said. "You okay?"

Amos brushed off the question. "Yeah, I'm fine. Just got in a tussle."

"Those cuts look fresh. Was the fight recent?" the other officer asked, the hurry in his voice worrisome, hinting that he'd jump to conclusions.

Rubbing the back of his head, Amos looked to the floorboards. "Eh, you know how it is."

"Actually, I don't, Amos," the officer said as he moved deeper into the house, his hand hovering at his firearm's holster. "Did that happen in a public place? Who else was involved and was anyone hurt?"

Pete sighed and patted the air between him and the other officer. "It's alright, Travis. Unfortunately, this isn't anything new, and it's nothing to worry about. No need to be so jumpy. You can calm down."

As slowly and quietly as the shadow of a sundial, Johnny backed away, noting that Officer Travis tensed upon the command to calm down.

The sheriff turned to Amos and said, "Travis just started last week."

"And I heard twice as much about the Boyles than everyone else combined," Travis said.

"Jesus, Travis, c'mon!"

"S'alright, Petey," Amos said. "But Archibald and Mercer are out of town."

"Actually, Amos, we're not here to see them. I was wondering if I could talk to Hank. Or Rand or Riley."

Amos chuckled, clearly attempting confidence, but looked every bit nervous. "The Winters boys? Why would any of them be here?"

The sheriff uncrossed his arms and let his hands rest by his hips, by his holster. Travis unbuttoned the strap over his firearm. Calmly, soothingly, the sheriff answered, "Well, Amos, Travis and I were on our way to the Winters' ranch, and Amanda mentioned that her boys came here with Mercer, and then Hank followed with Ramos. As to why they'd be here, Amos, I was hoping you could share that with us, especially since Hank's truck is parked right outside."

Amos audibly gulped, and Johnny was suddenly dejected – he was about to lose his only student before class began. Then a smooth, baritone voice from Heaven called down. "No need to worry, Petey. The boys and I are just fine. You can head on out now."

All eyes went to the second floor, but no one was on the landing.

"Hank?" the sheriff asked, a little louder to get his words up the stairs. "Where you at?"

"Like I said, Petey, no need to worry."

"If I'm pressed for the truth, Hank, I'm more than a little worried about this situation. It's not what I'd call normal. How about you step out where everyone can see you, and you let me know what to tell Amanda when I get to the ranch."

Silas walked out and rested his forearms against the railing, a wicked smile across his face.

The sheriff scuffled a few steps backwards. "Rand? What are you doing here? Where's your father?"

"Well, Petey," Silas said. "You do look confused."

The sheriff gasped, eyes going wide. "Wha...? What in the hell? You sound exactly like your father?"

"Isn't it obvious? My balls finally dropped."

"This ain't right!" Travis shouted, drawing his weapon. "Something ain't right here."

"Travis!" the sheriff shouted. "Holster your weapon!"

"Something ain't right!" The rising pitch in Travis' voice told Johnny that the young officer might be on the verge of losing his mind.

"Travis!" the sheriff shouted again, but no words were reaching him.

The situation was quickly barreling toward critical mass, and Silas had a penchant for taking tense situations past the point of no return. Johnny almost smiled when Silas leaped over the balcony.

Travis got off one shot, but missed.

Silas grabbed Travis' wrists and bent back his arms. With the gun's barrel pressed against the officer's nose, Silas pulled the trigger. The blast turned Travis' face inside out. Crimson slop splashed the wall, greasy chunks sliding down the *fleur-de-lis* patterned wallpaper. Johnny winced at the loud bang, covering his ears. Silas tore the gun from Travis' twitching hands and aimed it at the sheriff.

The sheriff reached for his gun, but before he could draw, Silas had squeezed the trigger. Johnny pressed his hands tight against his ears, anticipating the pop of small thunder this time. A burst of blood sprayed from the sheriff's face as his hat flew off. A half spin, but he didn't fall; he stumbled into the night, slamming the door shut behind him.

Frowning, Silas said, "I got 'em, right? I mean I popped him square in the face, didn't I?"

"Not necessarily," Johnny said. "If you shot him in the cheek, then his cognition would still function. Even if the bullet passed through his brain, that doesn't equate to automatic death. He might retain his full motor skills and the mental acuity to use them, depending on what portions of the brain were injured."

"Well, fuck!" Silas yelled as he ran to the door. He flung it open just as the sheriff's cruiser tore out of the parking area. "Double fuck! Where's he going?"

Instead of heading down the driveway and south onto the road, the sheriff raced past the pigpens, east toward brush-filled rough terrain.

"Looks like he's going toward the Winters' ranch," Amos said.

"Interesting," Johnny said. "The connection between the brain and the mind is a very noteworthy relationship. Even though his brain might be damaged, his mind is holding on to the thought of going to—"

"Stow it, Doc! You take the car! Amos, give me the keys to Hank's truck!"

As soon as he had the keys, Silas sprinted to Hank's pickup and Amos ran to his.

Johnny rushed to the car. Uncertain how a Ford Taurus would handle the prairie, he revved the engine, and put it in drive. A weird sense of ownership over Silas, along with the mentor-protégé relationship with Amos, compelled him. Besides, he had no intention of missing out on how this scenario would play out.

CHAPTER 35

Amanda racked the shotgun with a sharp clack, loading the chamber for action. The ratcheting prompted horrified gasps from Tilde and Barnes. Maybe they hadn't seen a gun before or been this close to one. Or maybe they were surprised she was using her kitchen as a staging area to prepare for a situation where a gun might be needed.

"Mrs. Winters?" Javi asked, his brown eyes wide and wet.

"Nothing to worry about, Javi. I just want to be prepared in case I have to visit the Boyles. Sheriff Pete is probably there by now with everything under control." She hated to lie, but adding concerns to a young man whose head was already full of them would do no good.

"Want me to come with you?"

Javi and his father had worked the ranch for four-or-so years, and Amanda knew Javi's idea of conflict management was to first avoid it, then hide from it. "No, that won't be necessary. I'd rather you stay here to keep an eye on things."

Jut-jawed and resolute, he nodded. "Yeah, I can do that."

Five rounds filled her Remington 870, and Amanda loaded the last few loops of the ammo belt. Seventeen shells ready to go, she wrapped it around her waist and buckled it snuggly.

"It's okay. She'll go over to the Boyles only if she absolutely has to. I'm sure Sheriff Pete has everything under control," Javi told Tilde and Barnes, reiterating as if they hadn't already heard Amanda. She appreciated him trying to sound brave, though she could use some of that confidence herself.

It was easy to be brave when Hank was around. It was easy to be brave when flanked by her strapping young sons. Without Hank and the boys, she had to dig for bravado, and it was buried deep within her. Sure, when it came to the Boyles she'd had her fair share of dealings, but it was usually to shoo Amos from snooping around their property, or to stand up to Archibald when he bad mouthed the Winters' name in townhall meetings. But something strange was happening over on their property right now, and her innards told her it was hindering Hank and the boys. Yes, Petey was probably there, but even police needed help from concerned citizens now and again. And no one more was concerned than Amanda.

She didn't know what was in store for her tonight, but wanted to plan for anything, so with hair long enough to be a nuisance when introduced to a breeze, she tied it tight in a ponytail. What she hadn't planned on was almost plowing over Nixon when she opened the door.

"Whoa!" he said, backing away, hand primed to knock. "Sorry about that, Mrs. Winters, I— *Whoa*!" The second exclamation had come when he realized she was holding a shotgun. "Heh. Wow. That's not for me, is it?"

"No, Nixon. It's not."

He backed a few more paces from her as she brushed past him toward the parking area.

"Okay. Whew! I know I've been a nuisance lately, but damn! Didn't think my crossing the line required a shotgun."

"You're fine. I'm just taking my truck to our neighbors. Hank and the boys are there and it's time they get back home. And when we come back, I trust no one will be loitering around the front of our house?"

Giving "aw, shucks" eyes, Nixon removed his hat to tame his hair. He slipped it back on his head, then sheepishly glanced around. "Well… That's what I was coming to talk to you about."

About a dozen crew members were milling around, a few with lit cigarettes. Had her ire been focused anywhere other than the Boyles, she would have snatched the tobacco sticks from their mouths and stomped them under her boots. As it was… "Nixon, I don't know how many times I need to remind you that you're the boss. I can't do it for you. They work for *you*. You tell them to call it a night and they should call it a night."

"That's the thing, Mrs. Winters. If we were on a studio lot, then they'd just head home at quittin' time. Here, they go to their RVs and trailers, but they're still together. And right now, all they'd be doing is stewing and speculating. You know how people get when they're agitated and lack information."

"I do, but I don't see how I can help with that."

"I just came to ask if it'd be okay if the cast and crew spread out a little bit longer. Another hour or two. If they pace round a bit, they'll work off nervous energy."

Amanda pinched the bridge of her nose and wished Hank were here, while at the same time, grateful that he wasn't. He would've handled this situation before it began and kicked them back to California, likely causing all kinds of additional problems. "Nixon, I can't—"

"There you are!" Bo yelled, laser-focused on Nixon as he stormed his way over. "Why are you always running to—? Holy shit! She's ready to shoot people!"

As tempting as the thought might be, Amanda huffed. "I'm not going to shoot anyone, Bo."

"You're holding a fucking gun!"

"This is the ranchland of New Mexico. You're more likely to see women carrying these than purses. A gun is nothing to fear."

"If it's nothing, then why do you have it?"

Turning the tables for once, Nixon came to Amanda's rescue. "Because it's none of your business, Bo. What do you want?"

Bo's gaze remained on the gun and his frown intensified. "I want the same thing as the rest of the cast and crew. Direction. Information."

"Information? You're the one with the fucking information!"

"Not all of it! Where's Miles? He's been trying to clean up your mess."

"My mess?" Nixon pointed down the driveway to where the producer paced in circles, on his cell phone. "He's been on the phone with the investors trying to talk them out of pulling the plug because of your stupid ego."

Damn it! Amanda would need to walk around Bo and Miles to get to her truck, and Lord only knew what fit either of them would throw. But then Miles slapped his phone closed against his thigh and headed toward the house, pulling at his hair with both hands. "Fuck! Fuck! Fuck!"

"We lost funding, didn't we?" Bo said.

"Worse! Maddox is pissed and said he's coming here if we can't get Brett back—" Like Nixon and Bo, Miles pulled up and froze in his tracks when he saw Amanda holding a gun. Unlike Nixon and Bo, Miles reached behind his back to pull out a revolver. "Fuck! What's going on here?"

Nixon tensed and raised his hands in surrender. Bo backed away, angling closer to Amanda. A few gasps were elicited from the loose gathering of cast and crew conglomerating behind Amanda. She had already steeled herself to the possibility of wielding the shotgun, but she assumed it'd be on the Boyles' property, not her own.

"Jesus, Miles!" Nixon yelled. "Why do *you* have a gun?"

"Didn't you hear what I said? There's a good chance that Maddox will be coming. That's why I have a gun!"

Amanda didn't like the sound of this. "You're afraid of Maddox? Is he one of your Hollywood investors?"

"God, woman, are you fucking stupid? There are no 'Hollywood investors.' There is only one investor. A psychotic motherfucker named Maddox."

Amanda tightened her grip on her shotgun and stepped forward. "Did you just imply that you're bringing a member of organized crime to *my* property?"

Almost laughing, Miles lowered his gun. "A member of...? Yes, Amanda, Maddox is a fucking gangster. And *his* boss, Roger Templeton, is the worst of the worst, but he was the *only* person willing to fund Nixon's dream project. I ran the numbers up and down and left and right, and even if this movie tanks, it will *still* make a profit. But there needs to be a fucking movie and I am doing *everything* possible to make sure that happens, including driving the PA's truck to Albuquerque and hitching a ride back after Sasha disappeared so I could keep the cops away. I'm even willing to double Brett's salary, but we need her back." He raised the gun again, this time accompanied by a cackle, and pointed it at Bo. "How's that coming along, Bo? Did you get a hold of Joel? Did he say she's coming back?"

Bo reared back. "Wait! Waitaminute! Don't do anything crazy!"

Miles' face twisted with mania as he pulled the hammer back.

A squeak of old shock absorbers.

The rev of a car engine.

A police cruiser burst from the darkness and plowed into Miles, mashing him to the ground. Blood spurt from his mouth like an over-ripe tomato, the rear tire parked on his back.

The driver's door opened and Petey tipped out, falling to the ground.

With part of his face missing.

CHAPTER 36

The police car in front of him suddenly came to a halt, and Silas thought he was fucked. He was making a half-assed attempt to drive Hank's truck, knowing the steering wheel made it turn and the pedals down by his feet made it go and stop. Which pedal did which? Right pedal to stop? No! Left! Trouncing both feet on the left pedal while turning the wheel, he narrowly avoided the police car, crashing through a wooden fence and smashing into the back corner of a barn. A blast of white smacked Silas in the face.

What the holy fuck just happened?

Silas took a breath, the air made powdery from the steering wheel's exploding bag. His jaw throbbed. His nose throbbed. A quick feel told him it was bleeding and broken. A sting behind his eyes when he twisted his nose to reset it, but the pain quickly subsided, replaced by the warm tingle of his body healing itself. He was now ravenous, but not in his belly. Were these new pangs a desire for blood? Yes, and the mere thought made his joints itch. Time to get some.

Silas pressed and pushed the deflating bag out of his way. The truck must have hit something electrical in the barn, because all the lights were now off. When he opened the truck door, he heard horses fussing. And people.

Women screamed, a couple men, too. Silas stumbled his way toward the screaming. The police car was parked on some guy, his throat making funny wheezing noises as blood spattered from his mouth with every cough. The half-mangled sheriff opened his car-door, mouth opening and closing like a fish on land as he attempted to say something – maybe call for help or warn everyone that Hell was coming for a visit – as red drool flowed over his chin. Either way, his words fell to the ground and so did he, his eyeball popping free when he hit the dirt. More screams.

Amos and Johnny remained in their vehicles behind the police car, engines idling, headlights on. In front of the police car, the chaos.

Let's make some more!

Hands in front of him, Silas eased his way out of the shadows, strolling carefully between the paddock fence and the police car. By the time he made his way past the dead sheriff and gurgling man under the car's wheels, Silas got a good gander at the situation.

A man in a black cowboy hat stood next to a guy who had what looked like one of them cellphones to his ear. A green haired girl and a blue haired guy clutched each other. A dozen or so people formed a perimeter behind all of them, all gawking with mouths open wide enough to catch flies. But standing closest to him, not more than ten feet away, was a woman wielding a shotgun. Amanda.

Hank had a picture of her in his wallet. Silas had rifled through it, and Amos had explained who she was. This was the mother of the boys whose skin he wore.

Silas didn't have a plan. But the creaking in his joints, the stiffness in his arms and legs, the desire to wet his tongue all told him that he needed these people. Needed their blood. He needed to grab the reins on this state of affairs.

Rand had wielded his smile like a weapon, so Silas decided to give that a try. Taking a step forward, he flashed his pearly whites and said, "Hey, Mom. I can explain—"

Amanda shot him in the face.

More horrific screams.

Silas turned just as Amanda fired again, the blast catching him in the side of his chest. Nowhere else to run and with the paddock beside him, he climbed up and over, landing inside the paddock with a thump.

Pain. Everything hurt. Even the skin and muscle not torn away by a shotgun blast. He wanted to put a barrier between himself and Amanda to gather his wits, his lungs burning with every scratchy breath. A click of a latch and the paddock door opened. Silas had to get to his feet.

Making God mad was always one of Silas' talents, and he'd been mostly lucky enough to avoid God's wrath. Neither talent nor luck on his part was going to stop Amanda from cocking the gun and stomping into the paddock.

"Amanda, what are you doing?"

"No!"

"Her son! She's shooting her own son!"

"Oh my God! Somebody stop her!"

Unphased by the voices swirling around her, Amanda raised her gun.

Silas held up a hand as if it stood any chance of blocking the shot. Amanda pulled the trigger to a new chorus of screams. A demon's kiss later, his fingers and part of his hand flew off his body.

He roared in pain, strips of meaty skin flapping against his wooden forearm and nub of a hand. Frustration coursed through him. He had finally got a body – a damn near perfect human body – and this bitch was mangling it. He wanted to wrap the fingers of his good hand around her neck and drive his jagged and charred stump through her eyes.

She cocked again and yelled, "Devil!"

He needed cover and the barn was the closest option. Gaining no more than a step-and-a-half when an explosion in his right leg matched the eruption from the shotgun.

Shreds of denim and globs of gristle flew from his hip and upper thigh. He cried out again, but didn't fall. Hobbled, he pushed past the inferno burning through his body. One foot in front of the other, he raced to the barn.

"Devil!" Amanda repeated. The last time she hollered that invocation, she conjured hellfire. And once again, parts of Silas' body exploded with splinters of goo-covered wood spraying the ground before him.

Running was impossible since he'd lost feeling in his right leg, using momentum to swing it forward whenever his foot thumped the ground. Another step, two, three. The sounds of the gun cocking and shells being jammed into it. Maybe he had some luck left after all?

With his good leg, he launched himself across the barn's threshold and rolled deeper into the safety of the darkness. Panting, he propped himself on his elbows and saw Amanda's silhouette in front of the barn, unmoving. As he had hoped – she didn't breach the black to follow. But now what?

Hand gone. Leg useless. Joints stiffening. And the hunger. Dear God, he was getting hungrier by the second, his body letting him know that if he didn't get blood soon, he'd stiffen to paralysis. Might as well be dead if that happened. Then… he laughed when he realized what ol' Johnny had been yapping about.

Ya damn idjit! You're in a barn. With horses!

Blood is blood. Wood is wood.

CHAPTER 37

Wherever the devil stepped foot became Hell. A local colloquialism Amanda had grown up with, but she never understood the saying, until now. Her barn, a building she had known and loved for decades, a place she could navigate with her eyes closed, now looked foreign. The pitch-dark interior was like a hungry maw ready to swallow her whole. All because a devil – hiding behind her oldest son's smile and looking through her youngest son's eyes while speaking with her husband's voice – had run into the barn. And Amanda couldn't bring herself to follow.

Spooked from the devil walking among them, the horses brayed and slammed into the stall walls. Amanda wanted to help the animals and run into the barn with her gun blazing, but the obscurity put her at a disadvantage. The only thing she knew about the creature in there was that it had taken the form of her family. *What kind of monster is this*?

Amanda held her breath and focused on the noises inside the barn, hoping she might determine that thing's position. At the very least, right or left of her, front or back of the barn. But all she heard was the stomping of horse hooves and the torrent of blood rushing through her ears to the rapid beat of her heart. And the voices behind her, outside the paddock. The murmurs. The confusion.

"What's happening?"

"She shot someone?"

"Who?"

"I think… I think she shot her own son."

No. That wasn't Rand or Riley she'd shot. Or Hank. Whatever it was, it looked like Rand. Rand's smile, the cocky smirk when he was looking for trouble. But that wasn't his soul behind those eyes – Riley's eyes. It was built like her youngest son, his muscular frame, his height. God only knew why it sounded like Hank. Though, Amanda felt in her heart and soul that God had nothing to do with that thing, which was why she'd been so quick to pull the trigger.

And she was right to do so.

When she blasted away the parody of her son's face, she revealed the demon beneath, made of... wood? It looked like wood as did the nub when she blew away its hand. Was it wood? That made no sense, impossible. Someone else had to have seen it, right? Seen that it wasn't bone under the skin. Seen that it wasn't either of her sons. But the whispers around her were getting louder.

"Oh my God, she shot her son?"

"Why? Why did she shoot him?"

"Because she's fucking crazy!"

Wait... She recognized that last voice. It belonged to Bo. That scum sucking lowlife. This was all his fault. If he hadn't been such an ass to Brett, she'd still be here and Amanda would have been able to keep an eye on her children. She should turn the shotgun on him!

"Shut up, Bo!" Nixon shouted. "Just stop fucking talking!"

"No! We need to do something. There's a woman with a gun shooting people. We need to call the cops."

"If you hadn't noticed, dipshit, one came blazing in already."

"And he fucking ran over Miles! Another reason we need to call for more police."

From behind her, two lights pierced the darkness. The lights danced as Javi and Tilde approached the paddock, directing handheld spotlights inside the barn. They rested the lights on a crossbeam and the beams of light converged at the barn entrance. Still not enough illumination to see inside.

"She's not crazy, you asshole!" Nixon yelled somewhere in the background, a part of the peripheral Amanda didn't have the capacity to care about.

"Didn't you see what everyone else saw?" Bo yelled back. "She's hunting her son! She shot him and cornered him in the barn."

"There... There has to be a reason for that!"

Oh, there was a reason all right. And she was going to prove that thing wasn't her sons, but there was no way on God's green Earth she was going to step foot into the barn's darkness. The spotlights were a good idea, but not bright enough. Should she call Tilde and Javi into the paddock with her? Could she put those kids in danger? What if it really was Rand or Riley and she had succumbed to the madness of the movie set, of Bo, of Miles, and she had pulled the trigger before having all the information? Her hands shook as she stood there ready to play back what she had thought she'd seen, but her breath hitched when something streaked across the light. Was that the creature? Amanda took a step closer, hands steady.

"This is lunacy!" Bo yelled again, this time a few voices agreed with him. "Someone has to do something. I am going to do something."

"Bo, stop talking shit," Nixon said.

"Fuck off, loser!"

The small crowd mumbled in tune to what sounded like someone hitting the ground. Amanda turned while taking a few steps to the side, getting a better look at the commotion while keeping an eye inside the barn. Sure enough, Nixon had been thrown into the dirt, and Bo was taking long strides toward Pete's patrol car.

Now, what in the hell is that shit heel doing? No. No, he can't be this stupid, can he?

Bo crouched down next to Miles' body, and took his gun. Face pinched into a frown, he stormed through the open paddock gate, and stopped about twenty feet from Amanda, pointing the pistol at her.

Shotgun still trained on the barn entrance, she asked Bo, "What are you doing?"

"I'm putting an end to this!"

Amanda doubted he'd hit her should he pull the trigger. Even if the safety was off, he was holding the gun sideways with one hand, stupidly believing the fiction of action movies.

"An end to what?" Amanda asked.

"You! You shooting up the place."

"I'm not shooting up the place, Bo. I shot some kind of creature."

"You shot your son, you crazy bitch!"

"That *thing* wasn't my son!"

"Do you hear yourself? Do you hear what you're saying?"

Dear God, was Bo right? None of the people around the paddock were in a tizzy about a wooden creature looking like her sons, sounding like her husband. None of them came to her defense. Javi and Tilde were helping with the spotlights, but they weren't voicing any disagreement with Bo. Should she drop her shotgun? Should she run to Rand or Riley? Was one of them lying in the barn, bleeding?

A whinny. A bray. A scream.

The terrified wail of an animal in pain while it thrashed around.

Everyone froze, even Bo's face seemed to register that an unexplainable evil was within the barn. The sound of agony ceased, but the horses continued to snort and kick against their stalls. Gun-hand shaking, Bo's expression changed from indignation to fear, his eyes darting from Amanda's face to the barn in a silent plea for guidance. Fully facing the barn, she aimed inside, feet planted in the dirt, shoulder muscles tight.

A minute passed, sweat trickling down into her brow.

Two minutes passed, sweat running down her spine.

Then insanity broke out from inside, multiple horses crying out in pain. Pops of wood cracking, boards splitting. The building creaked as it shook. It all happened so suddenly and loudly that Amanda didn't know how to react to the cacophony. Then, as unexpectedly as it started, the noises stopped.

Dust danced through the spotlight beams and there was silence. But as she stared and listened with expectation, she realized things weren't completely silent... sloshing noises, wet noises. A snap. Another. Then nothing.

Amanda panted as if she had sprinted a marathon, sweat matting her hair and gluing her shirt to her skin. Finger twitching, she hovered it on the trigger.

A massive object flew out of the barn and struck the ground between Amanda and Bo. At first, she thought it was a giant hand with five fingers, but as she stared, she saw that each fingertip bore a horse's head. The thing writhed in the dirt, muscles flexing and twisting. And then the creature with five horse heads started to rise.

Screams – human screams – pierced the air behind her.

Muscular legs emerged beneath the thing, elevating its mass above the ground. Stomping, clomping, pawing at the dirt, bare hooves grew from under the monstrosity, unnatural in number and more than she cared to count. As the mass continued to rise, the horse heads whipped about independent of each other, wide-eyed in confusion.

Amanda's guts liquified when she realized that this thing was all five of her horses sewn together in one massive beast. Palomino, grey, chestnut, and two roan coats fitted together at odd angles like a jigsaw puzzle of the damned, seams rippling like discontent worms. The chestnut head closest to her swung around and locked eyes – *oh God, Buster!*

"What the fuck?" Bo shrieked, his voice hitting a pitch Amanda had never heard from a man before. "What the fuck is that?"

It was a nightmare. And the longer it trod the ground, the uglier it became. The index finger of the devil's hand – the one with Buster's head – pointed at Bo. The elongated mouth opened, horse-teeth jutting forward.

Bo stood soldier-straight, shaking with palsy, the gun in his hand pointing impotently at the ground. "Amanda! Amanda, help!"

Amanda was frozen in shock by the abomination before her.

As Buster's mouth opened wider, a slim wooden hand reached out. Knotted, twisted fingers grabbed a fistful of Bo's shirt and pulled him off the ground. Bo shrieked as his chest slammed into Buster's awaiting muzzle. The horse mouth opened impossibly wide, pulling Bo inside. The actor's wails split through Amanda's head as he folded backwards into a V-shape. His flapping arms could not prevent the back of his head from touching the back of his knees as Buster's distended cheeks accommodated Bo. Wet, snapping bones replaced the screams. A second later, Bo was gone, and the distorted face of Buster was smiling.

A bulge that was once Bo slithered down the horse's throat toward the base of the mass. With a rippling tear, the bottom of the neck opened to create an orifice big enough to expel slop-covered clothes and bones picked clean of meat. Buster raised his head to the sky and whinnied as the hole closed, sealing itself as if it'd never existed. Then the chestnut's head turned to Amanda.

She readied the shotgun to blow away Buster's head, but when a wooden hand dripping with slime extended from the mouth like a pink wooden tongue, she caught her breath. It blinked? A sky-blue iris surrounding a dark pupil was embedded in the palm. The eye blinked again and Amanda knew it was Riley's. The wood split horizontally below the eye, forming a slim mouth. It spoke with Hank's voice, pleading, "Amanda. Don't. I love you."

Her throat tightened from nauseating realization – this monster didn't just take the form of her family, it assimilated her family the same way it assimilated her horses. The wooden hand reached closer, and Amanda was too wracked with grief to defend herself.

A bright circle of light shined directly into Riley's eye. The wooden hand flinched, its fingers curling closed. Amanda snapped from her stupor, every ounce of sadness replaced doubly with fury and wrath. She raised her shotgun again, but the Buster head then turned, the arm extending from its opened mouth toward the light's source.

Toward Tilde.

"No!" Amanda screamed, blasting the horse's neck when its wooden tongue latched onto Tilde. With an effortless yank, it pulled the young woman through the paddock's beams, her green hair whipping through the air, and Amanda fired twice more. The buckshot shredded red horse-flesh from the mutated beast and exposed the goo-covered wood beneath but did nothing to stop Tilde from being twisted in unnatural ways to fit into the chestnut's stretching mouth within seconds. As if he'd been chomping on green hay, Tilde's hair hung from the horse's muzzle. Amanda unloaded her last two rounds into the horse's head.

The shotgun stripped away most of the horse's face, and flaps of meaty skin flopped around as the finger of the giant hand writhed. Amanda ejected the empty shells, reloading while staring at the horrid beast. The mangled horse-flesh pulled tightly against the wooden parody of a skull and melded into it.

Amanda aimed again to shoot, but then other fingers of the multilegged mass writhed and vinelike tongues whipped out of the mouths; two grabbed hold of bystanders daring to stand too close to the paddock. As with Tilde, the fence-beams were merely toothpicks as the beast consumed the screaming crewmembers.

The gnarled mound of flesh that was Buster's head expanded, meat oozing along the burled wood. The five headed beast once again crapped out clothing and bones through a freshly made orifice, and that was when Amanda determined that it only consumed skin, blood, and muscle.

The remaining cast and crew members scattered in all directions, running for their lives. This monster was probably fast enough to catch each man and woman since it was an amalgamation of horses. She had to lead it away from there.

Crossing in front of the monster, she blasted one of the roan heads, and then sprinted out of the paddock to Rand's truck. As she fired up the engine, a stump of wood slammed against the bed, rocking the truck. The gray horse head stared at her as the wooden vine snaked back into its mouth. There was a malevolent intelligence in its eyes, the kind only possessed by a human, and there was no creature more wicked on this Earth than that.

Gear in drive, Amanda tromped the gas pedal, kicking up a rooster tail of dirt just as another wooden tongue smashed into the side of her pickup. The impact shattered her driver's door window, pebbles of glass bouncing off her. No time to worry about cuts or bruises, she tore around the paddock and aimed north toward Fake Town. Too many panicked cast and crew members were running around for her to consider any other option.

The monster gave chase, but in her mirrors, Amanda saw its initial cumbersome steps falter as it crashed through the fencing between the paddock and the playpen. The space in the playpen gave it ample opportunity to learn its legs, build mobility and momentum. The thing learned coordination quickly, and gained on Amanda.

The tongue-in-groove fence of wooden beams ran all the way to Fake Town. As the creature thundered closer, she thought about pulling away from the fence between her and the monster, but it'd simply break through and continue its chase. Instead, she could use the fencing as a weapon.

Hoof-falls of five conjoined horses reverberated through Amanda's chest as the beast raced side-by-side the truck; three heads looking at her, two watching where it was going. The terrain rattled her bones with every bump and divot. The fence was running to an end and Fake Town was coming up. Now or never.

Despite running on more than a dozen legs, the creature had learned to keep the heads steady, allowing them the opportunity to scrutinize, plan. Buster's head aimed between the two roans' and all three opened their mouths – a wooden tongue from the roan at the truck's bed, a wooden hand from Buster's mouth, but nothing from the roan in front.

Lifting the shotgun from her lap, Amanda pointed it at Buster. She'd heard that a person couldn't go deaf from their own screams, so hoping it'd help keep the shotgun from blowing away her hearing, she screamed and pulled the trigger.

Gunfire obliterated the hand, tearing through part of Buster's face. As Amanda had hoped, the other two heads went on the offensive and attacked as Buster reeled back. The wooden tongue pierced the truck's bed while the roan's thick teeth latched to the door, head where her window had been. A furnace of hot breath plumed from its nostrils against Amanda's left arm. She screamed again, this time with grit as she yanked the steering wheel right.

Unrelenting, the beast stayed with the truck. Its massive body crashed through the fence with ease, snapping the planks like twigs. But after a few more strides, it slammed into a post that splintered and sent two horizontal pieces into its chest. A fraction of a second later, the front tires of the truck left the ground.

The beast tumbled, taking the driver's side door with it, tearing it from the hinges along with a hunk of the bed's fiber glass. When the pickup's tires landed on the dirt, Amanda's head smacked against the steering wheel. Disoriented, fighting to see through stars bursting in her vision, she overcompensated and jerked the wheel. Before she had time to correct, the driver's side wheels lifted. Muscles tense, she braced when the passenger side hit the ground. After it skidded to a stop, she grabbed her shotgun and half fell, spilling out of the truck.

Not a cloud in the sky to hinder the bright moon, Amanda saw the creature twitch, trying to get to its feet. Vision slipping between double and single, she couldn't think. Her scream before pulling the trigger had helped, but the shotgun blast started a jet engine roaring between her ears. *Hide,* was the only thought she could form. The wrecked truck wouldn't be a good enough hiding spot, and the first building of Fake Town was only thirty paces away.

First steps uneven, listing to her right from wooziness, Amanda approached the building from the side. Once she got to the porch, she wrapped her arm around the corner post. Panting with her head against the wood, she took a moment to assess.

The creature lumbered to the pickup, the horse heads wriggling like worms, and dropped its weight onto the truck.

No more time to think, she shoved herself from the post. Hurrying across the porch, she ducked into the first doorway. The hardware sign on the building made her hopeful for weaponry inside, like hammers and nail guns and saws, but to her chagrin, this storefront was designed to be seen and not used. The room was completely empty. The lone window allowed her to see that the monster had finished mauling the pickup and was now lumbering toward Fake Town.

The back of the store had a doorway to the neighboring store, and Amanda hurried through. She couldn't remember what inaccurate place of business this was supposed to be, but it had no furnishings either. *Damn it!* By the looks of the lumber stacked on uneven plywood planks against the wall and the dozen paint cans in the corner, this place served as storage for the construction crew. The other corner looked helpful – the secret smoking area.

A full ashtray rested atop an overturned plastic bucket, two plastic lighters next to it. Amanda grabbed both and kicked through a small pile of cheap, lightweight screwdrivers and wrenches, pliers and hammers. Having no idea if anything would come in handy, she grabbed one of the sturdier looking hammers as well as a small hatchet, and slipped both through her belt, one on either hip. Then froze. Moaning came from outside.

This windowless store had a doorway with no door. Careful to step on the floorboard seams to reduce the wood squeaks, she crossed the room and peeked outside.

The beast roamed the center of the dirt street between the two buildings, the moonlight catching every disturbing detail of the atrocity. It moved slower than Amanda anticipated, as if struggling. Many of its legs dragged while Buster's and the palomino's heads hung limp. Fist-sized wounds in its chest from where the fence splinters had pierced glistened in the pale moonlight. It was slowing down. *Could it be killed?*

Right outside the store where Amanda hid, the monstrosity stilled. A shiver. It wriggled like a dog shaking away water, then stilled again. A gooey line formed vertically along the height of its body, and split open. The two wounded heads went limp like the fingers of an empty glove. The flaps of skin spread, exposing pink oily wood underneath the wounded horse heads – wood in the rudimentary shape of skulls. The chunks of wood fell away from the monster, thumping to the ground. The beast shed the two ruined horses, flaccid skin sloughing away and onto the ground, along with three, four, five massive branches. *No, not branches – legs.*

The flaps of skin rejoined, a seam merged then disappeared, and the wounds no longer existed. The three-horse mashup of a creature moved fluidly as it trotted to the other building, looking into windows.

It can be killed. Amanda didn't know the ins and outs of how this demon-thing worked, but she wagered that since it had tossed away its wounded parts to heal itself, it'd run out of parts and whatever fueled it. The three rounds in her shot gun and two shells around her waist might not be enough. But one of the four storefronts across the street was a blacksmith shop – with a working forge.

Bo had insisted on it, even though neither he nor his character knew anything about the profession. The entitled shit thought it'd be cool, and

Amanda was grateful he'd been such a spoiled brat about it and that Miles and Nixon had caved to him. *Now, how can I sneak—?*

The head of her gray horse poked into the doorway. It looked right at her.

"Shit!" she screamed as she squeezed the trigger. The buckshot tore bloody strips of skin and chunks of wood from under its chin. Crouched and unbalanced, the force of the gunshot sent her tumbling deeper into the room. This worked to her favor, aiding her retreat her from the wall as the horse-monster crashed into the building.

The wall exploded inward and pieces of splintered wood sliced her cheek as they zipped by her face. Unphased, she planted her feet and blasted away the rest of the gray's head. The beast reeled back, and just as it had on the street, it sloughed away the damaged skin and ejected the wooden frame of a horse's head, as well as a chunk of the chest and a few branches of unnecessary legs. The shedding process happened fast but it gave Amanda enough time to run through the back doorway to the next store – the saloon.

As with the blacksmith shop, the saloon's bar was fully functioning – another insistence from Bo, showcasing how he knew his way around a bar – and stocked shoulder-high along the connecting wall with high proof booze.

Down to the size of two horses, two roan heads charged through the doorway, the rest of its body violently widening it, black eyes wild as it forced its way through. Amanda took advantage of its recklessness and emptied her shotgun at the bottles of liquor on the shelves. The liquids splashed the beast, coating the rippling skin. Amanda pulled one of the lighters from her pocket and ignited the alcohol as she ran toward the double doors leading outside.

The woosh of flame warmed her back and the thin wood of the structure caught ablaze. She stumbled to the center of the dirt street, chased by the piney, petroleum smells of burning paint and biting odor of booze on fire. Panting, she cracked her shotgun open, her hands shaking as she removed the last two shells from her belt.

A slam against the saloon wall from inside as the monster smashed through the exit, blowing the swinging doors from their hinges. Fire consumed its entirety, both roan heads twitching and screaming as the flesh bubbled with popping blisters. A few shaky steps and the legs gave out from under the horse-thing, its chest digging into the ground. One head drooped then went limp; the other locked eyes with Amanda. And opened its mouth.

Bo's face appeared in the horse's maw under a curtain of pink slime. Once his head birthed free, Bo shouldered out his arms, and then grabbed the horse's upper and lower jaw. Bo slid out with his slop of afterbirth – naked with no signs of injury.

Amanda clacked the gun shut and racked it. She swung it around to blow his face off, but Bo was too fast. On his feet and in front of her, he grabbed the barrel, sending the buckshot impotently into the night air.

Bo smiled, crimson ooze dripping off his lips and chin. With Hank's voice, he said, "Hi, honey. I'm home."

"You're not Bo, and I'm not your honey. What are you?"

"Name's Silas, and I am a god!"

Amanda replied by tightening her grip on the gun and yanking. But his hold was too tight. Droplets of slime splattered her cheek as he said, "Careful, l'il lady. You'll hurt someone with this thing."

Amanda growled. "I have every intention of doing just that."

"Your need for this gun is your weakness."

"Oh yeah? Your nut-sack is yours."

Amanda brought the steel tip of her work boot to his crotch. This creature wasn't Bo. It probably wasn't even human, but the spot she kicked was human enough to call forth a squeal reserved for a pig slaughtered on the Boyles' farm. Both of his hands grabbed his sensitive spot as he doubled over, releasing the gun.

His face was now close to the barrel.

BLAM!

The thing wearing Bo's body jerked, dodging as Amanda pulled the trigger. Half of his head, neck, and shoulder smoked as chunks of charred meat and burned skin flopped over the broken wood underneath. Fingers curled to strangle, he lunged forward.

Amanda jumped back, avoiding his attack, but stumbled. Balance lost, she slammed onto the dirt, rear first. A lightning strike of pain blasted from her tailbone to her forehead as she dropped her shotgun.

The Bo creature also hit the ground, and immediately reached for her. Amanda tried to scrabble away, but her hands lost traction in the dirt. Shifting to her right hip, she delivered the sole of her left boot to what was left of his face. Again and again. She tore away his nose and sent his right eyeball flying. Cheek parts splattered through the air, and he started to slow down.

Digging her elbows into the ground, Amanda pushed herself away. The thing glared at her with one eye as it pulled itself closer, reaching. Reaching. Amanda screamed and kicked the hand away, the dirt scraping her skin as she braced herself. Another kick. Harder. Faster. With one last twitch, the Bo creature dropped its face to the ground, and its arm went limp.

Amanda took a beat to catch her breath, but as she shifted to stand, two sticks sprung from Bo's fingertips and pierced her calf.

For a fraction of a second, Amanda wondered about the noise the night air made as the world shredded around her, but from the burn in her throat, she realized it was her own shrieking. The darkness closing in on her peripheral vision pulsed to the speeding beat of her heart, threatening to take her to a blackened eternity. Blood flowed along the wood – her blood, being syphoned from here leg – and the Bo creature stirred.

She twisted and flopped, fingers scratching against the ground. She didn't manage to get anywhere, her hands impotently flailing about. Reaching or slapping, she didn't know, until she felt a cold chunk of metal by her waist. The hatchet!

A quick tug and she pulled it from her belt. Four, five, six whacks and she separated the wooden prongs from his fingers. Not soon enough. The Bo creature drew its hand closer to its body for support as it started to stand.

"No!" Amanda yelled.

Fighting for balance on her good leg, she stood just as the Bo-creature got to its feet. Putting everything she had into a downward swing, she drove the hatchet's blade into what remained of its forehead. The mangled skin folded into a frown, then its lone eye rolled back into its head. It collapsed once more.

As soon as it hit the dirt, Amanda grabbed the handle and jerked the hatchet free. She swung again and again and again. Over and over, crying and spitting out every curse she could think of, she cut away the skin and split its wooden head in two.

Physically unable to lift the little axe anymore, she took a few steps back. When she saw headlights coming her way, she dropped to her knees, relieved and thankful.

Her first thought was Javi, maybe Barnes with him, but as the pickup truck got closer, the headlights didn't look right. They looked familiar, but they didn't belong to Ramos' truck, nor anyone's from the ranch. Why did she know those lights?

No! No no no no no! Amanda mouthed, fighting through the blinding pain in her left leg to stand.

The pickup skidded to a stop, mere feet behind the thing that was once Bo, spotlighting it with its headlights.

The doors opened.

Out stepped a nebbish man with glasses.

And Amos Boyle.

CHAPTER 38

Amanda glanced at her gun. On the ground, ten feet away, but with the pain pulsing up her leg, it might as well be ten miles. Even if she somehow got to it without her leg falling off, she had no ammo. The hatchet wasn't an option either, buried in the gore-covered splinters of what used to be Silas' head.

The nebbish man ran to him.

Amanda was confident she could whoop his ass, even in her current state of fatigue and confusion, but there was something chilling about the way he scurried to the remains of the creature that called itself Silas. Crouching next to the mess of wood and meat, the man with the thick glasses cocked his head like a bird as he examined it. Voice calm and small, he said, "Fascinating."

"Yeah, yeah, yeah," Amos said as he hurried to the back of the truck and dropped the tailgate. "Now get your ass over here, Johnny, and help me with this."

"I'll fix you," Johnny said to the pile of meat as he got up and ran to the pickup.

What the hell are they doing? Amanda wondered what was important enough to ignore her.

Keeping an eye on the creature she had just killed, she limped around it on her way to the pickup. The headlights illuminated the area between the truck and the corpse. Amos and Johnny were dragging something along the ground and Amanda froze when she saw what it was.

A body.

A young man. One of the bit-part actors with such a tiny nose that Amanda doubted he was born that way. She didn't remember his name, just that he had two parts in the movie and the ensuing argument between Nixon and Miles about him – the producer insisting they use him twice instead of shelling out a few more bucks for a different actor. Amanda wondered, if

Nixon had won the argument, then which poor actor would she be looking at?

Amanda hustled to the men, putting as little weight on her bad leg as possible. They still paid her no mind until she hobbled close enough to shove Amos. He windmilled his arms, then fell to the ground.

Holding the actor's corpse by the wrists, Johnny paused, eyes wide and looking to Amos. With a sick smirk on his face, Amos got to his feet and said, "Take him to Silas and get the others. I'll take care of this bitch."

Others? Amanda retreated to the back of the pickup, using it for support along the way. Four more dead bodies lay in the bed. "What have you done, Amos? What the hell have you done?"

Amos laughed. "Done? I elevated myself. I've grown bigger than any Winters. I've gotten out from under my brother's shadow. I've become a chirurgeon."

"A chir-what? You're making no damn sense, Amos! Why did you kill these people?"

"To experiment, Amanda. To learn. To grow. I'm helpin' Doc experiment and learn about Silas. But first we need to recharge him."

Amanda looked to the mess that used to be Silas. Johnny struggled with the body as he dragged it closer. Recharge? Did he mean revive? Amanda guessed earlier that this thing needed flesh and blood to live and now these two confirmed it. And she'd be damned if she was going to let them revive this monster.

Broken glass swirling through her left leg be damned, Amanda took off in a limping sprint to stop Johnny.

Amos slammed into her. He'd come flashing around the other side of the truck, and she was unable to plant her left foot to keep from falling hard on her shoulder. Breath fled from her in a hard puff. With a wheeze and a hiccup, Amanda struggled to breathe. Panic tore through her as Amos sauntered toward her, but he was content to lord over her like a proud god.

"I need your assistance, Amos." Johnny stood about ten feet from Silas, adjusting his glasses. His sweat-slicked skin glimmered in the light of the burning building, the fire still dancing a bright orange.

"You're doing good, Doc. I gotta take care of this first," Amos said.

Johnny dragged the body another two feet closer to Silas.

"You're sick, Amos," Amanda mumbled.

"What was that?" Amos growled, stepping closer. "Are you finally admitting that a Boyle beat a Winters?"

Another big tug and Johnny was two feet closer.

"No!" Amanda shouted as she drove the heel of her boot into Amos' knee. A wet snap followed by a piercing scream, and Amos was on the ground. By the time Amanda got to her feet, Johhny was another couple feet closer to Silas with the body. Even though she stumbled, she had enough push behind her run to drive her shoulder into Johnny's ribs and lift him off his feet. The tackle was awkward, but she put her full weight into slamming him to the ground. His head bounced off the dirt. Not taking any chances, she punched his cheek hard enough to bounce his head again.

Squealing like the pigs he raised, Amos climbed to his feet and rushed her. Stumbling, he swung when he was close enough. Amanda dodged his punch, his weight taking him with the follow through, but he twisted and grabbed her shirt. Taking her with him as he fell, her other shoulder absorbed the brunt of the impact. Lanky arms and legs acted like whips, fast and hard to predict. He didn't have much power behind his strikes, but when a knuckle hit her temple, bright streaks of color flickered across her vision. And when a stray heel connected with her injured calf, her world shattered. A knuckle punch to her cheek sent lightning down her neck. Enough! It was her turn.

Yelling wildly, her punches and kicks were just as crazed, barely focused. She hated that she was reduced to flailing, but she needed a lucky connection to give her enough time. Got it! A great strike – middle knuckle to nose – and Amos rolled away. She mashed her lips and squeezed her eyes shut, brought her bad ankle to her good thigh and yanked the wooden prongs from her calf. A clenched-jaw-scream and her peripheral vison swirled, blackness closing in. Her world shrank to a small tube of flickering orange.

Fire.

The burning building.

A shape passed in front of it. What was it? Amos! It was Amos. *Snap out of it!*

As Amos lunged, Amanda sat up and drove both tips of her wooden prongs into his right shoulder. They both screamed as she yanked them out. She desperately wanted to stab him again, but he shoved her to the ground as he snapped back.

"You dumb bitch!" Amos howled, his wailing turning into laughter. Now cackling, he repeated, "You dumb bitch!"

Both hands pressed to his shoulder, blood pouring through his fingers, he stood and limped to the Silas creature. And splashed his blood on it.

A whip made of muscle and brain pieces shot from Silas' head to the dead man that Johnny had dragged from the truck, connecting the monster to the corpse. Both bodies twitched with spasms, but the one that looked like Bo started to reform, to heal. The tendril of gore pulled the dead body closer. Like a massive snake, the split head acted as a mouth – the old body consumed the new one. Bo's body distended as the bulge moved through it with bones, organs, and clothes being ejected out his other end.

Like fingers folding together, the two halves of Bo's head sutured itself, though a scar lingered from where Amanda had hacked into him with the hatchet. Standing, his sick smile was unphased. "Amanda, Amanda, Amanda. I think we—"

Amanda charged at the Bo-Silas thing. She jammed the tips of the wooden daggers into his new eyes and drove them through the jelly and into the hollow as far as they would go.

Screaming, thin vines pierced through his skin and whipped around like feelers in the air. Amanda dropped to the ground and rolled away from the thrashing miscreation. Far enough away, she grabbed a fist-sized rock, popped to her feet, and ran to the building that wasn't in flames.

Much like the other structure, the plaza was devised of four stores with doorways in the back connecting them. Pushing past the agony blasting through her leg, she ran across the porch and through the first door. She hobbled through the backdoor into the second room – the blacksmith shop.

The forge was not period accurate and ran on propane. Unsurprisingly, the crew had left six tanks in the far corner. She opened five of them and took the sixth with her as she limped to the third room. She almost stumbled when she heard her husband's voice boom from the first room, "Bitch! Where are you? I'm gonna fuckin' kill you and wear your skin!"

"It's not Hank. It's not Hank," she mumbled under her breath, running as best she could to the doorway leading outside. Once she hit the porch, she ran back to the blacksmith shop, arriving just as the creature entered the back of the room. She tossed the rock through the window, punching a hole in the corner of the glass, and then grabbed one of the lighters from her pocket. It lit on the first try. Dropping the flaming lighter into the newly made hole, she hobble-sprinted away.

Propane ignited with a woosh, rattling the windows. Amanda smelled her hair singe as heat slapped the back of her neck. She ran off the porch into the middle of the road. Amos' truck was gone, and Johnny started to stir. Red and blue lights flashed in the distance. This wasn't over; Amanda could feel it.

Just like the other building, the fire spread quickly, the newly applied paints adding fuel as it burned easy and hot. Dirty sweat flowed over her face, quick backhand swipes wicking it from her eyes. Something moved within the flames, and Amanda gripped the handle of the propane tank tighter. A dark shape formed, growing larger. The remaining glass shattered as the creature in human form jumped through the window.

Amanda cranked the propane tank's knob, the hiss and odor immediate. Still resembling Bo, the creature howled and charged at Amanda. Blisters bubbled and popped along its body, flames having their way with it. The creature reached out, sharp-tipped wood snaking from its fingertips and leading the way. Amanda raised the tank.

With both hands, she aimed the pressurized liquid at the monster, the stream igniting like dragon's breath. There was the risk of backdraft; the fire could extend into the tank and cause an explosion, but it was worth it to burn this thing back to Hell.

More inhuman cries of anguish as the creature pulled up. But it didn't stop. Neither did Amanda as she continued to blast it with fire while backing away. The thing's pace slowed, its steps toward her shorter and shorter. Skin and muscle liquified and the wooden mannequin beneath charred. Then the wood split and released another human-shaped likeness, this one only about three feet tall.

It moved fast, almost reaching Amanda before she realized what was happening, but the plume of fire stayed constant, and the wooden creature caught ablaze. Like the larger version, this thing kept coming.

The propane tank was getting hotter, and Amanda wasn't sure how much longer her luck would last before an explosion became inevitable. Arms shaking, she prayed this monster would stop advancing. When it finally did, she was about to sing hallelujah, but the wood split again, releasing a smaller wooden humanoid.

Howling, a little creature only about four inches tall launched itself at Amanda's face. One more shift of the tank and the muscles in her shoulders burned as hot as the flame. She blasted the little wooden fucker before it reached her.

It fell from the air and Amanda was quick to hose it with the blaze the second it hit the ground. It lay there unmoving, but Amanda didn't relent, screaming as her hands burned from the heat of the tank. She was set to use every bit of fuel to burn this creature from existence, but a small spark of reason flickered in her mind. Before she caused her hands any more damage, she set the tank down and closed the spout. All that remained of the tiny wooden figure was a pile of black ash, not even big enough to fill a shot glass. Amanda stomped on it, crushing it into the dirt.

A noise from behind her, and she whipped around. Johnny was on his knees with his fingers laced behind his head. "I give up."

"I don't care," Amanda growled as she searched the ground, the fires from either side of the street lighting up Fake Town and muting the red and blue police lights. There! Amanda grabbed the hatchet and strode toward Johnny.

"This would be murder," Johnny said with such a calm demeanor that Amanda caught a chill between two infernos.

"Still don't care."

Stopping stomach-to-nose in front of him, Amanda focused on his forehead, and raised her weapon.

Two police cruisers turned the corner onto Fake Town's only street and skidded to a stop. Four doors flung open and Amanda recognized the officers. One had his gun trained on Johnny while the other three held out their hands as if dealing with a barking dog. Officer Curtis took point and stepped closer. "Amanda, please put down the weapon."

"He needs to die."

"It's not worth it."

"Oh, yes, it is!"

"Officer," Johnny said as calmly as ordering the weekly special at a local diner. "I'd like to confess to the murders of over two dozen people, including, but not limited to, the six bodies that can be found in the Boyles' residence."

"Amanda!" Officer Curtis was louder this time, his hand drifting close to his sidearm. "He's unarmed and turning himself in. You can't do this."

"I can and I must!"

"I have to take one of you to jail, Amanda, and I'd much rather it be him."

Shit. He was right. If she sought justice this way, then she would pay for all the crimes Johnny had committed. She dropped the hatchet and stepped back, allowing the police to swarm Johnny. As they cuffed his wrists, he smirked, signaling that this was all going according to his plan.

By the light of the two blazing buildings she'd set while charring an abomination, she realized there was still one monster left.

Taking a deep breath, she swore she'd find Amos and make him pay.

CHAPTER 39

A week. It had been a week since Amanda had last been to Fake Town. A mere week ago, she and Hank stood right here at its edge and marveled at how quickly it came to be. The breeze still carried the deep grumbles of Hank's protests every time she suggested that he was the mayor. Amanda smiled at that. Then melancholy fingers glided over her cheeks and her smile fell away – she was now mayor of Fake Town. *A thriving metropolis of two burned down buildings with eight empty storefronts.*

The lone dirt street ran the entirety of the town, all one hundred feet of it. Her first step brought a sudden flare up from the medical boot on her left foot. She needed to assess what was left, needed to know what to tell the real estate agent for their first meeting tomorrow. That was a lie. The agent was going to tour the property regardless of Amanda's visit to Fake Town. Had she been more introspective, she'd admit that it was morbid curiosity. She told herself that she *had* to be here, because it sure wouldn't sit well if she had an inkling that she *wanted* to be here, at the scene of the crime.

That phrase had been used a lot during the investigation. "The scene of the crime." The real crime was committed against nature by the abomination that named itself Silas. But Amanda left that piece of information out of her retelling of the tale. Who would have believed her? The only two other people who knew the truth were Amos Boyle and Johnny Ghastson. Amos was missing and Johnny was adding more than enough information to incriminate himself for all the murders on her property and in the Boyle house. Hell, he even confessed to other murders around the Albuquerque area, offering evidence that could be found in his downtown holistic medicine shop. But he wouldn't give up Amos. In fact, he said Amos was dead.

When questioned by the police, he insisted that he had killed Amos and fed his body to the pigs on the farm, which was how he got unfettered access to the Boyle house. Amanda and Javi were the only two who testified that Amos was with Johnny. A few other witnesses stated that Johnny had an accomplice, but it was dark and there was too much commotion to get an accurate account of what had happened. Amanda would have pushed harder if she hadn't used that very excuse as to why her horses were found at Fake Town – "It was dark, and the fence got damaged. The horses got out and must have run north to get away from the commotion."

The reason was flimsy, but it was good enough for the police. Not for Amanda. There would be no reason good enough for her unless God Himself whispered the explanation into her ear. Though she knew the explanation was found in the eternal inferno below, not in the infinite paradise where Hank and her kids dwelled.

Hands in her pockets, she stepped onto the porch of the one building, though little remained to call it that. A husk was more like it, and that was a stretch. She had a vague idea where she'd been hiding when she first saw the creature discard part of its wooden skeleton. A half dozen paces of stepping over fallen wall studs so charred she imagined they'd just turn into black powder should her boot graze against them, she thought she had moved into the second store front. She still had no idea what it was supposed to be, the outside sign now charcoal.

She continued her tour, now in the saloon, judging by the larger chunk of blackened wood she assumed to be the bar. The monster had discarded more of its wooden innards here as well.

Something caught Amanda's eye. Three small islands of white floated in an aggressive ocean of jagged black. Aware of the boot-cast's cumbersomeness, she was careful not to trip as she hurried to the anomaly. Pictures. Three Polaroid pictures.

Of Riley and Javi.

A sob escaped as she clutched her chest. Using the back of her hand, she wiped away the sudden stream of tears while she steadied her shaky breath. There was an extra twist of hurt that came from how happy he looked, truly happy to be himself. Defying the warmth in the late afternoon air, a chill blew through her entire body. *Where were these taken and by whom? And how did they get here? Wait...* Pictures where often tacked to the Devil Tree by locals superstitious enough to believe that was how to access its power.

Looking northwest, Amanda squinted as if that'd help her see the accursed blight to the land a mile away. Did the tree really have something to do with this? The Silas creature was made of wood, after all, no matter what skin it wore. Amanda shivered at the thought.

She slid the pictures in her back pocket and limped away from the charred remains of the building, toward the center of Fake Town's only street. The packed dirt was streaked with black, the faint smell of burnt wood, cooked meat, and propane still in the air. This was where she had fought and killed a monster. She wasn't thinking about it at the time, but this was also the spot where she had avenged her family.

So many questions with no answers. She didn't even know where to begin. Javi wanted answers and had mentioned that he was going to find them, the fire of youth fueling him. Barnes said he was going to help. Amanda didn't want answers. She wanted her family and answers weren't going to bring them back. She made sure that Javi knew he had a home with her no matter when he was done searching and no matter what he found.

Something itched at the back of her skull, compelling her to hobble closer to the exact spot where she had turned the monster into a pile of ash. But… It wasn't how she'd last seen it.

Putting her weight on her good foot, she crouched down and marveled at what had happened. Black cinder was still there, but it was no longer in a pile.

No more than four inches tall, its arms and feet spread-eagle apart with a circle of dark ash making the head. All around it were dead ants and bug carcasses.

Then it twitched.

No. Never again, Amanda thought as she removed the bandana from around her neck. Careful not to touch a single piece of ash, she placed her bandana over the cinder and scooped it up. No movement inside her bandana, but she kept her fist tightened over it all the way to her truck and the short drive to her workshop.

The last time she was here, she was sharing beers with Brett. Despite her reservations about allowing someone else into her space, it was a fond memory, one with laughter and bonding. Friendship. Amanda had been dubious about that at the time, but welcomed it now. As soon as the news broke about what had happened on the ranch, Brett reached out and offered the moon and the stars to Amanda. Once the sale of the property went through, she'd book a trip to New York to visit. But first, time to end this terrible chapter of her life.

After clearing a space, Amanda set her bandana and the remains wrapped within on her workbench. Then she put on gloves and a filter mask before mixing a small batch of resin. She pulled out a cast to make a sphere and filled it about halfway. Next, the cinder and then the rest of the resin.

Amanda had no idea what the creature was, but it needed to take life to live, that much was obvious. Destroying it seemed nearly impossible, so the next best thing was to imprison it. After a couple of hours in the chiller, Amanda now held a baseball-sized globe of clear, colorless resin, the black ash in the center like an exploding dark star. It was Silas' fault for putting her on whatever path she was about to traverse. And now she was going to bring him with her everywhere, to make him watch.

EPILOGUE

Amos showed his driver's license to the officer at the visitor check counter and bit his tongue to stifle a giggle. "Charles Urjin." The inside joke was known only to him and the prisoner he was visiting, but it would never not be funny.

A pat down, a metal-detecting wand wave, a signature, an escort, and Amos was now sitting in front of Johnny Ghastson, The Chirurgeon.

"How've you been?" Amos asked. "Sorry, kinda dumb question."

Johnny repositioned his glasses and smirked. "Not at all. And I'm well. I'm acclimating faster than anticipated."

Amos winced. "Really? No offense, Doc, but almost all the guys in here are bigger than you."

The smirk remained, unwavering. "They're smart enough to know that I'm smarter. And rumors travel fast. Most of those in here have committed homicide only once or twice. One gang member killed nine people in four separate occasions, but..." Johnny shrugged. "I can always tell when an inmate learns of my number. A look in their eye. No matter how hard they try to mask it, I can always see that little spark of fear."

Amos nodded. "Yeah. I get it. You're an impressive fellow, Doc."

"Thank you, Amos."

"Actually, thank *you*, Doc, for taking the heat. And telling everyone I'm dead."

"It's all part of the mission to start an institute, Amos. A chance to spread my theories, my hypotheses. To share and collect knowledge. What I know and what I have yet to learn. I believe that many men in here would be interested in our institute, Amos."

"That's awesome."

A guard stepped closer. He cleared his throat and rotated his hand with index finger extended, the universal gesture to wrap up the conversation.

"Sure don't give you much time, do they?"

"Not yet. But they will. How have you been faring?"

"Real good, Doc. First class tonight. Got six students."

Johnny stood, prompting Amos to do the same. One last smirk and Johnny said, "Excellent news, Professor. Teach them well."

*

Amos parked his new Ford-150 next to three other pickups and some kind of station wagon. The smell of pigs hit him as he opened the door. Since he no longer lived on the farm, the odor was noticeable every time he came back to the area. It had been two months, but the pig smell from the Boyles' farm still existed and reached all the way up here to the Tomlin's property. It'd been two months since he last used this barn as an operating room.

A month ago, a man named Roger Templeton bought this property as well as the Boyle farm. Since Amos was presumed dead, it took some trickery of paperwork to complete the transaction, but Roger had paid him a pretty penny for information about the movie being filmed at The Winters' place. Amos didn't know much, but he offered everything he knew to the guy who had lost a shit-ton of money on the failed movie. Roger was definitely someone who didn't take kindly to losing money. Amos didn't know how much, but since Roger not only bought these two pieces of land and the Winters' ranch as well, he assumed that Roger equated money to power. Roger was the man Archibald had wanted to be.

Amos chuckled at the notion of how Archibald would have probably looked at Roger like a dopey-eyed kindergartner, star-struck by a movie idol. As he got his duffle bag from behind the driver's seat, Amos grinned at another thought – he was now the movie star!

He walked into the barn to waves, pats on the back, and a personal greeting from each of the six men waiting for him. Another perk about the real estate transaction – Roger didn't care what Amos did here. He just wasn't allowed to live in this house, his old house, or the Winters'. As Roger had said, "I don't want a man who should be dead caught living in one of my properties." If Amos knew two things, it was he shouldn't be where he shouldn't be, and not to disobey a direct statement from a man like Roger Templeton.

"Greetings, everyone," Amos said as he set his bag on a small table next to the large, wooden dining table in the middle of the barn. A few strings of light bulbs ran across the rafters as well as a few more strategically placed utility lights. No one was around for miles, but Amos didn't want to take chances by making the barn any brighter than need be. "I just came from seeing The Chirurgeon. He sends his well-wishes and has expressed his pleasure with the Institute so far. He asked me to report to him immediately on how our first class goes, so let's make it a good one."

As the six men cheered and clapped, Amos unzipped his bag. First, he put on his surgical mask, then green-paper operating gown. Finally, the latex gloves, giving them a satisfying snap against his wrists.

The students procured their own scrubs from whatever bags they had brought with them. For the most part, they all looked like a bunch of residents with a few exceptions – one man's bushy beard made his mask look like a postage stamp, one fellow wore a pair of pink kitchen gloves made for scrubbing dishes, and another guy wore an apron that read: "Kiss the cook." Amos would give the group a B plus for attire. Now, for the equipment.

Amos procured a shiny new, high-grade scalpel, per Johnny's recommendation. The other six men did also, not a single dull edge among them. That was A plus effort! Next, the subject.

A dead man lay on the table. Naked, the paleness of death just setting in. Mangey hair and beard, dirty fingers and toes, a few scars here and there, but he looked sturdy enough. Amos assumed he had been homeless. For this, he'd give his students an A minus. They were off to a good start.

"Alright, the first thing we're going to look for is this man's gillgites. Then, per our professor's standing request, we're going to look for the mind's eye."

Like vultures hungry for new carrion, all seven men converged on the corpse, scalpels ready to slice.

The first class of The Chirurgeon Institute was in session.

The Progeny of Devils series, book 1

THE TRUTH
IN THEIR BLOOD

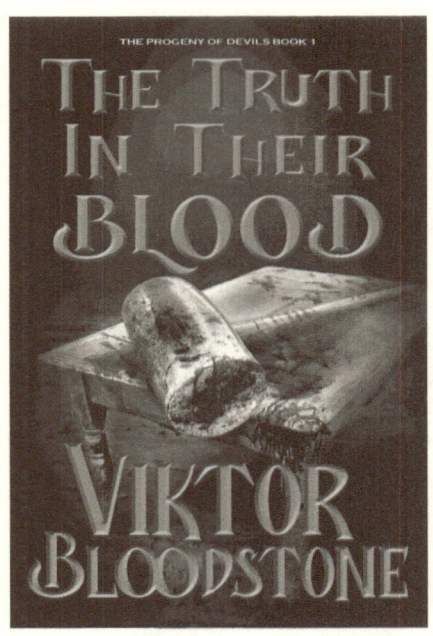

www.fortresspublishinginc.com

The *Legacy of Devils* series:

Hammer and Blood

www.fortresspublishinginc.com

The *Legacy of Devils* series:

The Dream Eaters

www.fortresspublishinginc.com

The *Killer of Devils* series:

BOOK 1: CLOWNS

www.fortresspublishinginc.com

Discover the secret origins of Johnny!

His story can be found in

Hellbent

An anthology by Hellbender Books.

Viktor Bloodstone

is

Brian Koscienski

Chris Pisano

Jeff Young

www.novelguys.com

www.ingramcontent.com/pod-product-compliance
Lightning Source LLC
Chambersburg PA
CBHW031213020726
47499CB00002B/573